# Sacra Obscurum

## By
## Todd Allen

Damnation Books, LLC.
P.O. Box 3931
Santa Rosa, CA 95402-9998
www.damnationbooks.com

Sacra Obscurum
by Todd Allen

Digital ISBN: 978-1-62929-211-3
Print ISBN: 978-1-62929-212-0

Cover art by: Dawné Dominique
Edited by: Avril Dannenbaum

Copyright 2015 Todd Allen

Printed in the United States of America
Worldwide Electronic & Digital Rights
Worldwide English Language Print Rights

*For my Michelle, my everything.*

*Special thanks to Bill Toner and Martha Vowles for tirelessly reading the scribblings of a total novice, and to Simone Seguin for her keen eye and thorough, yet gentle notes.*

# Chapter One

The late afternoon sun poured through the observation room's tall windows. Matt and Tammy sat on the bench in silence, a conservative space between them. He read from the clipboard on his lap and readied his pen to update the page. Tammy turned slightly to steal a look at his notes. She scowled as though they were the source of all her problems. When he was finished reading, he raised his practiced grin to her and said, "So...how are you feeling today?"

Tammy returned her gaze to the windows and squinted against the glare. Her yellow hair came untucked from her ear and hung slack in her eyes. "Better," she said. She leaned forward and her hospital johnny spread at the ties down her back, revealing a black bra strap.

Matt glimpsed the undergarment and immediately cast his gaze to the floor. He cleared his throat. "Umm...are you still experiencing headaches?"

"They're better," she said as she picked at the plastic bracelet on her wrist. "They'd be totally gone if you'd just let me have a smoke."

"I'll see what I can do about that," Matt said. "First, you need to talk to me before we can grant more privileges."

"Privileges," she snorted. "What fucking privileges?"

"Well, for starters, if you earn it, we can allow you to get your clothing back. Then we can see about getting you a temporary pass, so you can go outside and have a cigarette a few times a day." He leaned forward to mimic her position and lowered his tone. "Before any of that happens, you've got to work with me."

She sighed and said nothing.

Matt took that as assent. "So?"

"So what?"

"So, you've been having a hard time out there. I'd like to talk about why that is."

"Hey, I've been taking my meds. Ever since you guys gave 'em, I've been taking 'em."

"Yes, but you've also been using narcotics." She did not respond, only picked harder at her bracelet. "You were told that using drugs and alcohol will have an adverse affect on your medication."

She grunted.

"So why turn to drugs? What prompted you?"

"What prompted me? Are you serious? I don't know...fucking *life* prompted me." She raised her head and scanned the bright green room. The paint scheme was intended to promote patient serenity and encourage the all-round positive attitude so vital to successful rehabilitation. Both Matt and Tammy knew she had little to be positive about. "I don't even need it. I'm not hooked or anything. All I really need is a smoke."

Matt had read her address from the clipboard. She was from an older neighborhood in southeast Edmonton, not far from here, and he had a pretty good handle on the lifestyle that came with it. There were gangs, crack houses, prostitutes—the usual smorgasbord of criminal activity one might expect in the low-income part of town. He figured if he had grown up there he just might have ended up hitting the pipe too.

She looked at him with tired, black-ringed eyes. "Just tell me what you want me to say, and I'll say it."

"I'm sorry, Tammy," Matt said. "I can't give you that yet."

"Why not?...Please."

He rubbed his eyes, then ran his hand over significant beard stubble. "We have a lot of work to do before we get there." He flipped the page on the clipboard and read the one underneath. It was a Form Ten, commonly used by Child Protective Services when they have imposed custody. "Do you know where Crystal and Chase are right now? Tammy...do you know where your kids are?"

She tugged on her bracelet and stared out the window. "I want a fucking smoke."

Matt waited a moment. When he was sure that she had nothing more to offer, he clicked his pen and speedily scratched red ink across the top page on the clipboard.

The speaker in the corner of the room crackled to life and a breathy voice announced, "Doctor Dawson, please report to Station One. Doctor Dawson, report to Station One."

"I have to go, Tammy. I'm going to keep you at one milligram of Clonazepam for now." He completed his paperwork and stood. "We'll talk again tomorrow."

\* \* \* \*

As he left the observation room, Matt put on the phony smile he had come to perfect over his five years of residency at the D. A. McLaughlin Center. It came in handy from time to time—especially after dealing with a mother who was too ill to care about the welfare of her children. He showed the smile to the patients who were playing cards in the recreation area as he passed by. He shared it with a colleague emerging from the elevator. And, as he approached Station One, he showed it to Nurse Foster. "You beckoned, m' lady?"

"Yes I did," she said. "You are the lucky winner of whatever's behind door number three." She handed him a new clipboard.

"What have we got here?" he asked as he started to read.

"Police Department drop off. Apparently, this gentleman was picked up on a public disturbance call," Nurse Foster said as she shuffled through the admission forms she would have to fill out. "The officers decided that he wasn't quite lock-up material, so they brought him in for an assessment."

"Oh, very good," he said. "It looks like they are finally learning the difference between the common criminal and a person with mental health issues." He pulled the pen out of the breast pocket of his lab coat and made a few scribbles on the form. "Where can I claim my prize?"

"I told them to bring him around front." She leaned over the counter to look at the main entrance to the left of the lobby. "Yeah, there they are."

Matt made his way to the entry where two police officers, dressed in their dark blue attire, flanked a gray-haired man whose head hung, his hands behind his back. The man had the slender build of the malnourished and looked as though he would collapse to the floor had the officers not been holding him. Matt scanned his card on the wall reader to unlock the glass doors and motioned for them to enter the secure area.

"Hello, I'm Doctor Dawson," he said to the thin man as the police ushered him in. "Let's sit him down right here." He pointed to a bench just inside the doors and turned to the officers. "What's the story?"

The officers looked at each other, as though trying to decide who should do the talking. Finally one said, "We picked him up at Crosswinds Market. He was screaming nonsense at people about the end of the world and the devil returning or some kinda stuff like that."

Matt looked at the man whose head still hung. He figured the man was homeless—he certainly smelled that way. Long oily hair, and his face bristly with salt and pepper whiskers. He wore a tattered green army coat. Matt figured he had either gotten it as a handout or had stolen it, but he got a sinking feeling when he wondered if the man had actually served. Afghanistan had done a number on many veterans, some of whom Matt had treated.

"Anyway, he doesn't have any identification on him," the officer continued. "It doesn't seem right to put him through the system. We figured this was more your kinda thing."

"Yeah, you brought him to the right place," Matt said, though he knew the difference between someone trying to do the right thing and someone pawning their problem off on another. "You can take the handcuffs off him."

"*Geeze*, I don't think that's a good idea," the other officer said. "It wasn't easy getting them on."

"I think he's pretty calm now. Besides, I can't give him a proper assessment while he's bound."

The officer raised his brow in a *you're the boss* expression and bent to key the John Doe's cuffs open. With his restraints removed, the man brought his hands to his lap and rested them on his knees.

"Sir, can you hear me?" Matt knelt on the floor in front of the man and tried to get a look at his face. "I'd like to examine you, if I could." He fished through his hip pockets for his penlight to test the man's dilation.

John Doe slowly raised his head.

Matt saw his eyes between the curtains of greasy, gray hair. They were vacant, dark. They seemed to look through Matt to the brightly painted wall behind him. A different shade of green from that of the observation room, the wall was intended to create a soothing atmosphere. It failed.

The man lunged forward and tackled Matt to the floor.

Matt sprawled, the crazed transient writhing atop him. John Doe screamed and clutched fistfuls of Matt's hair as he thrashed about. The officers shouted indiscernible words. They grabbed the man and tried to pull him off, yet his grip on Matt's head held fast. Teeth stained the color of urine snapped at Matt's neck. He felt the heat of rotten breath on his flesh and putrid spittle flecked his face.

He seized the man's wrists and wrestled them away from his head, fistfuls of his hair tearing away. He struggled from under the pile of men and rolled free. With trembling hands he went to the keypad near the entry and pressed in the emergency code.

A robotic voice took control of the public announcement system. *Emergency, Main Entrance, Emergency, Main Entrance...*

Matt clutched his chest over his hammering heart. The officers fought to get the handcuffs back on the transient, whose small frame belied a wild strength. The cuffs finally gave a metallic *clink* that Matt barely heard between screams from his attacker.

"*We see you...*" John Doe screeched. "*We see you...*"

The squeaking of tennis shoes on the tiles told him the orderlies were coming around the corner. The two men dressed in white scrubs looked to him, but Matt couldn't speak. He merely eyed the leather case on one orderly's hip and nodded. The seasoned employees of the center knew what to do. The men responsible for policing the patients on the inside went to where the officers were holding the transient face-down on the entry floor.

The orderly unzipped the pouch on his hip and produced a syringe. In it was five milligrams of Midazolam, the standard sedative used in cases where patients became violent. Midazolam was known to pack a wallop and work directly—ideal traits when a tantrum must be stopped as quickly as possible.

Matt caught his breath as the orderlies and the police coordinate the injection.

"Hold 'em down."

"Stick him in the neck."

"Careful, he bites!"

John Doe howled when the needle pierced his flesh. Then his screaming ceased. He lay on the tiles, chest heaving.

"We see you," he said again, this time calmly. "We see you, Doc."

Matt studied the transient. Dilated eyes, all black, stared at him. Knowing eyes—deep, like vast wells. Matt fell into them.

"Doctor Dawson!" Matt saw the orderly looking at him with puzzlement. "Should we take him to Exam One?" he asked impatiently, as though he had posed the question a time or two already.

"Yes," Matt tried to say, though his voice was lost. He cleared his throat. "Umm...yes...Exam One. Oh, and stay with him. I'll be along shortly."

The officers helped to hoist the man into a wheelchair. By then, the entry area was filling with curious staff members who had also heard the robot's declaration of emergency. Matt went back to the keypad and entered the code again to reset the alert condition. "Okay everyone, back to work," he said to the on-lookers. "The situation is under control. Please, clear the area."

"Are you okay?" asked one of the officers of Matt as John Doe was wheeled by. Matt was about to answer when the vagrant raised his head. It lolled on his neck like it was supported by wet noodles. Weary, black eyes met Matt's again.

"Ring, ring, Doc," he said with a slow rolling chuckle, showing his tainted smile. "Ring, ring..."

Matt watched John Doe as he was escorted toward the examination rooms. It wasn't the first time he had been assaulted by a patient and it would scarcely be the last, but it was the first time it had left him completely unnerved. It was different. This man was not simply screaming. He was screaming *at him.*

The public announcement system crackled again. The robot's voice was replaced by Nurse Foster's soothing tone. Her message, however, did anything but ease Matt's anxiety. "Doctor Dawson, you have an urgent phone call on line 312." His breath went short again as the message was repeated.

He returned to Station One to take the call. On his way, he searched unsuccessfully for his phony smile to wear for the young nurse. In fairness, when he arrived he saw she wasn't wearing one either. In fact, her brow was furrowed with what seemed to be genuine worry. He reached for the phone receiver and keyed the line.

"Hello?"

"Oh, Matty, it's Aunt Joan. I'm so sorry to have to call you like this…"

*Urgent indeed.* He hadn't heard from his aunt, or any other family member for that matter, in a good long while. Yet, the sound of her voice, coupled with Nurse Foster's demeanor, told him that it was not a call to catch up.

"Joan, is everything okay?"

"Matty, I have bad news. It's your father…"

Matt felt a bone-deep chill. He looked in the direction of Exam One as his aunt delivered her bad news.

*Ring, ring, Doc.*

# Chapter Two

Matt stared dully over the shiny black casket where Stanley Dawson lay. He studied the mouth and nose that looked like his, the prominent brow. The resemblance was undeniable, save the thirty-plus years of strain that were etched into Stanley's brow. And, of course, his expression was serene. Matt's was not.

"He looks peaceful...at rest, doesn't he?"

Aunt Joan had joined him at the casket. Matt hadn't noticed. He forced a smile and showed it to his father's sister. "Yes, he does."

She reached for his hand and gave it a squeeze. "This is nice with everyone here. A right proper send off."

Matt looked around the room, surprised at the group that had amassed while his attention was on the casket. How long had he been looking at Stanley? How long had he waited for him to stir and wake, and answer the difficult questions swirling in his head?

Formally dressed mourners and well-wishers filled the room, standing shoulder-to-shoulder in the modest space. Matt questioned the sense in holding the viewing in Stanley's study, but Joan had insisted. "It was his most favorite place in the world," she had said. "He would want to have it here." She was right. Stanley spent a great deal of his time in the study among his many books and journals. In fact, most of the conversations Matt ever had with him took place within these four walls.

In his youth, Matt found the room intimidating. The dark-mauve papered walls, the deep mahogany wainscoting, the cases of texts rising overhead. The room always seemed dark, like it held secrets among its many books. He would imagine those thick volumes toppling from the shelves, crushing him with the combined wisdom of the world.

"Can I have your attention, please?"

Matt turned and found Robbie Bentley holding up a glass. He was one of the first guests to arrive that afternoon and had introduced himself to Matt as Mayor Robbie Bentley. "...but call me Bud," he had said. "Everybody does."

He seemed like a pleasant sort. His plump, well-fed face wore what looked to be a permanent grin. The only sign of his age came from the deep laugh lines that edged his bright eyes. He had extended Matt his most sincere condolences and added the customary: *if there's anything I can do...*

Bud was the kind of man that wanted to be everyone's *bud*, always networking, always campaigning.

"Your attention, please," Bud continued. The murmur hushed. "We're here today for our dear friend Stanley. There isn't a one in this room that isn't sorry to see him go. There isn't a one among us, he didn't touch the life of in some way. He has been both a good friend and good leader to this community. He was among my dearest friends and when I heard news of his passing, well, I got to thinking about the old days."

Matt looked around the study. Everyone hung on the mayor's words.

A man who Matt didn't know from a hole in the ground handed him a tall, frothy glass of beer. It was a little early for such an indulgence, but Matt politely accepted it.

"When we were kids," Bud went on. "We used to hang around in his father's boat when it was put-up for the winter. Oh his father didn't like us using it, but we used to sneak in there all the time and get up to no good. This one evening, we were entertaining the McCaffery sisters on the boat when his father showed up in the yard. 'Stanley Dawson,' he says. 'You get your bony arse down here on the double.' Well...Stanley near jumped out of his skin and he went to climb down the ladder from the cradle. He was in such a rush, he tripped and down he went—right off the side of the boat." Bud slapped his thigh to punctuate his words.

Many laughed.

Aunt Joan said, "I never heard that before."

Matt hadn't either, but he was less surprised. There were likely many stories about Stanley he would never know.

"It was a good ten foot drop, and Stan laid there in a pile under the ladder and he said, 'Dad, I'm hurt.' His father said, 'Boy...you don't have *time* to be hurt.'"

There was more laughter, especially from the men in attendance.

"Well...it seemed like Stanley adopted that motto from that day forward. When his father passed and he had to become the man of the house, he didn't have time to be hurt. Twenty years ago, when he lost his dear Susan to cancer..."

Matt clenched his jaw.

"...he had his patients to look after and he didn't have time to be hurt then, either. All these years he spent taking care of others and now it's finally his turn to rest, isn't it Stanley?" Bud said to the casket. "That's right," he said as though Stanley had answered. "Raise a glass in honor of our dear friend."

"To Stanley," some said. All tipped a glass.

"Let's wake him up," someone shouted from the back. It was the cue to strike up the band. A fiddle screeched to life accompanied by guitars in a spirited East Coast jig.

Matt looked around for the instruments. The quiet viewing he'd expected had morphed into a lively shindig. Men were handing around more glasses of beer. A few ladies circulated trays of sandwiches and cheese. Raucous laughter erupted from a huddle in the corner.

A woman with a heaping plate of finger foods approached Matt. "Poor Dear," she said. "You must be hungry. Look, I made a plate for you."

"Oh, thank you, Mrs...."

"Finney, Mrs. Finney. I was in the Rotary Club with your father. We're going to miss him so. He was such an active member...always giving."

Matt took the plate and set it on his father's desk. "Actually, I'm not very hungry at the moment." He set his beer glass down as well.

"Are you going to be in Saint Andrews long?" she asked.

"I'm not sure. I have to oversee Stanley's practice until I find a new doctor to manage it."

"Oh, are you a psychiatrist too?"

"Yes, I practice at the D. A. McLaughlin Center in Edmonton."

Mrs. Finney smiled and nodded. "Oh, that's nice, dear. Is there a Mrs. Dawson?"

"No, there isn't."

"Surely, a young doctor like yourself must have a girlfriend," she said with a coy smile.

"Umm, no, I've been concentrating on work lately."

"Well maybe you'll meet a nice girl while you're home."

*Home? This place hasn't been home since I was fifteen*, he thought, but smiled, nonetheless. Then he looked around the room for help. Where was Aunt Joan when he needed her?

"Here ya go, young sir," a man said, reaching around Mrs. Finney with another full glass of beer for Matt.

He accepted the cold glassful and said, "If you'll excuse me Mrs. Finney, I need to check on something."

"Oh yes, dear."

Matt made his way through the crowded study. He glanced at Stanley as he passed by the casket and he wondered how he managed to spend so many years among these folks. He must have had another side—one he never showed to his son. These people would not have gathered to mourn the passing of the serious, driven man that raised Matt. Men like that were seldom missed.

When he reached the hall, Matt crossed into the dining room where he found the band. He nodded to the trio who were just starting up a new jig. The floor boards bounced as they stomped their feet in rhythm and Matt felt the sides of his head swell. The flight east had left him exhausted and the entertainment was a little more than he could bear. At the far end of the dining room was a door to the veranda that wrapped around the front of the house. Matt forced himself to smile at a few more unfamiliar faces and handed his beer off to a fellow whose glass was running low, before he reached the exit.

\* \* \* \*

A trace of fog on the soft breeze, tasted faintly of the sea. Down the sloping streets about a half-mile was the Saint Andrews waterfront. The mighty Bay of Fundy skirted the town's business district and it could be seen from most anywhere in town. Matt had forgotten the feeling the bay brought about. It was an all-powerful presence, a vast abyss that could nourish and provide, but too many times, took away.

There was nothing like it in Edmonton. Their famed North Saskatchewan River was a mere trickle in comparison. When Matt first traveled west to attend university, he was out of sorts and didn't know why. He had difficulty sleeping and usually felt fatigued. It was another expatriated east-coaster who told him the reason. "You miss the water is all," he had said. "The air here is dry as a popcorn fart, but you'll get used to it." He did.

And now, years later, Matt mused that he would have to get used to the Atlantic air again. It was so damp and thick, it felt more like he was drinking it than breathing it. And that bay—so ominous.

"I'd expect it to warm up tomorrow," a gravelly voice said.

Matt had thought he was alone on the veranda. "That's good," he said to the man who stood further down the deck, looking out to sea.

"That fog is a good sign of it," the man said, taking a haul off a cigarette.

Matt moved beside him, though he was careful to stay up-wind of his secondhand smoke. "Matthew Dawson," he said offering a hand.

The man shook it. "I know. I was chums with your dad a way back. Arthur Sullivan."

Beyond the smell of burnt tobacco, Matt detected another odor emanating from Mister Sullivan. The unmistakable smell of fish. He was not in his Sunday best like the others in attendance. He wore dirty work pants and a matching vest over a wool sweater. Atop his curly gray head sat a ratty ball cap.

"Different professions, ya know," Sullivan said. "I didn't do too good in keepin' up with your old man."

*You and me both*, Matt thought. "Do you fish?"

"Not anymore. Too old for that. I just run the boats now," Sullivan said, still looking to sea as though he was reading distant messages from it. "You put on a nice wake for 'im. Lots of folks showed."

Matt agreed, though he felt like he had of a house full of strangers more than he had a *nice* anything.

He looked around the sweeping yard surrounding the house. The manicured pitch was outlined with tall cedar hedges that parted only at the entrance of the driveway. Three mature cherry trees grew near the street. Soon, they would blossom. Matt figured he would have to find out who did the groundskeeping and work out payment. It was yet another detail that needed attention. Who knew that dying could mean so much work for the living?

As his eyes wandered to the hearse parked beside the house, he considered what came next. Stanley's earthly remains were to be cremated in accordance with his wishes. He would concentrate on that. First things first.

"That fella a friend of yours?" Sullivan asked.

Matt followed his gaze to the mouth of the driveway where a man stood near the hedge, watching the house. He wore a dark coat with the collar turned up. "Do you know him, Mister Sullivan?"

"Nah. I figured you might..."

The man must have seen that the pair on the veranda had noticed him. He moved on, disappearing behind the hedge.

"He ain't from around here, either."

* * * *

"It was so nice of Mrs. Finney to stay and help with the dishes," Aunt Joan said.

Matt lifted a stack of plates into the cabinet. "Yes it was." Though he could have done without Mrs. Finney giving him the rundown on every eligible bachelorette in town.

With the house finally empty and the cleanup complete, the effects of the long day took their toll on Matt. He stretched and yawned.

"Thought I might put the kettle on," Joan said. "Care for a spot of tea?"

"Sure," he said and sat at the small kitchen table. There were two chairs at the table, one of which he just knew had not been used since his mother died.

Joan ran water into the kettle then sat it on the stove burner. She readied two cups with tea bags and spoons. "It doesn't feel right to dirty these," she said. "We just got them put away."

She sat down at the table and sighed. She, too, was weary after a long day.

Joan was an attractive woman. Even the passage of time couldn't hide it. She had big, bright blue eyes—wise eyes—like her brother's. They had seen a lot of hardship, including the death of her own spouse. Matt wondered what it was with Dawsons outliving their mates.

"So, what's next?" she asked.

Matt drew a breath as if describing his *to-do* list meant he would have to be long-winded. He exhaled slowly. *One thing at a time*, he thought. "Well, first I meet with the lawyer about settling the estate. Then the cremation is in the afternoon. I plan to get down to the hospital for a look around after that. That's tomorrow. What then, I don't know."

"Just take it as it comes, Matty." She smiled.

"What about you? Are you going to stick around for a while?"

"I'm going back to Saint John in the morning. I have things to do at home. Besides, I'd rather remember dear Stanley the way I saw him today rather than in some jar on the mantel."

They sat in silence for a moment.

Matt wondered how *he* would remember Stanley. It was not an easy thing to figure. On one hand, Matt was sent away from home when he was very young. On the other, he had been given every opportunity under the sun. He could have done anything with his life, so long as he did it someplace else.

"Your father loved you, you know," Joan said breaking the silence. She held him in her icy blue gaze.

"He had a strange way of showing it."

"Maybe so." She wrapped her hands around her empty tea cup. "He had a hard time after he lost your mother."

"I know...we both did, but he was a psychiatrist. He made a life out of helping people in turmoil." Matt played with his cup. "Why couldn't he help himself?"

The water in the kettle started to roll and steam whispered through the spout.

"That's the last person any of us helps," she said.

\* \* \* \*

Matt said good night to his aunt, but did not seek out his bed. He decided to stay up for a while and have a look around his childhood home. There were four large bedrooms on the second floor. A grand staircase descended the center of the house into the main hall. From there, right and left were two parlors; one formal, one a little less so. Toward the front of the house were the kitchen, the dining room, and the study. Matt found himself in the doorway of Stanley's favorite room. He seemed to gravitate there.

When their guests realized they had failed in their efforts to *wake* Stanley Dawson, they packed up their instruments and their beer kegs and went home.

It was then that the men from King's Funeral Home came in to close the casket. Only Matt and Joan had been in attendance for that part; the last surviving family members. She wept. Seeing this, Matt pretended to. The men expressed sympathy, then wheeled the casket to the back door and loaded it into the hearse.

With the casket gone, the doctor's desk resumed its customary position in the center of the room. Matt sat down behind it. It felt too big.

He pulled open the top drawer to his right. In it were pens, a stapler, and a stack of papers. He leafed through them, stopping when he came to a pink slip. It was a copy of a work order. Weed-Out Landscaping was written across the top, and at the bottom was a total of fifty dollars for services rendered. Matt grinned. He could strike one item from his growing *to-do* list.

He closed the drawer and grasped the handle of the deep one beneath it. It was locked. In the upper right corner of the drawer face was a small key hole. Matt figured the contents must be important, possibly hospital business, and would therefore be something he would need to see. He pulled the shallow center drawer open in search of a key.

Matt slid the empty drawer closed and was scanning the study for a place he might find the key when he was startled by a noise from outside.

*Thunk—thunk.*

Matt swiveled in his chair to face the lone window in the study. He saw only his reflection in it.

The noise came again.

*Thunk.*

"Aunt Joan," he called. "Are you up?"

When Joan didn't answer, he rose and made his way to the window with tentative steps. He would have to switch off the lights in order to get a good look at the darkened yard. Knowing a thing and doing a thing are mutually exclusive, he mused. When he reached the window, he laid a hand in the casing and leaned forward, tilting his head right and left, trying to get a look at the grounds. The meandering fog off the bay had reached the house. It shrouded the night sky, extinguished the stars, the moon.

Then his mind coughed up a memory that made him feel ill—the man who had been watching the house earlier. The one who *ain't from around here, either.* He wore his collar up the way sinister sorts in old crime movies did and he had quickly moved along when he was discovered.

Could he be trying to break in?

*Thunk—thunk.*

Matt jerked back from the window.

Whatever made that sound was very close. His heart raced. *Get a hold of yourself. It's the wind. The wind is slapping a branch against the house. Maybe it was too loud to be a branch, but it could be a...a shutter. That's it. A shutter has come loose and is knocking on the siding. It wouldn't be the first time it's happened to this house.*

He took a deep breath, and his heart rate slowed.

*Thunk.*

With a likely explanation, the noise was far less menacing. In fact, it shrank to an annoyance. Another thing that needed fixing, needed his attention. He decided to go to bed before his chore list got any longer.

He turned off the study lights and went to the stairs. Before he reached the second tread, another sound manifested, this one from below. He recognized it at once. Something else in need of repairs and had been for many, many years. The effect of a strong wind on the old house. His mother had told him so several times, though her explanations always rang a little hollow. As a child, he'd refused to accept that it was the wind he was hearing in the night. He knew better. It was the reason he had lain awake in his bed, the reason he feared to venture to the cellar.

Matt had forgotten the noise, forced it beyond the borders of his memory. While the loose shutter had given him a start, this sound chilled him to the core. Matt, the adult, knew it was simply the result of the wind and he continued up the stairs. There was no way he was going to investigate that particular problem. He couldn't. And he was okay with that. He knew from his profession that childhood traumas left lasting scars.

# Chapter Three

Arthur Sullivan was right. It did get warmer. In fact, for an early spring day, it got downright hot—too hot for the black suit Matt wore. He had considered Stanley's cremation to be a part of the funeral, so he dressed appropriately in the morning. Though the beads of sweat now pooling at the small of his back, made him regret the wardrobe choice immensely.

With Stanley's earthly remains processed, Matt accepted the urn his father had selected to spend eternity in. At first Matt thought Mister King, the funeral director, was playing a prank on him, but the man's solemn professionalism precluded such ideas. The urn was eighteen inches tall, with a chrome finish and looping handles on either side. It would have looked at home in the hands of a hockey player hoisting it overhead or a golfer at the eighteenth hole.

Matt tucked the urn under his arm and made his way to the hospital. The thing he liked most about Saint Andrews is that he could walk everywhere. He had walked the three blocks from the house to King's Funeral Home, and three more would have him at the hospital. He headed south on Adolphus, turned right at Water, passed Mary, and found himself at the gated walkway into Saint Michael's.

The rusted wrought iron gate squealed when he opened it. He winced through the nails-on-chalkboard sound and continued up the concrete walk. It was split and chipped away in several places. For a moment Matt wondered if he had the wrong address. The place before him couldn't be Stanley's immaculate little institution. He had not seen it more than twenty years, but one look at the bronze plaque mounted next to the front door confirmed the location.

Maybe Weed-Out Landscaping took care of these grounds also—they were certainly well kept. However, little else was inviting. Everywhere, dingy white paint peeled from the building's cedar clapboard siding. Windows missing shutters. Curled up and split roofing shingles promised a serious leak, if it had not happened already.

How did the town officials stand for the appearance of the building? Saint Andrews was a tourist town and went to great lengths to maintain a postcard image—especially on Water Street. It was home to many inns, restaurants and boutiques, and drew visitors in droves. His father had a great deal of pull in the community, though even that had its limits when it came to running a dump like this.

Standing on the walkway, he took in the two story manor-turned-hospital. Then it occurred to him why the hospital was allowed to fall into such poor condition. It was the old stigma. It was never far from center when considering the nature of his profession. Mental illness was seen as shameful. It was a sad, pathetic affliction of the weak-minded. It was best to ignore like a dirty secret. Perhaps the town had. Perhaps that explained why officials did not enforce upkeep laws and let the once-gorgeous building go to seed. It did not, however, explain why Stanley Dawson had let it happen.

\* \* \* \*

Matt entered the hospital unchecked and headed directly for Stanley's office. He hoped to get a look at the books and the charts before meeting with the hospital staff. They would no doubt have several questions for him and he wanted to be well informed before attempting to answer them. Though at the second floor nurse's station, Matt found himself surrounded by worried staff members, and the questions flew.

Matt introduced himself to orderlies John Cundiff and Tyrone Klewes and Nurse Wanda Cooke. They all wore expressions like the façade of the building itself—tired, rundown. Even the absurdly extravagant urn he held drew little interest.

Cundiff, a strapping lad with closely cropped, brown hair and a straight jaw line, threw the first hardball. "Are you staying on long term?" he asked.

"No, I won't be," Matt told them. When he saw their deflated reactions, he quickly added, "I plan to find a suitable doctor to assume long-term supervision of hospital operations."

"Are we gonna lose our jobs?" Klewes asked, cutting straight to the heart of the matter. The tall black man cut an intimidating figure. Built like a defensive lineman, with long limbs and thick with muscle. Yet, what Matt detected in his voice was not hostility. It was fear.

The three waited while the question hung in the air. Matt guessed Wanda was nearing retirement age, but the others were not even close, early thirties, if that. They could see the signs of closure all around them—the condition of the building, the death of the founding doctor, and the emergence of an absentee son to take over.

"I haven't looked at the books yet." Matt chose his words carefully. "Though, barring any unforeseen catastrophe, I plan to keep Saint Michael's open for a good, long while." He watched relief flood the faces of his new employees and prayed he was not leading them astray. "This hospital represents Stanley Dawson's life work and I won't see it close without a fight."

"See?" Cundiff said to Klewes. "I told you he was gonna take care of business."

Klewes grinned widely. "Chip off the old block."

"I plan to address the entire staff when I have a better grasp on our situation. For now, I'd like to have a look around," Matt said. "Is the office still at the end of the hall?"

Wanda assured him that it was.

The hallway smelled of Lysol disinfectant and the bright blue linoleum tiles had a coat of sparkling polish. Despite the building's shabby exterior, the inside seemed to be well kept by a staff that took pride. Matt could not detect the faintest evidence of dust or grime. Even the groove between the white wall and the buffered handrail that lined the hallway was clean. *A very good sign.*

Patients' quarters occupied either side of the wide corridor. Their blue doors matched the floor tiles. Above each door was a transom window that allowed for ventilation. The old building had no central air conditioning and the transoms, coupled with the slow-turning ceiling fans mounted every ten feet in the hall, were the only means of circulating air. Still, the environment was fresh enough and Matt hoped the same could be said of the patients' rooms.

He looked through the small rectangular observation window in the door to his left. Inside were a folded-up cot and a small dresser. The next room was the same. However, the last room in the corridor was occupied.

A man seated in a white plastic deck chair faced the sunshine flooding through the window. His shaven head was slumped and Matt guessed the man was asleep. A push on the door proved it locked. The name on the plaque under the room number read, Dykeman. Matt made a mental note to check the man's chart when he got settled, then moved on toward the office.

The office door had a large window, through which Matt could see his father's desk. It was well positioned to keep an eye on the entire corridor and the nurses' station in the center of it.

"You're back, Doctor," he whispered to the urn.

Drawing a deep breath, he steadied himself for the monumental task ahead. On the other side of that door, he would step into Stanley Dawson's shoes. It was something that he always prayed he could avoid, but it was impossible. He had been on a collision course with this office since the day he chose to pursue psychiatry.

He reached for the doorknob.

"I was the one who found him," a voice said from behind.

Matt flinched. He turned to find Cundiff in the corridor.

"Sorry," the orderly said. "Didn't mean to sneak up on you."

"That's okay. It's kind of a jumpy day."

Cundiff's deep brown eyes fixed on the urn.

"You said, you found him?"

"Yeah, I came in for the morning shift and I saw him in there at his desk. He was leaned back in his chair, you know. I thought he was asleep." He smiled. "It wasn't out of the ordinary for me to come in early and find he spent the night sleeping at his desk. Usually, I'd wake him and he'd just get right back to work."

Matt was smiling now, too. That was Stanley in a nutshell.

"That morning, I went downstairs to the kitchen and put the tea pot on. I talked to the night nurse while it brewed and when it was ready, I poured a cup for the doc and brought it up. I thought we'd sit and have a cup and talk baseball..."

Matt watched Cundiff battle tears. The orderly had that same glint in his eye that Mrs. Finney had when she considered Stanley. Just then, Matt felt tears burning his own eyes. He didn't miss Stanley like these people did, and that was what hurt. He was not Rotary club-mates with him, he did not talk baseball over tea with him. He was never *anything* with him.

"Anyways," Cundiff continued. He cleared his throat. "I'm very sorry for your loss."

"Thank you," Matt said. Though he wondered if condolences should have been offered in the other direction.

\* \* \* \*

"So, what do you think?" Klewes asked the nurse.

Wanda shrugged and looked at Cundiff and Matt talking at the end of the hall. "Seems all right, to me."

"I hope he is," he said. "He's the man now."

"You shouldn't expect him to be the Doctor Dawson we knew. He was a rare gentleman, our Stanley. One in a million."

"With any luck the apple didn't fall too far from the old tree."

"You seem worried, dear."

"Well, I'm in no hurry to look for another job is all."

"I doubt it'll come to that."

"I hope you're right. There's no work around here. I lost my belly for bagging fish meal and they don't take my people on the boats. Suppose, I could always try the cannery in Black's Harbor..."

"Oh hush, now," Wanda said waving a dismissive hand at the orderly. "You're not going anywhere. It won't take the new doctor long to figure out your use. And you two lads do more than most attendants...and take less pay to do it."

"Wait...we do?"

"Well, the orderlies in Saint John get union rate."

"Do you think they're hiring?"

Wanda gave him a hard look. "Get back to work, Mister Klewes."

\* \* \* \*

Phillip Prichard sat in silence while across the desk, Matt leafed through the ledger. Much to his surprise, the chartered accountant offered to meet with him directly to go over the hospital's financials. He had expected to make an appointment—sometime in a week or so. Amazingly, Prichard told him over the phone that he would be along in a few minutes. There was a definite perk to doing business in a small town. For Matt, that was the end of the good news.

"Am I missing pages or something?" he asked, not looking up from the book.

"That is everything, Doctor Dawson," Prichard said.

"This is a lot of red ink."

"Yes, it is."

Matt closed the ledger and looked up. The man across from him was close to Stanley's age, early seventies. He had a thin face and it made the considerable glasses he wore seem all the bigger.

"I guess I'm wondering why," Matt said after a moment.

Prichard leaned forward. His gray suit jacket floated on his slight frame. "It is not difficult math," he said. "Saint Michael's operates with six full-time staff, two of whom are nurses who command a significant salary. The hospital has a sixteen bed capacity, of which only nine are filled. Of the nine patients, none pay the full residency rate and two are free-stays. So yes, under the current model, there is bound to be a lot of red ink."

Matt was stunned. When he had seen the condition of the building, he'd known that Stanley had let things slide, but he never would have imagined this. This was far beyond letting the building go...this was business suicide.

He looked around the office as the accountant's grim news sunk in. He looked at the volumes of texts in the cases lining the walls, the cabinets of records, and imagined it all going away. His eyes fell to a two-foot wide stain on the beige carpet beside the desk. It was the likely result of John Cundiff dropping two full tea cups when he found that Stanley was not simply sleeping in his chair.

"I should add that I didn't handle your father's personal finances. It may be a case where running the hospital at a loss provided for personal tax shelter, but I can't say for certain." Prichard leaned back in his chair.

"Aren't there government grants or programs he could have taken advantage of?" Matt asked.

"Yes, I made him aware of more than one. There was even a program available that would have covered much of the cost of a renovation to the facility, but he declined. Other programs he was ineligible for, due to low occupancy."

"As his accountant, you didn't steer him in these directions?"

"I did my duty as his accountant," Prichard said flatly. "I made him aware if his options. I gave him the best advice I had to offer. In the end, it was up to him to accept or decline that advice."

Matt rubbed his eyes with the heels of his hands. He had told the staff that Saint Michael's would remain open for business barring any unforeseen catastrophe. Well there it was, right in front of him—a catastrophe written in red.

"You know," Prichard continued. "My recommendation to increase his rates fell on deaf ears, as well. Your father only charged $1200 a month for a bed. He hadn't increased the rate since the early nineties. I told him that, to keep in line with growing expenses, the rate should be at least $1600 a month, and that is at *full* capacity. The cost of insurance alone would account for nearly half of his gross."

"How are the doors even open today?" Matt asked, as much of himself as the accountant.

"You will notice in the ledgers that he was injecting large sums from a personal account into the hospital to cover salaries and operating expenses over the past few years. How long he planned to keep that up, I can't say. Yet, I think we can agree, it is a model that obviously cannot be sustained."

Matt knew that better than anyone. He had just looked at Stanley's estate and knew his accounts had been running on fumes. He could not understand how this had happened, how Stanley had allowed it to happen. There had always been money in the family. His lofty tuition had always been paid without hesitation. His living expenses had been covered through a comfortable allowance over the ten-plus years he'd spent in university. Matt had been in his thirties before he earned his first dollar. In fact, he still had some of that allowance money in investment funds. How could Stanley be broke?

He was silent while he considered Cundiff and Klewes and the rest of the staff he had yet to meet. He imagined telling them the hospital had to close, that their jobs were gone, that the fight was over before it had started.

This was exactly the kind of thing Stanley should have kept him around for. Matt could have helped him with the finances when they became a problem. *That is what families do for each other*, Matt thought...*well, good ones anyway*. Matt scarcely knew his family, he was sent from home so young. And why? He had been a well-behaved teen. He didn't act up or rebel like so many other kids.

Regardless of that, he was shipped off to a private school hours away, then a distant university, then a medical school farther still. Yet, he always expected to get the call one day—the call from Stanley that said, okay Son, it's time you came home. For Matt, there had never been reason in getting too comfortable in his new surroundings. There had been no use in fully furnishing an apartment or making friends. There had hardly been reason to unpack. He remembered thinking that he wouldn't be in Rothesay for long, nor in Red Deer, and certainly not in Edmonton. Yet, the call to return home never came.

The only one that did brought news of his mother's death. He hadn't even known she was sick.

Matt loosed a long frustrated sigh. He could not control any of these things. It was the past. *I should be spending more time with the patients who need me and less time dwelling on money problems*, he thought. *Of course, if I can't fix these problems, all these patients could end up on the streets.*

"Mister Prichard," he said finally, "would you be willing to share your recommendations with me?"

"Yes...of course," Prichard said, seemingly surprised that a Dawson was not too proud to ask for help. "It is the least I could do. I don't want to see Saint Michael's fail. I have known Stanley since we were both young lads."

Matt disagreed, but he kept it to himself.

Like him, Prichard only *thought* he knew Stanley.

\* \* \* \*

The dense evening fog had once again made its way up the hill from the waterfront to the grounds surrounding the Dawson house. It left a film on Matt's skin when he took the air on the veranda. Maybe it was the dampness that had him feeling breathless. Maybe his system was still adjusting from the thin, dry mountain air to which he had become accustomed. Yet, Matt blamed the bad news contained in Saint Michael's ledger for knocking the wind out of him.

He wished Aunt Joan were still here. She had left early that morning, but not before making a meatloaf and a pasta casserole for him. Matt found them in the fridge along with reheating instructions written on a sticky note. Although he had little appetite, he forced down some of the casserole with a glass of merlot. What he really hungered for were answers. The files stacked on the desk beside his half eaten plate of noodles and cheese provided none.

If not for the late hour, he would have called Joan to ask if she had noticed any strange behavior in her brother, if she could think of any reason why he would allow his life's work to simply go down the drain. Had he confided in her?

Instead of calling, he was limited to searching the files for some clue to Stanley's reasoning. As he sifted through the records, a worry began to stretch through his mind like a shadow in late afternoon. Maybe Stanley had fallen ill like the patients he had dedicated his career to treating.

Most of the files Matt found in the study were for patients Stanley had treated and discharged, but one of them contained a recent dose record. Among the names on it, one caught his eye.

*Dykeman.*

Beside the name was typed, *Olanzepine—40 mg once daily* and *Lithium Carbonate—600 mg once daily.* Matt read it again to make sure he was not mistaken. *That sort of cocktail could tranquilize a polar bear,* he thought. *It would render an average man catatonic and likely lead to cardiac arrest.* Matt closed the file. He could think of no case in which he would medicate a patient to that extent. Even if the patient was prone to violent outbursts, other measures could be taken. Restraints, isolation, transfer to a high security facility—Matt would have visited any of these before resorting to that kind of over-medicating.

"What was going on with you, Stanley?" he said to the empty study.

This was not like the man at all—to overdose a patient, put him in a room, and lock the door. If he was willing to treat a human being like that, the poor state of the hospital was suddenly not farfetched in the least.

Head spinning, Matt got up from the desk. He needed to rest. As he made his way to the stairs, he looked at the photographs that hung there. His mother smiled from one. She was standing by one of the cherry trees in their front yard. Matt sighed as he remembered happier times, when the Dawsons planted those trees, one to represent each of them. In the next photograph, a thirty-something Stanley stood beside the front doors of Saint Michael's. The bronze plaque was captured at his shoulder. Though it was far too small to read from the picture, Matt knew its inscription from memory. "Saint Michael's Hospital," he whispered. "Dedicated to the vitality of Saint Andrews and the well being of her people."

He continued up the stairs toward bed, but paused midway. In the diminished hallway light, he waited for ghostly sounds to emanate from the cellar. He knew what he had heard the night before was only the wind passing through gaps in an ancient foundation, but that was adult rationale. Matthew Dawson, the child, was not convinced. He had wanted to rush up the stairs and get under his covers. Thankfully, for both of them, the dead were at rest on this night.

# Chapter Four

Elmer Savoie loaded several slices of bread onto the conveyor of the industrial sized toaster in the hospital kitchen. He hurried over to the gas grill to stir the contents of a large pot then wiped his hands on his dirty apron and readied a margarine container for the coming landslide of toast.

Nurse Wanda Cooke stood on the other side of the heated pass through, chewing on her breakfast. "What do you think of him?" she asked between chomps.

"I tink he's okay, him," Elmer said, pulling a stack of large plastic plates from under the counter. "He tole me to call him *Matt*," he added with a slight air of pride.

"Well, aren't you quick to get up his arse?" Wanda said before another bite of her toast.

Elmer only smiled back.

"Are you worried at all that there'll be changes coming?"

"Nah, I don't worry for stuff like dat, me. Dis place will stay open as long as der are da crazy. And if dis place is open, it will need a kitchen to feed da crazy. And if it need a kitchen, it need Elmer." Toast slid from the toaster and the French cook went to work slathering bright yellow margarine on each piece.

Wanda laughed. She could not deny the man's logic. He had been the one and only cook to work the kitchen since she had been hired on ten years before. He would probably be the last employee to go. In all likelihood, he would be wearing his silly white paper hat until the end of his working days. Pushing sixty, he was probably ready to retire anyway. The hairs that escaped his hat were gray going on white. Deep lines around his eyes and mouth showed proof of a lifetime of labor. The tattoos on each of his forearms had faded to light blue in the many years since he got them while in the service of the navy. He already had the service pension to look forward to, and rumor had it, he never spent a nickel if he didn't earn two. He would be okay. Retired military seemed to have a knack for managing money and he was no exception.

Tyrone Klewes entered the kitchen through the swinging doors. "Elmer, you got the truck keys?" he bellowed. "Give 'em here."

"I need da truck for go at da store, me," Elmer said as he situated toast on each plate and set them on the pass through.

"After I serve breakfast, I need to go to the shipper's. I'm gonna need that truck," Klewes said as he readied a pile of serving trays beside Wanda.

Elmer went to the grill and began filling plastic bowls with oatmeal from the large pot. "Okay *Klew*," he said. "After I make da breakfast, I go at da store. You serve da breakfast in time for me to return and I pass da truck to you."

"After breakfast, you're gonna *pass* the truck to me?"

"I pass it to you," Elmer reiterated gruffly.

"Okay, you pass me the truck," Klewes said and he winked at Wanda.

She shook her head at the orderly in mock disgust. "Don't you get him all wound up, Mister Klewes. He's got to make it through lunch and supper before we're done with him today."

\* \* \* \*

Matt opened the door for Bobby Clark, owner and operator of Clark Builders. "This is the head doctor's office," Matt said once they were inside. Clark carried a clipboard and scrawled notes on it feverishly as he strolled around the perimeter of the room.

"It'll be a shame to get rid of all these built-in bookcases," he said, not looking up. He wore faded blue jeans and a matching jeans jacket. When Matt was a kid, this ensemble had jokingly been referred to as the redneck tuxedo. He couldn't help but smile when he recalled the barb.

"Yes, it will be," Matt agreed. "We need to add beds, and space around here is at a premium. We don't have much choice."

Clark walked over to a shelf and laid a hand on it. "Solid maple...too bad."

Matt cleared his throat and steered the conversation ahead. "I'd like to get all this shelving out of here and get the carpet torn up. Maybe you could get floor tiles to match the ones in the hallway."

Clark nodded as he jotted his notes.

"Oh, and replace the door. See if you can get one like the existing doors, with an observation window in it. We will need a couple new light fixtures in here, and new paint, I guess—white like the rest of the place."

"Okay," Clark said. "Is there anything else?"

"Yeah, there's a utility closet on the main floor. I'd like to make it the new office. So, I guess I'll need some plugs installed. Oh, and a data line too."

"The utility closet...that's gonna be kinda small, don't you think?"

"I won't be needing all these books in there. The beautiful thing about technology is everything in these pages will fit on my tablet. All I need is enough room for a small desk and a couple of chairs."

"Hmm...I guess so. Way of the future, eh?"

Matt grinned. "Way of the future." He considered the other benefit of the change—he would not have to work out of Stanley's office, where every square foot bore some small reminder of the man. It was Phillip Prichard who had recommended adding beds to increase hospital revenue. If they were to add beds, the office would have to be sacrificed. And though he would never admit it, Matt was happy for the excuse to give it up.

"So, that's a scrape and paint job on the exterior, fix the gate where needed, a reno in this room, and convert the utility closet to an office."

"Yeah, just make the utility a workable space."

"This is...umm...turning into a lot of work," Clark said. His brow was raised as he said it. It was the kind of look that begged, *am I going to get stiffed if I take this job?*

"We have a pretty good budget set aside for the work, so just get us your numbers," Matt said. He felt obliged to add, "The hospital is under new management and has a new investor."

Clark nodded and tucked his clipboard under his arm. He took a few more steps around the room, as though he was searching for stable ground from which to ask his next question. "Are my guys gonna, you know...be safe working here?"

There it was—the old stigma. It was never far from center. People feared what they didn't understand, and no one cared to understand mental illness. They didn't even want to think about it. "Yes, of course." For a moment, Matt considered the locked door near the office—the one with *Dykeman* on it. "No question about it."

\* \* \* \*

John Cundiff was seated at the second floor nurse's station when his new boss emerged from the office with Bobby Clark. He heard the men talking as they neared. "I just need to look at the utility closet and take some measurements on my way out," Clark said. "After I run the numbers, I'll be in touch with my quote."

They shook hands and Doctor Dawson thanked him for coming in.

Clark then turned to Cundiff. "Are you playing ball this year?" he asked.

"Wouldn't miss it," Cundiff said.

"Well then, I guess I'll see you Wednesday." Clark nodded and made for the stairs.

"What about you, Doctor Dawson?" Cundiff said. "Would you be interested in playing baseball with us? It's not softball, but we don't have any fire-ballers, either. We just sort of muck around and have fun."

"Umm...no thanks," the doctor said, scratching his stubbly chin. "I'm not much of an athlete."

Cundiff figured as much. He had just met Stanley's son a couple of days ago, but already the doctor looked worse for the wear. His hair was unruly, and his eyes were red and puffy. He looked like he needed a few good meals and then a few good hours of sleep. This worried the orderly. The former head doctor had always seemed at the top of his game, even when he wasn't. He gave the impression that he was in control, that running the hospital smoothly was child's play. His son did not. Cundiff could read the stress in his eyes.

Doubt was infectious and in a small group was bound to spread. Already, Klewes had voiced his concerns. He was genuinely afraid that Saint Michael's would close its doors, that Matthew Dawson couldn't fill his father's shoes. Cundiff had tried to assuage his fellow orderly's fears, but now he began to have doubts himself. Wanda had said that the meeting with the accountant did not go well and now Bobby Clark was here to give an estimate. On what? Might they be turning the hospital into an inn? An inn would be a whole lot easier to manage from a distance than a psychiatric facility, and it would be far more profitable to boot. Suddenly Cundiff could not wait for Wednesday to roll around so he had an excuse to talk to Clark and find out what he knew.

"Mister Cundiff," Doctor Dawson said. "What can you tell me about the patient at the end of the hall? I can't seem to find any of his records."

"There's not much to tell, really," Cundiff said. "He doesn't give us any trouble, if that's what you mean."

"I don't imagine he would, with all the sedatives he's given."

Cundiff shrugged. "I really don't know anything about pills and doses. Wanda administers all the medication."

"Well, I can tell you that his dosage is probably double what is needed. In fact, it's dangerously high. Can you think of any reason why? Is he a danger to others or himself?"

"I've been here for five years and that whole time, Mister Dykeman has been the same way. Like..."

"Catatonic."

"Yeah, that's it."

The doctor stared at nothing in particular, in thought.

"Wanda has been here the longest," the orderly offered. "She's the one to talk to."

"Dykeman's door is locked. I've checked the other patients' rooms and his is the only one. Do you know why?"

"Oh, that was Doctor Daw...that was your dad's orders. He told the staff that door always had to be locked."

"He doesn't seem like a flight risk. Strange rule, wouldn't you say?"

Cundiff grinned at the doctor. "No...I *wouldn't* say. With respect, that sort of statement is above my pay grade." He meant it. When he was hired and Stanley Dawson told him that he would have to wear white scrubs and white running shoes to work every day, he did not question it. When he was told he could not wear a wristwatch or his necklace or even his high school grad ring, he did not question it. He said, 'Yes, sir' and nothing else. In Saint Andrews, people learned young that loose lips sink ships. When you lived on the ocean, you took it to heart.

"Okay," Doctor Dawson said, turning back toward the office. "I'll talk to Wanda. Oh, and if you happen to find Dykeman's chart around here, please get it to me right away."

"Sure thing," Cundiff called after him.

Then he was left alone with his doubts.

\* \* \* \*

*Saint Michael's, Office of the Head Doctor—sunset:*

He woke to the sound of music. *Such a strange dream.* A fiddler played one of his favorites, *The Hills of County Downe.* Matthew was there. He stood beside Joanie, his hand in hers, in solemn reflection.

*Strange.*

Even now, at his desk, Stanley Dawson could still hear the final resonating notes of the song. They were slowly fading and all memory of the dream was sure to follow once wakefulness took hold. How long had he been asleep? The office was faintly lit by the sparse glow of the setting sun. It gave everything a slight brassy tinge, deepened the shadows. He stretched in his desk chair and rubbed his eyes.

The wall clock read 7:30. It seemed too dark for it. *Wait.* The second hand was frozen still. Stanley pulled his pocket watch from his lab coat. It agreed with the clock. It had stopped counting as well. He pondered the odd coincidence a moment then was distracted, as always, by the photograph of Susan he had years ago clipped and fixed to the inside cover of the watch. For Stanley, checking the time was no longer a measurement of the day. It had become a countdown until he would finally see his wife again.

He closed the watch, wound it, and replaced it in his coat, all while trying to shake his disorientation. He simply had to stop sleeping at his desk. What the staff must think of him. At the very least, he should make use of one of the vacant beds when fatigue sneaked up on him. At his age, he was lucky to wake pain free on his pillow-top at home. Sleeping in his old roller chair was asking for trouble.

He rose and looked at the corridor beyond his office door. Klewey was on duty tonight, he remembered. He and Nurse Tait should be helping the patients to their beds soon. Rory would start his cleaning rounds. Stanley wanted to catch him before going home, ask him to change the batteries in his clock.

When he reached the door, it refused to open. The knob would not turn. It was completely seized. *This place is falling apart,* he thought. He strengthened his grip and tried again. Then he put his weight on it, put his shoulders into it. It wouldn't budge. The hall outside was empty. It was not like his staff to leave the nurse's station unattended. He knocked on the door and waited, helplessly.

"This is ridiculous," he said to himself as he went back to his desk. *What was Rory's number again? With any luck, he'll have his phone on him.*

Stanley reached for his handset and stopped. A bolt of searing pain thrust though his chest and down his left arm. His knees buckled and he collapsed into his chair. With his right hand he clutched his chest as his left fell lifeless on his lap. His heart raced—he felt it thrumming under his palm. *Heart attack,* he thought. *Damn!* He slumped forward and seized the handset, but could not summon the strength to lift it from the cradle. Then another thought flashed through his reeling mind. *I've felt this before. This already happened to me once.*

He fell into the cushioned back of the chair, eyes shut tightly, waiting for the pain to stop burning like it had stopped the last time. Once again, he saw Matthew and Joanie holding hands. *What were they doing?* He approached them from behind, then he saw beyond them—the shiny black casket.

# Chapter Five

Darcy Collins dodged the foot traffic on the crowded sidewalk. She edged past seniors with white legs in shorts and socks in sandals, eating ice cream. A group of Asian tourists posed for photographs beside an arrangement of lobster traps and sun-bleached buoys in front of a seafood restaurant. Navigating the busy stretch was made more challenging by the three inch pumps she wore. She must have been out of her mind to take Nancy's advice. What made her an expert on what to wear to a job interview, anyway? What did appearing taller and firming up one's calves have to do with proving her qualifications? Darcy would have given anything to be in her comfortable black flats as she reached the iron gate.

She opened her appointment book and confirmed the address. Number 238 Water Street, Saint Andrews. This meeting had been a long time coming. She had achieved her PhD, won highest honors in her class, faced down fearsome final exams. Before that, it was a bachelor's in science, before that, high school, elementary, birth...life was turning out to be one hurdle after another. Each time she approached one, each time she felt the butterflies swirling, she promised it would be the last. Outside the gates of Saint Michael's she promised herself again.

Taking a moment to compose herself, she smoothed her skirt and straightened her jacket. She adjusted the collar of her blouse and felt for any stray hairs that may have escaped her conservative ponytail. "You can do this," she breathed. She clutched the shoulder strap of her bag tightly and pushed the shiny black gate open.

The hospital was not at all what she had expected. It looked more like an old Victorian house than a psychiatric ward. The yard was abuzz with construction workers. There were men on scaffolding climbing the west side of the building, scraping off old paint. Men on the ground painted shutters supported by saw horses. Others threw old boards and other debris into a dumpster in the side yard. Darcy got the sense that she had come at a time of drastic change, that the timing of this opportunity could not be better. Perhaps she could play a major role in something very special.

As Darcy made her way up the walk, the work stopped. All that could be heard was the *click-clack* of her heals on the concrete. She felt eyes crawling all over her body. The few workers who had not seen her heard her and dropped what they were doing to join in the ogling. A whistle came from somewhere on the scaffolding, but she did not look up. She had placed her entire focus on trying not to stumble on the cracked, uneven walkway in heels that felt too clumsy. Why had she listened to Nancy? If she were in her flats, she'd be able to hurry indoors.

Thankfully, she reached the stairs leading to the main doors without incident. Inside, she was sheltered from the leering men, but, as her eyes adjusted from the bright morning sun, she realized she still had an audience. Two stout-looking men in white scrubs had turned their attentions her way. One stood on the second step of a winding staircase, the other leaned on the banister. It appeared that she had interrupted their conversation.

"Can I help you?" the black man asked.

"Yes, I'm here for a meeting with Doctor Dawson," Darcy said in her most formal voice.

"You're here to interview," he said.

"Yes."

"That's great." He smiled, displaying a row of pearly teeth under his thick beard. The other man smiled too, and Darcy wondered if he had blinked yet. "The doc's office is down that hall and to the right. It's the door is marked *utility*. You can't miss it."

*Utility? Was that a joke?* She read the man's face for a trace of mischief. His warm smile seemed genuine. "Okay...thanks," she said. She took a breath and started down the hall toward her next hurdle.

\* \* \* \*

"Holy shit, Klewey. Is she ever hot," Cundiff whispered as he watched the young lady walk away.

"What? Are you shittin' me?" Klewes gave his coworker an indignant smirk. "She's way too bony."

"Nah, she's just slender...fit."

"Would you get outta here. There's no way that backyard is big enough for this kid to play in."

Cundiff laughed and shook his head.

"Yeah," Klewes continued. "You want a rump roast that's big enough to put some sauce on, ya know what I'm sayin'."

"It's always about barbeque with you, isn't it?"

"Hey, is that a race thing?"

They laughed quietly.

"Well, I hope she gets the job...for more than one reason."

"Me too," Klewes said, watching after her. "She's the only one who bothered to come for an interview."

\* \* \* \*

Matt had the date, June 27th, circled on his desktop calendar, with *Doctor Collins* written in the circle. He leafed ahead a couple of pages to the next date he had circled: August, 31st. The last day of his sabbatical from D. A. McLaughlin. The board had been more than gracious to award the break from his duties under the circumstances, and he was grateful. He was hell bent on resuming his residency before the end of the summer and giving the center his best years of service. It was the least he could do for their generous reprieve to deal with his family business. Yet, the issue that was most paramount remained unresolved—the issue of finding a replacement doctor to take the reins of Saint Michael's.

It was proving a difficult task. The salary he had in mind precluded most established psychiatrists, so he searched for relative newcomers with a few years of experience. Most discussion with prospective replacements ended at the phone call stage. When it came up that the available position was at a sixteen-bed, private hospital in tourist country, Matt usually heard *no thanks, not interested* or just *not interested* and one time he simply heard a dial tone. He decided to refocus his search.

He had phoned Doctor Kipping, the only university professor who Matt had kept in contact with after graduating. Usually they bounced two or three line emails back and forth, so on the day Matt called, Doctor Kipping had been surprised—even more so when he heard his former student's reason.

"You want me to recommend a fresh graduate from this year's class, with no experience, to run a facility for you?"

"Yeah. What do you think?"

"I think you'd better check yourself in to that hospital of yours."

"I meant, what do you think about a candidate?"

"Hmm...a head doctor's position in a quiet hospital in scenic Saint Andrews...maybe I'll take the position."

"Really?"

"No...not really."

Doctor Kipping said he would make a few calls and be in touch. A few hours later, he emailed Matt to say that he should expect a call from a Darcy Collins. She had graduated at the top of her class, was a very dedicated young woman, and may be the only fresh graduate capable of filling such a position.

Now Matt sat at his tiny desk in his tiny office awaiting her arrival.

Clark Builders had done a decent job in sprucing up the utility closet. They had put in a drop ceiling that hid the tangle of wires overhead, and the newly tiled floor and freshly painted walls brightened the room. They could not, however, do anything about the electrical panels, nor the water heater that serviced the next door bathroom. There was room for little more than a desk, a guest chair, and a filing cabinet.

Also, Matt had not anticipated the low frequency drone of the panels. The noise was akin to the relentless buzzing of a beehive and, after a week, had driven him half mad. He heard the noise everywhere he went. However, like new homeowners next to the airport get used to the comings and goings of planes, Matt acclimated to the former utility closet and no longer noticed the buzzing.

He eyed the latest transfer statement from the bank on his desk. It denoted the most recent cash infusion he had made from his personal account into the hospital's coffers. The sight of it sickened him. He stashed it in the top drawer.

"Doctor Dawson?"

Matt looked up from the desk and saw legs. Reflexively, he looked away. "Yes."

"I'm Darcy Collins," the woman said.

Matt rose. This time, he made sure to make eye contact with her. "Welcome," he said extending his hand. "Please, call me Matt."

Darcy shook it and was invited to sit.

"How was the flight?" he asked.

"Fine, thank you."

"Did you get situated at the inn?"

"Yes."

"Oh good. Is the room to your liking?"

"Yes, it's lovely, thank you."

"Well, let me know if there is anything I can do to make your stay more comfortable."

She smiled.

Matt was suddenly lost. He had prepared questions for the interview, but now they escaped him. He had not expected her to be so pretty. Kipping should have warned him. "So...U of A, huh?" he said.

"Yes." She pulled a folder from her bag and set it on the desk. "Here is a copy of my resume and transcript," she said as she handed Matt the sheets. "I also have a few reference letters from job placements I've done."

*Great,* he thought. *Maybe she can lead me through this whole interview process.* He read the transcript then read it again. 3.99. He made a mental note to never share his lackluster Grade Point Average with her. "Where did you do your placements?"

"In clinics close to the Stratford area." She bunched together three print-outs from the folder and passed them across the desk as well. "I'm from there and I wanted to be close to home."

Matt scanned the letters. They shared common assessments of the new doctor: very bright, intelligent, highly motivated, dedicated. One Doctor Stafford closed his letter with, *Miss Collins is sure to make a fine psychiatrist and will prove an invaluable asset to any facility's roster.* "Clearly, you have some fans," Matt said once he had finished reading. "Doctor Kipping also gave you a sterling endorsement."

Darcy shifted in her seat. "I enjoyed his classes the most."

"Me too." Matt leaned back in his chair, folded his hands across his lap, and tried to remember his carefully planned direction for the interview—the direction that fell from all reckoning the moment he laid eyes on the inter-viewee. While searching for a question to ask, the silence between them grew to the point of discomfort. He became aware of the ambient electrical buzz in the room.

There were no answers in her emerald green eyes or her deep brown tress-es. He immediately dropped his gaze to the desktop, the letters atop it. "I guess I should tell you a little about the position." He cleared his throat. "I am seek-ing someone to replace me as head doctor here. The successful candidate will oversee patient care directly. You will need to devise and update treatment plans accordingly, not just in the sense of therapy and medication, mind you, but also with respect to patients requiring special treatment like physiother-apy or speech pathology, or whatever the case may be. So there will be some required coordination with outside therapists."

Matt found a measure of comfort, as he usually did, when he discussed his work, and his words flowed freely. Venus herself could not unnerve him once his mind was set to his trade. "You would also manage the operations of the staff. There are two full-time nurses, two orderlies, one kitchen staff and one janitor, who for some reason, is also willing to perform as maintenance man without a pay increase. Let me know if I'm throwing too much at you."

"You're not."

"In addition to the day-to-day operations of the hospital, you will also be required to oversee expenses. Our accountant, Phillip Prichard, will help with the bookkeeping. And while the head doctor does all the hard work, I will get all the glory as I am to become president of the hospital. It is a new position and as such, the only duty I will perform will be the hiring and firing of the staff. What do you think, so far?"

"I think it will be a challenge for whoever gets the position...and a worthwhile one."

"Well..." he said. "I haven't told you about the salary yet."

"I gathered that it would be a little on the low side." She shifted in her seat again and added, "I mean...I guessed that's why you're interviewing a recent grad like me."

*Smart girl.*

"Still, you are paying in a currency few others are willing or *able* to pay in."

"Supervisory experience."

Darcy smiled. "Exactly."

*And hopefully, by the time you are ready to seek more money elsewhere, Saint Michael's will be healthy enough to see that you get it right here.* "The position draws forty thousand a year to start, plus accommodations." Matt winced and waited for her reaction. "I'll take it as a good sign that you are still here. I know it is half of what you could earn on the open market and there will be increases. They'll come when the hospital is running smoothly."

"I take it there are a lot of changes happening."

"Yes, from top to bottom. My fff...Doctor Stanley Dawson, opened the hospital in 1965 and was its one and only doctor. So, now I'm taking steps to update the facility. You probably noticed all the activity on your way in. We are adding beds as well. When the renovation is complete, there will be room for eighteen patients."

"How many patients do you have presently?"

"We are up to twelve. I put the word out to other facilities in the area that we can accept six more. It shouldn't be long before we're at full capacity. Beds in long-term private facilities usually fill quickly."

"As they do with most premium service providers. I wrote a paper on the comparison between public and private mental healthcare services."

"Oh, and what did you conclude?"

"That, while the public system is the only avenue for people of low income or those without health insurance, the services rendered are often lacking and at best inconsistent from hospital to hospital. Public doctors are often overworked and commonly carry too great a case load. Unfortunately, that has been shown to result in incorrect diagnoses and the over or improper medicating of patients."

Matt watched Darcy's confidence building as she shared her findings. She sat a little taller in her chair, her eyes hardened.

"In the private system, the proper patient-doctor ratio is more likely to be maintained, leading to better care of the patients and ultimately more face time for therapy. In a properly funded facility, patient stays can go on as long as they need to, so patient progress and response to treatment can be properly monitored. It is nothing like the revolving door public system."

"You and my father would have gotten along famously," Matt said, but he was thinking that he could show her pages of red ink that made deep-pocketed public care something to envy. "He told me the same thing every chance he got."

"Oh?"

"Yes. You see, I'm one of those overworked, overmedicating public doctors."

Darcy's confident visage went slack. "I am so sorry."

"That's okay," Matt said, grinning at the sudden flushing in her cheeks. "Like I said, I heard it all from my father before. What was it that he called what I do? Oh yeah...*triage* psychiatry. The idea is to take in the ill, diagnose, detox, prescribe and get 'em back on the streets as fast as possible because there are more on the way."

"It must be difficult to work in those conditions...to be on the front line like that."

"It is, and you're right. Very few of the people I treat can afford health insurance. Most of them are poor or homeless. After all, there's ultimately a good reason for people being poor or homeless—but they're still people. You just want to do your best for them with what you have to work with."

Darcy shifted uncomfortably in her seat and said, "You probably see a very rude, very cocky person before you."

"Not at all." He waved a hand in the air. "We don't have to agree on everything. It's better for me to hire someone who is pro-private healthcare into this position because this is obviously a privately run facility.

"So, I'm still in the running?"

"I think so," he said. "Besides, it would make Stanley happy to have a doctor of like mind at the helm of his hospital."

"Did he retire?"

"No, he expired."

"Oh...I should have known that coming in. I'm sorry for your loss."

"Thanks." Matt found himself nodding at the sentiment then stopped abruptly, fearing it wasn't the appropriate response to condolences. He quickly changed the subject. "So, tell me about your career goals."

"I have broken my goals into five year plans. First, I'd like to get a job...*any* job in the field and gain some of that experience you mentioned. Then, I'd like to work my way into a clinic near Stratford so I could be closer to my parents and my sister, with the end goal of opening my own practice someday."

"That's ambitious."

"I'll go one step at a time."

"Say you were offered this position. How would you feel about moving here?"

"I would be excited for the opportunity. I looked up Saint Andrews online after we spoke on the phone, but the pictures don't do it justice. It's a beautiful town and the water is just gorgeous. I love all the little shops and restaurants on Water Street, too. It's like being in a postcard."

*You say that now, but wait until winter hits and the wind off that gorgeous water is minus twenty-two.* "What about moving away from family and boyfriends? Would you be up to that?"

"Well, my parents already know that I will probably have to move where the work is and there are no boyfriends to speak of. I've been concentrating on school recently."

Matt felt his own cheeks get a little rosy. "Perhaps you'd like a tour of the place."

"I would very much."

\* \* \* \*

*Stupid!* Darcy fumed to herself as she followed Matt between the few tables and chairs that made up the dining area. *How did I not find out his father died before coming to the interview? He's going to think I don't know how to prepare. Oh, and I just had to shoot my mouth off about public healthcare. I'm so screwed.*

"...and there are a few patients' quarters on either side of the corridor here as it leads to the patient lounge," Matt said, pointing from his sides like a flight attendant showing the emergency exits on a plane.

They entered the lounge where a half a dozen patients were gathered to watch the muted television securely bolted to the wall or to gaze out the tall windows. There was a bookcase filled with well-used paperbacks, and the shelf beside it was home to a precarious stack of board games. Padded tables were set up for activities and ample, soft-cushioned furniture for resting. Darcy spotted the orderly that had greeted her sitting beside a middle-aged woman in a bathrobe. They were seated on a love seat in front of a round coffee table. He read to her from a magazine.

"This is Tyrone Klewes," Matt explained. "He's one of our capable orderlies."

Darcy shook his hand. "We sort of met when I arrived. I'm Darcy." She looked at the woman beside him. She was unkempt and stared blankly at the floor. Darcy felt a compulsion to brush the woman's hair. "Who would this be?"

"This is Margaret," Klewes said. "She's one of our longest standing guests."

Darcy bent before her. "Hello Margaret. It's nice to meet you."

The woman didn't respond. Eyes remained fixed on the floor.

"You were reading to her?" Darcy asked.

"She seems to like the baseball news," Klewes said, then looked up at Matt, smiling.

"Keep up the good work, Mister Klewes," Matt said, shaking his head. "Shall we move along, Doctor Collins?" While they continued toward the lobby, Matt told her a little about Margaret's condition. "Among her more serious symptoms, Margaret is prone to outburst. She must like you. She would have no trouble expressing herself if she didn't."

Past the lobby, they came to the main stair across from the front entrance. Beside it was a small lift that looked as though it was seldom used. Matt was explaining the wheelchair entrance at the rear of the building and how the lift was to be repaired to meet with accessibility standards. Darcy's attention was drawn to the other side of the staircase where a sculpture stood atop a white pedestal. The pedestal, fashioned after a roman pillar, stood four feet tall, the sculpture at least another four. The piece depicted a winged man holding a staff. Darcy moved around the stair for a closer look. The staff turned out to be a spear and at the man's feet was a coiled snake. The spear ran it through.

"Ah, yes," Matt said, watching her. "Stanley's old friend. If it wasn't so blasted big and heavy, I'd have it removed. I think it's real marble."

"Who is it?" Darcy asked looking up at the beautifully crafted man, his smooth features, the detail in his feathered wings.

"This is the archangel, Saint Michael, himself. As the story goes, he was sent by God to cast Satan out of paradise."

"That's the devil?" she said, regarding the serpent at the end of the spear.

"Stanley saw a kinship with Michael—enough to name the hospital in his honor. He felt it was his duty as a psychiatrist to help people exorcise their demons, much like the archangel did on behalf of the Lord."

"Was he very religious...your father?"

"Not really. He was more of a history buff and he had a keen interest in Christian lore in particular. He had several books on the subject. Come, let me show you the second floor."

Darcy stared into Michael's milky, pupil-less eyes. She half expected them to blink. When she was a child, her parents had taken her and her sister to church every Sunday. On the walls of their chapel hung carvings depicting Christ's climb of Mount Calvary under the burden of the cross. She had found the carvings so real, so lifelike, that she thought of them as living things—like they were listening as the congregation paid tribute. She imagined that when the church closed and everyone had left, the carvings came to life—the whips lashed, the spear pierced and the cross rose. During prayer, she would watch the nearest carvings intently for slight movements...a momentary lapse from the pose, a blink, any sign they were listening. She would stare until her head ached.

Matt was waiting for her. All she needed was to behave strangely in front of him. That would be the final shove over the cliff for an interview that was teetering on the brink of disaster. "It's beautiful," she said, to show that it was her appreciation of the piece that had given her pause. "Where is it from?"

"I'm not sure," Matt said, turning to the staircase. "It's very old and I think my father spent a small fortune getting it here."

Darcy watched Michael as they climbed and Matt went on about Stanley Dawson's pride in the sculpture. She thought of the carvings in her old chapel and of a time when her prayers were still heard.

\* \* \* \*

"This used to be the office," Matt said. He stood beside Darcy in the doorway as two of Bobby Clark's carpenters went about their work inside. The office bore little resemblance to its former self. The furniture and books were gone and the carpet was removed, as were the built-in cases. "Soon it will be patient quarters."

Matt walked briskly past Dykeman's room. If Darcy were to ask of Dykeman's condition, he would be forced to show his ignorance. Weeks after arriving at Saint Michael's, he still knew nothing of the man aside from the ridiculous amount of sedative Stanley had given him. Matt had been gradually reducing his medication, but saw little change in Dykeman's condition.

He spent his days seated at his window, once Cundiff or Klewes got him out of bed. They would feed him there, change his sanitaries, take him to the bath every two days. Always in pairs. No one was ever alone with Dykeman. Like the locked door, Matt figured it was another of Stanley's rules. It seemed even cremation could not keep him from running the place.

No family had come forward for Dykeman. For this, Matt was relieved. He was afraid the man had suffered permanent damage and there would be no explaining it to loved ones, let alone the College of Physicians. Matt cringed at the idea of a explaining himself at a hearing. He could not even explain the situation to a fresh graduate.

Minutes later, he had her safely back in his office. There would be a time and place to tell her about Dykeman, and the job interview was not it. He had watched her interact with everyone they met on their tour and she had impressed. She had a warm quality when talking with patient and staff alike. It was a quality that would probably fade with time and frustration in the practice, but it was a trait that was totally absent in most doctors. She exhibited trade knowledge and a keen interest. His mind was made up. The position was hers. In fact, Matt spent most of the tour trying to convince himself that he had not decided the moment he saw her legs.

Once they were seated, another question occurred to him. "Why psychiatry?"

Darcy's gaze dropped to the desktop. Matt was surprised that the question seemed to catch her off guard. He did not think it was much of a curve ball. He himself, and likely most of his colleagues, would have simply said the work is interesting and rewarding—something of that sort, something safe. He would never admit that he pursued the practice out of desire to gain Stanley's approval.

After a few moments, she replied, "There is a history of mental illness in my family. I grew up with it in the next bedroom. I have seen what it can do to people...and their loved ones. I thought, if I could work to improve the quality of life for people like my sister, Dianne, it would be a career well spent. I might even be able to help patients' families along the way—people like myself."

He smiled and said, "Welcome aboard."

# Chapter Six

It took a moment for him to get his bearings. The room was foreign. Wires hung from holes in the ceiling like waiting vipers. The walls were opened, the windows naked. Rough floor timbers were covered with dust and debris. The door that once proudly bore his name and title was gone, leaving a mere gaping hole. The furniture, his desk, his books—all had been taken away. All his books. Stanley felt like crying, though he did not know if he was even capable. Why wouldn't he lose that too? He had lost everything else.

The sun was setting again, even though his pocket watch insisted it was half past seven. It felt like a great deal of time had passed since his heart attack, but he couldn't tell how much. He did not know where he went, only that it was a black, empty void. Now he was back, but for how long? *When* is it, anyway? By the looks of things, the hospital may have been closed, the building condemned.

He was afraid to go to the doorway, to look down the corridor and see what had become of Saint Michael's. Did it die when he did? He paced the floor while trying to make some sense of the senseless. *Why do I keep coming back here? Next time I return, will it be to a parking lot...a field? Will I linger here for eternity?*

Stanley looked at his feet. They had left tracks in the dust. On some level he was pleased that he managed to affect his environment, if even in such an insignificant way. It meant that he was part of this world, not some afterthought blown in on the wind. Such as it was, this was still *his* hospital. He turned to the doorway, balled his fists, and marched.

The hallway opened before him. It was just as he remembered it: gleaming blue tiles and doors, bright white walls under warm lights. He smiled. Maybe the nightmare was over. He hurried down the corridor in search of the staff. He would have given anything to find Cundiff at the station, to ask him how the Blue Jays had been playing. Maybe he would find Klewes and ask him about his latest female conquest. Hell, it could be Wanda, for all it mattered. Even her crankiness would make for a welcomed reunion.

The chair at the nurse's station was empty, as was the far end of the hall. Stanley called out, "Hello?" and heard no response. Furthermore, he heard *nothing*, as though the entire building had been placed inside a vacuum where sound failed to propagate. He went to the stair and descended, calling for his people as he did. The lobby was void of patient and staff alike. The surge of joy he had felt leaving his office had gone as fast as it came. He was alone.

Save for one other.

Stanley went to the statue by the staircase. He smiled at Saint Michael and said, "Hello, old friend. I'm glad you haven't abandoned me." He leaned against the wall and slid down it to the floor. There he sat, arms around his knees, in the shadow of his angel's marble wings.

\* \* \* \*

Matt ate dinner in the study again. He had cleaned his plate and stacked it on the pile of dirty dishes, from previous meals, left on the corner of the desk. Somehow the kitchen table felt off-limits to him. It had been his parents' table, the place they had shared so many discussions over steaming cups of tea. Open before him was the hospital's ledger. He surmised that Saint Michael's should reach the break-even stage by the early fall. That would be a miraculous turnaround, albeit a painful one. His bank statements were the paper equivalent of a prize fighter in the ninth round—ugly and getting uglier.

He focused on the good news of the day. He had found his replacement. That meant he could soon return home—to his *real* home.

*Darcy Collins may be a little green*, he reasoned, *but what she lacked in experience, her drive and her charm more than compensated for.* She had been so pleased when he gave her the job. Though after a few moments of reverie, her smile began to fade and Matt could tell that she was already raising a new goal at the outskirts of her reach.

"So, what do you think?" Matt had said, basking in her brief delight. "Report for duty in a couple of weeks? That should give you some time to settle things at home."

"Why don't I just stay? That is, if you're ready for me to start right away."

"Umm, yeah. I'm ready for you tomorrow. Are you sure?"

"Yes. I'd really like to get started and besides, there isn't much for me to settle at home. My parents can ship whatever I need in a few days, so I'm pretty much ready to get to work."

"Okay then. I'll arrange an apartment for you. I planned to make Stanley's house available to the new head doctor once I go back to Edmonton. Until then, I'll line up something sufficient...fully furnished, water view."

It felt like a safe decision and he assured himself that he would have chosen her even if there had been scads of applicants. He typed those very thoughts in the form of a *thank you* email to Doctor Kipping. Then he indulged some of his more intimate thoughts of the new doctor. *Why didn't I offer for her to move in with me? The house is plenty big. We could have used the time to get to know one another. Right...I almost forgot, maneuvering like that is reserved for men who aren't downright terrified of women.*

Matt hoped she would like the house. He assumed she would, after all, she didn't have a history with it like he did. It was a beautiful home, built in the 1890's when everything was still made from real wood and brick. Its doors were solid and it boasted high ceilings with elaborate moldings. Each bedroom had a fireplace with unique masonry and mantelpieces. It was like each room had a personality of its own. *Which one would she choose to be hers?* he wondered. *The warmly stained oak over the red brick hearth? Likely the white painted mantel over sandstone.*

He liked the idea of her someday occupying the house. In a way, it already made him feel closer to her. The house deserved to hold life again. Once she was comfortable, she could use it to host parties and dinners. She could become a Rotarian and hold meetings in the parlor. Of course, he could stay there when he came to visit. His mind wandered into a spring setting, perhaps next year, in which he would be in town to check on things at Saint Michael's. They would have dinner at home in the evening, sit on the veranda sharing the view of the bay, and sip a flavorful Vouvray, no, Champagne, (of course, they're celebrating his visit). They would discuss the past months and the thing that is missing from each of their lives.

*Next year...*he thought, longingly.

*Thunk—thunk.*

Matt was roused from his fantasy of wine and conversation. It was a few seconds before he could decipher the noise, determine where it came from.

*Thunk—thunk.*

*That blasted loose shutter.* He had forgotten all about it and now a stiff night breeze served reminder. Matt made a mental note to mention it to Bobby Clark in the morning. Maybe he could send one of his men to fasten it down. Matt went to the window and saw more evidence of the blowing wind. The cherry trees near the edge of the grounds were dancing on the gusts. They were in full bloom and even the diminished evening light could not hide pink blossoms that shimmered like cheerleader's pompoms.

He admired the trees for a while before leaving the study. The report of the loose shutter followed as he made his way down the hall. He paused briefly by the door to the cellar stairs and listened.

"Nah," he said aloud, dismissing some wild inner notion. He continued toward the kitchen, then stopped. He was uncertain what made him do so, but he returned to the cellar door. Perhaps it was simply for old-time's sake—or maybe he really heard what he thought he heard.

Several seconds passed and he began to feel a little foolish for indulging in his flight of fancy. He was walking away when the elusive phenomenon returned. This time, he *did* hear it. *Moaning* from below. His spine tensed.

"The spirits are restless tonight," he said to himself. Then he chuckled, though he did not find the situation funny in the least. It was distressing that he was still afflicted by this immature fear in his adult years. He forced himself to open the cellar door. Slowly, he pushed it wide. There was nothing but blackness. He reached an arm inside and flipped on the lights. The rickety, old steps illuminated under a soft glow. Matt stuck his head into the stairwell and stole a glimpse. There was not enough light to entice him any further.

*Just go down there*, he thought. *It would be a good exercise.*

More than thirty years had passed since the last time he had dared venture to the cellar and the memory of it still unsettled him...

Matthew's mother was wearing a black dress. He leaned in the doorway to her bathroom and watched her put in dangling diamond earrings. "Sweetie, we rarely go out. I'm sure you can handle one night without us," she said, looking at him in the mirror.

"But, I don't want a sitter," he whined. "Why can't I come with you?"

"I told you, it's a dinner for adults. There won't be any other kids there."

"Well, can I stay home alone?"

"Yeah, right. You're nine."

"Fine, I'm gonna stay in my room all night."

"Come on, Matthew." She cocked her head to the side and gave her son her best *don't be silly* look. "You're going to like Chrissy. She's very nice and she happens to be very cute, too." Her expression morphed to a coy smile.

"When are you coming home?"

"You'll be long asleep in your bed, but I'll come in and give you a kiss."

Matthew looked at the floor. He wasn't getting anywhere. Maybe he should fake a bellyache. That old ploy always worked.

"Oh, and I got a video for you guys to watch."

"Which one?" he droned.

"I think it's called *Space Wars*, or something..." she said absently as she applied eyeliner.

"Do you mean *Star Wars*?"

"That's it. The young man at the store said it was pretty popular."

Suddenly the evening did not seem so bad. Forget Chrissy, he would be spending it with *Luke Skywalker* and the *Rebel Alliance*. "When is she coming?"

His mother smiled at his reflection.

She was right—Chrissy happened to be very cute. She had long, curly blond hair and big brown eyes. Matthew was enamored watching her interact with his parents at the front door. She carried on with them as though she was nearing adulthood herself, though she was only four and a half years his senior. "There is soda in the fridge and chips in the pantry. Don't let him have too much of either," his mother said while his father coaxed her out the door. Matt frowned, not for the limits on junk food, but for his mother's mothering him in front of his company. "See you in the morning," Matthew said in his best attempt at sounding grown-up.

When his parents had gone, he turned to Chrissy and said, "We have a video to watch," and handed her the case.

She took it, read it, and set it on the coffee table. "I have a better one," she said. She searched her bag and pulled out a case. "Go ahead, put it in the machine."

Matthew looked quizzically at the cover. It had a long word he was not familiar with. Seeing his struggle to decode it, Chrissy read it for him. "It's called *Poltergeist*. I heard it's really cool."

Matthew could sense, since he couldn't even read the title, that he was probably too young to watch the movie. Yet, as Chrissy smiled at him in anticipation of watching something that was *really cool*, he was compelled to put it in the machine. He did not want his company thinking he was...well...a little kid. He removed it from the case and took it over to their floor model television and stuffed it in the video player atop it.

"I'll get us some movie snacks," Chrissy said, going to the kitchen. She returned to the couch cradling two glasses of cola in her left arm and holding a bowl of chips in the other. "Did I miss anything?" she asked Matthew as she sat beside him.

She sat close. Their legs touched and it gave him a rush of excitement. Over the next hour and a half, as they watched the haunting of the Freeling household, Matt experienced many rushes of emotion—none of them good. He had stopped sipping from his glass in the first five minutes and simply squeezed it in his hand throughout the remainder of the movie. What little soda he did consume sloshed and fizzed in his belly as the horror played out. *I have a closet, too*, he had thought. *Just like the one that swallowed that little girl*.

At different points in the movie, Matthew tried to think about more light-hearted things, like his army action figures and his baseball card collection. He even tried to focus on the sound of Chrissy chomping on potato chips, but he was always sucked back into the film, just like that girl was sucked into her closet. He tried telling himself that it was just a story, that they were all actors, but the grown-ups in the movie were so genuinely frightened that he could not help but be frightened too. Toward the end, Matthew closed his eyes tightly and hoped that Chrissy would not look his way and catch him chickening-out. Though, if she did, that would be better than watching the monster attack that poor family. It would be the lesser of two evils.

"That was awesome," she said giddily when the end credits finally rolled. She shifted on the couch to face him. "What was your favorite part?"

Matthew continued to face the television. He was frozen—afraid that, if he moved, one of those coffins would burst through the floor and open in front of him to reveal a yawning skeleton. "Umm..." he started, but his voice was scratchy, his throat dry. He swallowed hard and said, "I don't know there were so many..."

"I know, eh. How about when the skin fell off that guy's face? That was so gross."

Matthew remembered. He swallowed again.

"Remember when the mother fell in the pool with all those dead bodies?"

"Umm...yeah." He still could not bring himself to look away from the credits passing through the screen.

"Oh, you didn't drink your Pepsi," she said.

"I don't really like it," he managed to say.

"Well, I'll take it to the kitchen for you." She reached for it.

Matthew made minimal movements to hand the glass to her. When he did, his hand was shaking. He hoped that she didn't notice. Sadly she had, just like she had noticed him shutting his eyes during the movie. And when she returned from delivering the glasses to the kitchen she wore an impish smile.

"You know, the most interesting thing about that movie is that the haunting takes place in an ordinary house. It's not even that old. It's nowhere near as old as this house. It wouldn't have half the history this one has."

He wondered what she meant by that. He forced himself to face her though his neck was stiff from what seemed like hours of heightened nerves.

"You do know what happened here, right?" She looked at him without the slightest hint of humor.

Matthew's heart sank to his tummy. *What do you mean,* he wanted to say, but he couldn't. He could not make a sound.

"Oh...you haven't heard about the little boy..." she said in amazement. "The one who died here."

His eyes widened.

"Well...it happened before you guys moved in, even before I was born. I'm not surprised your parents didn't tell you about it. It's so sad."

Matthew had an urge to get up and run to his bedroom—to pull the covers over his head and wait there until morning light, but he had been drawn into the horror movie and was now being drawn into the sitter's story. "...What happened?" His voice was little more than a whisper.

Chrissy lowered her voice to mimic Matthew's. "One day, the kids who lived here were playing hide and seek outside. The youngest boy wanted to find the best hiding place, and he did. It was perfect, a place only he was small enough to fit in and no one would ever think to search for him there. You see, he had discovered the old coal chute at the back of the house.

"Years and years ago, most of these houses were heated by coal furnaces. They were dirty things. People kept piles of coal in their basements to keep 'em going. A truck would deliver it. They would shovel the coal off the truck, down the chute and into the basement. Over the years, people switched to oil furnaces and all of the coal burners are long gone. But the coal chutes remain. My house down the street still has one...and, of course, so does yours."

Tension mounted in Matthew's shoulders again. His neck went stiff.

"The metal door was almost too heavy for the little boy to open, but he managed. He got in and pulled it shut behind him. Too bad he didn't know how steep the chute was when he decided to hide in there. He fell to the bottom and..."

Chrissy clapped her hands together. "*Wham!*"

Matthew flinched.

"He hit his head. He was unconscious while the other kids did their seeking. Hours passed and it was getting dark. Finally, the kids told their parents about the missing boy and they went out to look for him, too. When they couldn't find him, they called the police and put a search party together. They combed the neighborhood, the woods, even Garnett's field, and the whole time they were hunting high and low, the boy was in the chute.

He woke up and tried to climb out but couldn't. It was too steep. He tried to get the door open at the bottom of the chute, but it had been padlocked on the inside to keep burglars out. All he could do was scream for help while the search party moved farther and farther away from the house.

"The chute was dirty and it wasn't long before his lungs filled with coal dust. His throat went dry and pretty soon all he could do was moan...moan and hope for rescue. At some point he fell asleep and he never woke up."

The air went cold and it felt like ice was forming in Matthew's chest with every breath he took.

"They didn't find him until the family noticed the smell. His mother watched as his father opened the chute door in the basement. The boy's body fell onto the floor. The very sight of his blue skin caked in black coal dust drove his mother mad. They buried his body in the Greenock Church cemetery, but people say his spirit never left this house. Rumor has it that if you are quiet at night, you can still hear him moaning for help."

Matthew had heard him all right—too many times to count.

He was pushing forty, and he still heard him. He still heard Chrissy's story.

"Doctor, heal thyself," he whispered.

Matt switched the cellar light off and closed the door.

# Chapter Seven

"Look what I got here, Margaret," Klewes announced as he entered the lounge at Saint Michael's. "The new *Sports Illustrated*." The woman looked up from under a hay stack of gray hair at the magazine the orderly was holding. "It's got an article on Derek Jeter," he said. Margaret's gaze fell back to the floor. "I know, I'm pumped, too. We can check it out after my rounds."

"Mister Klewes," Wanda Cooke barked. "Don't you go getting our Margaret all worked up. There's more than enough excitement around here in a day."

Darcy smirked. She had been discussing a patient with Wanda when Klewes made his boisterous entrance, and the interruption clearly perturbed the nurse.

"Yes ma'am," he said, raising a hand in mock salute as he approached them. "Congratulations Doctor Collins, I'm glad to hear you got the position."

"Oh, thanks," Darcy said, tempted to add *call me Darcy*. Still, she liked the sound of *doctor* before her name and decided to let it go for a while.

"You must be eager to get to work, starting the next day and all."

"No time like the present."

"Ain't that a fact. Hey Wanda, you seen Cundiff around?"

"Mister Cundiff is upstairs," the nurse said absently.

Klewes headed for the staircase and as he passed by the couch where Margaret was seated, pointed at her and said, "Derek Jeter, baby. I'll be back."

"He seems to get along well with the patients," Darcy said to Wanda.

"Oh yes. Both of our orderlies are very good with them. They may look like ogres, but they are very nice boys...young Mister Cundiff especially."

Darcy smiled as she considered the other orderly. "He keeps offering to make tea for me."

"I think he just wants to do something nice for you, dear."

After a moment, she said, "I guess I'm just not used to that."

"Not used to what?" Wanda asked. "Drinking tea or getting attention from men?"

* * * *

Matt stood in the kitchen doorway as he spoke to his cook. Elmer Savoie was busy preparing sandwiches for the approaching noon serving, and Matt wondered how much of what he said to the cook was getting through. At the best of times, he wondered how much Elmer understood him, but this was important, so Matt persisted.

"So, Elmer, the new patient will be here on Monday and we really have to be aware of her food allergies."

"Okay der," Elmer said, focusing on his work.

"She has a pretty nasty peanut allergy," Matt continued. "So we'll have to be *really* careful. She is allergic to soy also. So, that's like double trouble. You'd be surprised what has soy in it...lots of stuff."

"All right, den."

"So this is the form the clinic sent over listing all of her allergies," Matt said, holding up a sheet for Elmer to see.

"Okay," Elmer said without raising his head.

"I'll just leave it here by the pass-through," Matt said. "Tell you what, maybe I'll come back to review it with you when you're not quite so busy."

"Okay, see you later, Matt."

Matt stopped in the doorway before leaving and had a thought. "Would it be easier for you if I printed the form in French?"

This time Elmer did look up. "What's dat?"

"Do you prefer to get paperwork in French?"

Elmer seemed to think it over for a few seconds. "I can read bote French and de English, but neider one too good, me."

"Okay, I'll come back." At that point, Matt just wanted to get out of there.

"Okay, pin me on da board," Elmer said.

"What?" *Pin him? On the what?*

"Pin me on da board, dat form. I don't wan it getting lost, me." Elmer nodded at the wall beside the door. Matt turned to where the cook indicated and found a bulletin board. Delivery slips, invoices, order forms and other bits of paper were thumb-tacked neatly to it. Elmer seemed to have a system in the works. Matt added the Patient Allergy form to it and thanked him.

"There he is," came a voice behind him.

Matt turned to find a portly man among the tables and chairs of the dining area. It took him a moment to register that he was looking at Robbie Bentley. "Mister Mayor, how are you?" Matt said, as he left the kitchen.

"Hey, I told you before...call me Bud."

"Are you here for business or treatment?"

"Some days I wonder," Bud said smiling. He seemed to use his whole face to do so. "I just wanted to stop by to see how you were getting on."

"Well, let's have a seat in my office," Matt said, leading the way. Matt was not a big fan of politicking, but the mayor's office had been lenient with the hospital when it fell into disrepair. The least he could do was some harmless glad-handing. When they reached the door to Matt's office, Bud's smile disappeared.

"What's this? Don't you use your father's office upstairs?" he asked.

"Not anymore. It's been devoted to bed space. Pull up a chair."

"That's a pity," Bud said as he sat and took in Matt's confining work space. "It was a grand office with the big wooden desk and all the books."

"Yes, it was very nice. It just wasn't very practical in a building with limited room."

"The last time I was by, your father and I talked up there and I remember looking around the room at all those books and thinking, my God, how many are there. There must have been five hundred."

"Maybe more."

"What happened to them all?"

Matt found it odd that Bud was showing such a keen interest in the fate of

Stanley's book collection, but chalked it up to limited things for them to converse over. "I had them packed and sent up to the house. The boxes are stacked in the dining room for now. When I get some time, I'll go through them. I was thinking I might donate most of them to the town library."

"Well, I'd appreciate a look at them, before you give them away."

"You would probably find most of them quite dry since you're, you know... not in the profession."

"Yeah, I figured. It would just be nice to have a token reminder of Stanley."

*Ah.* Matt nodded.

"Besides, it might help my image if I had more than *Hardy Boys* books on my shelf at home."

"I will be sure to have you over before I send any off."

They went on to discuss the state of the hospital and the high cost of renovations. Bud mentioned seeing the paperwork for the building permit go through the town office. He proudly proclaimed that he had waived the processing fees when he realized it was for his friends at Saint Michael's Hospital. "So don't let that Clark boy charge you for town fees," he said.

Matt thanked him for the heads-up. He noted the time and said, "I'm sorry, but I have an appointment scheduled in a few minutes. Some writer is coming in to ask some questions about the hospital." *It will be another significant waste of my time, I'm sure*, Matt thought. *It's time that I could be spending with Doctor Collins, showing her the ropes.*

"Oh, is he doing an article for a magazine or something?"

"I'm not sure what he's working on, but in the past, he has written true crime books and that sort of thing. Just how *true* his work is remains questionable. I read one of his and thought it was a little over the top, but I'll answer his questions. It might be a good opportunity to get the hospital's name out there."

"Any publicity is good publicity."

*And who would know that better that you?* "That's what they say."

Bud rose from his chair and extended his hand. "As always, if there is anything I can do for you, please let me know."

"Actually, come to think of it, there might be. I've heard through the grapevine that you dabble in real estate."

"You could say that." His smile suggested that *dabble* was an understatement.

"We have a new doctor here and I'm looking for an apartment or condo that is move-in ready—something that would be suitable for a professional, young woman. Do you think you could find something?"

"Absolutely, I could. Give me a couple days and I'll find you what you need. I'm thinking a secure building in the center of things with lots of closet space."

"You know your market."

Bud winked.

"Come on," Matt said. "I'll walk you out."

\* \* \* \*

Matt and Bud crossed the lounge on their way to the front entrance. Klewes was seated beside Margaret on the couch, reading a sports article to her. He claimed that she responded to the stories, but Matt had seen little evidence of that. More evident was the fact that the *orderly* enjoyed reading the articles to her. Either way, Matt saw little harm in it, though he wondered if Margaret would get the same treatment from him if she preferred gardening magazines.

Klewes paused the article long enough to share a greeting with the mayor. Always campaigning was the official.

A gentleman was standing alone in the lobby when Matt and Bud arrived. Matt guessed he was the writer. He wore a dark jacket and a weather-beaten leather satchel hung over his shoulder. Matt expected someone a little older, more distinguished. The man had a lanky posture he found vaguely familiar. "Hello, you must be Eric Fisher," Matt said, offering his hand.

"Yes. Doctor Dawson, I take it."

"Welcome." Matt sensed Bud's desire for an introduction and almost reminded the mayor that Mister Fisher was from out of town and therefore ineligible to vote in the township of Saint Andrews, but instead he said, "This is Mayor Bentley."

"Mister Mayor," Fisher said, shaking his hand.

"Call me Bud," he said with his customary whole-faced smile. "Everyone does."

Matt suddenly felt his friendship with the mayor was a little less special. He would have been hurt, had he cared in the least.

"On behalf of the people of Saint Andrews, welcome. It is an honor to have a writer of your esteem in our midst."

Matt nearly laughed as he watched Bud in action.

Instead, a booming voice from behind startled him.

"*Bastard!*"

Matt spun around to find Margaret looking in their direction. Her usual distant expression replaced by a furious scowl. "*Dirty rat bastard!*"

Klewes attempted to calm her. He stood in front of her, took her hands in his and tried to draw her focus away from the men in the lobby. "Hush now, Margaret," he said quietly. "He's not going to hurt you. It's okay."

"I'm sorry," Matt said. "I think Margaret is having a bad day."

She continued to glare in their direction. "Bastard...rat bastard," she muttered.

"No worries," Fisher said. "I'm a writer. I get that all the time."

They shared a less than comfortable laugh together, and Matt invited Fisher to his office. Bud took his leave with the promise that he would call soon regarding their real estate business. Matt hurried Fisher through the lounge so as not to upset his patient further, though as they passed the couch, Margaret was not looking their way. Instead she stared at the front door as the mayor made his exit.

\* \* \* \*

Darcy Collins was seated at the second floor nurse's station, reading from a stack of patient charts to familiarize herself with the people she would be treating. She learned about the elderly Curtis Ford who suffered from acute dementia. She could have guessed that when she met the man earlier and he informed her that he was heir to the Ford Motor Company fortune.

She closed the chart. Under it was the file on Mallory Killen, wife and mother of three and at the mercy of bipolar disorder. Under that one was the history of Hannah Wilkins, not yet eighteen and diagnosed with clinical depression and given to manic episodes. Reading these case histories was the bane of any good mood. Darcy had to remind herself that it was what she signed up for. She wanted badly to make a difference, and she wanted to do it sooner rather than later. So that someday, when she opened a chart, she would be greeted with encouraging news as opposed to gloomy diagnoses.

"Enjoying a little light reading?"

Darcy looked up to find Orderly Cundiff smiling warmly.

"The cure for insomnia." She lied with the interest of fitting in.

"Well, it's almost break time," he said. "I was on my way to the kitchen for a cup of tea. I could fetch something for you...not tea, I take it."

"No thanks."

"Okay, catch you later," he said going to the stairs.

Darcy remembered what Wanda said. Then she considered that she had not left her room at the inn since arriving in Saint Andrews other than to go to work. She had promised herself that she would start living after school. She was supposed to make friends that had not been classmates first. It was a hurdle she was finding it difficult to vault.

"Umm...I'm really more of a coffee drinker."

The orderly stopped and turned back to the station. He considered that for a moment, then said, "There is a diner down the street. I'm told their coffee is pretty good. They have one of those cappuccino machines, too. I can take you there if you like."

"Really?" Darcy was pleasantly surprised by the prospect of a gourmet coffee and even more so by the invitation. *Hmm*, she thought. *See what can happen, if you just speak up?*

\* \* \* \*

It was another gorgeous summer day. The sun was high and without a cloud to rival it. As soon as Darcy and Cundiff stepped out of Saint Michael's, she could smell the beach. She was thankful each time she tasted the seaside air. It was a reminder of her youth and family vacations when they had still been able to take them.

The painters had moved their scaffolding to the eastern face of the building to continue their work. They had hung off it like great apes, hooting as she had entered the building that morning. It seemed they were getting crasser by the day. Now, as she crossed the yard alongside the stout orderly, they were strangely silent. It was golden. She looked at her coworker, offered a brief smile. He was tall and broad shouldered, qualities she was beginning to have an appreciation for, but what she had noticed first were his hands. They were wide across the palm. Strong. The boys she had gone to school with did not have hands like that and on the rare occasion that a greeting involved a handshake, she often found them damp and clammy. She imagined that Mister Cundiff's hands would be rough and warm. They were hands that did more than grip a pen or type on keys. She allowed herself to imagine those hands balled into fists for her honor.

"Another beauty."

Darcy snapped out of it. "I'm sorry?"

"Another beauty of a day, huh?"

"Oh...yes. I had no idea it got so hot here. There seems to be a misconception about east coast weather, that it's always foggy and cool."

"Jealous lies," he said grinning.

She agreed. She was indeed jealous. Only it was of the passersby on Water Street's sidewalk. They wore tank tops and camisoles, shades and hats against the sun. Darcy had the good sense to doff her lab coat before venturing out, but her collared dress shirt was still proving to be the wrong attire. Mister Cundiff's scrub top hung loosely on him, and Darcy could see that becoming her uniform of choice.

They crossed Water and joined the lazy foot traffic on the south side. Behind the row of buildings was the vast expanse of the bay. It always drew her attention. She had spent hours watching it from her window at the inn. She favored the view over anything on television. She watched a string of ten brightly colored sea kayaks paddle by, rising and dipping on gentle swells. Her gaze followed the guided tour until it was blocked by the three-story Sand and Surf Inn. Everything in Saint Andrews seemed to be a converted something or other, and the inn was no exception. It looked like a former state house, full of grand wooden paneled windows flanked by stark white shutters against the pale yellow siding. Contrasting it was the steep roof with shingles black as pitch. Atop it, a weathervane adorned with a large bronze fish indicated that the warm, subtle breeze had turned north.

"Wow, they came a long way," Cundiff said, nodding at a car in the parking area in front of the inn. The plate read Tennessee. Beside that was one reading New York, the next Quebec.

"It must be a little strange, living in a tourist town with all these people coming and going."

"It is," he said somberly. "It's like the town is in a constant state of identity crisis or something. The folks who come here seem to know what Saint Andrews is all about, but most citizens don't have the slightest clue. I guess because so much of our identity depends on tourism."

"Do you like that all these people come here? I mean it must be kind of weird to go about living your life while so many are just passing through."

"Personally, I don't mind the crowds. Our economy is based on people visiting us, staying in the inns, taking tours and shopping. So, if we want to survive we have to abide a little traffic." Cundiff waved to a police car passing by ever so slowly. "Hey Chief Lumley," he shouted as his wave was returned. He turned back to Darcy again. "Don't get me wrong, a lot of people are happy to be rid of the tourists come the end of the season. I think that says a lot about them. They must be *the glass is half empty* people. In a way, I feel sorry for them."

Darcy regarded him again. Wanda had told her that he was a nice young man and she could see that plainly. She could also see evidence of the thoughtful nature that belied his imposing exterior.

"It's kind of funny. In the winter you forget about the crowds, and when spring rolls around and the tourists start coming back, they sort of surprise you. One day you get up, go outside and the streets are full of people in shorts and ugly shirts. Everywhere you go there's no elbow room. You have to wait in line at the store. It's all hustle and bustle."

She snickered and thought about the effect a big city would have on him. A group of people in front of them had stopped to window-shop at a small gallery where local works were hung. They had to walk on the street to get around them, serving a timely example of Cundiff's meaning.

"By the fall, you're so used to them, they become the norm. Then one day you find the streets empty—everyone's gone. Sure it gets easier to eat out or shop, but I get this feeling of...I don't know...isolation. Not long after that, the seasonal businesses close down and it's like they roll up the streets around here. Then the snow comes. It must be a legit form of depression—post tourist season depression, or something."

"Well, seasonal depression is a real problem for many. The fact that the seasons here are so different likely intensifies symptoms."

"What do you recommend for it?"

"Vitamin D."

"And get a life?"

"Not in so many words," she said, laughing. "Though it *does* help to stay active. Studies done in northern communities show that people who attended social events on a regular basis during the winter months—" She caught herself before quoting percentages and fully revealing her nerdy side. "...umm, were much happier." *I'll shut up now.*

"Well, I'm afraid, you'll find out if that is true after the leaves fall off the trees and there's nothing pretty left for tourists to look at. Hopefully you won't be affected by the winter blues like I usually am."

As they strolled past a restaurant with a full patio abuzz with laughter and lively conversation, Darcy found it hard to picture the street in the dead of winter. She watched a waiter set down a tray holding two gleaming red lobsters with side salads and frosty glasses of beer. Visiting that restaurant shot to the top of her *to-do* list. Even the hardware store next door was a hive of activity. On the side of the two-story structure was a grand mural of a seascape painted in vibrant colors. It had attracted a group of shutterbugs and Cundiff altered course accordingly.

They crossed King Street and Darcy could see the bay again. King ended at the beach and a large wooden wharf extended several yards into the water. There was a fishing trawler craning its catch into the back of a truck while half a dozen men looked on. A slight surge of excitement welled in her at the sight. She knew that whale-watching tours left from that wharf, but she had no idea that actual work went on there, too. As a girl, her parents had taken her and her sister to Cape Cod for vacation. Even in her youth she found those coastal communities to be a little fake. They were made to look like quaint fishing villages, but she knew most real fishermen could not afford to live there. It was all façade. She was happy to see that Saint Andrews was more than that. She was about to ask Cundiff about the boat, but he spoke first.

"Here we are," he said and opened the door to the diner for her.

She thought such gestures were all but lost to the world. He did it again as they left, each with a large steaming cup. Darcy shifted her French vanilla cappuccino from one hand to the other like a hot potato. She questioned the drink selection on the humid afternoon as the sun resumed its assault on the sidewalk. Cundiff must have been thinking the same thing. He hoisted his cup of orange pekoe and said, "This should warm us up in no time."

Crossing King, Darcy looked toward the wharf again. The truck that had been getting loaded when they first walked by now rolled toward them.

And it picked up speed.

Cundiff put a hand on Darcy's arm to slow her and in an instant the truck skidded to a stop in their path. Darcy's shock stole her voice and before she could find it, the exchange had already started.

"Oh hey, Cund," the driver of the truck said. He said it *Cundt*. "I didn't see you there." He had long greasy hair and a scruffy jaw and his grin displayed crooked yellow teeth. There were three men squeezed into the cab of the truck and each of them was just as repulsive. "Who's you're little friend?" All three showed their ugly smiles. Cundiff eyed them unblinking and spoke in a gruff tone that Darcy had not before heard from the orderly. "None of your business, Ricky. Just know, if she wasn't here, I'd slap you around like the last time you ran your mouth at me."

The fishermen only laughed at that.

"Hey sweet thing," Ricky said. "If you want to try out a real man, there's room for you in here."

Darcy grabbed Cundiff's hand before the situation got out of control. She tried pulling him to the front of the truck and around it, but he was anchored where he stood. "Come on, John," she said. When he heard her voice, he softened and she was able to coax him away while the men in the truck burst into more laughter.

"That's right, *Cundt*, walk away," Ricky called after them.

"Don't look back," Darcy said, her hand still locked on his. "Let's just go."

The truck squealed out onto Water Street. Its horn sounded along with the whooping of the trio inside. Many people on the sidewalk frowned at the spectacle the fishermen made of themselves as they sped away.

"Assholes," Cundiff said, sounding more himself. "I'm sorry about all that."

"What was that about, anyway? How stupid can those guys be? I mean, I saw the name on the truck, I could describe them to the police."

"It wouldn't do any good."

"Why shouldn't I? They threatened us, nearly ran us down."

"*Because* of the name on the truck."

"*Sullivan Fisheries*...what has that got to do with anything?"

"Arthur Sullivan is hands-down the richest guy in town. The police won't do anything to him or his family and that dirty faced loser behind the wheel was his son."

"That shouldn't matter."

"You're absolutely right...it shouldn't."

"Why did he do it?"

"We have a history. It goes back to when I worked for his father on one of his lobster boats. It was years ago..." he said thoughtfully.

"What started it?"

"I quit when they needed me."

"There must be more to it than that."

"No, not really. I couldn't do the job. I don't expect you to understand, but around here, it's a pretty disgraceful thing to quit on a boat. It's not something you ever live down."

Darcy gave his hand a squeeze. He was right, she did not understand, but she did not have to, to see the pain it caused him. It was an old hurt, one he had lived with for too long. Maybe she could help him through it. After all, it was what she did.

\* \* \* \*

Matt had been telling Eric Fisher a little about the history of the hospital and about its founder, but it did not take long for him to see that the writer had no interest. He had not taken a single note since sitting down across the desk. Matt began to feel a bit like Mayor Bud, talking for the sake of talking, and was dismayed that his valuable time was again being squandered.

"I get the feeling that you're not here to talk about Saint Michael's."

Fisher had a thick head of black hair that looked like it was hand-styled rather than combed and wore a neatly trimmed black goatee. He gave a wry smile and the goatee slanted on his face. "I may have misled you when we spoke on the phone," he said. "I apologize, but I was worried that you wouldn't see me if I told you my intentions up front."

Matt raised his brow and said nothing. He nearly stood and asked Fisher to leave, but he was curious as to why the man would deceive him. He waited.

"In short, I'm working on a new project and I would like access to one of your patients."

Matt leaned back in his chair and crossed his legs. "I can't allow that," he said, unsuccessfully stifling a laugh at the absurd request.

"I haven't even told you who."

"Mister Fisher, it doesn't matter, *who.* Hospital policy states that only family is permitted access to patients and only during limited visiting hours. Even then, the visits take place in a controlled environment. Conversations that upset patients are quickly ended and the visit terminated. The last thing I'll allow is a patient to be interviewed for the purpose of drumming up the details of something they did or witnessed in the past."

"I think you misunderstand my intent."

"Oh, I doubt that. I'm familiar with your work. In fact, I saw one of your paperbacks on the *Take One, Leave One* shelf in our lounge."

Fisher's goatee slanted with that jab.

"I've even read the one you wrote about the so-called monster in Hammond River that you said was responsible for the murder of eight police officers."

"It was four police officers and four civilians," Fisher corrected.

"Plus one raccoon if memory serves."

"It doesn't matter. It will pale in comparison to my new book: the story behind the most grisly crime scene in this region's history. Doctor Dawson, I *will* write this story and Morry Dykeman *will* be on the cover."

Matt felt like he was kicked in the chest.

"It's a compelling story and people will want to hear it. They'll want to know about the hometown boy who murdered his family in cold blood, who was found criminally insane and sentenced to a psychiatric facility like this for life. But it wasn't *this* facility, now, was it Doctor Dawson? No sir. He was sent to the high security wing of Centracare in Saint John to be locked up with the rest of the criminally insane. Then one day in '68 he got a transfer and ended up here, at Saint Michael's. My readers will want to know why."

Matt's mind was reeling. *Why? That's a good question—an excellent question. Why, Stanley? Why would you allow a transfer like that? This facility isn't equipped to handle such a dangerous patient.* The locked door, the abundant sedatives...Stanley's concerns were not unfounded, *but why? Fisher thinks I know. I have to keep him talking. Got to find out what he knows about this Dykeman.* "The transfer...it may have been a reward for good behavior," Matt offered.

"Yeah, I'm sure. Dykeman has been pumped so full of drugs since he was thirteen that he's pretty much a zombie. I'm not sure, Doctor, are zombies known for exhibiting good behavior?"

"I can't comment on my patient's condition."

Fisher ignored him. "The funny thing is, despite my best work, I can't find any records of the transfer. Usually a court-ordered stay in a hospital requires the approval of a judge and a hell of a lot of paperwork for a change of address, but I can't find anything."

"Maybe you're looking in the wrong place."

"Maybe I am." Fisher glanced at the filing cabinet behind Matt.

"If you want to browse my records, you can forget it."

"Doctor Dawson, I might have been born at night, but it wasn't *last* night. I know there are no transfer records. There are never any records from that kind of backroom deal. That's exactly what it was. The previous head doctor of Saint Michael's, *Stanley* Dawson, brokered a deal with some higher-ups to get a cold-blooded killer brought to his little hospital by the sea. Why he did it is where my next book lies."

Matt was silent for a moment. He had to admit, it made for a good mystery. It had all the required elements: murder, secret motives...danger. At last he said, "Mister Dykeman was from the area. Did you ever consider that he had family that wanted him moved closer?"

Fisher's goatee slanted again. "Oh, I'd just love to get my hands on the visitors' log—see exactly how much family Dykeman has entertained here over the years."

"I told you before Mister Fisher, I can't..."

"I know, I know," Fisher said, waving his hand. "You can't show me the records."

"Well, what do you want then?"

Matt waited while Fisher seemed to muster his nerve to make his request.

"I want ten minutes in a room with Dykeman."

"Absolutely not," Matt said with a chuckle. The writer had him shaking his head yet again.

"I don't intend to interview him. I just want to sit across from him, to look in his eyes."

"I think we're finished here."

"Doctor Dawson, you may not like my work, but there are many who do and they all pay to read it." Fisher produced a folded piece of notepaper from the inside pocket of his coat. "That is why my publisher bankrolls my research. He has very deep pockets." He laid the paper on the desk between them.

Matt picked up the note, read it. He stared at his desktop for a few seconds then slid the paper back toward the writer. "You know what? I recognize you, Mister Fisher. It took me a while to place where I'd seen you before, but it came to me just now. You were at Stanley's wake. I saw you sneaking around by the front yard. Now, I have no doubt that you approached him with your proposal. I also have no doubt what his reply was."

"He suggested that I go, and make love to myself, in not so pleasant terms. It would seem that he had no use for money. I was hopeful that his son was more practical."

Matt leaned forward over his desk. He was not as accustomed to confrontation as Fisher clearly was. Anyone brash enough to approach a doctor with such ludicrous demands had likely been met with his share of conflict. Matt's heart was racing, but it felt surprisingly good. His frustrations had been mounting ever since Stanley's death and he finally had the chance to vent some of them. He relished the moment. "The answer is *no*. It is the only answer I have for you. I would never let a glorified tabloid-trash writer like you come in contact with any one of my patients, regardless of what they did in the past or how they came to be under my care." Matt stood up without taking his eyes off Fisher. "Now, you'd better leave before I call on my orderlies to help you leave."

Fisher hung his head and got up from his chair. He slung his satchel over his shoulder and said, "Thank you for your time. If you change your mind..." Fisher went into his breast pocket again, this time he pulled out a business card and set it beside the note paper on the desk.

"I had better not see you nosing around here again," Matt said.

The writer took his leave.

Matt sat back down and rubbed the back of his neck. He tried to breathe deeply to shake off the last few minutes. He gathered the business card and note off the desk. *$10,000* was scrawled on the paper. Matt crumpled it and tossed it in the recycling bin beside his desk. He almost sent the card in after it, but after a moment of thought, tucked it in the desk drawer.

He eyed the recycling bin with half a mind to give it a kick. Instead he leaned back in his chair and fumed. He gave his head a good scratching and asked the empty room, "What the hell was going on here, Stanley?" After pondering just that, he swiveled his chair to face the filing cabinet. *And do what,* he wondered, *search it for like the tenth time for Dykeman's chart?* He had searched everywhere for the thing. The staff did, too. Dykeman probably never had a chart to begin with. It was useless. He turned back to his desk, opened the drawer and looked at the business card inside. *Margaret was right. He is a dirty rat bastard.* He closed the drawer with a heavy *thump*. At that moment, it occurred to him—he had not searched *everywhere*.

* * * *

Cundiff opened the door for Darcy and she walked inside from the bright afternoon. Near the foot of the staircase she stood awkwardly with him for a moment, as though unsure of the appropriate manner to bring their stroll to a close. Would a handshake be appropriate, a high five?

The orderly wished he could let her off the hook, but he was at a loss as well. He blamed Ricky Sullivan for the awkwardness. Before he showed up, their conversation had been natural and unforced. There was none of that reaching for things to talk about like he did with most people. He was comfortable with her, as if he had known her for far longer than a couple of days. Only now, that comfort was receding. Nerves were rising in its place as she looked at him, evaluated him. *Don't be stupid*, he thought. *Say something.*

"Well," she said, breaking the mounting silence. "I'd better track down Doctor Dawson. Thanks for the coffee."

"My pleasure." *Don't blow this.* "Maybe we could make it a...thing that we... do like everyday...at break."

She smiled at him.

*You blew it.*

"Yeah, it would be nice to go for a walk just to change the scenery. Still, we should probably avoid the wharf for a while."

"Good idea."

"So...I'll see you in the morning," she said, backing her way toward the office.

"Afternoon," he corrected. "I'm on tuck-in duty tonight, so I start late tomorrow."

"Oh, okay."

"Klewes and I alternate...it's my turn...tonight, so..." *Just shut up*, he thought as she continued to make her way down the hall.

She raised her coffee cup and said, "Thanks again."

To that he simply waved, having gotten control of his tongue, albeit too late. He cursed himself for being such an idiot and marveled at how one minute of clumsy exchange could undo a walk that started with such promise. "Oh, well," he said to himself then grinned. "I gotta tell Klewey."

Cundiff turned toward the staircase to seek-out his friend, but stopped abruptly. He was taken by the weirdest sensation. It was reminiscent of the late winter mornings he spent hauling traps on the lobster boat. On those mornings before the sun was up, the world was dark and frozen. The air was so wet and cold that it penetrated all layers and ultimately bit through the flesh. It settled in the center of the chest and every breath became a thrust from a dagger. Only swigs of spiced rum could counter it and the boys on the deck passed it from glove to glove. Even the lowly haulers were handed the bottle. No one deserved to suffer that kind of cold.

The orderly suffered it now.

He laid a hand on his chest over the icy ache and held his breath, hoping it would warm inside him. Shuffling forward, he decided to sit on the steps and rest a moment. As he climbed to the second tread, he felt warmth envelope him again. His temperature rose as quickly as it had fallen, the ache in his core faded. Was it simply a draft that he walked through? Perhaps that coupled with the nerves Darcy had stimulated in him?

A long, slow breath escaped his lungs as he composed himself. He glanced at the statue of the archangel, Saint Michael—the only witness to his awkward parting with Darcy and the episode that resulted.

"What are you lookin' at?" he asked.

He had never liked the sculpture. It was beyond him that such a creepy thing would have a place among people that were already haunted by their share of troubles. Today it looked especially eerie to Cundiff. He kept an eye glued to it as he got up and bound his way up the stairs.

# Chapter Eight

Rectangles of golden light stretched across the blue tiles, leaving green patches like lily pads on a stream. Stanley had not noticed. He did his best to ignore the perpetual sunset. It only served to swell his feelings of foreboding, dread.

He had not left the statue's side in what felt like days, though there was no way to mark the passage of time. Despite his incessant turning of the winder, his pocket watch continued to insist that it was half past seven. Winding it had become a way to busy his hands while new questions and thoughts came upon him like crashing waves.

"Did I die at 7:30?" he asked the angel. "Is that why my watch is stuck there?"

Saint Michael remained silent, eyes warily locked on the serpent at his feet. He had not been much help, though proved a sympathetic ear for Stanley's numerous inquiries. *Why do I remain here? Why hasn't the light come for me? Am I damned? If so, where is hell... Is this it?*

Stanley had even flirted with the idea that he had not expired, that he had lost his mind. He had always loathed that peasant's term for psychotic episode—*lost his mind*. However, wrapped in the perfect silence of the hospital that was how he felt...lost. Was his body strapped securely to a gurney in some facility, perhaps his own, while his mind wandered through these empty halls in a haze?

"Perhaps it is a combination of the two," he reasoned. "Can I be the *insane* dead? Is that why there is no place in heaven for me?" Mental wellness was simply the ideal balance of natural chemicals in the brain. There was no such thing as perfect sanity, but treating mental illness was the pursuit of achieving a chemical balance that was as close to the ideal as attainable. He looked up at his angel again. "Do I even have a brain anymore?"

Michael ignored the question, his entire focus on the never-ending task of exiling Satan from paradise.

Stanley stopped winding his watch and opened it. *Susan.* He sank deeper in his mire of despair as the question that hurt most flared again. "*Where are you?*"

The only reason he had been able to linger on into his seventies, that he had been able to survive these several years in their empty house, was that he was safe in the knowledge that they would one day be reunited. He had worn the idea like armor, dressed in it every day to face the battles of the world. He had envisioned meeting her in a green pasture under a solitary cherry tree in full bloom. The sun would be high and a gentle breeze would be fanning the meadow grass and swaying her white sundress. As he drew nearer, his many years would drop away, his skin would smooth, his hair darken. He would recede into his fifties—the age he was when she had left him. Their embrace would be the stuff of dreams—warm and fierce yet tender as the pink petals that fell about them.

Stanley snapped the watch closed.

He could not even cry. Even that release had abandoned him.

"You were supposed to protect me," he said to the angel. "How many times did I pray to you...*directly* to you? O glorious Archangel Saint Michael, Prince of the heavenly host, defend us in battle and in the struggle which is ours against the principalities and powers... No? Maybe you don't speak English. *Sancte Michael, defendenos in proeliout non pereamus in tremendo iudicio...*"

Stanley glared at the statue, at eyes both beautiful and cold. He felt all strength bleed out of him and he slumped to the floor in a pile. There he stayed, wishing that the empty void would return and swallow him. In the perfect blackness, he had felt nothing.

It had been a godsend.

Then a door slammed.

Stanley lifted his head, turned to the front entry. He saw nothing. Slowly he rose, ears trained. At the foot of the stairs, he waited for another sign. The noise had been close, or so he thought. Could it have come from upstairs? Before he could reach a decision, a most peculiar sensation washed over him. It felt as though he had descended into a warm bath. Only the tepid water more than saturated his flesh, it permeated deeper, ran through his very core.

Then it was gone.

Stanley wrapped his arms around himself. The chill returned to his skin and bones, all the more acute after feeling the nurturing touch of heat.

Behind him came a *thump*. It was followed by another.

He turned to the staircase, mind made up. He would pursue the noises and he would find that he indeed was not alone. He knew footsteps when he heard them.

\* \* \* \*

Matt increased his pace along Adolphus Street. The afternoon sun had begun its lazy descent toward the hills and though hours of daylight remained, he felt as though it was fleeting before his eyes. Still, no amount of sunshine was enough to ease the burden of the task in front of him, and if night fell before he could begin, it would go undone altogether. He would stand at the top of the cellar stair, helpless to continue. Indeed, the daylight may be all that would allow him to dare venture into the bowels of the house. He would hurry down the steps, collect his prize, and return to the light like a diver returns to the surface of the sea with tank near empty. That was the plan, anyway.

Cresting Adolphus, he turned right on to Prince of Wales as knots tightened in his chest. He hoped they would not overcome the determination that had been all ablaze when he left the hospital only minutes ago. So driven was he that he had left without a word. His walk had been more of a run. Though as he drew near Stanley's house, he could not bring himself to look up for fear he would turn in his tracks. Instead, he followed the cracks snaking though the asphalt sidewalk, looked at the houses he passed, and thought of the happy families that dwelled within. Surely they would be making plans for barbeques and evening strolls. Matt's own evening would find him hunting for the records of a murderer—records Stanley had seen fit to hide.

Anger mingled with the angst in his chest. That sleazy trash writer had schooled him on his own patient. Fisher knew much, and of course, he likely knew a lot more than he had shared. Whatever it was, it had been enough to bring him to Saint Andrews to nose around. He had thought he could dupe Matt into divulging information, but the joke had been on him. Matt knew nothing. All of his efforts to learn about Dykeman had failed. Even Wanda, the senior member of the staff, the nurse responsible for administering all medications, could not tell Matt why the patient was overly sedated. All she could tell him was that it had been Stanley's wish, and she did not question her employer as a rule. Stanley had done a good job surrounding himself with loyal and obedient people. It had allowed him to keep his secrets.

No more.

This night, Matt was getting answers. Even if he had to tear the house apart, if he had to brave the darkness of the cellar and the company of the unsettled dead, he would get answers.

Matt raised his gaze to the sprawling grounds, the gray house atop the slope. There it brooded like a raven on a perch, dark and sullen despite the brilliant afternoon sun. His stride broke into a jog. He met the graveled drive-way where the hedge gave way and sprinted for the house. He ran passed the cherry trees, crossed the lawn and climbed the veranda steps to the front door. Before he allowed any doubts to derail his determination, he was inside, going down the hallway. He would see this ugly business done.

Then the cellar door stopped him cold.

Sweat beaded at his temples and his breath, short from his run, could not be reined in. He panicked. The drive that had him bolting from his office was all but expired now that he faced the cellar door and the dim stairwell beyond.

He closed his eyes and searched for the will that had abandoned him. He saw Fisher seated across the desk, his coy grin. He had such a wry, cocky face— a downright punchable face. Matt found something else within—rage. Though it was not born of a noble desire for truth, it was still the fuel he needed to descend the cellar stair.

"Fuck you, Fisher," he said aloud.

In one fluid motion, he turned the door knob, swung open the door and reached inside to light the way. Then he was on the stairs. It was like his body was put on autopilot, operating solely on instinct, and he watched his actions from some remove. The ancient steps creaked and whined as if warning him not to go any further. The air was stale—a mixture of mold and dust. Matt was compelled to cover his mouth for fear of aspirating some foreign spore and infecting himself with whatever was so wrong with the place. He stepped off the bottom tread onto the concrete floor. Grit crackled under his shoe and the sound gave him a start. He paused, surveyed the silence.

The room was too big for the few bare bulbs tasked with lighting it. Darkness consumed their weak yellow glow before it reached the walls. Everywhere were pockets of black: in the corners, under the stairs, behind a pile of boxes, beyond the wide brick chimney that ran up the center of the house. For a mo-ment, Matt considered what the darkness concealed behind the chimney that had once served the long-gone coal burning furnace. Then he hurried onward.

The snapping of grit and debris underfoot followed him to the western wall where the light was somewhat stronger. Under one of the dust-covered bulbs, pushed tightly against the wall, was a modest wooden workbench. It was exactly where Matt expected it to be. Stanley had been a creature of habit, and though it had been thirty years since Matt had seen them, he knew where to find Stanley's hand tools. They were cluttered atop the bench, blanketed with layers of spider web. He fumbled through the pile, dropping some to the floor. His hands were shaking so badly, it was a chore just to grip anything. The thin sounds of metal rubbing metal bounced off the stark concrete walls, surrounded him and fuelled his panic.

Autopilot kicked in again. Matt found himself backing away from the bench. It was as though his body had decided the mission had failed and it was time to abort and return to the sunshine above. He forced himself back to the tools, knowing full well he would never allow himself a second chance at this. Then his left hand found a familiar shape. He held it up to the light. A hammer. That was a start. He tucked it under his arm and went back to the search. He slid his fingers down shafts of screwdrivers, felt the heads, until he found the slot driver he needed. It went under his arm, too. After a few of the longest seconds in Matt Dawson's life, he found a small black pry bar and happily allowed himself to make for the exit.

As he walked to the stair, he watched the dark corners for anything that might emerge and lay chase. He looked to the red brick chimney and the void beyond. He stopped. The memory came upon him like a fever.

Chrissy had coaxed him into the cellar for the grand finale of her ghost story. She led him behind the chimney. Matthew had tried so hard to be brave while he waited for his eyes to adjust to the darkness like she said they would. He wanted to stay close to her, but she kept moving toward the wall, farther from the light. All he could do was lay a hand on the red bricks of the chimney in hopes of anchoring himself to the real world, while his sitter showed him a more frightening one. He could make out the shape of a rectangle on the wall. It was about the size as their television's screen.

"This is it," Chrissy whispered. "The coal chute door."

Matthew shivered when she said the words.

"I told you we'd find it here."

"I believed you," Matthew said. *Can we go upstairs, now?*

"It is said that when the little boy's spirit moans, if you come down here and open the chute, you'll see him trapped inside waiting to be saved."

"Don't open it...my parents might get mad." *Why didn't they tell me about this?*

"They don't have to know. It could be our secret."

Chrissy raised a hand and touched the door. There was a scraping sound and a metallic *clink.*

"*Don't!*"

"Come on Matthew, we might get to see him. I want to be able to tell the kids at school I did."

There was an awful screech as the door opened on its rusted hinges. The shrill sound spurred Matthew into motion. He let go of the chimney and ran for the stairs. He was halfway up when Chrissy released a blood-chilling scream. Bravery failed him. He did not stop or even look back. He did not see what she saw—did not see the ghost, but he did not have to. His nightmares would fill in the blanks for years.

Matt took his hand off the chimney. He backed away from it and the wall beyond where the coal chute remained. Then he hit the stairs, taking them two at a time. When he reached the safety of the main floor hallway, he closed the cellar door and leaned against it. He hugged the hand tools to his heaving chest. Perspiration soaked his hair, left a wide wet spot on his back that felt cool where it pressed against the door. The air seemed so fresh compared to that of the cellar. He tasted the rich aromas of old hardwood mingling with coffee and traces of the pasta dish he ate last night.

"I went to the cellar," he said, panting as he reflected on his triumph. He was drenched with sweat and still shaking, but he granted himself a small measure of pride. "You're still thirty-nine and afraid of the basement, but...it's a damn good start."

\* \* \* \*

Stanley ascended the stairs as quickly as he could, though running proved a challenge. He tottered and yawed from side to side like he was trying to find his sea legs on riled waters. The phantom footsteps he chased up the staircase had faded to whispers before falling completely silent. When he reached the second floor he scanned right and left but found only empty corridors lined in blue doors under slowly turning ceiling fans. He wondered if he had actually heard the footfalls in the first place. He could not count on anything in this place aside from the never-ending sunset and, of course, that it was 7:30. *Always* 7:30.

He walked behind the high counters of the nurse's station. The desktop was normally cluttered with all manner of paperwork pertaining to the everyday business of the hospital: prescription forms, charts, medical records. There also had been the personal effects of the staff that irked him so. How many times did he tell them to clean up their newspapers, novels, and the ever-present sports magazines that Klewes favored so much? Yet, this desktop was empty, perfectly clean. He would have thought he'd appreciate that kind of tidiness, yet confronted with it, he felt worse. Clutter, after all, had been a sign of life, of the staff, his friends. He missed it like he missed them. He would have given anything to find a folded issue of *Sports Illustrated* that Klewey claimed he kept around to read to Margaret. The young man thought he had capably conned Stanley into allowing him to read sporting news on the job. The memory of the innocent deception made Stanley smile. It was just like Cundiff thinking that his many tea breaks would be overlooked so long as he made a cup for the boss, too.

*Those boys...my boys*, Stanley lamented.

With a shaking hand he rubbed his lined face, scratched at his hairline. In the diminished light of the setting sun, he eyed the desktop again and this time found someone looking back. Glossy, lifeless eyes seemed to look directly at him. Stanley moved closer, studied the face, the image. Sydney Crosby graced the cover of a hockey magazine over bold text reading, *The Next Great One*? How did Stanley miss that? The desktop had been bare...hadn't it?

Stanley raised his head, eyes darting about the place.

He called out. "Hello...is anyone there?"

He listened to the perfect silence for a moment then dropped his eyes to the desk and the mysterious magazine that had appeared from nowhere. Sydney still looked back and now, beside his cover issue, was a white paper cup—the kind they used at the diner down the street. Stanley gasped. He may have over-looked the magazine, but he was certain that cup was not there a second ago. Watching the steam rise from the dark fluid inside the cup, Stanley fought the urge to run back down the stairs, to cower at Saint Michael's side.

He went to call into the emptiness again, but the words hitched in his throat. True, he was not alone, but if his company was friendly, why had they not made their presence known?

Sydney had no more answers for him than did the stone angel downstairs. He simply looked through Stanley with mocking eyes. Stanley passed his hand over the cup and yanked it away. The steam from the drink was scalding. It felt like he had plunged his hand into flames, and yet there was no trace of a burn when he inspected his fingers and the pain quickly faded away.

"Jesus!" a voice beside him said.

Stanley screamed in surprise and flung himself away from the station in reflex. His feet moved faster than the rest of his body and he nearly went to the floor. When he turned back, his dread evaporated. Pure elation flooded his chest. John Cundiff occupied the chair behind the desk.

Stanley laughed aloud. "You scared me out of my skin, lad. Sorry if I startled you, but I..." He trailed-off as it dawned on him that the orderly was completely unaware of his presence. Even though Stanley had screamed, Cundiff showed no sign of acknowledgement.

"John!" Stanley yelled. He moved closer and waved his hand through the orderly's field of vision. "Johnny! Can you hear me?"

Cundiff offered no reaction. He merely sat, staring at the distance and rub-bing his arms to warm himself. "Why is it so friggin' cold in here?" he asked.

Stanley almost answered, almost said that he did not find it cold in the slight-est. Then he realized the question was not intended for him. He watched the orderly pick up the phone that now waited on the desktop amid all sorts of pa-perwork and office implements that were not there only seconds ago.

"Rory, are you messing around with the furnace?" Cundiff demanded. "Well, it feels like there's cold air blowing through here." Stanley placed a hand on Cundiff's shoulder and tried to shake him to attention. The orderly's muscled shoulder did not yield, though when he lifted his hand, Cundiff rubbed fiercely at his shoulder as if to warm it. "Well, it's freezing up here," he reported bitterly into the phone.

Stanley bent close to the young man and studied him. He yelled into the receiver pressed against Cundiff's head, "Rory! Hello Rory! Can you hear me? Hello?" He listened intently for a response.

"I don't know," Cundiff said after a moment. "It's static on the line or some-thing. Look, I'm more concerned with the temperature in here. Feel free to fiddle around with the phone lines when you get the furnace fixed. Okay, let me know."

Cundiff hung up the phone and, after brief contemplation, got out of the chair and left the nurse's station. Stanley stepped back to let him pass, then followed along. The orderly turned right and headed down the corridor. "Hey Wanda," he said. "Do you find it cold in here tonight?"

*Wanda*, Stanley thought. *Maybe I can get through to her.* He tailed Cundiff as he met the nurse at the end of the hallway. She was dressed in her white uniform, complete with the nursing cap she pinned to her tied-up hair. Stanley had never enforced the cap as part of the mandatory attire at the hospital. The veteran caregiver wore it anyway. Standing by her medication cart and making notes on a clipboard, she looked every bit the part.

"Not particularly, Mister Cundiff," she replied without looking up from her writing.

The two discussed the temperature while Stanley sidled up to the nurse. Like Cundiff, she could not detect his presence either. He entertained the idea of yelling at her or touching her arm to gauge her reaction, but was suddenly distracted by the door at the end of the hall. It had once been his office door. Now it was like all the others, painted bright blue with a small rectangular observation window. He moved in front of it and looked in. His former office now boasted two cots flanked by small dressers with rounded corners. It was patient space. He did not know how to feel. On one hand, he was a little gladdened that no one would claim his desk, his books. On the other, it was like he had been erased.

"Did you tell Rory to have a look at the furnace?" Wanda asked of Cundiff.

"Yeah, he said he'd get back to me in a few minutes."

"Well, that's good, because now that you mention it, I am feeling a bit of a chill."

Stanley watched his staff members walk in the direction of the nurse's station, Cundiff pushing the cart for his senior. *What to do?* Stanley lamented. *They don't know I'm here. I can't make them aware that I am. All I can do, apparently, is make them cold, and that's something I'd prefer not to put them through. They were, after all, good friends in life. I don't want to haunt them. What to do?*

Stanley fished in his coat pocket and pulled out his watch. He needed to see Susan's face again. If there was ever a time he needed to draw strength from her smile, this was it. He read the time, as always. It was like taking the good with the bad. He got to see his beloved and yet he was taunted by the report of 7:30 all over again. It reminded him that he was stuck in this limbo—a place where time no longer marched on. This time, he read the hands twice, three times. He could not believe it.

They read 6:05.

"That's right," he said aloud. "Wanda's giving medication…it's six. It's six!" He looked up from the watch face. Saint Michael's was brighter. Outdoors, the sun was higher. Everywhere shafts of brilliant daylight pierced the corridor, illuminated the dust floating on the drafts like fresh snowflakes. He watched Cundiff and Wanda speaking by the staircase and wondered who else might be here. *Matthew…could he be?*

He turned to his right, to the patient quarters nearest his old office. It was his choosing to keep this patient close, under a watchful eye. He went to the door and looked through the window. There, seated in his white plastic deck chair, was a very old acquaintance. Morris Dykeman had his back to the door and faced the window, bathing in the sun's rays as he liked to.

*I'm dead and his days continue to drag on.* It hardly seemed fair. Worse yet, Dykeman was left behind for the staff to deal with. Stanley hoped they were still obeying the rules he had enforced for so long. He hoped they would not take Dykeman lightly now that he was gone. It would only be too easy. The patient was old—seventy or more. He was withered and drawn, made meek by decades spent in this room. Though Stanley remembered his works. He knew what he was capable of.

For a few minutes, he watched the man who was watching nothing in particular. He had done this many times when they were alone together. The permanently scuffed floor tiles in front of Dykeman's door were a testament to that. Stanley looked at the pale blue floor around his ghostly feet. The worn tiles were perhaps the only remaining evidence that he had ever been there. When he looked up, another shock jolted his body like an electrical current.

Dykeman was *watching* him.

The old patient had shifted in his seat and now looked over his shoulder at the door. It was likely more movement than he had done on his own in months. Yet, he had turned his stern countenance to the doorway, to Stanley. His pupils were dilated, the whites of his eyes nearly eclipsed. They were like windows to the darkness inside the man.

Stanley moved slightly from side to side. Dykeman's black orbs tracked his movements. There was no mistaking it—he knew Stanley was there. He could *see* him.

Goosebumps ran down Stanley's flesh and he backed away from the door. Cundiff and Wanda were gone. The corridor was empty and it grew dark again before his eyes. The bright shafts of daylight had dimmed to a deep golden hue and he did not bother consulting his watch—he knew what it would read.

He went to look into Dykeman's room again. Surely the patient had vanished along with Cundiff and Wanda. In that case, he would have been relieved. He turned to the door. Dykeman's dark visage filled the window. Stanley staggered backward until he fell into the adjacent wall. Then his feet carried him from the corridor as quickly as they were capable, running for the archangel's side.

\* \* \* \*

Matt tipped the wine bottle and took a hearty swallow. Cool chardonnay raced down his throat and chilled his stomach. He had not eaten much today, and the wine was already going to his head. He had grabbed the bottle from the refrigerator before going to the study, hoping it would help to calm his fraying nerves. After another drink, he put the bottle down on the desk and went to work. He slid off the chair and knelt in front of the bottom drawer on the right side of the desk—the only one that was locked. The hand tools he had retrieved from the cellar waited on the floor. Matt picked up the pry bar first. He slid the straight end of the bar through the drawer's pull handle and braced it against the desk frame. Then he pushed. He heard the pleasing sound of wood snapping and splitting, giving way to the pry bar. It seemed for a second or two that breaking into Stanley's locked drawer would be easier than Matt first thought. Then the resistance was gone and he fell shoulder-first into the desk. When he straightened up, he found that he had simply torn the handle free, screws and all, while the drawer remained unopened. Matt released an exasperated breath.

He decided to change his approach and picked up the hammer and screwdriver. The drawer facing fit neatly into the frame of the desk, but around it was a narrow gap. He fit the blade of the screwdriver in and pounded it in with the hammer. Then he pried on the driver until the gap widened and repeated the process. He chiseled at the edge of the facing for several minutes, splintering the fine mahogany piece with abandon. Rivers of sweat ran from his unkempt hair as the sound of splitting wood filled the air. His efforts resulted in a pile of wood chips around his knees and a gap big enough to fit the pry bar into. He helped himself to another gulp from the bottle then placed the bar. Immediately the cracking began, louder now, and he could see the front of the drawer beginning to bow. He put more weight into it. Drops of perspiration dotted the floor as he strained the bar. He thought about the possible contents of the drawer and the chance that it was empty or held nothing of use. He pushed those thoughts away, told himself that the desk definitely held secrets. If it didn't, it would not hold on so tightly.

There was a loud popping sound and the drawer face went slack. Matt set the bar down and easily pulled the facing off. Such a pity, he thought, that he had to damage the desk so. He slid the drawer open then surprise fell upon him like dousing water.

In the drawer was a handgun. Matt knew next to nothing about firearms, but he guessed the shiny revolver with the black grip was a .45 millimeter based on the labeling on the box of bullets beside it. *What is this doing here?* Matt thought. In all the time he lived with Stanley, he had never seen him with a gun, had never known him to go to the firing range. Matt realized the only reason Stanley would have a gun and he took another drink. It was for protection.

Under the firearm and ammunition was a folder thick with pages and wrapped in an elastic band. Matt picked it up by the corner, slid the revolver off without touching it. He plopped the folder on the desk and sat before it. *This is it...*He did not need to read a single word. He knew exactly what it was. *It was under my nose the entire time. It waited for me to find it and open it.* Sitting in Stanley's study, about to learn his secrets, Matt wondered if he *should* open it. Would it do more harm than good? He may learn what kind of monster Dykeman was, but he was more afraid of learning what kind *Stanley* was. There were already so many questions surrounding his decisions at the hospital and about his treatment of patients. Matt wondered if he could handle more questions...more disappointment.

He knew the situation was bigger than the Dawson family. What happened at Saint Michael's affected more than just Matt. He had to think of the staff in his employ and the patients he was sworn to help. He took off the elastic and opened the folder to the top page. It had a recognizable heading: *Psychiatric Evaluation.* It gave him a degree of comfort to see the terms of his trade on the page. It was familiar territory, something he could understand. Soon he lost himself in the text...

*Psychological Evaluation*
*Centracare Psychiatric Facility*
*Subject: Morris "Morry" Dykeman*
*Case No: 289566*
*Building No: 2*
*Admission Date: 9/10/52*
*Dates of Evaluation: 9/12/52*
*Date of report: 9/14/52*

*Purpose for Evaluation: Initial inpatient assessment for Morris Dykeman; a white male, 14 years of age, from the town of Saint Andrews, New Brunswick. Custody of the subject was turned over to Centracare and its staff by order of the Court of Charlotte County. Under the criminal code, Mister Dykeman was deemed unfit to stand trial for his alleged crimes by Doctor S. Freeling of the Chief Medical Examiner's Office. Doctor Freeling cited acute psychotic disorder and perceptual disturbance in the subject in his summary report (enclosed).*

*The purpose of current evaluation is to screen for particular psychosis in order to decide appropriate treatment method and to determine risk, if any, to general patient population.*

*Assessment Procedures:*
*Clinical Multiaxial Inventory-III (CMI-III)*
*Multiphasic Personality Inventory-2 (MPI-2)*
*Mental Status Examination*
*Review of Prior Medical Records*
*Clinical Interview*

*Patient participated in three hours of testing followed by a brief diagnostic interview. Tests were administered by Michael Fry, M.S. and interpreted by Brian Metcalf, M.A.*

*Background Information: Subject and immediate family have no prior history of mental health deficiency. Student records obtained from the school district office show a tendency for disruptive behavior which was exacerbated in recent months. Subject had not been administered any form of medication prior to admission.*

*Mental Status Examination: Results of examination revealed highly agitated behavior given to aggressive episode. Subject displayed evidence of excessive distractibility and poor conversation tracking. Subject was poorly groomed. Orientation was disrupted and subject could not track time and place. Vocabulary and grammar skills were suggestive of intellectual functioning beyond average range of age and development of the subject. Eye contact was appropriate. There was no abnormality of gait, posture or deportment.*

*Speech functions were appropriate for rate, however volume and fluency were highly varied throughout testing.*

*Memory functions were grossly fragmented with respect to immediate and remote recall of events and factual information. Subject's thought process was disorganized. Thought content revealed evidence of delusion, paranoia and homicidal ideation. Social judgment appeared impaired, as evidenced by inappropriate interactions with staff.*

*Results/Summary: Results of psychological evaluation reveal a psychotic disorder characterized primarily by disturbance of thought content, with relative degradation of thought process and clear indication of perceptual disturbance. The current clinical rating appears to represent an acute exacerbation of a chronic psychotic disturbance which had its onset approximately three months ago. Currently, Mister Dykeman appears extremely distressed, anxious, paranoid, and delusional. He lacks sufficient capacity/ motivation to rely on external supports and lacks sufficient personal insight to cope independently at present. The patient appears to be attempting to cope with his illness though use of aggression. Subject is believed to be a significant physical risk to himself and to others.*

*It is recommended that efforts to aid Mister Dykeman be conducted through individual therapy so long as exposure to general patient population remains a risk. Once his aggression has been relaxed, it will likely be beneficial to explore psychosocial issues present at the time Mister Dykeman carried out his alleged crimes. Additionally, the patient will benefit from use of Fluphenazine injection for its sedative agent and proven record of discouraging psychotic episode. Confinement to personal quarters in a security level three environment is highly recommended at this time.*

*Brian Metcalf, M.A.*
*Psychology Associate*

Matt found himself tipping the bottle again. Fisher had indicated how ill Dykeman was and Matt had believed it, but reading the assessment brought to it another level of validity. It was all there in black and white. The evaluation was carried out by qualified personnel—professionals whom Matt would have seen as peers if he had practiced in the fifties. He considered closing the folder. Something told him the pages that followed would only bring more bad news.

The study was dark, lit only by the lamp at the corner of the desk. Across the room, Matt could see the shape of Stanley's trophy-styled urn at home on the fireplace mantel. On either side of the fireplace were those tall cases holding volume after volume of ponderous texts. In the dim light, Matt could not read their regal spines, could not tell just what knowledge they so proudly claimed to possess. They may have intimidated him in his youth, but keeping to the shadows, they lost power over him. In the company of the thick and tattered folder on the desktop, they were nothing to fear.

Matt summoned the will to forge ahead and flipped to the next page in Dykeman's chart. It was a Centracare dose record. Twelve and a half milligrams of Fluphenazine in a fourteen day cycle, it read. The next pages told more of the same with brief notes on Dykeman's response to treatment. There was a medical report in which the attending physician described the patient's physical conditioning as *above average*. Matt continued to leaf through the chart and was beginning to think that Dykeman's stay at the facility was without event. He had been holding out hope that the patient had been transferred to Saint Michael's as reward for good behavior. Then he came upon an incident report.

*Incident Report*
*Centracare Psychiatric Facility*

*Patient: Morris "Morry" Dykeman*
*Patient No: 289566*
*Building No: Three*
*Admission Date: 9/10/55*
*Date of Incident: 2/3/56*
*Date of report: 2/4/56*
*Parties Involved:     Mary Cooper, R. N.*
*Syl Goodwin, Orderly Unit Three*
*Description of Incident: At approximately 06:30 Nurse Mary Cooper was administering required dosage to Mister Dykeman in the patient's quarters. Patient became agitated and physically assaulted Miss Cooper. Miss Cooper called for the aid of the orderly on duty. Orderly Syl Goodwin was at his post and responded as per procedure by blowing his alert whistle to summon additional support. Orderly Goodwin then entered Mister Dykeman's quarters and attempted to subdue the patient. With the aid of two more orderlies, Mister Goodwin was able to confine Mister Dykeman to his cot where restraints were applied. Medication was administered by the duty supervisor, Doctor F. Kennedy, and sedation of the patient followed soon after.*

*Consequences of Incident: Miss Cooper sustained a fractured right wrist as well as numerous fractures to her right hand where the patient seized her. Miss Cooper was also struck in the face resulting in severe bruising. Mister Goodwin suffered three broken ribs as a result of his altercation with the patient and required emergency surgery to stem internal bleeding. Both injuries will result in significant loss of man hours.*

*Corrective Action: Procedure to be altered to require an orderly be present when nurses and doctors visit patient quarters in all level three areas. Mister Dykeman's medication is to be increased to 1200 milligrams Chlorpromazine administered on a daily cycle to discourage repeat incidents.*

> *Mister Dykeman is to remain under restraint until the effect*
> *of new treatment tool is determined.*
> *Report Prepared By: Doctor F. Kennedy*

A turn of the page revealed another incident report. It was more of the same—violent behavior followed by punishment. This time, Dykeman managed to bite an orderly despite being restrained to his bed. That earned him lockdown and a dose increase. Matt saw a pattern emerging. Dykeman had been doped up, restrained and kept under lock and key for more than fifty years, but it had started long before he was placed in Stanley's care. *How did he survive all that time?* Matt pondered. *What could possibly be keeping him alive when his body has been poisoned with drugs like this for decade after decade?* Ordinarily, Matt would sympathize for the patient. Clinically speaking, Morris Dykeman was a very ill young man and the years had not improved his state. Speaking from the heart, Matt saw Dykeman as a homicidal madman who was kept in Stanley's hospital mere blocks away from his home, where he grew up, where his mother lived. Dykeman had been there the whole time, while Matt attended elementary school, went to Boy Scout meetings, played barefoot on his lawn. Dykeman was there like a beast lurking in the shadows.

After he emptied the wine bottle, Matt flipped through more pages. There were more incident reports, but he could not bring himself to read them. He had the gist. As he got to the bottom of the chart, there were fewer and fewer dose records and none of them bore any notes by attending psychiatrists. If there was no change in condition, there was nothing to write about. How could there possibly be any change when he was kept in a vegetative state? He became the forgotten patient. And when Stanley came calling, Centracare was probably thrilled to be rid of their guest. Dykeman was finally someone else's burden.

Strangely absent from the chart were Stanley's notes. Matt had assumed that he would have performed his own patient evaluation, but maybe he didn't bother. After all, Dykeman's records spoke for themselves. It was clear that the patient would never be well. He could never improve to the point of reentering society, or even achieving any quality of life, so why waste time on him? Then again, why bring him to Saint Michael's in the first place? Matt may have found Dykeman's elusive chart, but he still did not find any answers.

Matt groaned and rubbed his tired face. There was another wine bottle chilling in the fridge with his name on it. He was about to stagger to the kitchen to retrieve it when he noticed the envelope at the very bottom of the folder. He flipped to it, pulled it free, and pushed the chart away. On the front of the manila envelope, *Saint Andrews Police Department* was stamped in red ink. Matt opened it, dumped its contents on the desk. There were some pages stapled together and half a dozen or so eight-by-twelve black and white photographs. The first one took a moment for Matt to comprehend. When he did, the Chardonnay he had consumed attempted a comeback. Tears stung his eyes as he swallowed hard against the tempest in his stomach. He took a breath.

"They're crime scene photos…Dykeman's crime scene photos," he said softly. "It's okay. You've worked on cadavers before…you can handle this."

Indeed, he had. Matt had even dissected a human brain in the course of his studies. Yet, there had not been any blood. That made all the difference. Though the blood appeared black in the pictures, there was no mistaking it. It was everywhere—splashed on the floor, climbing the walls, dripping from the ceiling—everywhere.

He looked back to the photographs. He had never seen anything like it. What used to be people was rendered to bits and pieces. What was once Dykeman's family was mere gore strewn about their kitchen. Matt shuffled the pictures to the next. It was a close up of a housedress—white with flowers dotting it on the parts that were not blood-soaked black. The next depicted a pair of hedge clippers resting on the kitchen table. "Oh, my God..." escaped Matt's lips. He brought his hand to his mouth. The image of the huge shears slick and dripping, froze the breath in his chest. *How does one use those to butcher people...to butcher family?* Stunned, Matt looked to the next photo. It was a shot of a weird symbol painted on the kitchen wall. No, wait, it was not paint, it was drawn in *blood.* By hand, too. Matt could see streaking made by individual fingers in the gruesome drawing. That was enough for him. He put the stack of photographs face-down on the desk.

# Chapter Nine

"Here we go, sweetheart," Darcy said as she wiped at her patient's glistening chin with a folded napkin. "Let me just get that for you." She spoke to Hannah Wilkins in a soft and nurturing tone, a mother's tone, though she was only ten years her senior.

A thick strand of Hannah's bronze, shoulder-length hair fell in her eyes. Darcy pulled it away and tucked it behind the girl's ear. She did not know why. It was not bothering Hannah. Nothing was.

Hannah, still a minor at seventeen, had been signed into the care of Saint Michael's by her parents two weeks before Darcy's arrival. Doctor Dawson had concurred with the assessments of Hannah's previous psychiatrists and labeled her manic depressive. He decided on a treatment plan, and Hannah had been in a stupor since. "An adjustment period" was what he called it when Darcy voiced her concerns. He had explained it to her as though she was a first-year student. "Once the patient adjusts to the medication, strides toward improvement in her condition can be taken," he had told her without looking up from his desk.

"You look very pretty today," Darcy said. She was seated beside Hannah in the patient lounge. She checked on her there every morning once Cundiff or Klewes helped the girl from her quarters. Hannah could not walk on her own without stumbling. She was loaded into a wheelchair like human cargo, then dumped onto the couch where she stayed among Saint Michael's other lost souls until the next meal was served or bath time rolled around.

Darcy's compliment went unheeded. Hannah's gaze fixed firmly on the floor in front of her. Like her stumbling and drooling, incoherence seemed to be another part of her "adjustment period."

She wondered how she could ever be of any help to Hannah in this state. How could she help any of the patients, for that matter? They were all either past the effective treatment stage or in drug-addled comas. How was she supposed to help patients get to the root of their problems, when therapy seemed to be a forgotten art to Doctor Dawson? That had become abundantly clear when he told her he would be seeing to the treatment of that poor old man on the second floor, Mister Dykeman. How he could call *that* treatment was beyond her. She had seen the man's dose records, she knew what kind of dope he was on. To her, it was simply abuse, and the College of Physicians would likely agree.

These times, when frustrations took hold, Darcy felt the walls of Saint Michael's close in around her. The atmosphere of the place pressed against her flesh. And the silence—it was the worst. Out of all the hospitals and care homes Darcy had visited, Saint Michael's was the first that was perfectly quiet. Moaning and wailing was commonplace in such a facility, especially in the night. Yet, Saint Michael's remained silent to the point that Darcy's ears rang at times. She could see only one reason for that.

Still, how should she approach Matt about the medication he gave his patients? How could she advocate on Hannah's behalf when poor girl's own parents did not seem to care? They had not even come to visit the poor thing. *Human cargo*...the words echoed in Darcy's head. She could have cried. Hannah's story was all *too* familiar.

*Soon*, she thought. *Things around here will be different soon.* Matt would return to his position in Edmonton and the running of Saint Michael's would be left to her. Then she would see to the proper care of these people. She would practice exactly like she imagined when she was in school—her reward for studying all those long hours.

Darcy wrapped Hannah's hand in hers. She tried to picture her as a normal girl, without the yellow plastic bracelet and hospital-issued robe and johnny—without those blue-black bags beneath her eyes. She could see her happy again, smiling, among friends. She could help her get there and she knew where to start.

\* \* \* \*

Darcy waved to Klewes as he emerged from the basement stairwell. He gave her a warm smile and a greeting as she climbed the stairs toward the second floor. That was the one nice thing about Saint Michael's—the people made her feel welcomed. John Cundiff, Klewes, that funny cook, Elmer, everyone was so nice. Even the owly nurse, Wanda, was warming to her. She could never say there was anything wrong with the hospital staff. They were the lone bright spot in this otherwise gloomy place.

The construction work had finally been completed in the weeks since her arrival and the building looked much better for it, but for Darcy, the greatest improvement was the departure of the construction workers. She did not miss their leering in the slightest.

When she reached the second floor, she steeled herself for an encounter with Doctor Dawson. She knew where he would be—outside Mister Dykeman's room, watching his patient. It was where he spent much of his time now. Only God knew why.

"Doctor Dawson, I wonder if we might have a word," she said firmly when she neared her boss at the end of the hall. He did not seem to hear, his focus on the room's occupant. "Doctor Dawson..." she said again. Darcy's concern piqued. She wondered for a moment if he had been taking his patient's meds. She touched his shoulder. "Matt."

He flinched, his trance broken. "Doctor Collins...yes?"

His appearance was shabbier than usual. His beard was thick and wild, his face drawn. Stress lines webbed from his eyes and the corners of his mouth. It was like he had aged overnight. Darcy guessed that he had not *slept* overnight, or in any recent nights for that matter. He wore the same shirt and pants he had on the day before, and smelled accordingly. She was so taken aback by his condition that she momentarily forgot what she wanted to discuss with him.

Matt turned toward her, placed his hands in the pockets of his lab coat and straightened himself. He labored a smile and said, "What can I do for you?"

His expression was so rigid, so ingenuous, that it looked painful to wear.

After a few moments of searching her memory banks, Darcy recalled her purpose. "I wanted to talk to you about Hannah Wilkins." She had anticipated a confrontation in which neither side would easily back down, but having seen Matt's state, she was at a loss. It appeared that he needed someone to intervene on his behalf as much as Hannah did.

"Hannah...yes."

"I am concerned about her response to the Topiramate we have her on," Darcy started. *There*, she thought. *No turning back now.*

"Yes?"

"I feel that I haven't seen significant improvement in her side effects to warrant further use. Her loss of cognition and coordination is becoming a concern."

"I see."

"I wondered if a change to Lamotrigine might help with this. It has a proven record of discouraging manic episodes while reducing side effects in some subjects. It may help Hannah to reach her target level."

"Lamotrigine...Lamictal...I'm familiar with it." Matt furrowed his brow while he pondered Darcy's request. "Is she exhibiting any numbness now?"

*He doesn't even know.* "She drools."

"Okay. Make the change. You can sign for it. Tell Wanda."

Darcy released the breath she had mustered in anticipation of the argument that never came. She relished the moment, the small victory, and envisioned more to come. She almost told Matt *thank you*, but caught herself and said, "I'll make the arrangements."

Matt nodded and returned to the window to Dykeman's room.

"Doctor Dawson...Matt...are you all right? You sort of look a little...tired."

He loosed a deep sigh and slouched as though he had expelled the last of his energy. "It's been a grind, Darcy." He spoke quietly, like his words were not meant for sharing. "Stanley left me this...this mess."

Darcy had heard from the others that the hospital was in financial trouble when Stanley Dawson passed away and Matt had inherited the burden. He had been carrying the load on his own since—the state of the hospital, the patients' health, the staff. It was enough to break the strongest of men. She had lost sight of that. Instead of being at odds with him over medicine, she should have been sharing the load. One day it would be hers, once Matt had done all the heavy lifting and the hardship had taken its toll. She suddenly felt small. "If there is anything I can do to help, I'm ready for more responsibility."

Matt turned his red and weary eyes her way. He attempted to force a smile and failed miserably. It was as though he was on the verge of spilling his problems out in a landslide, but before he spoke, seemed to rein himself in and merely nodded again and turned his attention back to his patient.

"You don't have to do it alone anymore, you know," Darcy said softly and patted his shoulder. "I'm going to do the rounds. We can talk later, if you like." She started away, every bit as concerned for Matt now as she had been for Hannah.

"Oh...Doctor Collins," he said.

Darcy stopped, looked back at him.

"Good work with Hannah. Keep it up."

\* \* \* \*

After Darcy had left him alone, Matt continued to watch Dykeman. Over the last hour the subject had shifted his hanging head from one shoulder to the other and for a period of about fifteen minutes, appeared to be asleep, after which, he raised his face to the sun pouring through his window. Matt did not know what he was watching for. Perhaps he wanted to gauge the effect of the steady reduction in Dykeman's medication. A part of him hoped that Dykeman would suddenly shake his head to clear the cobwebs and rise from the deck chair ready to answer all of his questions. The rest of him prayed that Dykeman would never move again. Maybe he should return his meds to the dosage Stanley set. Maybe he should arrange for a pillow to accidentally cover his face while he slept. Matt pressed his forehead to the door.

Determining Stanley's connection to this man was proving futile. The records Matt liberated from the locked desk gave nothing in terms of answers. They only led to more questions, more blank spaces to fill in. The problem was, without facts, Matt was filling those blanks with bits of his worst nightmares.

Did Stanley know Dykeman before the murders? Did he somehow feel guilty or responsible for what happened? Is that why he went to such trouble to bring Dykeman here? Matt was appalled by the crime scene photographs but after the initial shock subsided, studied them more closely. He wondered how a fourteen-year-old could do such a thing. Accepting that he was morally capable in the first place, how could he even carry out the deed? He would have had to overpower a grown man in his father *and* his older brother. Not to mention, any full-grown woman could put up one hell of a fight when confronted with a life or death struggle. It did not add up—unless he had help...an accomplice. The idea made his stomach churn. Matt had to remind himself it was only an idea. He still did not have any facts.

He had considered going to the police with his concerns, but what would he say? Why would he inquire about a sixty-year-old murder case in which a judgment was reached, a sentence handed down? That would do more harm than good. The last thing he wanted was to get the authorities asking their own questions about Dykeman *and* about Stanley. That sort of thing could threaten the hospital.

Matt had already turned to one community resource. He had asked the man who seemed to know something about everything that happened in Saint Andrews. He had asked Mayor Bud.

They had been standing in the front room of the condo Bud had found for Doctor Collins. It was the perfect setting for a private conversation. Matt thanked Bud for donning his realtor's hat and finding such a great place. In addition to the *hat*, Bud also wore a professional-looking navy blazer and matching striped tie for the occasion. The paperwork was neatly laid out on the coffee table for Matt to sign while Bud continued his sales pitch even though the deal was virtually complete. It seemed he couldn't help himself.

"I figured our new doctor would want a unit that was big enough to entertain some company," he said for the third or fourth time, "and the view...

there's no sense living in Saint Andrews without a grand view of the bay."

"Yes, Doctor Collins will appreciate it, I'm sure," Matt said absently as he read over the forms. "I understand she is enchanted with the water."

"I'm guessing that she'll like that the unit is fully furnished," Bud added as though he worried that Matt may reconsider signing on the dotted line.

"That works also. Doctor Collins will be moving into Stanley's house once I return home, and it's furnished, so this situation makes good sense." Matt sifted through the papers. "That reminds me, this *is* a three-month lease, right?"

"Oh yes, I was adamant about that," Bud said proudly. "I even negotiated a price reduction for you."

"Yes, thanks again," Matt said, thinking, *you've only mentioned that about ten times now.* Satisfied with the terms of the lease agreement, Matt made his signature. When he did, Bud released a subtle but detectable sigh. "Good work, Bud," Matt said and they shook on it.

Mayor Bud collected the papers from the coffee table and went about stuffing them into a manila envelope. "It was my pleasure, Doc. And, if you decide to set up more housekeeping in this building, I can make it happen easily enough. Just let me know what I can do."

"That is appreciated." Matt rose from the contemporary couch centered in the living room and went to the large picture window overlooking the wharf and waters beyond, then broached the subject he had been eager to visit since they arrived. "Bud, can I ask you something?"

"Of course."

"It's about Stanley."

The mayor stopped fiddling with the envelope and regarded the doctor. "Yeah?"

"It's safe to assume, by what you said at his wake, that you knew him pretty well."

Bud hesitated before answering. His realtor's hat was off, replaced by his mayor's. When he gave his response it was with all the cautionary footwork typical of a politician. "Yes, I *knew* him pretty well. Years ago, mind you. People can drift apart as they get older, even in a town this small. Though, I'll do my best if you have questions."

Matt peered out at the bay, aglitter under the midday sun. It was alive with activity. Boats of every type went in all directions. They were under power of sail, motor, paddle, and oar. He could hear the cheery voices of citizens and tourists alike at play on the water. The scene was in painfully sharp contrast to the dark business he was about to conduct.

"You went to school with my father?"

"That's right," Bud said, then chuckled and added, "I'm a couple years older than him, but I was held back and we ended up in the same grade. Let's just keep that between you and me," he said with a wink.

Matt grinned. "Deal." *Another secret,* he thought. *For such a small town, Saint Andrews is full of them. It seems to keep as many as the deep blue sea outside the window.* "What about Phillip Prichard?"

"The accountant?"

"Yeah, he said that he grew up with Stanley also."

"Sure. He was around." Bud laid the paperwork down on the coffee table and stuffed his hands in his pants pockets. Matt recognized the posturing as defensive. "I could probably name fifty people still kicking around that we went to school with...folks who are near to our age."

Matt pivoted toward the window again and watched the water as he continued to fish. "Morris Dykeman is about your age too, isn't he?"

Bud remained silent. When Matt turned to look at the mayor, he found him seated in the arm chair, slowly wringing his hands. "Doctor Dawson...Matthew... please, come and have a seat."

Matt returned to the couch, eyes trained on the visibly shaken man. He suddenly looked like different person. The ever-smiling, ever-campaigning mayor had been replaced by a weary old man.

"You *do* know him, I take it."

Bud gathered a breath. "Yes. Everyone does."

"You know what he did?"

"Oh yes...small towns never forget. A case like that is something that will stick with you. What happened to Morry's family was monstrous. It hurt this community like you'll never know. Morry's father worked the boats. His mother sang in the church choir. His brother played high school hockey. Their loss touched everyone in some way.

"It's something you don't get over. The town never has, really. It's like a stain on our history and all that laughing and carrying-on you hear out that window can't ever erase it. We did our best to forget it. The Dykeman property was auctioned off, their house torn down, their presence all but wiped from the town. Folks stopped saying the name altogether, as though it was some kind of curse. After a while we got pretty good at pretending the murders didn't happen, but we *can't* forget...even though we'd sure as hell like to.

"I often think about the day the wagon from the city came and they took Morry away. I think that may have been the last day of my childhood."

"He's at Saint Michael's."

Bud did not flinch.

"You already knew that," Matt said.

"I'm one of the few who does...and for good reason. Morry's crimes were unspeakable. The citizens would be outraged if they caught wind that he was here and has been for years. We couldn't do with a mob storming the hospital, out for vigilante justice. Keeping it quiet was necessary."

"Bud, I'm sorry for stirring up the pains of the past, but there are things I need to know."

"You want to know *why*. You want to know why your father took him in to Saint Michael's."

"Yes."

"It's simple. It's as simple as the tides coming and going. Morry Dykeman is one of us, and despite the horrible things he did, he'll *always* be one of us. Your father saw that. He remembered Morry the classmate, the ballplayer, the boy, not the cold-blooded murderer. Your father brought him here so he could take care of him. You would do it too. The same blood, Stanley's blood, runs in your veins. It's in you to care for the people nobody else cares for."

Matt scratched at his burgeoning beard as he considered that.

"Now, I'm guessing this all has something to do with that asshole writer who's been snooping around town."

Matt was stunned by Bud's blunt account of Eric Fisher.

"Don't be surprised. It's the mayor's job to know what visitors to the town get up to, especially when it's a man like Fisher. He's no good. Now I have half a mind to see that he's prompted to move on. I can't have him flapping his gums about the Dykeman case all over town. People will start asking questions and I owe it to Stanley's memory to keep his secret."

*Fucking secrets*, Matt thought. As he stood outside Dykeman's door, studying the man inside, he cursed every secret he had ever heard. *Secrets are like cancer. They fester and swell until they kill relationships, families, even Saint Michael's isn't safe from its secrets.*

Mayor Bud did not shed much light on Stanley's ties to Dykeman. Matt saw that he was stonewalled, that whatever else he knew was secured deep within his vault, far from prying eyes. One thing Matt's profession had taught him was to be patient. He knew that successfully taking down one's walls was done over time. He knew when to press and when to wait. He was not done with the mayor just yet. He knew that too.

Dykeman had lolled his head from his right shoulder to his left. That was the sum of his activity over the last half-hour.

Matt leaned on the door and rubbed the bridge of his nose. He was beyond tired—depleted at the core. *A merlot with a strong bouquet would do wonders about now*, he thought. The corridor was quiet and still. Matt closed his eyes and felt himself dipping into slumber. He forced his eyes open. Looking down, he noticed that his clothing was a road work of wrinkles and it occurred to him that he had not changed in recent memory. Then something else caught his eye. Beneath his feet, the normally shiny floor was scuffed and dingy. He looked at the tiles around him. They displayed the usual glossy sheen.

*Odd...Did I do this? No, I couldn't have. It looks like it would take years of wear...years of standing in this very spot.*

Matt raised his head to the small window in Dykeman's door.

Inside, Morry Dykeman sat in the sunlight, his head now hanging to the right.

Matt lowered his gaze to the worn tiles and decided to go home early. *Maybe that merlot is a good idea. That and a hot bath—it's absolutely freezing in here.*

\* \* \* \*

"Hey, it must be story time," Darcy said to Klewes when she met him en route to the lounge, *Sports Illustrated* in his hand.

"Yeah, it's about that time. Margaret will be waiting," he said with a wry smile that would be appropriate on a fox entering a hen house.

"What's today's article?"

"Oh, it's about how a salary cap in major league baseball would affect the sport."

"Ooh, sounds kind of dry," Darcy said, wriggling her nose. "I hope Margaret likes stories about sports business."

"Yeah, I sort of wind up scraping the bottom of the barrel every month before the next issue comes out. She doesn't seem to mind, though."

Darcy smiled. She could see that nothing would deter the orderly from his reading and respite. "Umm, before you go, I wondered if I could talk to you about something."

"Okay," Klewes said quickly. "I took the truck to the Coffee Stop drive through. I know I'm not supposed to, but Elmer does a lot more with it than I do. I mean, you gotta know he's full of shit, right?"

Darcy pursed her lips and shook her head. "You lost me."

"Oh...all right...forget I said anything." Klewes cleared his throat. "So, wassup?" he asked, cheerful once again.

"I wanted to talk to you about Cundiff."

"Well, he works real hard. He's also willing to take shifts the rest of us..."

Darcy raised a hand to slow the orderly's journey down a new sidetrack. "No, I'm not asking as head doctor or as a supervisor or anything, I'm just asking as...a girl."

"Oh." Klewes reached understanding a moment later. "Ooohhh..."

"It's not like that. I was just curious about what's going on between him and those Sullivan fishing guys. I ask because a couple weeks back we were leaving the diner and we had kind of a confrontation with them on the street."

Klewes folded his thick arms across his chest and nodded as she told the story.

"Anyway, they clearly have a history. Cundiff said it had to do with him working for them or something. I just thought maybe you could shed a little light. I know he's a good friend, so if you don't want to tell me, I'll understand..."

"No, it's cool. Everybody knows about it anyway. It's pretty straightforward. Cundiff went to work on one of their lobster boats, but he had problems off the get-go. He never could swim very well. He knew that going in, but he took the job anyway. The boats are the best-paying job in town. Unfortunately, his fear of falling in the drink got to be too much after a while. I mean, it gets pretty crazy on the high water sometimes. Anyhow, he woke up one morning and couldn't bring himself to go to the wharf and get on that boat again. He called in and quit on the spot and the boat was left shorthanded. It's about the worst thing you can do in this town—leave a crew short like that. It's something people always remember...it's like a reputation killer.

"It was hard enough on him that he came to talk to Doctor Dawson about his problem. He told the doc the whole story and asked him what he could do about his fear of drowning. The doc had the answer. He always did. He hired him, right then and there. Next thing you knew, Cundiff wasn't a broken fisherman anymore—he was a perfectly good orderly."

"Well, he didn't have a problem in the first place. Fear of drowning when you don't swim well is completely healthy. If he had no sense of danger, *that* would be a problem."

"Try telling that to a kid from Saint Andrews. He's supposed to have salt water in his veins and gills on his neck."

"No offense, Mister Klewes, but that sounds like a lot of *macho* bullshit."

"Well, whatever it is, it's why the Sullivans and their boys don't like Cundiff too much."

"To the point where they physically threaten him? It's just stupid."

"I agree."

"Don't you think something should be done about it?"

"Doctor Collins, you should probably just let it go. The Sullivan family has a lot of pull around these parts."

"So I've heard."

"Hey, take it from me. They could treat him much worse. At least they gave him a chance on the boat in the first place."

Darcy considered his meaning. "Thanks Mister Klewes," she said. "I'd appreciate it if you kept this between us."

"Sure," he said and started toward the lounge. "And you can call me Klewey. My friends do."

Darcy called after him. "Hey Klewey, don't let me catch you going to the Coffee Stop in the hospital's truck again."

# Chapter Ten

Darcy sunk into the couch and laid her head back in its ample cushion. She just completed another day at the hospital, worked a total of nine hours, made three rounds, and actually helped zero patients. She was supposed to be making a difference. Getting to the root of a patient's problems and making breakthroughs, like she used to daydream about when she was studying, were proving to be the stuff of fiction. Her patients had real problems and all she could do was brush their hair, wipe their drool and hope for a positive response to drug treatment.

Tears welled in the corners of her eyes and overflowed when she raised her head.

Before her, the large picture window opened to the bay. The water sparkled as though the moon had fallen upon it and shattered into a million pieces. The whale watching expeditions and boat tours ended at sunset and the restaurants and bars along Water Street were just getting busy. Three floors down, people were chatting and laughing on the sidewalk en route to their dinner plans. It reminded Darcy of weekends at school when the dorm parties were starting and she had her nose in the books.

She was still there, minus the books, of course.

Drying her eyes, Darcy searched for a way to salvage her Friday night. Maybe she should call Mom. Sure, she would have to suffer the inevitable *did you meet a man yet* and *are you taking care of yourself*? Still, it would be nice to hear a familiar voice. She could tell her about her new condo and the large Dawson house that she would soon move into. Wait—that would sound too much like bragging, and that always led to argument. Mom always took good news as some kind of boasting. "Well, it must be nice. I never had a chance to do anything with my life," she would say. "I never got to go to university, let alone med school. I had to look after your father and your sister."

*Sister...Dianne. Now there was a gal who never had a chance.*

Darcy glanced at her watch and calculated Nancy's time zone. Her old classmate was always good for a phone-in griping session. Of course, when last they spoke, Nancy hadn't found a job yet and seemed a little short with Darcy when she described the head doctor's position she had lucked into. Better hold off on calling until her online status has been updated to *employed*.

*Why is everyone so jealous?*

*Seriously, is there anything about my life to envy?*

Darcy got up from the sofa and went to the bathroom. She winced in the harsh vanity light and regarded the slightly older-looking woman in the mirror's reflection. Crying had not helped matters. Her eyes were sunken and red, her cheeks puffy. She splashed cool water on her face and dried off with a hand towel. The reflection did not improve much. *Hmmm.* She pulled the elastic from her ponytail, shook her hair loose and shaped it with her hands.

*That's better.*

Darcy opened the medicine cabinet and picked up a tube of moisturizer from the shelf. She put it down and retrieved the small makeup case beside it. Most women would have exhausted ten of them before Darcy finished one. She opened it and considered the different shades on the small palette and she tried to recall when she bought it. She couldn't remember, nor could she remember the last time she shadowed her eyes with it. She snapped it shut and studied her reflection again.

*That's it. I'm going out. I'm going into my closet. I'm going to put on something that I wouldn't wear to work. I'm going to put on some makeup, and I'm just fucking going out...and not alone, either.*

\* \* \* \*

Stanley watched Cundiff sitting behind the desk of the nurse's station. He had been lingering for what seemed like an hour. Exasperated by his futile attempts to seize the orderly's attention, he was resigned to spying. Just like before, Cundiff was oblivious to Stanley's presence save the occasional shiver when he got too close.

Stanley had been at the main entrance, trying unsuccessfully to force the door open, when the *change* happened this time. He still did not understand what it was or how it happened; he just felt it. He could not nail down the feeling or give it a name, but at some point it stopped being 7:30 and the wan sunlight faded completely. The world—*his* world—simply *changed*. Stanley had fumbled his pocket watch open. It read 10:00. Suddenly the halls of Saint Michaels were illuminated by the sparse secondary lighting fixtures. It was customary lighting for the hospital during sleeping hours. The staff called it turning on the nightlights, and they did so every evening in the summer at 9:00 p.m.

The last time the *change* occurred, he saw Cundiff and Wanda on the second floor. As he pocketed his watch, he had wondered who he might see this time. Would he see Matthew? He dared not hold a hope. There was little room for it at Saint Michael's.

Stanley had abandoned the front door. There was no way for him to know how long this *version* of Saint Michael's would last and he wanted to make the most of it. His search for life brought him to the second floor again, and it was there he found the orderly.

Conversation proved impossible, so Stanley merely watched. At first he felt as though he was eavesdropping, that he should let the young man be. Yet, he craved human contact so badly that he just could not bring himself to leave his side. Besides, he reckoned, it was not as though he could tell anyone if Cundiff picked his nose or talked to himself when he was alone, so what was the harm?

Despite the joy of being in the company of another, the last hour had been largely uneventful. Cundiff had busied himself by reading patient assessments. Stanley had no idea he had such a keen interest in hospital business. He had never once asked a question related to patient care. Perhaps he and Klewes were no longer receiving the direction they needed to do their jobs properly and he was being proactive by learning patient requirements. Perhaps not.

Cundiff closed the file he had been reading. "*Coo coo,*" he said, much to Stanley's chagrin.

Stanley was considering laying a freezing hand on the back of the orderly's bare neck when the phone rang. Cundiff lifted the receiver and gave a greeting that sounded more like a groan. When he heard the voice on the other end—a female voice—he sat up in his chair straight as a pencil.

Stanley laughed aloud at his reaction. Curiosity trumped his reservations of snooping and he leaned in toward the receiver.

"What are you doing?" the woman asked.

"Not much...just hanging around." Cundiff winced and shook his head as though unhappy with his response. Stanley thought he might enjoy this exchange.

"I thought your shift might be over," she continued.

"Yeah, it's past ten. I can go anytime."

"Go where, exactly?"

"Umm, I was going to go to a thing with some friends...umm..."

Stanley told Cundiff to relax and breathe. He laid a comforting hand on his shoulder and did his best to give it a squeeze. When he did, Stanley experienced a sensation he had not felt since he first met his Susan, when they were still kids. It surged through his chest like a heat wave and settled in the pit of his stomach. Stanley took a breath himself. It did little to relieve the feeling he could only describe as extreme adoration mingling with undertones of lust.

"Actually...I was going to go home and have Kraft Dinner."

"Really?"

"No...not really...Mister Noodle. I don't know why I lied just now. Like Kraft Dinner is any better than Mister Noodle."

"Hey, I was a student for a long time and I can tell you that Kraft Dinner is *way* better than Mister Noodle."

"Maybe, but it's still embarrassing."

"Well, since you don't have any pressing plans, why don't you meet me at the Lobster Bucket for a drink?"

The tempest in Stanley's chest peaked and he pulled his hand away and wrapped his arms around himself. The moment his hand was clear, Stanley's emotional turmoil ceased. He looked back to Cundiff, and at once, he understood.

"Umm, yeah, a drink would be nice."

"Great, is twenty minutes enough time for you to get there? I mean nothing's far in Saint Andrews right?"

"Yup. I can be there in twenty."

"Okay, see you then."

"Okay."

The woman hung up and Cundiff slowly placed the receiver in the cradle. He seemed to be processing everything that just transpired. He slumped back in the chair and released a breath.

Stanley sympathized. He knew exactly how Cundiff felt. He felt it too, after all. Stanley held up his hand and examined it front and back. Somehow, when he touched Cundiff, their connection was more than physical—it had gone much deeper.

Cundiff bolted from the chair. "Twenty minutes," he said, bounding from the desk in the direction of the stairs.

Stanley watched him go. He would likely rush home to change from his scrubs into something he hoped would impress the young woman who had evoked such raw emotion in him. It was all too much for Stanley. He fell into the chair Cundiff had vacated, relieved for once that he felt nothing.

\* \* \* \*

Matt stared at the urn on the mantel in the sparse light of the study. From his seat behind the desk, the handles of the lavish urn looked like horns, the reflected hallway light like gleaming eyes. He hoisted a bottle and took a generous swig. Red wine fuelled the furnace in his belly and he reveled in its warm glow. Truly, everything was better with a little wine in the system. With it, he was able to eye Stanley's macabre urn without feeling much of anything. Even the gun beside him in the broken desk drawer no longer raised his nerves.

*Would anyone complain if I brought a few bottles to the hospital to help face the day?*

He smiled as he contemplated the possibility of working under the influence. It ultimately reminded him of his duties and he leaned forward and collected the pile of mail from the desktop. He shuffled through it: power bill, phone bill, insurance bill. *Ouch.* He hated seeing that one. Even partially intoxicated, he could not bear to read it. At least there was finally some cash flowing into the coffers, thanks to Prichard's aggressive plan to boost hospital income. The bills may hurt but they would be paid.

He flipped to the next envelope, which boasted that it contained over $100 in savings if its coupons were put to use. "Oh, this one's addressed to you," he said to the urn, and tossed it on the desk.

The next envelope in the pile was blank. Matt turned it over in search of a label. It was thin, perhaps empty. It had been sealed, though. Images of his dead body being discovered on the floor of the study flashed in his head. The coroner stood over him, beside the attending detective. "Just like I thought... anthrax," he said holding up a clear plastic bag with the suspicious envelope inside, white powder spilling from it.

"I should be so lucky," Matt said to the urn. He opened the envelope. Inside was a single folded sheet of notepaper that had been torn from a spiral-bound pad. It held a short handwritten message: *How about twenty grand?* It was signed, *F.*

Matt crumpled the note and envelope and threw them across the room. "Fisher!" He seethed. *He was here. He had strolled right up to the front door and slid the letter through the mail slot. And after I warned him, threatened him.* "The fucking gall!" Matt rubbed hard at his brow with both hands then looked up at the mantle again. "You should have to deal with this."

\* \* \* \*

"What can I get you, dear?" the bartender asked. He leaned over the wooden bar top, close to Darcy. The question left her a little doe-eyed. He was a man of about fifty with kind eyes and a welcoming smile. It was likely he could tell she was a little nervous. Professor Kipping had joked once during a lecture that one would make a pretty good psychiatrist if ever he was able to read faces as well as a bartender could.

Darcy had not made many drink orders in her life, and searched her limited menu for an adequate response. The bar was bustling with customers and the barman, while patient with her, would not wait long for her to make up her mind. She went with the choice she made last time she was out with Nancy. "A glass of the house white, please," she finally said.

He raised his brow as if he was quite certain of her inevitable disappointment. "Coming right up," he promised and went to the other end of the bar.

Darcy took a moment to check herself over. She had put on a burgundy V-neck sweater, a pair of faded blue jeans, and opened-toed shoes that matched her shoulder bag. Compared to the other girls in the Lobster Bucket, she was glaringly overdressed. Most of them wore shorts and colorful tanks or shorter shorts and halter tops. Even when she made an effort to dress casually, she managed to be the most rigid-looking person in the place. Oh well, at least she had put on some makeup and some jewelry. That was a step in the right direction. She touched her ears, making sure her diamond studs had not come loose, then the silver heart pendant that hung from her neck. Touching it always brought her a measure of comfort, a feeling of home. Dianne wore the matching one. She may even have been touching hers at that exact moment. That would not be the strangest phenomenon Darcy and her sister had shared.

"Here you are, dear," the bartender said, setting a long-stemmed glass on a coaster in front of her. "If it doesn't meet with your approval, I'd be happy to get you something else. We don't move a lot of wine here."

"Thanks. I'm sure it's fine," Darcy said, instantly regretting it when she looked at the glass and saw contents that were far more yellow than white. The bartender seemed to be waiting for her to try it before moving on to the next customer. Darcy took a sip. It was so tart, it almost brought tears to her eyes. She managed a tight smile for the nice man and said it was okay. Truth be known, she could not think of anything else to ask for other than the house red, which in all likelihood *would* make her weep. The barman nodded and took another customer's order.

Darcy breathed deeply to cleanse her palette and fought the urge to retrieve a piece of gum from her bag. She looked around the crowded restaurant. It was a kitschy place, with lobster traps hung from the ceiling and fishing nets festooned over rough wooden walls. A large custom-made light fixture comprised of old buoys lit the dining area, while rusty red lanterns turned into sconces illuminated the perimeter. It was what she imagined a pirate hangout might look like.

The place held a dozen tables with a few more on the deck in front of the restaurant. Each one was occupied by a group seemingly more boisterous than the next. Even the bar was at full capacity with no stools to spare. She imagined the other customers were regaling each other of days spent sailing or hiking or playing tennis. They were not the cool kids she had gone to school with, but they sure looked like them. They definitely went to school with some other geek that would feel equally uncomfortable in Darcy's seat.

The gentleman on the stool next to hers was recounting a lively fishing tale for his friends. His voice was ever rising and he was so animated in his gestures that he bumped her shoulder. Though an apology quickly followed, Darcy began to wonder if the evening had been a bad idea. It was nothing like what she wanted. She thought it would be quiet affair with a few drinks and some late dining and, most importantly, some pleasant conversation with John Cundiff. She had envisioned learning if he was someone she wanted to get closer to. Instead, the bar was rowdy, she stuck out like a sore thumb, and her drink could probably remove wallpaper with ease. Maybe she could sneak out. She could tell Cundiff that something last-minute had come up. *Whatever just came up in Saint Andrews, anyway?*

"Hi," she heard from her side.

Darcy turned to find her date. Her voice stuck in her throat as she involuntarily looked him over. He wore a green fitted tee shirt that revealed his arms. She felt more than a little superficial as she took in his muscled limbs. Then her gaze dropped and her appreciation of Cundiff reached a new level. Instead of shorts and sandals, like her, he was wearing faded blue jeans.

"Hi," she managed.

"I hope I didn't leave you waiting long. I went home to change."

"No...I just got here."

Cundiff looked around the room. "Wow, is it ever busy tonight."

"Yeah, it looks like all the tables are taken. Did you want to go somewhere else?"

"No, that's okay. Besides, you already ordered a drink."

Darcy looked at her glass and the urine-colored fluid in it. Cundiff went to their right, to the men that were exchanging *the one that got away* stories. He greeted them and said something. A moment later they got up and went to stand in the corner near the end of the bar. Cundiff plopped himself down in the stool beside Darcy's and smiled at her.

"What did you say to them?"

"A gentleman never reveals his methods."

Darcy laughed.

"Hey Chuck," Cundiff called down the bar. "How about a pint of Clover?"

"Lager or Ale?" the bartender called back.

"Ale, please."

Cundiff turned to Darcy. "I wondered if I'd find you in here wearing your lab coat. It's all I've ever seen you in."

"Come on."

"Seriously, I almost wore my scrubs so you'd feel more comfortable."

"I wish you had, Mister."

"Well, you look very nice tonight."

"Funny, I feel a little overdressed," she said, regarding the other patrons, "but, thanks."

"You're not overdressed. You don't want to look like them, anyway. They're tourists, you're a local now."

Darcy found the sentiment surprisingly nice to hear. Someone felt that she actually belonged somewhere. It was a first.

"One pint of Clover Hill Ale," Chuck said, setting a foaming mug in front of

Cundiff. "How's the wine treating you, dear?"

"Well..." Darcy started, feeling more comfortable after Cundiff's kind words.

"I gotta tell ya, Chuck," Cundiff said. "That looks a lot like pee."

"You should taste it," Darcy said, getting a laugh from the two.

"You're too nice, dear," Chuck said, taking her glass away. "Most of the ladies that come in here would have thrown it in my face if they didn't like it. Can I get you something else?"

"What would you recommend for a girl that needs to get an awful taste out of her mouth?"

"Hmmm..." Chuck closed one eye, studied her, and said, "You look like a liqueur girl to me. I'll mix you up something that'll float your boat." He went down the bar to begin his creation.

"He seems very nice," Darcy said, watching the barman retrieve bottles from the shelf.

"Chuck? Oh yeah, he's great. He's been the bartender here for as long as I can remember. When Klewey and I were kids, we used to come here after hockey practice and sit on these very stools and eat fries and gravy. It was like a ritual—and, if no one was around, Chuck would let us have a small glass of beer."

"Really? You were *kids*."

"It was really good for us. It didn't amount to more than a mouthful of beer, but it made two boys feel like men for a few minutes. That is, until customers came in and Chuck grabbed up our glasses and hid them behind the bar." Cundiff grinned and shook his head at the recollection. "Maybe Chuck was just giving liquor to minors, but the way I see it, he was encouraging some confidence in a couple boys who could really use it."

"Hmmph." Darcy watched the bartender as he topped a concoction with a cherry and put a straw in it. He made his way back to them and placed the glass before her.

"This," he said proudly, "is called a cherry pie. It's made with amaretto. I think you'll like it."

Darcy thanked him, and like before, she did a taste test while he waited. This time, she was not disappointed—far from it. It was the perfect mix of sweet and sour. "Oh, my God," she said, still holding the drink to her mouth. "This is amazing." She took another sip.

Chuck's face lit up. "All right then. Hey, I got a few more recipes up my sleeve, dear. You say the word and I'll make you a drink that tastes like a chocolate sundae."

"I might be stuck on cherry pies for a while."

"Good job, Chuck," Cundiff said. "I've always said you belong behind bars."

The bartender scowled at the pun as though he heard it every night.

When they were left alone again, Cundiff said, "Well, we have a place to sit and drinks that work. I'm thinking we can relax for a while." He raised his mug to her glass. "Cheers."

She returned the salutation as they clinked drinks and she contemplated how easily she could become a drunk if all of Chuck's creations were so delicious. As she took another sip, she felt a comfort settle upon her, like she was sinking into her stool a little more. She felt all the tension she had been carrying around for days melting from her shoulders. She had discovered a day at the spa in a short glass. As she and Cundiff chatted about town life and he told her more of its history, she felt more and more at ease. She felt anchored to the place through him. He belonged and, in a way, that meant that she did too.

After her second cherry pie, Chuck threatened to make her that chocolate beverage again. She waited for Cundiff to finish his mug. "I'm getting a little hungry," she said. "Do you want to see about getting a table?"

"No, no, we can't eat here," he said, shaking his head emphatically.

"Why not? I've been craving one of those lobsters since I got here. I'm almost ready to tackle the next waitress that walks by with one."

"Oh, we can have lobster, just not *this* lobster. This is tourist food."

Darcy wanted to laugh but could not tell if he was being sincere. "So, where do locals get lobster?"

"Well, it just so happens that it's Friday night, so we're in luck. Let me make a phone call."

\* \* \* \*

"Isn't it a little late for going to someone's house for dinner? It's like 11:30."

"No, we're right on time. You'll see. It's more of a get-together than a dinner. Every Friday night, Klewey's family puts on this big spread. They'll have clams and mussels, crab legs, corn on the cob, and of course, lobster. They do it right, too. It won't be any of that tough pre-cooked canner lobster you get at the Bucket, either. It will be the best lobster you've ever had—the only lobster worth having."

Cundiff's car hugged the turns as it took them away from town and onto darkened back roads. Darcy remembered little of the country route that brought her to Saint Andrews on the day of her arrival. However, she did remember how twisty and hilly it was. Cundiff aimed the car with an ease that showed his familiarity with the road. It seemed he had driven it a thousand times and he knew what was behind every curve and rise.

When they left Water Street, the evening fog was threatening to overtake the beach and shroud the town in its misty vale. A few miles north and they were out of the fog belt altogether. Even the air was noticeably less briny.

"What is the name of the place we're going again?"

"It's called Mount Chamcook. It's really more of a hill than a mountain. It's just a name that kind of stuck."

"Do you come out here often?" Darcy was noticing that the further they went down the country artery, the fewer homes they passed. Many of the ones they saw were unlit and lifeless. The trees on the roadside grew wild here and closed in around them.

"I grew up out this way, not far from Klewey's. My parents still live here. In fact, if you take the third road coming up on the left, it will take you to a neighborhood called Gibson Lake. That's where they live." Cundiff turned the car off the main route and onto a nameless road that was even more narrow and dark. "It's only another five minutes," he said.

Darcy could see an ominous shadow to their right. It peeked between the trees here and there like a giant failing to hide his mass. "I take it that's the mountain," she said solemnly, trying to hide the nerves swirling in her stomach.

"Yeah, that's Chamcook. They live right under it. I guess I should tell you..."

Darcy's heart beat faster. *Tell me what?* She was beginning to think that this was a very bad idea indeed. She hardly knew Cundiff. She knew him enough to have a drink with him in a public place, but to go down a dark country road with him in the middle of the night, she must have been out of her mind.

"Some of the folks in town don't really care for the Klewes family. I hate to say it, but I think it's like a race thing. Anyway, some of those ignorant folks call the Klewes *mountain people*. The Klewes are a little sensitive about it, so try to avoid mentioning the mountain at all. As a rule, I just ignore that it's there."

"Okay," Darcy said, but her mind was dwelling on other matters, like how few people there were out here and how many places one could, say, hide a body if they had to.

The car made another turn, this one toward the mountain. "This is their road," Cundiff said. The Klewes' driveway was even more shrunken than the last road. Tall trees loomed over the dirt laneway on either side. The encroaching limbs joined together in places, forming a canopy of leaves that blocked out the stars. The headlights splashed against them, giving birth to myriad shadows that lurked behind their twisted trunks. Darcy felt like they were going off the map, that whatever they found at the end of the road had been seen by very few.

She had barely uttered a word since they turned off the main artery, and Cundiff seemed to sense her trepidation. "Oh, I'm sorry about the drive," he said. "I guess it can be a little nerve-wracking out here in the dark. I should have thought of that."

"I'm okay. Umm...are we going to be there soon?"

"Yeah, it's just around the next bend. Although, I'm thinking their place can be a little spooky at night too, if you're not really used to it."

Darcy released a giggle that contradicted her angst. "Where are you taking me, Buster?"

"Oh, the Klewes are great people. They're all like Ty and you think he's nice, right?"

"Well yeah."

"You'll see. They're very welcoming...they just live a little differently."

"What do you mean, differently?"

"We're here."

When the car straightened, the trees backed away from the road. The narrow laneway continued on now with wild grass growing tall on either side. Then a junked car came into view. The headlights shone across its surface, then another and another. They lined the left side of the road in succession. Darcy's heart was in her throat. *He is going to kill me. He's taken me to a junk yard to do it. They'll never find me.*

"Klewey's uncle restores old cars," Cundiff said of the wrecks. "Well...he collects them anyway. Come to think of it, I've never actually seen him work on one."

The explanation did little to assuage her mounting fears, and it meant absolutely nothing to her when the first ramshackle structure appeared. It was little more than a garden shed and it sat lopsided on its stone footings. The roof was missing several shingles and its wooden siding was split throughout. It screamed haunted house. So did the next building. It was bigger than the first, but was in the same state of disrepair. When she saw the newer-model car parked beside it, she understood that it was someone's home.

"Here we are," Cundiff said.

Darcy gripped the door handle, terrified that the broken-down shack was their destination. To her relief, the car continued on and eased around another slight turn. Then she saw lights—multicolored lights. They were patio lanterns like the ones her parents used to set up whenever they went camping in her youth. The long strings of lights were festooned between tall poles in a squared formation. Her tension abated when she took in the sentimental sight. Under the lanterns were three picnic tables, arranged end-to-end and covered with red and white checkered table cloths. Outside the square was an inviting campfire ringed with large, pale stones. Lawn chairs had been placed around it. There were people gathered around another long table to the left of the square. Between them, Darcy caught a glimpse of big, shiny pots.

Cundiff pulled in beside another car that she recognized as Tyrone Klewes'. She had seen it in the lot in the rear of Saint Michael's several times. Now it was parked in front of a modest bungalow with a charming roofed porch. It was a far nicer abode than the shacks they had passed by moments ago. It was a real home.

They got out of the car and Cundiff waved at the group near the table. Darcy looked around the small community. There were houses on all sides of the clearing, at least half a dozen. "They all live here..." Darcy lowered her voice to finish her question. "...like it's a commune?"

"Yeah, I guess you could say that. Come on, I'll introduce you to everyone."

"Well, looky here."

They turned back to the bungalow to find Klewes standing on the porch, smiling widely.

"I almost didn't believe it when you said you were bringing the boss over."

He stepped down and greeted his guests. "Welcome, guys. I hope you brought an appetite with you, 'cause we're having a big-old feed tonight."

"Sounds good, my friend," Cundiff said.

"We're gonna cook just about every damn thing you can drag out of the sea. You don't have any allergies, do you Doctor Collins?"

"Thankfully, no, and it's about time you started calling me Darcy."

"Alright...Darcy. Come on and meet my kin. They're all excited to meet my new boss."

Klewes led them over to the table where the group had gathered. It was a pretty impressive setup and it gave Darcy the impression that they had these cookouts often. Three huge pots sat atop propane burners, each supplied by individual tanks. Darcy could see shucked corn cobs afloat just under the surface of rolling water in one of the pots. There was a pail on the ground beside two Coleman coolers that was filled with the glistening black shells of mussels. She could smell the salty brine on them and it made her mouth water.

Klewes introduced his family. There was his father, Anthony, his mother, Mabel, Uncle Willie and his cousins, Deason and Devon. By then, Darcy was overwhelmed and she had yet to meet his sister, her boyfriend or her boyfriend's friend. She was normally very good with names, but keeping up was hopeless. Cundiff just laughed at her befuddlement.

Anthony shook hands with Cundiff and gave Darcy a warm hello. The family resemblance was striking. He was an older, shorter version of their Klewes, who possibly had enjoyed a few more meals in his day. His balding head gleamed under the patio lanterns. "Don't you fret, young lady," he said. "We'll get you fed in no time. God sakes, Cundiff, have you been eating off her plate?"

"No." Cundiff laid a hand on his midsection as if to measure his waistline.

"Well, she's a rail and you just keep on swelling every time I see ya."

The family laughed at Cundiff's expense.

"Can I get you two a drink?" Uncle Willie offered.

"A beer would be nice," Cundiff said. He looked at Anthony. "Better make it a light."

"And for you, Doctor? What can I get to wet your whistle?"

"Do you know how to make a cherry pie?"

"Lord above...what in the...would you be upset if I just brought you a beer?"

"That would be fine, thanks." Darcy already missed Chuck and his drink menu a little.

"It's nice of you to join us, Doctor," Mabel said. "It ain't nothin' fancy, but what's ours is yours."

"Well, thanks for having me."

"If you don't see anything you like, I got a lovely chowder in the house I can warm up for you. You just say the word."

Darcy watched Anthony lift the lid of a cooler and she saw the red lobsters within. Her stomach growled. "Oh, I like what I see."

Uncle Willie returned with cold beer. He smiled as he distributed the nicely chilled bottles. Willie looked a lot like his brother. He was husky and had the same short, white curls, only in different places. Unlike Anthony, he was not balding and he wore a beard that made him look more like his nephew. "Now, Anthony," Willie said. "You be careful you don't burn yourself, dropping them lobster in the pot. You know how stupid you are."

"Damn it, Willie. I stick your head in there, you don't shut up."

"Doctor Darcy," Mabel said, ignoring the brothers' bickering as though it was commonplace. "I don't suppose you could give me a hand getting some plates from inside?"

Darcy said she'd be happy to help and followed Klewes' mother into her house. Mabel was a large woman and limped awkwardly on what were likely weary knees. Darcy got the impression that this was one family that took food very seriously. Once they were in the kitchen, Mabel turned to Darcy and said, "The reason I asked you in is so I could get you alone for a minute. I just want to say thank you. I know the hospital is goin' through hard times and I wanted to thank you for keepin' my Tyrone on."

"Of course. You don't have to thank me, he's a great employee. He is very good with the patients..."

"Oh, I know he ain't the sharpest tool in the box, but he means well and...

well, we just really need his paycheck around here. His father is retired and our belts are already pretty tight. My nephew started work down at the jail, but even with that, it's hard to make ends meet these days."

"You don't have to worry about a thing. Klew...Tyrone isn't going anywhere. Not while I have a say in the matter."

"Bless you, child. Bless you, bless you."

"Please. Don't mention it. Now, where are these plates?"

"Oh yes. First, I want you to meet Tyrone's grandmother. She's already heard a lot about you. It will only take a second."

Mabel led Darcy into the living room. It was dark until Mabel flipped the lights on. When she did, Darcy was startled to find an elderly woman seated in a well-used armchair.

"Mabel?" the woman asked.

"Yes Mamma. I brought the new doctor to meet ya."

Darcy went closer to the woman, extending a hand. Then she noticed her milky white eyes and the darkened room made more sense. "Hello Ma'am," she said, feeling a little foolish for offering a handshake.

"Oh child, you call me Cecile. You say ma'am and I'll think you mean to talk to someone else," she said, turning her off-target gaze toward Darcy.

When she smiled, Darcy could see that she was missing several teeth. Her slack cheeks and forehead were liver-spotted and her neck was so thin it looked like she would have trouble supporting the weight of her head. She clutched a blue shawl around her chest with one slender hand, the other laid on the blank page of a book that rested on her lap.

"It's nice to meet you, Cecile. I'm a friend of Tyrone's."

"Friend ya say? Nice to know he's keeping better company these days."

"Umm, what are you reading?" Darcy asked, not knowing quite what to say.

"It's *Moby Dick*."

"That's one of the classics."

"Have you ever read it, child?"

"...No." Darcy felt foolish yet again.

"Well, this here's my third time through it. I don't have much of a library and Braille is still hard to come by around here."

"Doctor Darcy," Mabel interjected. "Cecile was hopin' she could get a look at you." She raised her hands to her face to mime her meaning.

"Oh...yeah, okay. That would be fine." Darcy stepped toward the armchair. "What—should I kneel down?"

"That would work for me," Cecile said. "You just tell me when you're ready."

Darcy got down on her knees in front of the arm chair.

"I'll get them plates," Mabel said and left the women alone in the living room.

Darcy took a breath. The situation was rather bizarre and she would agree with Cundiff's assessment that the Klewes were a little *different*, indeed. "Okay, I'm ready."

Cecile exerted herself just to lean toward the sound of Darcy's voice. She slowly raised her bony fingers to the young woman's face. "I'm sorry if my hands are cold, but I've had a chill ever since I came here. That was in 1938." She pressed her fingertips to Darcy's chin and worked them down the sides of her jaw. Yes, they were cold.

"Are you from a warmer climate?"

"Oh, heavens yes. I'm from down Louisiana. I met my late husband there when he was workin' the shrimp boats. I was young and stupid and after I married him, he brought me up here and I've had this damn chill ever since." Her fingers touched Darcy's ears then moved up the sides of her face. Her thumbs pressed into her lips and traced their contours.

"It is very damp here," Darcy offered. "That was the first thing I noticed about the place. The air is so thick."

"I guess that has something to do with it." Cecile's fingertips ran over Darcy's eyebrows and down the sides of her nose. "Oh, you're a pretty thing ain't ya? My, my. I bet the boys in town are beside themselves."

"I don't know about that."

"What color are your eyes?"

"They—they're green."

"Oh yes, that's what I thought...and your hair is dark brown with streaks of chestnut, ain't it?"

"Yes." Darcy figured that someone must have told her that.

Cecile finished *looking* at Darcy then leaned back in her old chair and rested her hands on her book. Her vacant stare settled somewhere on the floor. "I hope I didn't smudge your makeup too much."

"It's okay if you did. I don't wear it very often."

"Well, you did a nice job puttin' it on. It's good and even and you didn't use too much. That granddaughter of mine always wears too much of the stuff." She leaned ahead a little and lowered her voice. "Between you and me, I think she looks like a whore."

Darcy's mouth dropped open and she suppressed a laugh. "It's our secret."

"Well, thank you, child. It's always nice for me to be able to put a face to a name. So now I can picture you when my lunkhead grandson tells me about the goin's on down at Saint Michael's."

"It was my pleasure, Cecile," Darcy said rising from the floor.

"Now, you probably want to join the party outside."

"Why don't you come out, too? If you need a little help, I'm sure-"

"No thanks, child. I prefer the company of my books and besides, those boys of mine will start blaring their jazz records soon and I don't think I can take another note of that garbage."

"Well, if you change your mind..."

"It was sure nice meeting you, child. You just make sure you help yourself."

"No problem there. I'm starving."

"I'm not talking about food."

Darcy searched the woman for her meaning.

Cecile's empty eyes moved up to meet directly with Darcy's.

"I mean you've gotta help yourself...before you can help anyone else. I can tell you're having a hard time with that."

Darcy broke out in gooseflesh.

"You're a bright young thing. You just might have the world by the tail. Just remember, the brighter the light, the darker the shadow."

Darcy backed out of the room silently, her tongue paralyzed. She crossed the kitchen and stepped outside while Cecile followed her with those cloudy, white eyes.

* * * *

The Klewes family and their guests settled at the picnic tables under the patio lanterns and after a short grace led by Anthony, all dug in. Big bowls of clams and mussels and potato salad were circulated down the tables while Miles Davis provided the ambiance from Uncle Willie's record player.

Darcy looked up from the plate she had been picking at. Cundiff was nice enough to shell a lobster for her, but the ravenous appetite she arrived with had been frightened off by Klewey's weird grandmother and her even weirder insight. Most unsettling was that she felt that Cecile had hit some target that, up to now, she hadn't known even existed.

Aside from softly playing jazz, the clink of silverware and the occasional crack of shells, the table remained quiet as everyone ate in earnest. The only words muttered were for the purpose of offering or requesting certain dishes. Then, as dinner plates started to empty, the conversation livened. Local sports seemed the hot topic among the family. Then a slew of work-related stories passed back and forth. Some of them were set in the fishmeal plant where Anthony was a foreman, some on the road where Willie earned his living as a truck driver, but most came from Saint Michael's. Darcy was not sure what to think about those ones. They often centered around a staff member reneging on their duties or were to do with patients being the brunt of some joke. Still, she did enjoy the levity of the banter. It helped to take her mind off her strange interaction with Cecile. Though at the end of the evening, after she and Cundiff said their good-byes and they were once again alone on the dark back roads, the blind woman returned to haunt her.

"Are you feeling okay?" Cundiff asked. "You didn't eat much at dinner."

"Yeah, I just have things on my mind."

"The hospital?" Cundiff guessed. "You seemed kind of distracted when we were talking about it."

"That...and other things, family things."

"You miss 'em, huh?"

"It's a bit more complicated than that. I have a sister who requires a lot of care."

"Oh?"

"Dianne. She's a diagnosed schizophrenic."

"I see."

"My parents don't know how to look after her properly. They don't really *try.*"

"Well, they have your expertise to draw from."

"They don't. They only listen to Di's tired, old doctor. He put her on this base treatment that makes her really dopey. Because she's calm, my parents think it's working great. I mean, Di was showing severe side effects. She's developing tardive dyskinesia—it's like a tremor around the mouth—and they just ignore it. And, anytime *little Darcy* speaks up, they just say they'll look into it to appease me.

"There are other, far better treatments available. I was excited about one in particular, but my parents would have to take Di for regular blood tests, so my father passed on it."

"So they have an actual psychiatrist in the family and they don't listen to her?"

"Pretty much."

"That's fucked up. Pardon my French."

"No, you're right."

"It sounds a little like abuse. Can't you impose custody or something?"

"It's really not that easy. It would go to court for God knows how long and while we're fighting for her custody, Di's condition would only worsen anyway."

"I wish you could have met Stanley. He would have gone home with you to straighten your parents out. He was at his best when he was fighting for people who can't fight for themselves."

"That's what this job is all about, really."

"Maybe you should tell that to Matt."

"Yeah...Matt. I'm worried about him. He's been through a lot."

"All I can say is, I'm really glad you're here."

Darcy felt her cheeks flush and she looked out her window.

Cundiff must have sensed he overextended with the compliment and added, "I mean, the hospital would be in real trouble without you." They were quiet for the remainder of the drive to Darcy's condo—Cundiff afraid of saying too much, Darcy thinking about her sister.

"This is your building?" Cundiff asked, bringing the car to a stop by the front door.

"Yes, home sweet home."

"The mayor owns this building."

"I didn't know that."

"He owns a lot of the buildings down here."

"Does he own the half of Saint Andrews that the Sullivans don't?"

"Hmm, I guess you could say that."

Darcy realized a silence between them was growing again. With all the other things on her mind, she was not up to an awkward social interaction to top off the evening. Should she give him a good night kiss? Should she invite him in? What was the code for an invitation that would not imply sex? Darcy flung aside all possibilities by simply getting out of the car. She leaned in the door and thanked Cundiff for a fun night. Then before she closed it, curiosity got the better of her.

"Something has been nagging at me."

"What's that?"

"What did you say to those guys at the bar to get them to move?"

"I told them you worked at Saint Michael's and you had something catching."

Darcy's mouth dropped open.

"Kidding. I told them I needed the stool, because we were on an important...*date*." His tone implied he was asking rather than stating.

"Well, it was nice of them to move." Darcy smiled and closed the door.

# Chapter Eleven

"I'm a gonna told you something, *Klew*," Elmer said with utmost conviction. "Noting in da world can beat da Chevy Camaro."

"What?" Klewes was indignant and couldn't hide it. He paused with a tray full of plates in his hands as Elmer continued to bus the tables in the dining hall.

"For sure, it was da bess car I never had."

"As far as sixties-era muscle cars go, the sixty-five Mustang has no equal. Everyone with half a brain knows that." Klewes stowed the tray on the cart and moved on to the next cluttered table.

"No way. I was in a race once. He was a sixty-five Mustang. I was a sixty-eight Camaro."

"*You* were a sixty-eight Camaro?" Elmer had the orderly stopped in his tracks again.

"Yup." Elmer continued to collect trays from the tables, as oblivious of his linguistic error as he was of Klewe's mocking.

"Well, you've come a long way," Klewes said shaking his head.

"Anyway, we were race on da 127." Now Elmer took a break from his work to tell his tale. He pointed emphatically as he did. "Mustang, he was fass, but he can't andle as good as me. I kept lose him on da turn, and he almost catch up on me in da straight. At Edward Corner, I get ahead for good. When I hit da train track, I know I went six feet in da high. I leave dat Mustang in da dust."

"You lie like a rug."

"You lie on da rug, *Klew*. Back den, if you show up in any car, we would race and you would probably lost."

"I'll race you any day. Oh right, you don't have a car. Okay, you can drive the work truck and I'll kick your ass in my Corolla."

"No way. If I get caught by da police, I could lose my license of drive. Den you would always get da work truck. I will *never* let you always get da work truck."

Klewes tried to piece together what he was told. "You will never let me always...Good Lord, you're fucked in the head."

"Oh, look who's here. Da counter."

Klewes looked up from the dishes to witness the accountant, Phillip Prichard, knocking on Doctor Dawson's office door. "Does he look like he has good news to you?"

"I don't know, me. I don't worry for dat stuff."

"Well, you should. *Dat stuff* is the difference between you cooking here for a paycheck and you drawing unemployment."

"Nahhh...I truss da boss. He's a smart man, him."

"I hope you're right. There's a lot riding on the doc."

"You know what, he tole *me* to call him Matt."

\* \* \* \*

"Knock, knock."

Matt raised his head to find Phillip Prichard standing in his office doorway. "Mister Prichard, please have a seat." Matt lifted his rear off his chair and gestured at the empty seat across his desk. Prichard looked as though he had lost even more weight. His gray suit billowed on him and his shirt collar hung slack around his neck. Matt wondered if he was ill. It certainly was not out of the question for a man his age. He made a mental note to ask about his health after their business was concluded.

"You didn't forget about our appointment, did you?"

"No...not at all." Matt closed Dykeman's file and stowed it in his top desk drawer. "I was just reading up on some cases while I waited."

Prichard smiled. It made his considerable glasses ride-up on his cheeks. He reached into his bag and produced a file of his own. He opened it on the desk and was silent for a moment. Finally, without looking up, he said, "Cash flow has significantly increased. We are anticipating a break-even month in September. After that, if hospital capacity is maintained, we should be in the black by Christmas."

"That's great...but we already knew that," Matt said, also smiling despite the fact his patience was in short supply these days. "Have you heard anything about the grant money?"

Prichard looked up, his somber eyes magnified by his thick lenses. "I am sorry, Matthew."

"Oh, don't say it."

"Our application was denied."

Matt winced and flung his head into the chair's headrest. "You're kidding me. Wh—what reason did they give you?"

"It was their claim," Prichard started, thoughtfully. "That Saint Michael's did not meet certain regulatory requirements to qualify—"

"Regulatory requirements...like what?"

"Well, they believe some building systems, particularly the security and nurse call systems, are deficient for an active facility such as this."

"Deficient? They're nonexistent."

"Yes."

"But we're fully manned. We've never had a problem with someone trying to break in or out. The patients are well supervised..." Matt got out of his chair and paced his meager eight feet of office space.

Prichard watched him for a moment and said, "If we were to meet the requirements, we stand a pretty good chance of getting the application approved. We qualified in all other areas."

Matt stopped and leaned over the back of his chair. "There is no money in the budget for new alarm systems. I still need to get the roof replaced before winter and I can barely afford that. Hell, I just wrote another huge check to Clark Builders." He pushed his chair hard into his desk. "Godamnit! I needed that money!"

"I know, Matthew," Prichard said softly. "I know that you have paid for all of the updates to Saint Michael's out of your personal funds. You just need to hang in there for a while longer. The hospital is making strides, but it cannot turn the corner overnight."

"Mister Prichard, you are talking to a man who has depleted once-significant savings on a venture he cares little about. Hear me now...I am *ruined*. This fucking place has ruined me and you're preaching patience."

Prichard closed the folder and replaced it in his satchel. "Once again, Matthew, I truly am sorry," he said lifting his slight frame from the chair.

Matt followed him out of the office. "So, is this how it went down with Stanley? Is this how you served him? It's obvious to me now why his hospital was at death's door."

"Matthew, I understand how upset you must be, but when you have some time to look at things objectively—"

"Oh, very good, Phillip. All this time I thought *I* was the psychiatrist. Tell me, what am I supposed to do now?"

"Well, there is still the ten-thousand-dollar county grant. We can apply and it's likely we will succeed in getting it."

Matt cocked his head to the side and squinted as though he was hard of hearing. "I'm sorry, did you say ten thousand dollars? Really? Ten thousand? You might as well tell me to get a fucking paper route."

"Matthew, please, I only meant..."

"If that is the best you can do, I think I have seen enough. You're services here are terminated."

"Matthew, I urge you to reconsider. I have worked for your family for fifty years."

"Get the hell out of my sight while you still can."

Prichard regarded the doctor, his eyes wide with trepidation. "I'll have all the records sent over." He turned and walked swiftly down the corridor.

Matt watched him go, anger still mounting. If the accountant had not been so frail, he might have struck him. Instead, he fumed. He turned to go back to his office and kicked the plastic dining room chair in his path. When it did not satisfy his need to lash out, he kicked its mate across the room and toppled the table they belonged to. Plates, cups and utensils clattered to the floor. He closed his eyes and tried to get control of himself. Soon he was able to take a deep breath. Then he opened his eyes and was immediately flooded with shame. Elmer and Klewes had witnessed his tantrum. They were equally awestruck, Elmer stopped in the act of clearing the breakfast dishes as though frozen in time. Matt said nothing. What on Earth could he say to justify his actions? Perhaps the anxiety etched on his face as he returned to his office was explanation enough.

* * * *

Stanley stared at his son, mouth agape. He had wanted so badly to find Matthew, to lay eyes on him, to simply be in his presence. Now, he wanted anything but. Stanley had followed Phillip Prichard down the corridor after his arrival. He watched his lifelong friend walk over to what Stanley had known as the main floor utility room. Phillip knocked and opened the door, not to the expected bird's nest of wiring and piping, but to Matthew, seated behind a small desk. Stanley was elated. He felt a surge of heat flow though his normally ice-cold chest. He basked in it. Only minutes later, the blissful feeling was all but doused. The business conducted between the two was brief and ended badly, and as Matthew pursued Phillip into the hall, it only got worse.

Phillip turned and left without hearing Stanley's voice. Matthew didn't hear it, either, as Stanley yelled at them both, tried to broker a peace. When his son took out his anger on the dining hall furniture, he realized his pleas were pointless. Stanley followed him back to his utility closet, scolding him the entire time as only a parent could. He slipped inside before Matthew closed the door.

Now, he watched his son stew in his seat. He looked like a miserable cab dispatcher or fast-food manager in his cramped cubby of an office. Why did he favor this hole in the wall over the grand office left to him? Why did he utterly refuse to bring the slightest bit of dignity to the profession? Even his hair was long and tangled, his clothing a mess. Thank God, Susan wasn't here to see what had become of her boy. Stanley reached into his lab coat pocket and palmed his watch for comfort.

Matthew pushed himself back from the desk. He opened a drawer, pulling out a bloated file folder and setting it on the desk. It made a thumping sound that announced its girth. Stanley took one look at it and his mood worsened. It was Dykeman's file—the one he had kept locked away. Matthew continued to search the drawer for something. Stanley hoped it was not for the other item he had locked in his desk with Dykeman's chart. Could his son be so twisted by anger that he would put the gun to use?

Matthew found what he was looking for and sat upright. Stanley was relieved to find that it was not the gun, but rather a simple business card. He expelled an uneasy breath as Matthew considered the bent card for a moment then balled it up in his hand. Matthew brought his fist to his chin and continued his silent debate, agitation beginning to show in his face.

Stanley moved in closer. He eyed the heavy folder on the desktop. "This is why you had to leave Saint Andrews," he said. He reached out to his son, touched his unkempt head.

The emotions came in a flood.

Stanley gasped as deep, dark dread settled in the pit of his stomach. A pall descended, so ominous it seemed to dim the room around them. He shared in Matthew's complete despair, his sense of hopelessness and with it came sporadic thoughts of failure and fear that his next actions would make things worse. Stanley recoiled, unable to bear another moment of his son's turmoil. Reflexively, he rubbed his hand in an attempt to work the sour feelings from it.

Matthew seemed to reach a decision. He examined the business card and picked up the desk phone. The room filled with tension.

"Whatever you're planning on doing," Stanley said. "Don't."

It seemed that Matthew noticed his breath then. It floated on the air like vapor rising off the bay on a winter's day. He exhaled again and watched as his breath dissipated. Then he dialed and waited.

"Fisher...it's Dawson. You know why I'm calling...Yes, I got the note...Well, you're starting to speak my language, but I'll need more than...Really? Yeah, I think that could get it done...If you can get me the cash, we've got a deal... Fine...Tonight. My office."

Matthew hung up then slumped in his chair.

"What on Earth are you planning, Matthew?" Stanley asked as he watched over his son. The suspicious nature of his brief exchange on the phone told him it was not entirely above board. Any time the words *cash, deal* and *tonight* are uttered, one could be assured of that. Matthew spent a few moments in what appeared to be deep thought then he abruptly got up and made for the doorway. Stanley watched him go and contemplated the possible fallout from his son's seemingly shady dealings. When he reached the door, Matthew stopped as though something had caught his attention. He turned and looked directly at Stanley, where he stood by the desk.

"Matthew..." Stanley said aloud. "You know I'm here, don't you?"

His son's look lingered a moment and broke off as he shook his head. Stanley watched him, waiting for a hint of recognition to return to Matthew's gaze. Instead, the living Dawson walked out of the room and closed the door behind him.

\* \* \* \*

Darcy flashed her pen light in Hannah Wilkins' drowsy eyes. She was encouraged by their response. It had only been a few days since Darcy had convinced Matt to allow a change in the patient's medication, but already the new drug was showing promise. Darcy sat back beside Hannah in the comfortable couch in the hospital's patient lounge. She held the girl's hand and wished for faster improvement in her condition. She had to be patient, she told herself. Though, as she looked around the lounge and saw Marcie and Sam and poor old Margaret, each in somber convalescence in their respective corners, that patience was tested. She tried not to dwell on the lack of progress they were all showing, but when she was not concentrating on her work, her mind drifted back to Mabel Klewe's darkened living room—to Cecile's dead eyes.

*Make sure you help yourself,* she had said.

*You've gotta help yourself before you can help anyone else.*

The very thought of the blind crone's words sent a chill down Darcy's spine. She shivered with it and, because they held hands, Hannah shook too. The worst part is that on some level, Darcy knew she was right. Cecile knew something intimate about her. It was a thought she had never shared with another living soul. *How? Why did I let her touch me?*

She saw Cecile's spotted face when she closed her eyes.

*The brighter the light...*

*The darker the shadow...*

"Why so glum, chum?"

Darcy's eyes snapped open. They focused on Curtis Ford, standing before the couch, front and center. She knew him as Ford, Curtis H, age: sixty-seven, early onset dementia. He smiled at her and his whole face wrinkled. He was a slight man with a long hook nose that Darcy always found herself looking at instead of his eyes. "The rigors of the work day got you down?" he said.

"No, not at all. Spending time with you guys isn't what I'd call rigorous. You're good company."

"You think so? Even your young friend there? She hasn't said two words since she got here."

"Silence is golden," Darcy said, hoping he would take the hint. He did not.

"You know, when I was still in my working days," he started, folding his hands behind his back and turning to look out Saint Michael's stately windows. "...and I felt like I wasn't getting anywhere with a problem, I would remember some advice my grandfather once gave me. He said, 'failure is simply the opportunity to begin again.' He was a man who knew a thing or two about perseverance. Do you know why his first successful attempt at the automobile was called the Model T? Well it's because his failed attempts at it were named Model A to Model S. That's nineteen failures!

"Most folks don't encounter nineteen failures in their whole career, let alone before they get their first true taste of success. Now, I'm sure, when you consider *that*, your job doesn't seem so bad. I know mine didn't. Remember, it was all those blunders and mistakes that became the foundation of one of the finest motor companies the world has ever seen." He looked back to the girls on the couch. "Amazing, isn't it?"

Darcy was not supposed to encourage Curtis when he got sidetracked in his alternate reality, but she just wanted to get away from him before he could continue, so she said, "Thanks for the advice. You've given me a lot to think about."

He smiled proudly, wrinkles on full display.

"Now, if you'll excuse me..." Darcy gave Hannah's hand a squeeze and laid it on her lap. She left the lounge in search of refuge from advice that ranged from the cryptic to the absurd.

# Chapter Twelve

Matt paced the corridor outside Dykeman's room. His teeming nervous energy had him bouncing on his toes. A sea in turmoil splashing violently in the bottom of his stomach. A voice in his head, like distant thunder, reminded him over and over that he had made a poor choice.

He forced himself to stop his prancing in case the night nurse, Miss Tait, happened by and he had to explain his obvious jitters. Across the hall from Dykeman's door, he planted his feet, pressed his back against the wall, and clutched the handrail to keep his body still. The clock on the wall told him that Fisher had been inside with Dykeman for nearly five minutes. Was that all? The writer had paid a gross amount for a mere ten minutes with the patient, only now Matt did not think he could last that long.

*Maybe I should end this.*

*I could return some of the money...*

*Money*...the idea sickened him. He thought about the thick stack of it in his office. Over the phone, Matt had told Fisher to bring the cash, but he had not expected him actually to bring bank notes. Seeing the money inside the brown paper lunch bag Fisher handed him made the whole transaction feel all the more vile. If there was a hell, surely the road there was paved in dollar bills. His deal with Fisher marked the first time in Matt's thirty-nine years that he had done something purely for money and it was not sitting well. Was it because Stanley would not approve? Was it because it simply was not the right thing to do, or was Matt feeling ill because of the parties involved in the affair? He still didn't know enough about Dykeman to truly condone this kind of close contact. Then there was Fisher. He may have been the more dangerous creature of the two.

Matt envisioned Dykeman's face on the cover of a sleazy trade paperback. *I just want to sit across from him...to look in his eyes*, Fisher had said. What if those eyes end up on the cover? What would that do to Saint Michael's? Matt's mouth went dry. He felt like he was close to vomiting, though he pushed himself toward his patient's door. Before he could reach for the handle, it opened and Fisher stepped into the hall.

Matt swallowed the paste in his throat. He might have been looking at his own reflection. Fisher's forehead was beaded with sweat, his flesh blanched and he too swallowed hard. Matt looked over his shoulder for a glimpse of Dykeman before the door closed heavily. He appeared serene, seated in his deck chair, ogling nothing in particular.

Matt exhaled slowly, but much of the tension remained bunched in his shoulders. "Well?" he asked, studying the obviously shaken man before him.

Fisher breathed heavily like he had spent the last five minutes in a full gallop. His gaze darted about the tiled floor.

"Fisher, what happened in there?" Matt's voice was an urgent whisper.

"I...umm...I got everything I need."

"You weren't in there long."

"Long enough."

Matt peeked through the observation window at Dykeman. He had not moved. "Look, Fisher, I forgot to mention, I can't allow you to leave here with any photographs. You didn't take his picture, did you?"

"Don't need 'em."

Matt eyed the writer. "Well, what went on in there? I know you two didn't share a deep conversation."

Fisher raised his gaze to meet Matt's. "Have you ever just looked in those eyes? Do you have any idea what's looking back?" He seemed to shiver as he said it. "I think he *saw* me."

Matt looked at Dykeman once more and produced a ring of keys from his lab coat pocket. "Of course he did. He's not blind." He fumbled through the keys for the one that fit Dykeman's lock with fingers that were robbed of dexterity by his sheer angst. Before Matt could secure the door, he looked up to find Fisher walking briskly for the stairs. "Fisher...wait."

"He saw me, Dawson."

\* \* \* \*

Stanley had been waiting for hours for someone to happen by and open the office door. He felt like a dog waiting to be let outside to visit the fire hydrant. Being dead was indeed a major inconvenience, but for Stanley this was a new low. It was humiliating. *Conquered by a door,* he mused. *This old hospital was definitely not designed for the living-impaired.*

He had kept himself occupied for a while by attempting to float on air the way ghosts were so often depicted in movies. He concluded that was a lot of bunk. He then busied himself by trying to roll a pen across the surface of the desk, and while he thought he was getting close to making it happen, he decided the exertion wasn't worth the result. With nothing left to distract him, his worries once again became paramount. Matthew was planning to do something he wasn't proud of. Though Stanley wasn't sure what that was exactly, it was clear that Matthew needed help. All Stanley could do was pace the floor and wait for someone to let him out. He groaned in frustration. The feeling quickly morphed to anger and desperation.

Stanley funneled the emotion. He charged the door and seized the knob. He twisted it for all he was worth, grunting and putting his back into it. He poured every ounce of his being into turning that knob. It refused to give. He took a breath and resumed his furious struggle. He battled until the knob slipped from his grip and he stumbled forward. All at once he realized it did not slip *from* his grip. It slipped *through* his grip. Stanley froze, elbow deep in the solid wooden door. In reflex, he pulled his arm back and felt the inner substance of the wood pass between his fingers like thick gravy. Dumbstruck, he inspected his hand, rubbed his fingers together.

Fearing the ability wouldn't last, Stanley plunged his hand into the door again. It disappeared into its surface and the rest of his arm followed. When he was shoulder-deep, he took a step forward. Everything went dark for a split second as he pushed his head through the door. Then he broke the surface on the other side and entered the brightly lit dining hall. It was like wading through a deep snow bank when he pulled the rest of his body from the office. He fought through the resistance and, once free, he stumbled to the floor. He looked back at the door. It was as solid as ever.

He patted his body down where he lay, making sure everything was still whole, that nothing got left behind in the office. He allowed himself a fleeting second to consider his new-found ability and the freedom it might afford him if he was able to fully harness it. Then he turned to the eating area where the wreckage of Matthew's earlier tantrum had been cleaned up. Any thought he had of escaping the confines of Saint Michael's quickly vanished. His son was in trouble. It had something to do with Dykeman. All his troubles did. Sorrow descended over Stanley like a fog. It was not trace emotion left over from his contact with Matthew.

This dreadful feeling came from within.

Stanley hurried down the corridor and just as he reached the lobby, a man he had never seen before crossed his path and quickly left through the main entrance. He guessed it was the person Matthew had arranged the meeting with—the one he called Fisher while on the phone. Stanley was too late. Whatever business those two had, it seemed to be concluded. He watched him go and then checked his watch. It was a few minutes before midnight. Whatever Matthew and this Fisher were doing, they chose to do it in the cover of night, away from prying eyes. Stanley went to the statue of God's general to draw strength from him. The act felt hollow. As Stanley's gaze dropped to the serpent coiled at the archangel's feet, another feeling took hold.

\* \* \* \*

Down the corridor to the east, Hannah Wilkins writhed in her cot. So fitful was her sleep that she had tossed her sheets and the remaining bedclothes lay bunched at her feet. She kicked at them, pulled at her johnny shirt. Sweat matted the hair to her brow and glistened on her upper lip while she moaned indiscernible pleas. Her thrashing stopped. She lay rigid in her bed, arms and legs arrow-straight. Her eyes opened and searched the small dark room for the presence she was feeling. She followed it around the room, up the wall and across the ceiling. Above her bed, her eyes remained fixed.

\* \* \* \*

Stanley watched the snake, half expecting it to shed its marble skin and slither off the statue. The night lights in the corridor dimmed. There came a soft *thumpf* sound from the second floor, and he looked up just in time to see the top of the stairwell go dark. *Thumpf.* The west wing plunged into darkness. *Thumpf.* The east wing as well. Stanley looked at his watch. The sight of its hands at a perfect right angle sent a wave of the purest dread he had ever felt through his body. He said aloud, "three o'clock," then he and Michael were thrown into perfect blackness, as well. "My God, Matthew; what have you done?"

# Chapter Thirteen

"Holy shit!" Tyrone Klewes blurted when he entered the lobby at the hospital. He couldn't stifle his reaction when he saw the condition the statue of Saint Michael was in. "What happened here?" he asked of Darcy and Doctor Dawson, who stood side by side looking at the damaged marble figure. Saint Michael, the archangel Stanley Dawson had so proudly displayed, had been decapitated.

"Vandalism," Doctor Dawson said flatly.

Darcy regarded the headless angel in silence, a stony look of disgust etched on her normally warm face.

"Who did this?" Klewes said.

"We don't know. I found it this way when I came in this morning," Doctor Dawson replied. "Neither Miss Tait nor Rory saw anyone come or go during their shifts. I was here late myself and I didn't see anyone in the corridors." He pulled his key ring from his pocket and inspected it briefly before stowing it again. "It makes a strong case to have surveillance cameras installed."

Klewes stepped closer to the statue and examined the jagged edge that was Michael's neck. "Well, it must have made quite a noise. It looks like you'd need a sledgehammer to do this."

"Nobody heard anything." Doctor Dawson scratched his head.

"I just don't understand who would do such a thing," Darcy offered. "Why would someone go to all the trouble?"

"When people are ill, Doctor, they tend to do things that don't make a great deal of sense to the rational witness."

"You think a patient did this?"

"It wouldn't surprise me. I've seen all sorts of strange behavior over the years."

"I just don't know how they could. As Mister Klewes said, it would be difficult to manage and most of our patients aren't nearly physically fit enough."

Klewes looked the statue over as the doctors continued to disagree over possible patient involvement.

"It could have been local kids, I suppose," Doctor Dawson said, his stance weakening. "I'm sure most townspeople aren't exactly overjoyed at having a mental hospital in their neighborhood, let alone one that is expanding."

"Fucking assholes," Klewes said and looked back over his shoulder at the lady in attendance. "Umm...sorry for the sailor talk, Doctor Collins."

Darcy waved a dismissive hand at the orderly. "I couldn't have said it better myself."

"Well," Doctor Dawson said. "I guess this is the push I needed to dispose of the damned thing." He turned toward the west corridor, heading to his office. "I'll make some calls. With any luck, I can get it taken away before too many visitors see it this way. In the meantime, Mister Klewes, maybe you can find a sheet to cover it with."

"Sure thing, Doc." Klewes knelt to have a look at the base of the marble column and the layer of stone chips that sprinkled the floor like salt. "Just out of curiosity, where's the head?"

\* \* \* \*

Hannah Wilkins stared at the droplets spattering the tall window in the patient lounge. The fat spots of rain made stark *tick* sounds as they slapped the glass. Soon they were running together and sheeting down the surface of the window as the heavens opened above. Klewes had sat the girl in a high-backed wooden armchair near the window at Darcy's request, though he wondered aloud how much their incoherent patient would benefit from the view of Water Street.

"Good morning, Hannah," Darcy sang as she pulled a matching chair across the floor, closer to Hannah's side. "How are you feeling today?" She got herself settled in her seat and laid a chart on her lap. "Oh no...it's raining," she said comically. "That's no good is it?"

Hannah turned her head slightly in Darcy's direction. At once, Darcy dropped the chart to the floor and stood in front of the girl. Hannah's lazy gaze followed her. "Hannah!" Darcy said, smiling brightly as she got the penlight from her pocket. She flashed it in Hannah's eyes and smiled again, this time at her response. The doctor timed her patient's pulse, then performed a series of reflex tests on her arms and knees. "Can you follow my finger?" Darcy knelt before her and slowly moved her index finger from right to left. Hannah tracked it. "That's great."

Darcy got back into her chair and retrieved the chart from the floor. She made a few quick notes on the page inside then looked back to Hannah. "Welcome back," she said. For a few moments, she searched Hannah's still-bleary eyes. She wore a vacant look, though Darcy knew she was in there, near the surface and ready to break through and shake off the remaining tethers of her deep sleep. Then something strained Hannah's expression.

"Hannah, is there something you want to say to me?"

There was. Hannah struggled to find her tongue. Her jaw dropped open until her lips reluctantly parted.

"It's okay. Just take your time. Don't force anything."

Hannah's mouth gaped and air dragged across her dry tongue. Somewhere in the back of her throat, atrophied vocal folds began to coil. She managed a *click* and a *hiss*.

"Hannah, maybe you should rest for now. You'll be your old self before you know it."

Hannah continued *hissing* as her breath leaked uselessly through her throat. Obviously there was something she just had to say. At the end of her breath, she managed a moan. Deep and hoarse. More of the scratchy tone came out on her next attempt. Darcy leaned in closer, told her it was okay if she had to whisper. Then Hannah heard her own voice, so thin and dry it appeared to scare her.

"Go...Darcy..."

Darcy pulled back to regard the girl. "No Hannah. I'm not leaving you. I'm here to help you." Darcy grasped her hand and held it firmly.

Hannah continued her plea, "Go...away...not...safe..."

"What? Not safe...what do you mean? Hannah you *are* safe here. No one will hurt you here. What do you mean, you're not safe?"

Something seized Hannah's attention and she turned away from Darcy. She seemed to watch the hallway over her shoulder intently, then her gaze tracked something as though it was moving away. Darcy got up and looked from Hannah's perspective for whatever had taken command of her patient's focus. As far as she could see, the hallway was empty. Darcy sat down again and held Hannah's hand.

* * * *

"Hey pretty lady." Cundiff smiled as he approached Darcy, seated at the nurse's station. She raised her attention to the orderly and tried to brighten, but the smile she forced on her lips wasn't fooling anyone.

"What's wrong?" he asked.

"Nothing...everything." Darcy released an exaggerated sigh. "Hannah Wilkins. She's just coming off the wrong meds. I know it's just a matter of time before she shows some clarity, but she was *so* close today. She was actually able to say a few words."

"Well, that's good news, isn't it?"

"Yes. I mean, I guess it is. The problem is she also gave me some signs that she may be experiencing delusion or paranoia. It's frustrating because I didn't even have time to pursue it further with her before she was just gone again. As quickly as she showed improvement, it was all wiped away. Now I don't know what to think."

"Doctor, if I could be so bold as to share my humble opinion," Cundiff said, sticking his chin out in a mock display of pride. Darcy laughed in spite of herself. "I think you need to be patient with your patient. It was her first sign of progress, right?"

"Yes."

"You're pretty sure that this funk or whatever she's in is going to lift?"

"Yes."

"Then I say let it lift. In the meantime you can concentrate on other things like having dinner with me tonight...or like helping someone else with their problems."

Darcy squinted while she considered both options and said, "Who do you think I should help first?" Cundiff clutched his chest over his heart and groaned. He had her laughing again. It was just the medicine she needed.

"Oh, I know who you can help. Saint Michael."

"Oh, my God, did you see it?"

"Yeah, I was a little curious why a sheet was hanging over him. It was obvious once I helped myself to a peek."

"What a shame. It was a beautiful statue."

"Stanley sure loved it." The orderly folded his arms across his chest and leaned against the desk. He was silent for a moment then said, "It's sad really. His office is gone, now the statue. It's like the place is losing all trace of him. I don't like it."

"Maybe it can be fixed."

"Maybe. What did Matt say?"

"He thinks it was vandalism. Whoever did it took the head as a trophy."

Cundiff's expression went sour instantly. "Ooh, if I get my hands on the..." He took a breath to regain his composure.

"It's okay. I feel the same way." Darcy considered Cundiff and Klewe's combined anger over the loss of the statue and felt a twinge of pity for the unlucky person who got caught with the angel's head.

\* \* \* \*

The rain persisted all afternoon and when Matt stepped through the iron gate in front of the hospital to make his way home, the clouds seemed to follow. The normally raucous sidewalks of Water Street were deserted of tourists—their party spoiled by nature's wet blanket. The restaurants and shops had closed their patios and withdrawn their sandwich boards. Even roadside parking, normally in high demand, was abundant. The only sign of life was the post office a few blocks down where year-round residents of the seaside town went about the business of daily life. Matt was among them, heading home from his all-consuming job.

He had the foresight to bring his umbrella along in the morning, but as the winds increased and drove the rain sideways, it was of little use. He winced against the cold, hard bullets of water flecking his face. The offensive from the bay lashed the town as though its spite of the land was overflowing it. The seascape looked like an ever-changing, expansive mountain range with its black slopes and white peaks. Only when Matt turned the corner at Adolphus Street and put his back to the deluge did he get some relief. He braced the shaft of his umbrella against his shoulder, only now it pushed him along like a jib on a schooner.

He hated running. He hated most things that resulted in sweating. Though, as the wind shoved him up the hill, he found himself breaking into a trot. His wind-assisted jog got him to the top of the street in record time. That was good, because he was anxious to get home and start planning the investments he was to make with the proceeds from his deal with Fisher. Bolstering his ailing financial portfolio was finally something positive for Matt to think about. The interview between Fisher and Dykeman had turned out to be harmless aside from some rattled nerves, and it seemed all parties were satisfied—Matt especially. He would celebrate the occasion by grilling some red meat and chasing it with a fine merlot...but that would have to wait.

When he jogged between the hedges bordering his father's property, he saw that he had company. A Saint Andrews Police Department black-and-white was parked in the driveway beside the house. Matt slowed his pace as he approached. The driver looked in his rearview and waved. Matt watched as the officer placed a hat atop his head and got out into the rain.

"Hi there," Matt offered and pointed to the shelter of the veranda. The officer took his meaning and hurried up the steps behind him.

"A beautiful Saint Andrews summer day, isn't it?" the officer said, shaking the water off his jacket.

"I remember more rainy days than not when I think about this place," Matt said. He closed his umbrella and leaned it against the house.

"Sorry for the surprise visit," the officer said, presenting his hand. "I'm Martin Lumley."

"*Chief* Lumley," Matt said shaking his hand. "Nice to meet you."

"Likewise." The chief turned to look out over the sweeping grounds in front of the house. "I should have come to see you sooner. I've just been so damned busy this past while. Budget cuts have left us short on manpower. I knew Stanley pretty well. My condolences."

"Thanks," Matt said, unlocking the door.

"I know it's in bad taste as late as it is."

"Not at all." Matt opened the door and gestured for Lumley to enter.

The chief took his hat off when he stepped inside. His hair was waves of gray mingling with black. He filled out his dark brown jacket and stood half a foot taller than Matt. In his day, Matt figured Lumley was quite the intimidator. He still was.

Once they were out of the wind, the air filled with the strong essence of Old Spice. Clearly the chief was a fan. "Let's step into the kitchen," Matt said. "Can I get you a towel?"

"No thank you."

"Please excuse me for a moment," Matt said, leaving the officer to retrieve a towel from the bathroom down the hall. "Can I get you some tea or coffee... perhaps something a little stronger?" Matt called.

"No thanks, Doctor Dawson. I'm afraid I'm on the clock."

Matt was drying his ears with the towel slung around his neck when he entered the kitchen. Lumley leaned against the counter and eyed the slew of empty wine bottles that occupied it. "Oh, I apologize for the mess," Matt said when he saw Lumley's reaction. "I'm a little behind on my recycling. You're not the only one in town who's too busy for his own good."

"Think nothing of it." Lumley smiled at the doctor.

Matt could tell it was not genuine. Lumley's eyes gave it away.

"It must be hard enough to deal with the death of your father and then the added burden that goes along with running Saint Michael's. I'm sure it's almost too much to bear at times. I lost my father a few years back myself, and it had me draining a bottle or two."

"Right."

"Speaking of the hospital, how are things going down there?"

"Good...great. We're close to full capacity."

"It must be getting hectic with all those patients to look after."

"I'm getting lots of help."

"There must be a lot of new patients."

"Yes."

"I assume you kept Stanley's patients too."

"Yes."

"He wouldn't have any more than a half a dozen or so at a time, as I understand it. Have any of them been discharged lately?"

"I'm not at liberty to discuss particular cases."

"Of course not..."

"Unless, this is a formal questioning." Matt grinned, belying his growing unease.

"It's not. I just thought I'd get to know you a little better."

"Well, what else would you like to know about me, Chief?"

Lumley dropped his phony smile. The stony visage that replaced it looked more at home on his face. "Where were you last night?"

"That's kind of an odd question."

"Don't you answer odd questions?"

"I was at the hospital until about midnight."

"About?"

"Until midnight."

"Then?"

"I came here and went to bed. What is this concerning?"

"Can anybody vouch for your whereabouts?"

"While I was at the hospital, yes, but, I live alone here. Should I have a lawyer present?"

"You don't need one yet. I'm not here to arrest you."

"Arrest me? What is this about?"

"Phillip Prichard's wife found him in his study this morning."

"Found him..."

"A blunt instrument was used. Forensics thinks the time of death was between three and four in the morning."

Matt went to the kitchen table and sat down before his legs gave out.

"Mrs. Prichard told me that you two had a falling-out over some botched business."

"No...I..."

"You severed your business connection with Mister Prichard, didn't you?"

"I did, but..."

"You two had an argument?"

"Yes."

Chief Lumley sat in the chair across the table from Matt. "You know what this all means, don't you?" Matt just looked at him, shocked and speechless. "It means you have a weak alibi and a strong motive." Matt was lost in the chief's words. He tried desperately to make some sense of what he was hearing. All he could think of was Prichard and his poor wife discovering him. "Now, I know first-hand how hard things can be when you lose someone like Stanley. I watched you at his wake. I could see how lost you were and I remembered hoping for your sake that you'd be able to right the ship. I guess some blows are too hard to come back from."

Lumley looked again to the numerous liquor bottles littering the kitchen. "Anyway, your father was very well respected and I'm proud that I was able to call him a friend. That friendship is why I'm here—*off* the record. If there is anything you want to tell me about last night, it would be to your benefit to come clean. Turning yourself in with a full and voluntary confession could do you a world of good when it comes to sentencing."

"I didn't kill Prichard."

Lumley bared his teeth in a silent curse and cast his eyes to the floor. "Goddamn it, Dawson, I'm trying to help you, here."

"I don't need your help. It seems that I need a lawyer's."

"Now you listen to me. I don't care if you show up with Ben Matlock, if this thing goes to trial, *no one* will be able to help you. My men are gathering evidence as we speak, not that we'll need any more than what we got already."

"I don't care what you think you have, Chief. I'm innocent and I have nothing to worry about."

"We'll just see about that." Lumley dug into the breast pocket of his jacket and pulled out a scrap of paper. He unfolded it and passed it across the table. "What does this do for your worries?"

Matt looked at the paper. On it was a rough hand-drawn picture comprised of a circle and two vertical lines that ran through it. It was oddly familiar. He studied it a moment and it invoked an eerie, gut-deep feeling. Then it came to him all at once and his insides went to liquid. He saw the black-and-white photographs in the dark recesses of his mind. He saw the symbol. It was scrawled on the wall in the Dykeman family home—in their blood. Matt looked up at Lumley in disbelief. He did not need the chief to tell him that the same symbol was found this morning, this time drawn in Prichard's blood.

"Yeah...you know what that is, all right. You've seen it before. Too bad for your defense, not many others have." Lumley began counting on his fingers, a smug grin growing all the while. "There is Stanley who had a copy of Morris Dykeman's crime scene photos in his files. There is the original artist, Dykeman himself. There is the chief who holds the full report. Then there is you, the beneficiary of all the hospital's records. Now Stanley's dead, Dykeman's a vegetable, and me, I don't live alone so my alibi is solid. That puts you on some pretty shaky ground, Dawson. You're the only other person alive who may have seen this symbol and your reaction just told me without a doubt that you have. You're the only one who could have drawn it on Prichard's wall."

Matt was floundering. He didn't know what to say. Lumley was right—there would be no defense against these facts. He thought about the swollen folder he had liberated from Stanley's locked drawer. If he never got his hands on that file, he never would have seen the photos and this conversation would be over. It had been locked away for Matt's protection, after all.

A voice sounded within him then. It was like a semiconscious defense system had been put into action with the sole purpose of pulling his ass out of the fire. It sounded off again, and it provided Matt with an answer: *Fisher.*

"Eric Fisher," Matt said, looking at the crude drawing.

"Who?" Lumley scowled at the curve ball Matt threw him.

"He's another who may have seen this symbol. He knows all about our resident murderer. In fact, he's writing a book on him." For Matt, things started falling into place. What better way for Fisher to stir up hype for his new book than to have the story of a copycat murder in the press? The only thing that did not add up was the victim. *Why Prichard?*

It was Lumley's turn to go speechless.

Matt continued making his case. "Fisher has been in town for a while now, digging up anything he can find about the Dykeman murders."

Lumley went into his pocket again and retrieved a notepad and pen. He remained silent as he made a few notes. "Where can I locate this *Fisher?*"

"I don't know. Ask the mayor. Bud seemed to take a special interest in him."

Lumley was not at all pleased. Matt could see it on his face. And the mere mention of the mayor's involvement seemed to irk Lumley all the more. "You should know, Chief, that I'll take a polygraph to prove my alibi and when you don't discover one bit of evidence that says I was anywhere near Prichard last night, we're going to talk about this again."

Lumley stuffed the notepad in his pocket and put his uniform hat on, badge forward. He got out of his chair and towered over Matt. "I'll be in touch, Doctor," he said. Old Spice flooded Matt's nostrils and it stung his eyes. "I guess I don't need to tell you not to leave town."

"I trust you can show yourself out."

Matt watched the chief's deliberately slow gate carry him to the hallway. When he heard the door open and close, he exhaled. He fanned at the pungency that remained of the chief's cheap cologne. *It had to be Fisher*, he thought, but on the outside chance that it was not him, it could only be one other person. Matt had to make sure, as Lumley so eloquently put it, that person was still a vegetable.

# Chapter Fourteen

"Did you hear about poor Mister Prichard?" was the first thing out of Wanda Cooke's mouth when she met Tyrone Klewes in the second floor corridor. She parked her medication cart to greet the orderly as she did every morning, only today she skipped her customary salutation. Klewes didn't mind. He was bursting at the seams to discuss the matter.

"It's the talk all over town."

"I heard it was murder," Wanda said in her most discreet tone and the hard look she gave Klewes told him to use the same.

"Yeah, that's what I heard. He was bludgeoned to death right in his house."

"I know, and apparently Mrs. Prichard was home when it happened."

"Is she a witness?"

"Not that I heard. She just found him on the floor of his office in the morning."

"She must be one hell of a heavy sleeper. I mean, I can't imagine a bludgeoning is all that quiet."

"Odd..." Wanda said in her low, sullen tone.

"Also, I stopped at the corner gas on my way here and Gordy told me that it wasn't a robbery, either. Nothing was taken. Prichard had a wall safe that wasn't even touched. It looks like someone *meant* to kill him."

Wanda lowered her brow and considered the orderly's conclusion. "Who would do such a thing? Mister Prichard was such a mild man. I can't believe he'd have any enemies."

Klewes stepped closer to the nurse to up their level of secrecy. "That's what I'm worried about. If Prichard *had* an enemy, I can only think of one man it might be."

"Mister Klewes, don't be ridiculous." She knew he was referring to the scene in the dining hall. Elmer was telling everyone about it. "Doctor Dawson and Mister Prichard had a disagreement over finances and it was over as soon as it started. Even if Doctor Dawson was angry enough to harm Mister Prichard, he doesn't have it in him to commit cold-blooded murder."

"You weren't there. You didn't see what happened. The doc went nuts. He kicked tables and chairs over. If me and Elmer weren't watching, I think he would have killed Prichard on the spot."

"You're starting to sound like Elmer with his wild stories."

"I swear, this is one time Frenchie doesn't have to exaggerate. I'm worried. Things haven't been easy on the doc. His father died, he's losing money left and right, he's completely stressed, he looks like shit all the time, you gotta wonder if he ever sleeps. I'd be this close to snapping, myself."

"Feeling stressed is a far cry from murdering a man, Mister Klewes. I refuse to believe that our doctor could sneak into the Prichards' house in the middle of the night, commit the murder—undetected mind you—and sneak out again. That implies some sort of expertise."

"I suppose he could have hired a hit man."

Wanda slapped the orderly across his arm. "This foolish conversation is over. Doctor Dawson is a fine young man with more than his share of worries. He doesn't need you spreading a bunch of malarkey around behind his back. He only needs you to do your job and do it well." Wanda picked up a clipboard from the medication cart and continued her duties.

Klewes knew when not to press an issue with Wanda Cooke. He turned on his heel without further word and went to begin on his workload. He stopped when he saw someone ascending the stairs two at a time. "Speak of the devil," he said to the nurse before they parted ways. He watched Doctor Dawson emerge from the stairwell and hurry to the end of the east corridor.

\* \* \* \*

Matt flipped through the keys on the crowded ring. He found the one he desired and shoved it into the lock in Dykeman's door. He turned it and the lock clicked a warning. Matt ignored his apprehensions and stepped inside the room. The stale air greeted him, told him he was entering a place few visited.

Dykeman was seated in his usual position, facing the small window on the north wall of his sparse quarters. The staff believed he liked to bask in the glow of the sun. Apparently, he was also partial to lazing in the rush of beating rain drops. Outside, the storm continued. This morning the winds had increased and now whipped the stately old building with rain and briny spray off the bay.

"Hello, Mister Dykeman," Matt said, his voice uneven and labored. "I'm Doctor Dawson." Then he considered his father and corrected, "Doctor Matthew Dawson."

The patient made no response, not the slightest of movements or huff of breath to acknowledge his visitor. Had Matt not spent hours tracking the patient's tendencies from the safe side of the door, he may have suspected that he had died in his chair. Matt knew Dykeman had a talent for stillness. It was as though he had the ability to pause the reel of life itself. The room followed suit. It was silent, the air stagnant with the faintest essence of feces.

"I would like to examine you, Mister Dykeman."

The door banged behind him.

Matt snapped around.

The heavy blue door had swung shut. It had automatic closers on its hinges, after all. Matt decided its closing was reasonable and allowed himself to breathe again. For a moment, he eyed the transom above the door. It was hinged open a few inches, though it did little for the air flow in the small room.

"Sorry about the door," Matt offered. He turned back to Dykeman, not surprised to find the man had not budged in his deck chair. The back of Dykeman's neck was a field of wrinkles. It was liver-spotted here and there, and the blemishes spread to his scalp. Matt could see them hiding amidst stubby gray-white hairs.

"Let's have a look, then," he said, stepping beside the chair and taking a seat in the small cot adjacent. He studied the man before starting. Dykeman's pale blue hospital johnny and matching robe draped off of his wiry frame. His arms were streaked with blue veins under nearly translucent skin. Flesh hung from his high cheekbones and bunched under his chin in a significant waddle. Dykeman, the ruthless murderer, was gone, replaced by one of God's meager creatures in the twilight of life. Matt studied the brassy hue in his throat and cheeks. He was jaundiced from the years of medications poisoning his liver. He may not have been convicted for his crimes, but he had paid a stiff price, nonetheless. Doctors, Stanley included, had robbed him of life as capably as any noose could. Death would have been a mercy.

Matt slid off the cot to the floor in front of his patient. Dykeman's hollow stare remained fixed on the window and the streams of water it shed. "I'm going to check your pulse, Mister Dykeman," Matt said, reaching for his wrist. It was then he noticed that Dykeman did not even wear a hospital bracelet. He was an afterthought in every way. Matt pressed his fingers into Dykeman's leathery wrist and felt the slow, distant pump. He tried without success to reposition his fingers, hunting for a stronger beat. Matt decided that he would have a general practitioner give Dykeman a thorough examination in the near future. He continued by testing his reflexes at both elbows and knees. The results were discouraging. No reaction whatsoever. Even after a profound reduction in medication, Dykeman was still basically comatose.

Then he considered the bright side. There was no way Dykeman could have anything to do with that strange symbol appearing on Prichard's wall.

To complete his observations, Matt held his penlight before Dykeman's eyes. Matt aimed the light beneath his patient's deeply lined brow and wiry eyebrows. He flashed it in the right side and was stunned to mark no change in Dykeman's hazy brown orb. A second test yielded the same result. *Hmmm...* Matt considered the possibility of brain damage. Then he remembered what Fisher said. *Have you ever looked into those eyes? I think he saw me.* What the hell could he have meant? This poor man did not *see* anything.

Matt switched sides. He flashed the light in Dykeman's left eye.

Matt's body froze throughout in an instant.

Dykeman's pupil dilated. When it reached the brown iris bordering it, it overflowed and polluted all white, leaving nothing but a shining obsidian orb. His right eye inked over as well. Matt yanked himself back. He would have fallen over, but Dykeman grabbed his hand.

Matt gasped, unable to find his voice to let out a scream. He watched Dykeman, his beetle-shell eyes and blank expression, with his bony weathered hand wrapped firmly around his. The grip tightened. Matt felt his bones begin to bend. *Metacarpals*—the name for the little bones popped into his head for the first time since he attended anatomy class at the university. Those were the bones that really hurt when broken, that took so long to heal.

"Mister Dykeman—*please!*"

The patient was heedless. His grip continued to strengthen. Soon Matt would hear the snapping of those *metacarpals*. Would that satisfy the old man with the superhuman grip? What if it didn't?

"*Stop—please!*"

He looked for any sign of humanity in those black holes that used to be eyes. He found something else. A memory. It was of a transient he met months ago at the D. A. McLaughlin Center. He had attacked Matt too, tore out clumps of his hair, but what stayed with Matt, were his eyes—empty holes tunneling to the darkness beyond. Matt was looking into them again. He was certain. They were the same eyes.

*I think he saw me.*

"*Help!*"

The first crack of bone came. Matt thought he would be sick at the sound. He tried to look away, but Dykeman's stony countenance held him as firmly as his grip. He screamed for help again. Where was the staff? Another crunch emanated from Matt's burning hand. He began to swoon as the searing pain travelled up his arm from the grinding bones in his hand. Then he heard the squeak of tennis shoes from the hall outside and he knew help had arrived.

Klewes pushed on the door.

"Why is this locked?" he yelled.

Matt heard Wanda's voice. "Hurry, Mister Klewes, hurry."

He heard the panicked jingling of keys.

He heard more crackling from his hand. This new pain, he barely registered.

He heard the *click* of the door lock. The door flew open and the orderly dashed inside, Wanda at his heels.

Dykeman loosened his grip immediately.

Matt fell backward into the wall. He looked up in time to see the blackness ebbing from the old man's eyes just before they closed. Dykeman's entire frame stiffened and began to shake. His lips smacked and the flesh around them turned noticeably blue.

"He's having a seizure," Matt said, disbelieving.

Klewes grasped the patient by the shoulders just as the deck chair overturned. He lowered Dykeman to the floor as gently as possible as his thrashing continued. "Get the pillow," the orderly shouted. Matt held his throbbing hand close to his chest, the pain making it nearly impossible to think of anything else. Klewes shouted again, "Doc, get the pillow off his bed." Matt clued in. He reached for the pillow with his good hand and passed it to the orderly. Klewes placed it under Dykeman's head. "I need something to put in his mouth." Matt offered his pen light. "He could break that and choke on it!" Klewes barked, then had a thought and dug the wallet out of his back pocket. He pushed the worn leather fold into Dykeman's snapping bite. He barely got his fingers clear before they became the choking hazard.

"Now don't touch him," Klewes said shifting away on his knees.

A few minutes passed before Dykeman's spasms abated. Only when Dykeman's body finally went slack did Klewes dare to move him to his cot. Matt gathered himself off the floor, his fractured mitt throbbing worse. Wanda saw his hand, already swollen and purpling before her eyes. She escorted Matt into the corridor and left the orderly to watch over Dykeman. "We'll get you to the clinic for X-rays, Doctor," she said. "No doubt, they'll set you with a cast right away." She rubbed his back while he cradled his hand gingerly. "Does it pain you much?" Wanda asked. Matt told her that it was manageable. It was, but only because his mind was elsewhere—looking into the abyss at the bottom of pitch-black eyes.

\* \* \* \*

Wanda returned to Dykeman's quarters once she had enlisted Elmer Savoie to drive Doctor Dawson to the clinic to have his hand seen to. "He's asleep," was Mister Klewes' report when she asked after the patient's condition. The orderly joined her in the doorway.

"You did very well, Mister Klewes," she said. "You fell back to your training nicely in a situation that would have many out of their wits."

"Guess that's why the doc made us take the first aid training every year like clockwork."

"Stanley Dawson didn't do anything by mistake," she said with a tight smile.

The orderly closed the heavy blue door behind him. He had left his key in the lock during his urgent entrance. He turned it and the door gave up a metallic *clink* and Klewes pulled the key out. His expression went grave.

Wanda's smile broke. "What is it?"

Klewe's face was rigid aside from a faint tremor in his lower lip. "We saw the doc come up here alone, right?"

"Why yes." Wanda was not accustomed to seeing anything but confidence in the burly young man. She watched his anxiety mount.

"Did you see anyone else in the hall?"

"No."

"Me neither."

"What are you getting-" The orderly's meaning crashed upon her like frigid surf.

"You can't lock these doors from the inside," he said. "Yet somehow, the doc was locked in there with Dykeman."

# Chapter Fifteen

Stanley stood at the main entrance, inches from freedom. Despite being so close, it remained unattainable. He closed his eyes and balled his fists, his breathing slowed. He took control of his body, whatever form of life (or death) it now was. There were no textbooks, science journals, or manuals that could tell him what exactly he was. Nor could they demonstrate what he was attempting to do. All he had was the knowledge that he had done it before. Though, standing nose to the thick double doors, he did not know how.

He concentrated on his goal, focused his entire being on it, and when he thought he was ready, raised his right hand and stuck out his finger. It pointed at the door. Slowly, eyes still closed, breathing still controlled, Stanley moved his finger forward...and it stopped when it met the unyielding door.

*Blast*!

How had he done it before? How had he managed to pass through Matthew's door? His whole body had gone through, arm first, then head and shoulders, legs followed. It was like trudging through dense brush, difficult but achievable. Now, when it mattered most, he couldn't even get a finger through.

Stanley stepped away from the door and turned to the blank darkness of the hospital. The impenetrable black wall was all around him. It persisted. In the lobby near the stairs stood Saint Michael, but Stanley could not go to him. He could not bring himself to leave the entrance. He knew there was something else in the hospital with him, just like he knew that, if he could read the hands on his watch in this abyss, they would tell him it was 3:00. The very thought of it had Stanley back at the door, trying to open it again. He steadied himself, centered his mind on the task, and pointed. His index finger resumed its collision course with the solid wooden door...and stopped again on the unwavering surface.

*Damn*!

What was different this time? Was it because he was somehow attached to Saint Michael's—that it was impossible for him to leave the building? Could he pass through doors only so long as he didn't go outside? Stanley backed to the entrance wall and leaned on it. His head was a vortex of questions. He tried to bring order to them to deal with one at a time...*Time*. If only he had more. If only he had long enough, he could decode this existence as he had his life. Through trial and error, he could learn the rules, exploit them. He could earn his freedom—if he had time. Of course, he did not.

*It was 3:00.*

He turned back to the lobby and the stubborn darkness that suppressed everything. Only now, the perfect black showed the slightest blemish. Stanley eyed the indistinct mark, little more than a rust spot on his vision that disappeared when he looked directly at it. He watched it in his periphery. Stepped closer. The spot grew brighter. For the moment, he forgot about the door, about his escape attempt. He concentrated on the smear on the darkness that could only be evidence of some far-off light. It took on a definite red tinge, like looking at the sun with eyes shut tightly. Stanley moved further inside the lobby. He had witnessed the breaking of the void before, the return of life within the hospital. During those times the daylight returned without warning, as quickly as it had left. Soon after, he would see his staff, his friends, and he knew he was not entirely alone in his afterlife. This was different. Stanley could feel it.

The red glow strengthened. By the time Stanley put the entrance behind him, he had little doubt it was coming from upstairs. He stood still while it spread rusty tendrils downward. Soon he could make out individual stairs, the balusters like bars on a jail cell door. The radiance intensified and it reached his legs, painting his suit and his shoes in flame like everything else it touched. Stanley turned to his Michael, bathed in bloody brilliance, and something broke inside him. He went to the headless angel. He reached out, but did not touch. He did not want to know the feel of his protector in such a ghastly state, robbed of his beauty, his piercing eyes. Now, he was alone. Desolation settled upon him and he sagged under the weight of it.

Overhead, the haunting glare unfurled like a sail in a gust. Stanley ascended. There was little else for him to fear, he decided. He believed he had nothing more to give up. The notion allowed him to crest the stair, to seek the center of the queer radiance. The second floor of his hospital was otherworldly. It was taken from heavenly Saint Andrews and cast into a furnace. The very air shimmered in sightless waves of heat. The walls danced in the brilliance. Stanley understood that he was *inside* malice. He breathed hatred.

Stanley went into the hall and looked east, always east, always to Dykeman's door. It was open and Stanley knew he found the core of all that malevolence. The door yawned like the mouth of a dragon. It spat fire from within the room—from within the man. Stanley had watched it simmer beneath the skin of Morry Dykeman for nearly sixty years. Now it burned unchecked. Now he watched helplessly like he had watched the night it was ignited in '52. It sensed him. It hungered for him. It needed him to be complete.

Fire spewed from the open room and splashed on the floor. It spread from the doorway and came for him. The paint on the walls of the corridor blistered and steamed. Tiles split and cracked and exploded off the floor. Stanley backed away. He decided to take another crack at that front door. He hit the stairs as fast as he could manage without risking a tumble. When he reached the landing, he witnessed the railing burst into flame and the fire streamed past him down to the bottom, igniting the banister. Stanley forged ahead, made it to the lobby, and—

"Stanley..."

The voice was a whisper, dry and labored.

Stanley stopped abruptly and turned toward the west corridor. The voice was familiar. After all, it was one he had known from the time he was ten years old.

"Phil...Phillip, is that you?"

Stanley faced the darkened hall. He saw nothing in the black abyss, though he heard shuffling, the soft scuffle of feet drawing near.

"Stanley...don't go..."

The darkness released its stubborn grip and a figure stepped forward. It glowed like the floor above. Some thirty feet away, Stanley watched the red man approach. He lunged forward on one foot, dragged the other behind.

"Phillip...what in the hell..."

Stanley considered the door. He knew he should go, but what if Phillip was really here? What if he needed help?

He neared. Lunge, drag.

"Phillip, what happened—"

Then Stanley got a look at his lifelong friend and understood the ghastly light he was giving off. He was burning. Under a fine layer of smoldering flame, Phillip Prichard was being consumed. Charred and split flesh rolled atop the nearly bare musculature of his slight frame. Blackened skin hung from his limbs here and there. He was seared hairless, his eyelids and lips burned completely away.

Lunge, drag.

The ruined man closed in.

"Stanley..."

Prichard raised his hands. Scorched and denuded fingers reached for Stanley.

"No. Phillip, I'm sorry...I can't help you."

Stanley spun toward the front entrance and found his path blocked. Another burned soul stood in his way. Stanley pulled back. He regarded this new creature. Though it had not spoken, it was somehow as familiar to Stanley as Phillip. There was something in the way it stood and in the tilt of its head. Stanley circled around it, keeping a distance from the ever-advancing wreck of his friend. The second flaming creature raised torched arms toward Stanley. He stopped in his tracks. He *knew* this creature that moved to touch him and hold him. He had received a thousand embraces from it in life. He had loved, and been loved by this creature. He had dreamed endlessly of their reunion for so many years.

"Stanley..." Susan Dawson said.

His heart ignited. It was like the fires that consumed her spread to him and exploded in his chest.

"There was a price, Stanley."

Susan stepped closer. Her burnt and crusted bosom heaved.

Little of his beloved remained. Her beautiful hair was ash, her soft lips, embers. Even her eyes, the deep pools of heaven he used to lose himself in, were baked over yellow and bubbling pus. Stanley collapsed.

"There was a price, Stanley."

He crumpled on the floor and buried his face in his arms while his demons surrounded him. They called to him and he imagined leathery wings enveloping his body. Screams burst from within. He wailed and what remained of his sanity seemed to be expunged. Then they touched him. They pawed at him for help, for relief from the fires. With their touch came their feelings. Stanley writhed as the fires bit and tore his flesh. He experienced true torment.

It was enough to throw him backward. He fell away from the burned people and tumbled across the floor until he met with the solid door. They followed him to the entrance, their fires illuminating the space. Stanley clamored to his feet and backed to the door. Susan and Phillip pursued, grotesque hands extended. Stanley winced and felt himself sink into the wood at his back, felt the fibers and splinters in his hands. He was passing through. He turned and punched at the door and his fist sank deep and felt the cool night air beyond. With the demons nearly within reach again, he pressed forward into the door.

The breeze outside froze him. It sliced through him like he was not there. It did not feel like it had before, when he passed through Matthew's door. This was not passing through a snowdrift or tall grasses. This was painful. He yanked his hand back. He went to clutch it, to rub the hurt out of it, but it was gone. Stanley stared in disbelief at his arm that now ended at his elbow. He was breaking a rule. He understood now—he was not allowed to leave. He was as anchored to the place as the stone angel in the lobby.

"Stanley...I paid for you."

Susan beckoned him.

Phillip followed.

Somewhere on the second floor, Dykeman was emerging from his room.

And Stanley knew, on this side of the door, he would remain with them for eternity. On the other side he would find oblivion. Sulfur burned his nostrils as his red loved ones approached. Over their shoulder, stood his lifeless angel.

Stanley decided then. He watched Susan's spoiled body limp toward him and nearly told her that he loved her. However, this was not *his* Susan. It could not be. He threw himself at the door. It gave way, he sunk through it, he fell.

He landed on the cold hard concrete walkway before Saint Michael's.

He breathed of the misty air and tasted salt. It was the bay. The shore was across the street, waves breaking on the rocky coast. Above him, the night sky was a patchwork of clouds. Where the canopy cracked, he saw a star. Up there were the heavens, better places than this. Leaves rustled on the oaks that bordered the grounds.

A breeze kicked up.

It cut him at his core. He doubled over as the wind passed through him, wore him away. Stanley looked down at his good hand. It eroded before his eyes, pinky first, then the rest of the digits. They corroded away like a sand castle on a high wind. *This is better*, was Stanley's last thought. *This is better than that Godforsaken place.* His legs went boneless and he fell over. When he hit the walkway, he shattered into a billion grains and was cast onto the night air. Every last bit of him scattered to the wind.

# Chapter Sixteen

Matt unlocked the front door and waved at Elmer, who had parked and waited to make sure his employer got into his house okay. Elmer waved back and reversed the hospital's truck down the long sloping drive. Matt flicked the switch to illuminate the darkened hallway. He had been at the clinic for hours, first for X-rays, then to have his shattered hand set in a cast. The pictures of his hand revealed multiple breaks. Doctor Brown, the young general practitioner who had tended to Matt, suggested surgery might be required to deal with a nasty-looking bone chip that had broken free in his palm. Matt graciously declined the invitation. He had other pressing business and could not waste any more time in the snail-paced public healthcare system. Brown sent him on his way with a prescription for Tylenol Three. After Matt left, he tossed it and wrote himself a prescription for Demerol.

Elmer had patiently waited in the lounge the entire time. He had seemed content to sit in the uncomfortable chairs and flip through the germ-infested magazines.

When Matt emerged from the Emergency Department, he asked, "How are you feeling in da wriss?"

Matt grinned despite his obvious discomfort. Elmer was likely proud of the merit points he expected he'd earned with his boss. Yet, Matt was more troubled by the idea of his cook spending the day in the clinic waiting room while Tyrone Klewes likely served Coffee Stop donuts to his patients at mealtime.

They stopped at Cockburn's Corner Drug so Matt could get his pills. The rest of the drive home, he thought of nothing but downing four of the little yellow capsules and taking enough edge off his pain to get some sleep. Once inside the house, Matt dumped out the white paper bag Cockburn gave him and carried his pills into the study in search of a mouthful of wine to chase them down.

*Did I leave that desk lamp on?* he wondered when he entered the study.

"Broken wing, Doctor?"

Matt's stomach did a flip and he spun in the direction of the unexpected voice.

His shock turned to revulsion when he saw the person seated in the armchair by the fireplace.

"What are you doing here, Fisher?"

"Sorry for the intrusion, but we need to talk. Hope you don't mind, I let myself in." Fisher watched Matt intently from his dim corner. He had made himself comfortable. His jacket rested on the back of the chair and his beat-up satchel slumped at his feet. An opened bottle of red stood on the end table beside the chair.

"Is it okay with you if I sit?" Matt said. He rounded the hulking desk with the busted bottom drawer and gingerly lowered himself into the cushioned chair.

Fisher smiled that sly smile of his and the goatee slanted on his face. "If you're thinking about that big shiny gun in the desk, you can forget it. I put it in a safe place."

Matt eyed the writer's satchel and guessed where the gun had gone.

"I shouldn't have come unannounced," Fisher said. "I know that's just not good manners, but there is a police car parked outside my motel room and I didn't feel too good about going in."

"I wonder what they want," Matt said absently as he carefully laid his aching hand on his lap.

"Oh, I think you know. I had a conversation with Chief Lumley about my research and how it relates to a dead man named Prichard." Fisher snorted a laugh. "Don't worry, Dawson. No hard feelings. I probably would have rolled over on you had I been in your shoes."

"I'm guessing the focus of your conversation was a strange symbol you dug up in your investigation."

"It certainly was, but I think he still likes you for the murder."

"You framed me."

"Yeah, some frame job. The cops are watching me too. Look, if it makes you feel any better, I swear on my mother's grave, I didn't murder anyone. I have an alibi, but seeing as I'm kind of a loner, no one can confirm it."

Matt glared at his guest. "Is your mother even dead?"

"She will be someday."

Matt shook his head. The throbbing in his fractured hand reminded him that he needed to take his painkillers. With his right, he put the pill bottle on the desk and attempted to twist the safety top off with his fingers. His hand slipped. The bottle went skittering across the desktop and fell to the floor by Fisher's feet.

"How many of these bad boys do you want?" Fisher asked as he rose and scooped up the bottle.

"Four ought to do it," Matt said, frustrated.

Fisher opened the bottle and shook the pills out on the desk in front of Matt. He retrieved the wine from the end table along with two glasses. He filled the glasses and slid one across the desk. He sat back down, raised his drink and said, "To your health."

Matt lifted the pills to his mouth, said, "To yours," and rinsed them down. He considered their position for a moment. *Supposing Fisher wasn't involved with Prichard's murder, he may be of use*, he thought. *If he has to prove his own innocence, maybe I can use what he knows to prove mine.* "We can't be the only two people who know about that symbol."

"I find you difficult to read. What do you know, Doctor?"

"Not nearly enough."

"Tell you what, since we're in the same boat here, I propose full disclosure."

Matt agreed. Little would change from his point of view. He had nothing to disclose.

"Well to be honest, Phillip Prichard and the cops are the least of my worries right now. I need the book."

Matt was taking a drink when Fisher said it and he winced as he swallowed with difficulty. "What book?"

Fisher's goatee slanted again and he gave up a wry chuckle. Though, when he read Matt's face, his grin vanished. "Wait...you really don't have it."

"I don't have the slightest clue what you're talking about."

"Dawson, you're in this up to your fucking neck, and you don't know shit." Fisher's expression morphed to one of concern as he seemed to calculate things. "I continue to overestimate you, Doctor. I was sure your father left it to you."

"There's a lot you don't know about me and Stanley."

"Apparently, there's a lot *you* don't know about Stanley."

Matt clenched his jaw. Fisher was right, but he did not like to be reminded of his weak family bonds. He drew a breath. He had to be patient with Fisher, keep him on *full disclosure*. This was his chance to learn a thing or two about Dykeman and Stanley and their link. "So, what about this book?" he asked, looking at the shelves surrounding them. "Maybe it's in here."

"I sincerely doubt that. It's not the kind of book you leave on a shelf."

*Of course,* Matt thought. *You already searched these bookcases long before I got here.* His sore hand pulsed wave after wave of agony up his arm. It eroded his patience. "Look, it's been a long day, I'm exhausted and you're being a little too cryptic..."

"Okay, Dawson." Fisher paused and took a hearty drink. He seemed to regret his prior willingness to be open. "The book is what brought me to Saint Andrews."

"The one you're writing?"

"I'm not writing anything."

"I wonder if you ever tell the truth."

"Okay, here it is," Fisher raised his free hand as though he was putting himself under oath. "...the God's honest. Six months ago, I got a package in the mail. In it was an idea for a book from some anonymous person. He said he was a fan. At first I read through it and tossed it aside. I get stuff from crackpots all the time. You'd be surprised how many there are out there."

Matt exhaled audibly and shifted in his seat.

"Oh, look who I'm talking to. You of all people would know better than me. Anyway, there's always somebody pulling my leg or looking to send me on a wild goose chase or something. Sometimes they just want promotion for their supposedly haunted Bed and Breakfast. Usually the more detail they give, the more full of shit they are and, let me tell you, this proposal had a *lot* of detail. There was a background story, newspaper articles, photographs, the works. Like I said, I tossed it aside and forgot about it. A couple of weeks after that, I was researching an unrelated project and came across a hieroglyph in an old text. You know the one I'm talking about." Fisher drew a circle in the air with his finger then drew two lines through it. "I knew I had seen it before. It drove me half nuts trying to figure out where. I racked my brain for days until I finally remembered the package and a certain black-and-white photograph that was in it. I dug it out and sure enough, it was a match. Then I read some more."

Matt listened to the writer but found it hard to concentrate on what he was saying. He gave up on waiting for Fisher to make his point. Instead, he more or less waited for the painkillers to kick in. "Fisher, I find your ghost stories fascinating and all..."

Fisher gave Matt a look of sarcastic exhaustion. "I came to find out that the symbol isn't a symbol at all."

"Oh no?"

"It's a name."

"A name?"

"Yes, and I won't say it out loud, but it relates to the book Stanley had."

"You won't say—*Jesus Christ.*"

"Listen, I know a little bit about this stuff and you have to be careful when dealing with—"

Matt cut him short. "A man is dead, Fisher! Someone murdered him. I am a suspect, so are you. These are hard facts and you're handing me some superstitious bullshit."

"Come on now, Dawson. You know how I make my living. I've been all over the world researching supernatural occurrences. I have seen evidence of heaven and unfortunately I've seen far more evidence of hell. Dozens of other cultures accept it as fact. There are other forces at work in the world whether you can accept it or not. Some of them are dangerous."

"Spare me the theatrics, Fisher. I want to stick to the facts. Now you said whoever sent you that package has seen this symbol. Whoever it is probably killed Prichard. That is what we need to focus on."

"You want to know who else has seen this thing? I'll give you a hint. He has a second floor suite at Saint Michael's."

Matt could not prevent his indignant laugh from escaping. "I'm not going to listen to this. Morris Dykeman was not only confined to quarters, he was totally incapable of murdering Prichard. Even if I set him loose on the street, he doesn't have the cognitive ability to even find Prichard's house."

Fisher went silent for a moment. He drained his glass and set it on the end table. "Look, Dawson, I have chased tall tales all over creation, and yeah, a lot of them are nonsense, I'll admit, but I keep searching. Do you know why? Because one of these times, the story will be true. Someday I'll find something important, something profound, that we can't explain away with science and math. That's what I've found here. And it all goes back to that book Stanley had."

"Okay Fisher, wow me." Matt leaned back in his chair and rubbed his tired eyes.

"Try to keep up. Somehow, in 1952, five boys got their hands on it. I don't know how they came to possess it, but I found out the last recorded owner was a big deal in the shipping business in the nineteenth century. The interesting thing is, among many other places, Saint Andrews happened to be one of his ports of call. That may be how the book got here. Anyway, it was originally written in Prussia by some guy named Steiger in 1540 something.

"Years later, it was translated into both French and English, although the copies were strictly controlled. In fact, there may only be one English copy in existence."

"Which translation did the boys come across?"

Fisher ignored Matt's wit and continued. "This Steiger was reportedly big time into the occult and it's said he put everything he knew in the book. In it were rituals and ceremonies designed to allow the reader to commune with those on the other side."

"Like the devil?"

"Among others, yes. There are several notable demons in Satan's court. Did you know that it matters which one you proposition depending on what you want in return? Well, these boys were practical. All they wanted was money. They followed the directions in the book, found out which...umm *demon* to ask, and on the night of the summer solstice, they took the book into a barn and attempted to perform the ritual."

"Let me guess, something went wrong."

"Oh yeah. That is if by *wrong* you mean that one boy went to the dark side and never came back."

"I'm assuming he went mad? Isn't that what normally happens in the horror movies when the naïve character looks behind the curtain?"

"Not always. For example, in this one, the boy went home and killed his entire family with a pair of garden shears."

Matt had no humorous retort. The black-and-white image of the shears laid carelessly on the Dykemans' kitchen table flashed in his mind. They dripped sticky black gore, long hairs tangled around the blades.

"That's right, after that night in the barn, our friend Morris Dykeman was never quite the same."

Matt swallowed the remainder of his wine. He raised his brow and looked directly in Fisher's eyes. "Fisher, he was ill and that night he acted appropriately for a boy that was so afflicted and who regrettably, went untreated." Matt's tone was flat and even, implying that the fact was not debatable, although he was starting to wonder who was in need of convincing.

"That may be your prerogative, Dawson, but you should know he wasn't the only boy involved that night that you'd be familiar with. One of those boys kept the book. Do you know anyone around Dykeman's age who is good at keeping secrets, keeping things hidden?"

"Stanley." Suddenly Matt could not feel his fractured hand. He was distracted by the frost building in his chest. *Stanley.* He looked up at the urn over the fireplace.

"*Very good.* The others entrusted him with the book, and so far as anyone knows, he still had it when he died."

Matt's head was spinning as he tried to sift through this new information. His father never spoke of any rare book that Matt knew of. Fisher must have been lying. The only thing Matt knew about him with any certainty was that he had his own agenda and his interests were his first priority. Then it occurred to him. "The book...you came to Saint Andrews looking for that book. That's what you wanted all along."

Fisher sighed as though the last piece of his cover story had just dissolved. "Honestly, I thought you had it. I thought for sure that if I gave you a nudge, you'd bring it out double quick."

"What was the nudge?"

"Well...that's where I fucked up, Dawson."

Matt looked at the usually cocksure writer and tried to imagine what could possibly have him admitting to error.

"When I met with Dykeman, I didn't mean to sit there and look in his eyes or bask in his evil presence." Fisher paused as though he was having second thoughts, then went into his satchel and dug out a cell phone. "I played this for him." Fisher's fingers went to work on the touch screen. He went through a couple menus and pulled up an audio file. He held the phone up and hit play.

At first, Matt did not know what he was listening to. A single male voice droned in an indecipherable dialect. Then, gradually, other voices joined in the chorus. The chanting became repetitive, rhythmic. The voices bled together into one giant-like tenor. It filled the study and seemed to grow louder with each passing second. Matt and Fisher listened to the dizzying din while the desk lamp seemed to struggle against the night and the shadows stretched longer throughout the room. *How many voices is that?* Matt wondered. He looked to Stanley's urn on the mantelpiece. Shadows overtook it. On some primal level, Matt knew he was listening to something foul, something that was not meant to be heard by rational men. Had Stanley heard this as well? Did it play some part in what those boys did on that summer night in 1952?

Fisher stifled the chanting with a flick of his thumb.

The air in the study cleared at once.

"What the hell is that?" Matt asked. The flesh on his arms that was not covered by plaster had broken out in goosebumps.

"I woke him up, Dawson."

"Dykeman?"

"Not Dykeman...the thing inside him. The thing that killed Prichard."

"Fisher...no, no, no."

"It did. I know it. It caved in his head and then used his blood to write its name on the wall so we'd know who did it."

"Listen to me. There is no way, even if I could believe for a second that there is something evil living inside Dykeman, that he is physically capable of committing murder."

"You think it's limited by locked doors? Your father knew better than that. He knew who was looking back at him through those eyes."

*Perhaps.* Stanley *had* taken precautions with Dykeman. He had kept his patient doped up and locked down. Still, if Stanley really had dealings in the occult, if he truly bought into that foolishness, he may have been every bit as ill as Dykeman. *On the other hand.* Matt looked down at his plastered mitt. It was Dykeman who had done it to him, no one else. He had turned his cold eyes on Matt and he had attacked, just like the transient had done that night in Edmonton. Matt pulled his mind away from the image of the two black-eyed men. He could not allow himself to dwell on them, or the possibility they were cohorts, or even that they were one and the same.

"Well, I don't have the book. You will have to find some other magic spell to make you rich."

Fisher shifted uncomfortably. "All right...granted, it would have been nice to take advantage of the book. Now, I need it now for different reasons. I have to finish the ritual those boys started."

"You're going to fix their mistakes? How valiant."

Fisher leaned forward in his chair. He wrung his hands and tapped his foot nervously on the floor. "I *have* to. The thing inside Dykeman...it saw me. It is following me. Listen, Dawson...I see it everywhere. It's getting close and I know I'll end up like that accountant if I can't complete the ritual. I *need* that book. You must know where it is. *Please*, Dawson!"

"Sounds to me like you're getting what you deserve."

"Yeah, well, we both deserve something." Fisher eyed the bottle of painkillers on the desk. "What happened to your arm?"

"I bet you'd like it if I told you the devil did it to me, wouldn't you?"

"Oh, yeah, be smug about it. Just don't forget when it's done with me, it will come calling on you."

Matt studied the writer, his foot bouncing on the floor. He was exhibiting some pretty strong signs of paranoia and delusion. Matt figured he should be getting clinical treatment and the last thing he needed was for someone to buy into the fantastic story he was selling. But something nagged at him, something he had seen in Dykeman's hollow eyes. *Maybe the painkillers are starting to work*, Matt thought. *Maybe I'm high as a kite. I must be to go along with this.* "All right Fisher, I'll look for the book. What is it called?"

"*Sacra Obscurum.*"

"What is that, Latin?"

"It translates to *The Sacred Darkness.*"

"God Almighty...no one can say you don't have a flare for the dramatic."

# Chapter Seventeen

Matt stood before the wall of boxes. Twelve large cartons in total contained the collection of books from Stanley's office at Saint Michael's. The pile was nearly wide enough to eclipse one of the dining room walls. The mere sight of them and thought of the task ahead was all it took to flare the agony in Matt's fractured hand. He did not know how he was he supposed to go through them all singled-handedly, but he had promised he would just to get Fisher to leave.

Matt reached for one of the boxes on the top. He grabbed a corner and pulled. The entire stack of boxes teetered dangerously toward him. He stepped to the side and gave another tug. The column of cartons crashed to the floor, toppling two dinette chairs. The flimsy box from the top split and gave way in a landslide of books. Medical texts, volumes of science journals, and psychiatry periodicals spewed across the floor in a landslide of heavy paper. Matt looked down to where his feet were no longer visible under the avalanche of Stanley's collection. Suddenly, his hand felt worse.

He stepped back from the mess on the floor. Three tall columns of boxes still stood against the wall. Books were scattered from the fallen boxes to the far reaches of the dining room. They went under the table, under the chairs. Matt groaned.

*This is pointless*, he thought. *Even if I could search through all of these, what are the chances I'd find this voodoo book, anyway? If it's half as dangerous as Fisher says it is, Stanley would have hidden it away. He would have kept it in a safe place. Right?* Matt had to admit he didn't know. It appeared Fisher knew more about Stanley than he did. Matt did not even fully know the false façade Stanley showed the world to shield his true character. Trying to figure him was like trying to get to know an actor by watching his movies.

Matt went back to the study in search of the wine he had shared with Fisher. He eyed the urn over the fireplace as he entered. *Stanley was with Dykeman on the night he killed his family. What in God's name did he do?* Matt shuddered at the idea that Stanley had acted as accomplice on that bloody night. He snatched up the bottle from the end table and gulped it dry. He could do little else. This situation was undeniably beyond his control. Everything was. He was a suspect in Phillip Prichard's death, his patient had become a menace to everyone at Saint Michael's, and Stanley may have been a murderer. Matt rubbed hard at his brow. Then he realized there was at least one thing he could do. He picked up the phone from the corner of the desk and dialed the hospital.

Doctor Collins answered before the second ring.

"Saint Michael's."

"Hello Darcy. It's Matt calling."

"Matt! Oh, my God. I heard what happened. Are you okay?"

"Yes, I'm okay. I'm home now."

"How is your hand? Was it broken?"

"Umm, yes...in several places. I...I'll be all right."

"I could send Nurse Tait over if you need help at home."

"Thank you, no. That won't be necessary. The reason I called was to check on Mister Dykeman's condition."

"Well, he slept most of the day and we have been keeping a close watch on him. There were no further episodes. Doctor Brown from the clinic is checking him over now."

"Doctor Brown...he isn't alone with him, is he?"

"No, Mister Cundiff is with them."

"Okay, Darcy, I need you to place a watch on Dykeman. Can you ask Mister Cundiff to stay overnight? I will call Mister Klewes straight away and ask him to relieve Mister Cundiff in the morning. I want the two of them on twelve hour shifts for the time being."

"Sure, I'll ask, but I think Mister Dykeman is out of the woods now. Sometimes these *petit mal* seizures occur with a profound change in medication, but they're usually isolated. I mean, aren't they?"

"Yes. I'd just feel better if he was watched. Oh, and don't let the staff remove him from quarters. I am going to suspend Mister Dykeman's bathing schedule for a few days."

Darcy's tone dropped a gear. "What's going on, Matt?"

"Nothing, everything's fine. I just want to be cautious."

"I understand that, but it's starting to sound like you want Dykeman under *guard*, not under observation."

"I'm just concerned that he might harm someone else. The well-being of the staff is ultimately my responsibility, as well."

"Matt, we're taking all the necessary precautions."

"Please, Darcy, just help me with this, okay?"

"Is there something you should be telling me?"

*Yes.* "No...I know that asking you to bear with me is probably asking a lot right now."

"It is."

"I don't have all the answers yet, but when I do..."

"Can you at least tell me what the questions are? What is going on with you?"

"I really can't. I'm sorry."

"Well, just so you're aware of my position, let me be frank. I am supposed to succeed you as head doctor at some point and I'm finding that difficult because you won't inform me of *all* hospital business. And if I can be blunt, you are a *mess*, Doctor. Your entire staff sees it and they're worried about you and the future of this facility and now you want me to hand down a strange request that will have them even more confused than they already are. How am I supposed to do that? How am I supposed to continue under these conditions?"

"Please, Darcy, this is a difficult situation for me. I need a little more time to sort through it. There are some problems left over from when Stanley ran the hospital. I need to work them out, and when I do, I will be happy to explain everything."

"There is no time for that, Matt. You need to explain yourself now, to me and the rest of your staff, or you will know what it's like to truly be on your own."

"Fine. Arrange a meeting for tomorrow morning at shift change."

"I'll be looking forward to it. Try to get some sleep."

A *click* told him that she was gone.

Matt felt like he was being held hostage—first by Dykeman, then Fisher, and now by his own employees. What could he tell them? What was he certain of? Dykeman was a cold-blooded killer. Maybe Stanley was. The police thought Matt was, too. Don't worry. All will be fine if he can find the magic book for Fisher. Matt groaned when he realized that the most ridiculous part of this was the only one he could do anything about. He headed back to the dining room to sift through the haystack of books.

* * * *

Darcy hung up the phone. She wanted to slam it. This golden career opportunity was turning to lead before her eyes. She should have known it was too good to be true. It had fallen into her lap, after all. She had not toiled for years for the prime position. She had not sacrificed, suffered, like she had for everything else she'd earned.

Doctor Brown and John Cundiff emerged from Mister Dykeman's quarters. John locked the door behind them and they made their way down the hall to where Darcy was waiting for the GP's assessment. Doctor Brown was a relative newcomer to the profession, possibly Darcy's age. His hair was gelled back and he wore fashionable black-framed glasses. John stood beside the young doctor. He straightened his posture comically to show that he was a full foot taller, just in case Darcy was running a physical comparison of the men. She fought off the urge to smile and asked Doctor Brown his thoughts on their patient.

"His vitals are passable," Doctor Brown started. "Blood pressure is okay. He seems quite fatigued, but that is relatively normal in the wake of a seizure. Do you know off-hand what medications he is on?"

"He is given Olanzepine and Lithium Carbonate daily so far as I'm aware. I'm not his primary doctor."

"Right...umm, he'll need lots of sleep and try to get him to drink water when he wakes."

"Thank you, Doctor. If you would like more information, Doctor Dawson will be along in the morning."

"Yeah...Dawson. I had the pleasure of treating his hand this afternoon. I'll be sure to rush right over."

Darcy grinned despite feeling genuinely sorry for Matt and the reputation he seemed to be earning around town. Whatever his problems, he hid them poorly. "Thank you for coming so quickly, Doctor," she said.

"I'm available whenever you need me," he said and instead of making his exit, lingered a moment. "Umm, if you are free some night this week, maybe we could get together for dinner or something. This town is a pretty sorry excuse for a night out, but I can promise good company."

"I'm attached," Darcy said flatly. "Thank you anyway for the invitation."

Doctor Brown nodded and walked away.

John moved beside her and placed a hand on the small of her back. "You're attached? You really should have told me."

"Shut up," she said and started away from him.

"Is there anything else I should know?"

"Yes...you're working overtime tonight."

\* \* \* \*

As was customary for him, Cundiff did as he was told without so much as a question. He had wheeled an office chair into the east corridor on the second floor and took up position only feet from Dykeman's door. Every fifteen minutes or so he put down his magazine and checked on the old man through the observation window. Every fifteen minutes, Dykeman was the same—asleep on his right side, facing the wall. Years ago Cundiff had read an article in *National Geographic* about human behavior during deep sleep. Well, he had looked at the pictures, anyway. He remembered the photos of the slumbering test subject, taken every few minutes. Cundiff had been surprised to see the level of activity caught on film. Despite never waking, the subject flopped about the bed so much that he might have fallen out. Cundiff expected that looking through Dykeman's window every fifteen minutes would be a similar exercise. Yet, the old patient disappointed. He had not moved from his face-the-wall pose in hours.

Cundiff returned to his cushioned chair and eased himself in. When last he checked, it was about 11:30. He had not been at the hospital this late in recent memory. Everything was crypt-quiet except for the rare moan or wail from the main floor where the notoriously noisy patients were quartered in the west wing. They put them there so as not to bother anyone but each other. The arrangement seemed to work. The only people still awake in Saint Michael's were Cundiff and the night nurse, Miss Tait. Though she could be counted on to disappear for an hour or two.

The dimmed lighting in the hallway made it difficult for Cundiff to read. Soon the words on the magazine page were blurring together. *I've got to get a drink or something*, he thought. *If I don't get some caffeine in me soon, I'll be dead to the world.*

Cundiff got up from his comfortable chair. He went and stood beside Arthur Sullivan. The old salt adeptly steered the lobster boat through the ocean swells while a steady spray of water on the windshield obscured his view. Cundiff grabbed hold of the dash as they pitched and yawed side to side one instant, front to back the next. Outside, the bay was riled. The sky and the water were a sullen gray on gray. It was winter.

Sullivan stood letter-straight, feet shoulder width apart at the helm of the *Pact*. It was like he was a part of the boat. He looked straight ahead while the smoke from the cigarette tucked in the corner of his mouth funneled to the cabin ceiling. The deep lines around his eyes seemed darker than Cundiff remembered. Clearly Sullivan did not like what he was seeing through the distorted glass. "Them traps ain't gonna pull themselves," he said to the orderly. Cundiff looked to the back of the cabin. There was a door and beyond it was the deck, no doubt basted in a fine film of ice. The rigging would be cold, the hooks would be cold, the winch would be cold. They waited for him. He staggered toward the door and prepared to carry out his orders. He took a yellow slicker from the lineup of rain gear hung on the back wall and put it on over his white scrubs as he swayed this way and that. It fit him perfectly. He read the name patch on the front of the jacket. *Cundiff.*

He went through the pockets and knew he would find his black gloves and tuque. He pulled them on tight and went outside. Frozen spray pelted his face as he stepped from the warmth of the cabin. The sharp winds drove the icy pellets sideways, but he could see another hand on deck dressed in yellow rubbers and matching rain hat. Cundiff's first step out on the glistening and sodden deck had him sliding awkwardly. His tennis shoes offered no grip on the slick boards. He reached out and seized the edge of the bait table. Using it as a crutch, he worked his way to the winch on the trawler's starboard side. When he got there, he was greeted by a gush of seawater breaking over the boat. He slid again. The other mate did not. Like Sullivan, he stood steadfast on the deck.

"Lovely day," Cundiff shouted as he regained his footing.

The deckhand did not respond. He did not even turn his head. Instead, he readied hook and rope to cast out and snag the trap line. Cundiff looked out over the choppy water. Red buoys with yellow stripes—Sullivan buoys—bobbed up and down on the ever-changing seascape. They seemed near the boat one moment, far off the next, as the frigid water churned and spat.

The deckhand whirled the hook to his side then loosed it out onto the water. Twenty feet off the starboard side, it snagged the trap line. The hand pulled it in. When it was within arm's reach, Cundiff leaned forward, over the side. Under him the bay slapped the boat and foamed against the hull. He looked down at the dark water, black and bottomless, and an old fear flared within him like a struck match.

He grabbed a nearby deck cleat with one hand and with his free one, reached for the trap line and pulled it in. Only out of the water a few seconds, the line was already starting to freeze. He fed it through the winch like he had done in his brief fishing career too many times to count. The winch did the heavy lifting. It raised the trap from the rocky ocean floor. The men watched it appear from the secret depths of the bay. With a grunt, Cundiff hoisted the trap out and held it on the side of the boat for his mate. The other deckhand worked fast. He opened the lid and pulled the two dozen imprisoned lobsters from the trap and tossed them into the deep tote bin on the deck floor. When it was empty, he baited the trap with a sloppy handful of dismembered herring from the bait table. The hand never looked up, never said a word, just readied his hook for the next throw. Cundiff closed the lid and dumped the trap over and it was swallowed by the bay.

The hook shot through the air and fetched another line. *No rest for the wicked*, Cundiff thought as the trap line topped with the familiar red-and-yellow buoy neared the jostling boat. A few seconds later, it was in his hand, then threaded through the winch, then the trap was on the surface. Cundiff lugged it out and when he did, slipped badly and went down on one knee. Tennis shoes were evidently not the gear of choice in the fishing business, nor were thin cotton scrub pants. Rough and gritty ice dug into his knee when he fell and left a pink blotch on his pants. By the time he regained his footing, the orderly found that his mate had already emptied the trap and was baiting it.

"You're fast," he yelled to the deckhand. "I take it this ain't new to you."

The hand replied by slamming the lid of the trap closed.

*Not the most talkative sort*, Cundiff thought, eyeing his mate. Though, with his rain cap pulled low and the collar of his slicker turned up, he could not get much of a look at the man.

The hook was airborne again. It splashed down beside the next buoy in line and the next thing Cundiff knew, it was within his reach. Again, he grabbed hold of the cleat with one hand and reached with the other and soon the winch was resurrecting the trap. The orderly waited for the cage to appear. He knew he had to yank it out and fast if he wanted to match his mate's pace. If he could not keep up, Arthur Sullivan would not keep *him*.

The deckhand whacked the hook against the boat's gunwale while he waited.

The winch seemed to slow. It gave a whine as it struggled to raise its burden.

Cundiff carefully looked over the side of the boat for any sign of an obstruction.

The winch continued to emit the desperate squeal of metal-on-metal friction and it slowed to a crawl before stopping altogether.

The deckhand whacked the hook against the gunwale again.

He was clearly not talkative *or* patient. Who could blame him? If Sullivan had to come outside to find out what the holdup was, he would not be pleased in the slightest. Too many delays would see a pair of deckhands replaced by any of the dozens of sons of Saint Andrews eager to work his way onto a good-paying boat. The thought led Cundiff to hazard another look overboard. The trap line disappeared a few inches into the choppy gray water. The trap was nowhere to be found. It was like there was some unseen force keeping the trap seated in the depths. He swallowed hard as his imagination drew images of giant squid with a belly for fresh lobster.

The deckhand whacked the hook against the gunwale again. This time it was hard enough to send wood chips flying.

Cundiff seized the line, figuring he could pull the trap the rest of the way. It may have been only a few feet below the surface, for all he knew. It was impossible to tell. He pulled. The line gave half a foot, but when he went to replace his hand on the frozen cable, it eagerly took it back and the trap sank again. He took a breath. He would have to use both hands. That meant letting go of the cleat.

The hook whacked the gunwale, harder again.

Cundiff grabbed the line with both hands. He strained with his wide back and legs and pulled. He was able to gather a couple feet of slack in the line, and he pulled again. Hand over hand, he reeled the trap closer to the surface. Each time he pulled, the deck hand beat the side of the boat with his hook, adding an unspoken urgency to the situation. For a moment, Cundiff wondered why the winch struggled so mightily with the line. If he could reel it in under manpower, surely the machine could do so with ease. Then he felt it.

Something pulled back.

If he had not been wearing gloves, his hands would have been skinned by the friction. In an instant, he gave up most of the line he had pulled in. He clamped down hard on the cable, braced his knee against the side of the boat, and attempted to wrestle it back. His tennis shoes failed him again. He slipped. Then he was falling.

Time stood still as his momentum carried him forward. It was like he stepped out of his body and he was watching himself fall toward the deep unknown. He realized then what this meant. The one thing in life that truly scared him, the one thing that woke him, cold and sweaty in the night, was happening. He tried to scream but the frigid salt water flooded his mouth before he could. His nerves exploded in unison when he went under. A million icicles stabbed his body and he went stiff. The bay enveloped him in its frozen embrace. All was silent save the rumble of the *Pact's* engine, like a great beast clearing its throat.

And there was a voice. It came from within. It was his own voice and it screamed for him to *kick*. He slapped and clawed at the water, fought his way to the surface. When he broke the skin of the water, the noises of the world rushed back in. The gusting wind, the groaning of the trawler, and his own terror-ridden voice added to the din. He thrashed at the water frantically and continued to kick while he yelled for help.

Arthur Sullivan did not pay for his crews to receive survival training, and his boats were ill-equipped for rescue to boot. All Cundiff knew about falling in was what he gathered from the talk of the other mates. What came to mind first was something Ricky Sullivan once said. "When men go in the North Atlantic, their survival rate drops by seventy-five percent if they ain't pulled out in the first thirty seconds." The orderly knew he was on the clock. He turned to catch sight of the boat and get his bearings. Then he broke for it, fighting against the swells as best he could in the soggy rubber raincoat. It made his arms weigh ten times as much, but he was fuelled by adrenaline and fear. He yelled for the deckhand. He yelled for the hook. It didn't matter if it pierced him like he was a trout, he begged the mate to throw it.

The deckhand made no motion to help. He whacked the hook against the gunwale and he watched.

Cundiff begged for aid. He had done his part. He had fought his way back to within fifteen feet of the boat. Why didn't the hand throw the hook? Where was Sullivan? The orderly outstretched his hand and pleaded again for aid while briny water flooded his mouth and stung his eyes. The mate looked down on him from the safety of the deck. Cundiff stopped begging. For the first time, he saw the man's face beneath the soaking rain hat and knew there would be no rescue. The mate's long, square visage was hard and uncaring as though whittled from wood. His swollen eyes were monstrous. When Cundiff looked into those black-as-coal eyeballs, he saw nothing human behind them. He knew then that he would die.

He stopped fighting and the roiling bay carried him away from the *Pact*, or the *Pact* away from him—there was no way of knowing. He watched the man in the yellow slicker on the deck until he became small on the wide water. The man never took those weird eyes off him, Cundiff knew. Even when he could no longer see them, he could feel them.

Then something below the surface cut through the waters and moved by him. It nudged his thigh and his blood went as cold as the bay. He remembered raising the trap and how something fought against the winch—something strong. The vile deckhand was immediately flushed from his mind as he searched the black waters around him. It bumped him again, and this time the force put him under and he had to kick back to the surface. His heart stopped beating as the reality came crashing down on him. He would never be found. His family would bury an empty casket. His name would go on the bronzed plaque in the square by the Saint Andrews wharf with all the other souls. Like theirs, his name would bear the postscript: L.A.S. *Lost at sea.*

The thing from the depths came back. It wrapped itself around Cundiff's left leg and he screamed his loudest scream. No one heard. Even Sullivan's boat, with its cold and heartless crew, was gone from sight. The orderly battled to stay afloat and gulped at the air as the thing tugged at him from below. He could not see what held him—could not even bring himself to look, though his imagination told him they were tentacles. Yes, this sea monster had tentacles. One reached up his back and fell over his shoulder. It squeezed. It shook him.

"John."

"*John!*"

He wailed again and jerked in his chair.

"*John!*"

He sprang upright and opened his eyes to the searing corridor lights.

He was in Saint Michael's. He was not alone.

Darcy stood over him, aghast, with a pizza box in one hand and the other gripping his shoulder. "Are you okay?"

Cundiff fought to suppress the wetness that gathered in his eyes. He pawed at his chest and felt the hammering within. Darcy told him to breathe. It was like his body had refused to, like it was convinced he was really underwater and his next attempted breath would be the one that drowned him. He drew air and it started off a chain of dry coughing. Darcy set the box down and rubbed his back until he was able to catch his wind. "Oh, my God," he said at last. "I fell asleep...had a nightmare."

"I'd say. There was no waking you. For a minute, I thought I would have to give you an epinephrine shot."

Cundiff rubbed his eyes and groaned as he recalled the dream. His hands were shaking. His fear was genuine. It had been that real. He shivered as a chill worked its way through him from the inside out. "Shit. I can't believe I fell asleep."

"What did you expect? You shouldn't even be here. Fuck Matt and his stupid fucking requests."

"It's okay, Darcy."

"No, this is utter foolishness, making you sit and watch a door all night long."

"Really, I'm fine."

"In what way are you fine?"

"Is that a pie from *Olde Tyme Pizzeria*?"

"Yes."

"That's how I'm fine."

Darcy sighed at his absurd reasoning.

"You're here, too," he said. "That's better than fine."

"Yeah well, I thought we could have a picnic in the hallway since you're stuck here all night, but now I—"

"We still can. I'm all right now. Well...hungry anyway. I guess you work up an appetite when you're scared out of your wits."

"Well, I'm going to make you some tea at the very least. Then you can tell me about this dream of yours."

"That would be lovely."

\* \* \* \*

Darcy stepped carefully down the darkened staircase. She suppressed the almost overwhelming urge to scream. She felt like the same powerless little girl she was when her parents effectively told her to butt out of Dianne's care, that she did not have any idea what was best. *You just don't understand*, she heard them say again. Only now, it was Matthew Dawson telling her to butt out, to leave the running of the hospital and its staff to him. *You just don't understand*. She was compelled to walk straight out the front door when she reached the bottom of the stair, the way she walked out on her family and a hopeless situation.

The man she'd left on the second floor deserved better than that. He deserved her help, maybe more. If she left, who would stand up to Matt? Who would fight for the people here while his judgment continued to deteriorate along with his health? *This is it*, she told herself. *This is the line in the sand. We don't encourage Curtis Ford with his talk of being an auto-making mogul and we can't encourage Matt with his desire to post twenty-four-hour security guards at patients' doors.*

Morning could not come fast enough. Matt was supposed to explain himself to the staff first thing and Darcy had her mind made up. Despite whatever he had to say, she was going to demand that he resign his post. It was time for him to step aside and leave the running of the hospital to those who were fit to run it. If she had to threaten him with the promise of a frank letter to the authorities describing his recent decisions, so be it.

She started down the east corridor toward the kitchen, muttering curses as she went. The hallway was soundless as though Saint Michael's was listening to every word of her complaints. The only other noise was the *click clack* of her shoes on the tiled floor echoing fore and aft. Everywhere shadows gathered boldly under the sparse yellow glow of the hospital nightlights. Darcy looked behind her at the long, darkened corridor. It was like looking into the gaping jaws of a great snake. It was then Darcy realized she had never been at the hospital this late at night. It was a very different place when the sun went down. She wondered how Nurse Tait could bear the isolation of the late shift all these years. How had she spent most of the night alone in here? Once Rory finished his cleaning rounds, he went home and left her on her own. *Clearly Miss Tait, like Wanda for that matter, is made of tougher stuff than me*, she mused and the *click*ing and *clack*ing of her shoes on the tiles resumed. She had crossed the patient lounge and was near the dining hall when the voice startled her.

"*Darse*," it called out to her.

She stopped. Turning, she searched her surroundings for Nurse Tait, prepared to laugh at her mild surprise and say, *I was just thinking about you.* Working opposite ends of the day, they had only spoken a handful of times and

Darcy did not think they were on a first-name basis, let alone using nicknames with one another. Still, she could play along. What should she call her in turn? Taits, Taters, Taitsie?

Darcy scanned the patient lounge and decided Miss Tait was not in there. The low lighting in the hallway was likely to blame for concealing the nurse. Darcy took a few steps toward dining hall, the report of her shoes now uncomfortably loud in the cavernous space.

"Hello?" Darcy called down the snake's throat.

"*Darse,*" came back. The voice was hushed as though ready to share a secret.

It stopped Darcy again. The tiny hairs on the back of her neck stood erect as though brushed by a cold-blooded hand. That voice...*Darse*...it occurred to her that only one person had ever called her that. She tried to greet the unseen visitor, though her voice failed her and it came out but a whisper.

"Di?"

Saint Michael's went silent again. Darcy peered into the blackened corridor and listened for her sister. "Dianne...is that you?"

"*Yes.*"

Darcy's heart jack hammered in her chest. She ran toward the detached voice. The clomping of her footfalls in the empty hall was near deafening.

"Di, where are you?" she called.

The improbability that her sister had really come to Saint Michael's did not get a toehold in Darcy's mind. Foremost was her guilt of abandoning her and the guilt of not calling and not writing since she left for Saint Andrews. The urge to find Dianne and comfort her took control. When she reached the lobby, Darcy slowed down.

"Di, where are you? Can you see me?" She turned around and around, searching the shadows for a trace of her sister. *She must be so scared*, she thought. *She needs me*. Tears spilled the rims of her eyes at the notion of Dianne lost in a strange place, begging for help from the one person in the world who truly understood her.

"*Darse...*"

Darcy spun around to face the west wing of the hospital. "I'm here, Di. Where are you?" she said, her voice cracking as despair lumped in her throat. "Please, tell me where you are."

*Click clack.*

Steps echoed through the empty space again, only this time, they were not hers. Darcy looked for their source, but Saint Michael's conspired to hide it from her.

*Click clack.*

She dried her eyes and kicked off her shoes. Barefoot, she hurried from the lobby and down the west corridor, following the footsteps that she decided could only be Dianne's.

*Click clack.*

The footfalls continued down the west corridor, just out of reach, just beyond the range of Darcy's vision.

*She's so close. Why won't she come to me?* Darcy wondered as she closed in on the sound. Then she saw her. Out of the gloom of the hallway appeared the slender figure of a woman with long dark hair. She wore a burgundy sweater and snug-fitting blue jeans. It was something Darcy would wear, and while it was not unusual for Di to raid her closet, this was somehow different. For a moment, Darcy thought she was looking at herself from behind. Her build was exactly the same, her walk, her posture. Could she have forgotten what it was really like to look upon her twin?

"Dianne, where are you going?"

The woman stopped and tilted her head to look over her shoulder. Darcy stopped as well, struck by the expression Di wore. It was staid and serene. Gone was any evidence of inner turmoil, of the struggle to reason that had etched her face for all her days. The illness that had made her so radically different from her sister had finally loosened its grip. *"Why did you leave me?"* she asked.

The question swelled the lump in Darcy's throat and her eyes overflowed again. "I'm sorry, Di. I never wanted to...it's just Mom and Dad, they..."

"I needed you," Dianne said, and continued her pace down the hallway.

Darcy followed. "Di, please, let me help you now."

Dianne turned to her right and stepped in front of a patient's door. She slowly raised a hand and laid it on the handle. *"You can't,"* she said and the look she gave Darcy cut her deeper than any blade ever could. *"It's too late for that."*

"Di...wait."

Dianne turned the handle and walked into the room, the heavy door closing behind her like a thunderclap in the lifeless hallway. Darcy rubbed at her eyes and nose and followed, but when she tried to open the door, she found it locked. The back of her neck went prickly again. She looked through the observation window. The room was vacant—the cot folded up and pushed to the corner.

*Keys*, she thought. *Where are my keys?* She plunged her hands in her pockets, searching for her key ring while focusing on the empty room. *She's in there. I don't know how, but she is.* Darcy found the ring in her jacket and flipped through them for the ground floor skeleton key. Though, when she went to shove the key in the hasp, the breath was knocked out of her and the key ring dropped to the floor. Instead of reaching for it, her hand trembled and covered her gaping mouth. On the door handle hung a heart pendant on a chain. She recognized it at once. She wore its twin around her neck.

The sight of Dianne's pendant sapped her last ounce of strength and she fell to her knees on the unforgiving tiles. Her shoulders heaved as she gave in to the tempest in her chest and unreined sobbing took over. *She was here. She was.* Darcy balled the pendant up in her fist and squeezed hard as if to ensure it was tangible. *I'm holding the proof here in my hand.* All at once her tears were interrupted as an ugly thought nudged its way in. Darcy opened her hand and studied the bauble in it. Then she felt her chest. That familiar tiny swell under her top was missing. She reached a hand up her shirt and felt around for her pendant. It was gone. Again she looked in her hand at the pendant that could only be *hers*, and let it fall to the floor. She buried her face and wailed again as this new hurt dug in deep.

Then there was an arm around her. John Cundiff's touch didn't frighten her in the least despite his approach going undetected. She was numbed.

"Oh, my God...Darcy, what happened?" he said.

She could not answer him, only cry. He knelt on the floor beside her and she turned away so he would not see her grief-twisted face and running nose. Then another arm was around her and she sank in to the coarse fabric of his scrub top. He did not ask any more questions, did not tell her to hush or that everything would be all right. He merely held her at the end of the dark hallway where she had followed her demons.

\* \* \* \*

"So, what do you think?"

"I think it tastes like dirty sweat socks."

"Well tea's a good drink for times like this. It should give you a boost."

"Is there anything this drink isn't supposed to do?"

"I wish it could make you tell me what happened in that hallway."

Darcy looked up at the orderly sitting across the small table that served as Elmer Savoie's desk. She still could not make sense of what happened. All she wanted was to be alone for a while to sort things out and come to a reasonable explanation. It seemed that having someone around who cared about her meant that isolation was no longer an option. John's deep brown eyes bore the genuine look of concern. He planted them squarely on her and let the silence build. It was almost too much for her to handle. She looked around the kitchen. It was stark and cold under the fluorescent lights and the thick smell of congealing fry oil had overpowered the usual aromas of home cooking. Myriad pots and pans occupied a tall metal shelf beside the gas range. Elmer's knives were sheathed on a rack that hung on the wall. The stainless steel counters and appliances had been polished to a shine. It was sterile. It was as good a place as any to be dissected and studied.

"I thought I saw my sister." Darcy said it all at once, as though saying the words slowly would give her too much time to reconsider sharing. Then it was out there. She looked back to Cundiff, expecting a new expression on his face, one that involved his brow furrowing and eyes shifting away. Instead what she found was only more concern.

"I was coming down here to make some tea...and someone called my name." Darcy paused. "So I followed the voice down the west wing and that's where I saw her...I saw Dianne."

"Umm, what was she doing?"

"She went into one of the rooms...and just disappeared." Darcy touched the swell of her pendant, back at home on her chest. "I know she wasn't really there. It was just so real."

Cundiff leaned back in his seat and chewed his bottom lip as though processing what Darcy had told him. His gaze drifted around the kitchen at nothing in particular. Finally he said, "I think we've both been working a little too hard. Things like this are bound to happen when you put in long hours and don't get enough sleep."

"I know and I've been thinking about Dianne a lot lately. I always do. Sometimes these incessant thoughts can manifest." What she did not tell the orderly was that there has to be an underlying issue in order to experience such an episode, that the hallucination was not the problem, merely the symptom. She did not want to admit that to herself, let alone the man she was growing very fond of. She set her teacup down on the table. "I've been thinking about something else a lot recently, too."

"Oh?"

"It was something that happened the night we went to Klewey's place."

Cundiff wore a blank look.

"Remember I told you about his grandmother wanting to *look* at me?"

"Yeah, I remember you were a little freaked out after."

"It wasn't the touching that troubled me. It was something she said. Did Klewes ever talk to you about her? Did he ever tell you anything, I don't know, *weird* about her?"

"No." Cundiff put his teacup down and shifted in his seat. "He never talks about her, never has. Other folks around here sure do, though."

"What do they say about her?"

"Darcy, I don't really see how it matters what people say. I told you the Klewes were never really accepted around here. Folks say all kinds of stuff... whatever hurts, you know?"

"If I knew anything about her, it might help me make sense of something, that's all."

"This is stupid..." the orderly leaned forward and laced his fingers together. "Some people say she's like a witch or something. They say she's into some kind of voodoo she brought up here with her from Louisiana. Like I said, they say a lot of mean shit about that family and Klewey's my friend, so I don't listen and neither should you."

Darcy dismissed the notion of Cecile being a witch though she felt there was some small degree of truth to it. Not in what people called her, but in what led people to call her that. Sometimes the unexplainable is classified as supernatural. It makes it easier for people to categorize things that way. There are many who would likely say that she followed a ghost down the west corridor earlier.

"What does old Cecile have to do with any of this, anyway?"

"When she was...touching my face, I felt like she was reading more than my looks, it felt like she was...I don't want to say this." Darcy cleared her throat. "I was thinking about Dianne at the time. It was just a passing thought, here one second and gone the next, but I wondered if Cecile would be able to tell us apart. That was all."

"Yeah, so?"

"Then Cecile told me something...really strange. She told me I had to help myself. Then she said something like, 'the brighter the light, the darker the shadow'."

"That just sounds like gibberish to me. She's very old, you know."

"Well that gibberish summed up my relationship with Dianne in ways I've never admitted to anyone. You see, I was always the smart daughter, always the good one, the fun one. I got the academic awards. I was good at sports. I know I was the favorite.

"Then Dianne's behavior went bad. She started acting up in school. She slept all the time. Then came the imaginary friend. Not long after, she was diagnosed with juvenile schizophrenia. My parents took her out of school, she lost all her friends. It was a nightmare. Only, I kept on getting straight A's. I kept winning track meets. I kept being the favorite." Darcy gave up battling her tears and they ran free.

Cundiff pulled his chair closer and put a hand on her knee. "That's hardly your fault, Darcy."

"She was supposed to have so much more. She was supposed to have everything I had. Dianne and I...we're twins. We are two halves of the same embryo. We're practically the same person, or we were supposed to be anyway. Though, if you ask Cecile, I'm the bright light and Dianne's the shadow. The brighter I shine, the darker she is."

"Oh, Darcy, no. That can't be true."

"It is." Darcy's gaze fell to the floor. "That's the worst part of all of this...it's *true*. My parents would be the first people to tell you."

"Maybe, you should talk to them about this. I mean, it's no wonder you thought you saw her. I think you've been carrying this around far too long."

"Longer than you know."

"Darcy, there is nothing wrong with you trying to be the best person you can be. I think, in a way, you owe it to your sister to try because she can't do it for herself. You know what, I look at you and honestly I don't see a bright light. I see a beautiful woman who starts every day wanting to make the world a better place. I see a woman who works tirelessly to care for very troubled people. She understands that doing the right thing usually means doing it the hard way, but she does it anyway. She stands up for what she believes in and if you're lucky enough to be accepted in her life, she would do anything and everything you asked of her. Sometimes, when I see you walking the halls in this old hospital, I have to wonder if *you're* really there or if I'm just dreaming you."

Darcy did not know what to say. She could not imagine ever hearing anything so endearing again in her life. Tears were threatening once more.

"I said too much," Cundiff admitted, laughing uncomfortably.

"No...thank you, John." Darcy reached over and took his hand in hers.

"Oh, look, I've abandoned my post for almost an hour now," he said, looking for a way out of a situation that seemed to get away from him.

Darcy let the orderly make his retreat. "I hope your prisoner didn't escape his cell while you weren't looking," she said.

"Well, if he did, I hope he didn't eat our pizza."

# Chapter Eighteen

Matt limped up the front steps to Saint Michael's. The walk from Stanley's house was a challenge for a man who had awoken in a seated position on the dining room floor with his back against a large box of books. When first waking, he had felt almost comfortable. The cardboard had buckled under his weight and molded to the curvature of his back. Though as soon as he moved, his stiff body complained emphatically. His head began to throb and his hand joined in rhythm. He had to look at his cast to jog the memory of his fracture. Then it all came rushing back—Dykeman grabbing his hand and squeezing until it popped and crackled like bubble wrap.

When he hobbled to the kitchen, he read the wall clock. It was after eight. The sun was blazing through the eastern windows. As he teetered in the center of the kitchen, rubbing sleep from his eyes and yawning, he could hardly believe he had spent the night searching for the magical book that Fisher wanted. The task seemed all the more foolish as daylight burned away the superstitious conversation he had with the writer. What had been of the greatest importance the night before, now had him snickering to himself. He had bigger problems, besides. He had a dangerous patient on his hands. He had to address the staff and tell them about it. Not to mention, somewhere out there, was Prichard's killer.

As Matt crested the steps leading to the hospital's front door, he set his mind on striking one of those problems from his list. How much should he tell his staff? Was it enough to fill them in on Dykeman's history and the murders he committed? Inside the lobby he found that he did not have time to decide. They were waiting for him.

Wanda and Nurse Tait were there with Elmer and Rory. They stood conversing in front of the covered archangel statue. Mister Cundiff and Mister Klewes were seated on the stairs. Their chatter stopped abruptly when Matt entered and all eyes went to him. Suddenly he felt very conscious of his appearance. He made a futile attempt to brush the wrinkles out of the shirt he had slept in and tame his shaggy hair. Stepping forward to greet him was Darcy. She did not look well-rested either. "Good morning, Doctor Dawson," she said folding her arms over her chest. The look she met him with was anything but cordial.

"Good morning," Matt said. "Hi everyone."

They remained silent.

"Thanks to those of you who are staying after shift change. I appreciate you waiting around..." Matt lost any idea of what to say. He instantly regretted not planning his statement better. "I'm sure you all have concerns about some of the...umm stuff that's been going on around here and I will do my best to inform you of what I know."

"Why do you want Mister Dykeman guarded?" Darcy cut straight to the point.

Matt took a breath. His sharp young successor was not going to go easy on him and it came as no surprise. Her patience was near exhaustion. It was written all over her face. "I'm afraid that Stanley may not have been very forthright about the circumstances that brought Mister Dykeman here." Matt picked his way through his minefield of a response. If he blamed Stanley openly, he would lose the trust of the staff that had loyally supported him. "Also, I haven't been sharing all that I have learned about the patient, either." He paused while he tried to figure out the best place to start Dykeman's story.

"Why don't you tell us why that poor man has been kept in a medicated coma for as long as anyone here can remember?" Darcy urged.

"In short, it's because he is dangerous."

"He's an old man."

"He broke my hand."

"He was in seizure because you and your father had him over-medicated."

"It was necessary. Stanley took precautions with Dykeman. He knew what he was dealing with and now I do too."

"What he was dealing with...he's a human being, for God's sake."

The rest of the staff looked on like spectators at a tennis match while the doctors fired back and forth. Matt clenched his jaw and he shook his head. "You don't understand, Darcy. You don't know the whole story."

"Then by all means, fill me in."

"Yes, fill me in too while you're at it!"

Everyone turned to the front door where Chief Lumley made his entrance. One of his deputies followed closely—a thin young man who scarcely filled out his uniform. "I'd like to hear the whole story myself," Lumley said, removing his hat.

"Chief, this is a private meeting," Matt said. "I'd be happy to talk later, but for now I'll have to ask you to leave."

"I'm afraid you'll have to cancel your meeting, Doctor Dawson. You have more urgent business down at the station house." The officers strode into the lobby and flanked Matt. Lumley pulled the handcuffs off his belt. "I don't need to put these on you, do I?" he asked, eying Matt's cast.

"What in the hell is this about?" Darcy said.

The chief ignored the question and spoke directly to Matt. "Doctor Matthew Dawson I am placing you under arrest for the murder of Phillip Prichard."

Klewes and Wanda exchanged glances while the rest of the staff gasped.

"As well as for the murder of Eric Fisher," Lumley finished.

Matt locked eyes with the officer and his mouth went slack. "What...no... Fisher's not..."

"Oh, he sure as hell *is*..." Lumley corrected, "but, you know that, don't you?"

The deputy made his way over to the staff gathered by the stairs. They parted for him to pass and he went to the foot of the covered statue. He reached for the sheet and pulled it down. "Umm, Chief," he said. "You were right."

"Of course I was."

"Right about what?" Darcy asked and like her other query, it went unanswered.

"Doctor Dawson, you have the right to remain silent. Anything you say can be used against you in a court of law." Lumley continued to read Matt his Miranda Rights while the others looked on in awe.

*This is happening. This is really happening,* Matt thought. When the chief finished relaying his rights, Matt said, "I didn't do this. I have an alibi." It was intended for the staff to hear as much as it was for the police officer.

It was the officer who responded. "Tell it to your lawyer," he said. Then he gestured to the entrance. "Let's go, Doctor. Your car is waiting."

Darcy followed them to the door. "Matt, don't worry," she said. "I'll arrange a lawyer."

He looked back to her over his shoulder, his eyes bulging with panic. "Just take care of things here," he said. "*Watch* him, Darcy. You know who I mean. *Watch him.*"

\* \* \* \*

Darcy searched the drawers of Matt's desk for a directory or appointment book or something that might contain the name and number of an attorney Matt used before. The desk was empty aside from a box of envelopes, a few pens and some bills. She decided to give up and turn to the Saint John Yellow Pages. She knew Matt had dealt with a lawyer in Saint Andrews when settling his father's estate, but a local lawyer was likely the last thing he needed. Matt's troubles ran deep. Charged with two murders, he needed representation that would not have the slightest hometown bias. Phillip Prichard's murder was all anyone in town could talk about. That is, until this latest murder. Darcy imagined it was the new hot topic at the salon and the pharmacy. Of course the local authorities would turn to the man who came to town just as the murders started. She wondered why she was not a suspect. After all, she was new too.

*Two murders*, she thought. *What if he did...*

She shoved the idea out of her mind. Matthew Dawson was definitely a mess and a poor employer and a questionable psychiatrist, but a killer? *No way.* He was simply a good person who got in over his head with the loss of his father and trying to run this place and all. It could happen to anyone. *Right?*

She slumped back in the chair and tried to rein in her racing thoughts, but when she closed her eyes she saw Matt being escorted out of the hospital by the police. The look on his face, his wide eyes. It was honest fear. Though he was not afraid for himself. He told Darcy to 'watch him,' to watch Dykeman.

*I can't get caught up in that*, she reasoned. She pulled the top drawer open to search for a phone book. It was in there. So was a ratty, old folder bulging with papers. She laid it on the desktop with the intention of taking it to the cabinet later and filing it where it belonged. Then she read the name on it. *Hmmm...speak of the devil.* She studied the folder with its frayed edges and yellowed paper contents. Then she pushed it to the corner of the desktop. *No...I can't get caught up in that.* Darcy opened the phone book and flipped to the page populated by attorneys. She circled a few of the numbers and paused. She looked back to the thick file on the corner of the desk. Maybe she should wait to contact a lawyer. If she called now, there might be too much emotion in her voice...too much doubt. She did not want Matt's potential defenders to sense that she believed he might actually be guilty. She put the Yellow Pages down and eyed the folder.

"Watch him," Matt had said. "He's dangerous."

Darcy slid the file in front of her. "All right Doctor, you say he's dangerous. Let's find out why." She opened the folder and started reading the first page, and before long, she found out.

\* \* \* \*

Darcy flung her bag over her shoulder and hurried from the office. In her haste, she narrowly avoided a collision with Cundiff in the hallway. Reviewing Dykeman's file had left her nerves frayed and the near-accident hardly registered with her. She continued for the exit.

Cundiff looked puzzled as he watched her walk away. "Hey, where are you off to in such a rush?"

"I'm going to the station to see if I can talk to Matt."

"Hold on a second," he said.

Darcy stopped a few yards down the hall and waited for whatever it was he had to say. It seemed he was having trouble finding the words. He was likely trying to come up with a nice way to say, *you look like hell*. Darcy broke the silence first. "Why aren't you at home getting some rest? You were up all night."

"I slept for an hour after the meeting, but with all that's happened, I thought I should be here."

"This business with Matt getting arrested will be straightened out by the end of the day. Before you know it, things will be back to normal...or as normal as things get around here."

"I can only hope you're right." The expression he wore hinted at underlying doubt. It said, *what if he really killed those people?*

Darcy eyed the hallway anxiously.

"Do you want me to come with you?"

"Umm, no, that's okay. I just have to discuss a patient with him...if I can see him, that is. I shouldn't take long."

"All right, just don't go getting yourself arrested, too. We're shorthanded here as it is."

Darcy gave him a fluttering, nervous smile. She tried to come off calm and collected, but after reading Dykeman's file, how could she be? Her stomach was in knots. She was a lousy actor, and judging by Cundiff's demeanor, he was too. Despite his excuse, the only reason he had come in to the hospital was to see her. As unfamiliar with budding romance as she was, she could still see that. She made a silent vow to make it up to him. "See you soon," she said and made for the hallway.

The mood in the hospital was dour—more so than usual. It was like the people of Saint Michael's had themselves braced for the next inevitable catastrophe. The patient lounge was still and silent as she walked past. Even the residents seemed more mired in their various ailments today. Hannah Wilkins was slouched on the green couch beside Mallory Killen, but no words passed between them. Even Curtis Ford, who told endless stories of the car business, was keeping mum.

In the lobby she came upon Wanda and Klewes. Their hushed chatter ceased as Darcy approached. She smiled at them and headed for the main entrance. There was little doubt what they were talking about. The small-town gossip would be relentless now. *Gossip.* The very word heightened the tension in the pit of her stomach. She stopped and turned. "Wanda, do you have work to do?"

The veteran nurse stood straight, clearly taken by surprise at the tone the young doctor summoned. "Yes, Doctor. I'll see to it." Instantly she was walking away, leaving the orderly alone to face Darcy's scorn. He scratched the back of his head uncomfortably.

"Mister Klewes, I believe Doctor Dawson asked you to watch a certain patient's door."

"Yes, Doctor."

"I don't think it's down here."

"No...it's ah...I'm going." Klewes backed his way to the stairs and for a moment Darcy thought he might trip over the bottom riser, but he turned just in time step atop it. She watched him go. The bloated file in her shoulder bag had her taking precautions just like it had Matt and Stanley before him. Now maybe Matt could tell her why.

\* \* \* \*

She waited at the folding table in one of the police station's two interview rooms. Getting in had proved easier than she thought. Thankfully, Chief Lumley was out of the station on business so she did not have to contend with him or even his deputies. Instead, it was Deason Klewes who greeted her at the help desk. When she saw his youthfully handsome face, his neatly trimmed moustache, she was instantly reminded of Mrs. Klewes telling her that her nephew had taken a job at the jail. He smiled widely when he recognized her. "Hi Doctor Collins," he had said. Darcy knew then, that getting access to Matt would not be a problem. "The Chief didn't say he *couldn't* have visitors," Deason added. A minute later, she was waiting in the interview room.

The door opposite the one she had entered from rattled briefly and opened. Matt stepped through, accompanied by the young Klewes. If it was possible, Matt looked even more haggard than ever. His flesh had taken on a near-gray hue aside from the rings around his eyes that were red going on purple. The clothes he wore made him look more like a beggar than a doctor and she dared not get close enough to hazard his odor.

"I just have to discuss a couple of patients with the doctor. It shouldn't take long."

"When you're finished, just knock on that door, Doctor Collins," Deason said as he left the two alone. Darcy thanked him and wondered how long he could keep his job as turnkey if he allowed the prisoners to dictate the schedule. Matt got himself seated across the table from her. The room was stuffy and small, nearly ten by ten, and it was painted a grungy yellow that led one to believe the walls were originally white and had been nicotine stained. The customary one-way glass window that was a fixture in almost every police station in the movies she had seen was absent. Yet, it did little to assuage her feeling of being watched.

"How are you doing?" she asked, instantly feeling silly for saying it.

Matt just shook his head slowly. "Lumley confiscated my painkillers. I need them."

"I'll see that you get them. Legally, you can't be denied medication," she added as if he did not know. "I've arranged a lawyer. His name is Kelleher. He's on his way from Saint John, should be here soon. He said you're not to say a word until he gets here. I *Googled* him. He's got a pretty good track record with mur—" She caught herself before she said the ghastly word. Matt's eyes rolled up to meet hers. "...with cases like yours," she corrected.

"I hope he's skilled at working miracles. I haven't been formally charged yet, but they're already building the gallows."

"Matt, you're innocent and we'll prove it."

"The evidence...Darcy, you don't know. There's a link between the murders. Right now, it looks like I'm the link. At least you'd have to be crazy to believe otherwise."

*Crazy.* The word stung her. She hated that word. In other circumstances, Matt never would have accepted use of the term. In fact, he would have berated anyone who did. He would have said it was inappropriate, insensitive... facile. Stuck in this dire situation, the word spilled from his mouth with ease. When men are truly afraid, ideals are the first things to be lost. "Do you think it would be the first *crazy* thing I've heard?" she asked.

Matt gathered a breath and released it slowly. He reminded her of a patient who did not want to broach a painful subject. It was likely all he thought about minute after minute, but talking about it aloud would give it new life. "The crime scenes," he blurted. "There were markings on the walls at both crime scenes. It is some kind of symbol. I seem to be the only man in town who is familiar with it."

Darcy's eyes went to the bag on the floor beside her chair. She reached into it and retrieved the thick file. It grabbed Matt's attention when she set it on the table in front of her. "You're not the only one familiar with it anymore."

"You found...did you read it?"

"I've never seen anything quite like it."

"Then you know..."

"What the hell is a man like Dykeman doing at Saint Michael's? He should be in a high-security hospital, not some twelve-bed home."

Matt went silent again. Darcy let him take his time as his demeanor reflected signs of an inner debate. When he finally decided to share, little by little he told her the story. It was a story about a young Stanley Dawson and his childhood friend, Morry Dykeman, and the finding of an old book called the *Sacra Obscurum*. He told of the grisly murder that followed and Morry's subsequent incarceration. He told her all he supposed about the transfer that saw Dykeman placed in Stanley's care and the relative peace that endured until Matt took over the hospital and a man named Fisher came to visit. Then Prichard's body was found and next, Fisher's. He told her the whole ugly tale concluding with the evidence against him. "That bloody symbol was smeared on the wall at the Prichard murder scene. There was another one on the wall of Fisher's motel room where the police found his body. They found the most damning piece of evidence against me in that room, as well. Apparently Fisher was beaten to death with a large piece of marble."

Darcy thought for a second, then pictured the headless statue in the hospital lobby. A chill marched the length of her backbone. The killer was there. He had been so close. She released a wavering sigh as she tried to process everything. There had to be another explanation, something they were missing. Her gaze drifted over the open folder in front of her.

"It's got to be a copycat killer, someone who knows about the Dykeman case."

"Yes, that's what I told Lumley."

"What did he say to that?"

"Oh, he agreed wholeheartedly. Only he said *I* was the copycat. He accused me of trying to relive my patient's crimes."

It came to her all at once and she looked up at Matt, awestruck. "You think Dykeman did it."

Matt's brow stiffened. "It's the only explanation."

"Oh, my God, Matt, no. It's impossible."

"I would have said so too, Darcy. That was before he broke my hand." Matt winced as he closed his fingers as much as his cast would allow. "The strength he had...I couldn't break free for all I was worth. The way he looked at me. That wasn't the old man who stares out the window all day. It was *something* else. Now, I don't know what he and Stanley did with that book sixty years ago and the only man who might know had his skull crushed last night. I just know, whatever they did, it wasn't...natural."

"Matt, reason through this," Darcy said. "Dykeman couldn't have killed Eric Fisher. You asked for him to be guarded last night and he *was*. Mister Cundiff watched him all night long." *Well, aside from the hour he spent consoling me after I saw my sister strolling the halls.*

Matt rubbed his beard stubble with his good hand. "He found a way," he said resolutely. "There is something wrong at Saint Michael's. I don't know what it is, but it goes beyond all the troubled patients that have come and gone over the years. It's something in the fiber of the building. I can't tell you how many times I've felt eyes on me when I was alone in there. It's like the shadows are hiding things."

*The brighter the light, the darker the shadow...*

"Once it even felt like something touched my shoulder, but when I turned around, nothing was there. The sudden temperature swings, the strange smells and the noise...or lack of. Did you ever notice how quiet it is all the time? That's just not right."

Darcy was hardly listening. All she could think of was Dianne—how she picked up her scent as she followed her down the hall, the way that she *felt* her presence in that unexplainable way only twins can *feel* each other. To her it was real. Even the passage of time did not diminish the experience. *I agree with you, Matt*, she thought. *There is something wrong at Saint Michael's. And, if you're crazy, maybe I am too.*

\* \* \* \*

Darcy listened to the ringing and willed Cundiff to answer his phone. One more ring and his voice mail would kick in. How could she sum up everything she had to tell him in a brief message? It had taken Matt an hour to relate the story.

"Pick up, for Christ's sake, John," she said under her breath, though loud enough for the couple walking ahead of her on the sidewalk to hear. They turned in unison to ogle her. She pushed between them and hurried on toward the hospital. The sun had dipped behind the Appalachian foothills to the west, but its residual flares poured blood across the sky. Visitors to Saint Andrews were cramming the restaurant patios. Their jovial commotion filled the evening air. Glasses clinked, silverware scraped plates, but it was the incessant laughter that bothered Darcy most. *Blasted tourists*, she thought. *What was it John said? Our lives are going on here and they're just passing through.*

\* \* \* \*

Darcy found the orderlies talking in the second floor corridor outside Dykeman's room. Both were in uniform, seated on office chairs they had wheeled into the hall. Cundiff was there to relieve Klewey for the night shift. When they saw her crest the stairs, they both got up and greeted her. "How is the doctor holding up?" Cundiff asked.

Darcy did not know how to answer that. *He's not good*, she thought of saying. *He's in terrible shape*, would be more accurate. Her stomach turned with a profound sense of foreboding that told her if they did not act fast, something horrible was going to happen—maybe another murder—maybe one of them. "He's okay for now." Darcy fumbled with the shoulder strap of her bag. The heavy folder within, made it hang uncomfortably on her slight frame. She realized the burden was more than physical. A tension headache had settled in behind her eyes and it throbbed with her every heartbeat, her every blink.

Cundiff read her discomfort and took the bag from her. "So, what did he say?" he asked, setting the bag down on the floor.

"He's innocent."

"Of course he said that," Klewes mused.

"No...he *is* innocent. Someone else killed those people." She eyed the locked door down the hall behind the orderlies. How in the world could she make them believe the killer was behind it? Did *she* really believe it? "What details have you heard about the murders?"

"Lots," Cundiff said. "I don't know how much is true, though."

"Yeah, I heard they were occult style killings, like sacrifices or something," Klewes offered. "The rumors are out of control."

"Did you hear why Matt is a suspect?"

Cundiff looked at Klewes. He folded his arms and seemed to search the floor for a diplomatic way to respond. "Umm...I heard that there was something at both murders that only the doctor had knowledge of. I haven't heard what that is, but that's bad right? I mean it must be hard to defend against that."

"It's true. He has intimate knowledge of the murders, but he's not the only one who does. What did Stanley tell you guys about Mister Dykeman?"

The orderlies exchanged another look. "About Dykeman...*that* Dykeman?" Klewes asked pointing his thumb toward the door behind him. "What does he have to do with it?"

"Matt thinks he's responsible."

Klewes laughed aloud. Cundiff looked on Darcy with concern stamped across his face. "You're kidding, right?" Klewes said, his big grin starting to fade. "*Right?*"

"I wish I was, because I know how this sounds. The short story is, Dykeman murdered his family when he was fifteen years old and there are details about the recent murders that match that case."

"Well, it's got to be someone else doing these murders," Cundiff said. "I mean, Matt can't be the only one who knows about that stuff."

"Unfortunately, it was a pretty good secret. The only people still alive who know the particulars are Matt and Chief Lumley."

"This is...no...this is nuts," Klewes said, walking to the patient's door. He looked at Dykeman through the observation window. The elderly man was still in slumber on his cot. "You think this guy has been getting out of here when we're not looking and killing people? Really? I have to lift him from his bed to his chair every day. I have to feed him. I have to carry him to the bathtub. Darcy..."

"That man has been given enough Lithium to tranquilize a horse every day of his life since he was a teenager," Darcy said. "Until recently, when Matt lowered his dosage. That change in medication coincides with Prichard's murder."

"So, because his meds have been changed, he can let himself out now and *kill* people?" Klewes asked, his voice rising. "Then why do I still have to change his fucking diapers?"

Cundiff winced at Klewe's tone, but he did not challenge a word he said.

"I think he's had help getting out of his room," Darcy said. "I don't know how else to say it. There is something here at Saint Michael's...something, I don't know...off." Battling burgeoning tears, she could no longer look the orderlies in the eyes. Their expressions would tell her what they thought of her nonsense. "Matt has felt it too. He told me. Normally I would have blamed the pressure he has been under the last few weeks, but as he was telling me every strange thing he's experienced, all I could think about was how I followed my *sister* through these halls last night. She lives a thousand miles away, but here she was. I followed her. I spoke to her. *Fuck*, I could *smell* her." She rubbed her eyes. "If that can happen, if that is possible, then maybe a locked door can be opened."

Both men were silent for a moment while Darcy fought to rein in her emotions. She sniffed loudly and the sound resonated in the vast hall.

"Well, that's good enough for me," Cundiff said, breaking the silence.

Klewes gawked at his friend. Darcy could hardly believe his reaction, either. He went and stood in front of her and took her hands in his. "So what do we do now?"

"We need Matt."

"Okay," Cundiff said, turning Klewe's way. "We need Matt."

"Whatever," Klewes said with little interest. "I'm sure you can post bail after he goes before the judge."

"It may be too late by then," Darcy said. "We need him now. There are lives at stake."

"What are you saying, you want to bust him out?" Klewes said, stifling more laughter.

"It's not busting if Deason opens the door," Cundiff said. "He'd do it if you asked him to."

"Oh, no...no way! He'll be in a world of shit if he lets Matt go free."

"Not if Matt can do something to stop the murders and prove his innocence," Darcy insisted.

Klewes turned to Cundiff. "Whoa, whoa, whoa—stop and think about this. You really want to put us all in this kind of trouble just because...just because *the girl* you're chasing asked you to?"

"Yes," Cundiff said immediately. "Yes, I do. She's right about this. She's right about the hospital. There's something up with this place. I've felt it, too. She's also right about Matt."

"Fine, if that's true, let the court decide. If he's really innocent, they'll let him go free."

"Do you really think we can just leave it up to them? You of all people? You know better than anyone what happens when this town passes judgment. Matt deserves better than that. He may not be one of us, exactly, but he's Stanley's son. You remember Stanley, right? He was the man who gave you a second chance when no one else would."

"Yes, I remember Stanley," Klewes said, taking a step toward Cundiff. "I remember him every fucking day. Don't you *ever* think I'd forget what he did for me, John Cundiff! When everyone in this town was slurring me behind my back, he treated me with respect. He treated me like family. Saint Michael's became my family. Wanda, Rory, even that idiot in the kitchen means more to me than you'll ever know. And you know something else? If Stanley was here today, he wouldn't ask me to break his son out of jail.

"Now, I was raised in the belief that there are forces at work in the world that we can't begin to understand. I know what you mean about this place. There's another side to Saint Michael's, one you don't want to mess with. I respect that, but even so, I can't go along with you two...not this—"

A booming *thump* interrupted Klewes. Cundiff and Darcy looked past him, down the hall, where the sound originated. Klewes turned. His gaze settled on Dykeman's door just as it started to rattle in its jamb.

Klewes looked back to the others, and took a tentative step toward the vibrating door. Then Cundiff was beside him and they both closed in cautiously. Darcy called for them to stop, to keep their distance from the chattering door, but they paid no heed. The door continued to shake, violently now, as its lock was put to the test. The orderlies still moved in, half crouched as if sneaking up on some unseen burglar. They eyed each other as though attempting to formulate some silent plan, though each expressed only confusion at the situation.

Darcy wondered what they would do if they found old Mister Dykeman on the other side of the door, trying to force it open. She hoped they would have the good sense to keep it closed.

The door suddenly stopped vibrating.

The orderlies froze.

After a moment Klewes continued his approach, seemingly intent on stealing a peek inside the room. He went to his knees, touched the frame and began raising his head to the bottom of the observation window. His breathing became heavy as he slowly rose to eye level with the glass. He hadn't managed a look inside when another loud *thump* sounded overhead.

Darcy screamed.

Klewes fell backward and scrambled to get away from the door. When he looked up he saw the shadow of a hand on the inside of the transom window over the doorway. Then there was another hand beside it, like a pair of overgrown spiders against the frosted glass. Darcy yelled something incoherent and Cundiff grabbed his partner by the arm and pulled him brusquely away. Klewes got to his feet and the three of them watched the unspeakable sight unfold.

A pale and weathered hand appeared. It reached through the open transom window. The window had a slight, four-inch opening, but the arm passed easily through the meager gap and slapped the wall outside the room. Another arm shoved its way through the opening. Darcy's screaming ceased. Aghast, they all watched on without so much as a word until they saw the head emerge. It gave a crunching sound as it compressed and flattened like a deflated football so it could squeeze through. Klewes gasped as the hairless and liver-spotted head was reshaped. Darcy released another horrified shriek. Cundiff stood in front of her to shield her from the gruesome display. Once clear of the window, the mutilated cranium popped and cracked some more while it returned to its natural shape. Its blank eyes opened and it turned their way.

Snakelike, it dragged the rest of its unlikely body through the window. Hips and legs went boneless as they plied and molded to fit through the pinched gap. Hand over hand the thing climbed down the wall, unrecognizable body parts in tow, tangled in light blue johnny shirt fabric. It slapped against the floor like a wet garbage bag. For a moment it lay in a crumpled mass of ruined flesh. Then joints snapped back into place and bones set with sickening crunches. The thing began to resemble a man, not as divinely intended, but some mistaken recreation. It twisted and bent and soon it was standing, a more familiar bipedal form wearing a backward hospital johnny. While its grotesque skull held fast, the gangly thing twisted at the waist in a full circle so that finally torso and feet pointed the same direction. Black, lifeless eyes, doll's eyes, never moved from the trio of stunned onlookers.

Klewes pulled one of the chairs in front of him and held it there in crude defense. "S-stay back," he hollered, like a desperate hiker might holler at a hungry bear. Cundiff backed away with arms outstretched and herded Darcy back as well. She could hear him mumbling something in rushed words. Was he praying? Darcy continued backward, guided by Cundiff's retreat. If not for his prodding, she would not have budged. The thing down the hall, the thing her mind was unable to comprehend, had left her paralyzed. Even her voice had frozen over and—not for lack of wanting—she could no longer scream.

The creature that used to be Dykeman, that wore his lined and pasty skin, turned away from them and entered the room at the end of the hall.

"Where's he going?" Cundiff whispered. Klewes offered no answer. He stepped slowly after Dykeman, the office chair squeaking as it rolled before him. Cundiff followed and Darcy stood where he left her, still unable to move.

The orderlies approached the room—its door was half open, but the darkness beyond concealed all. The other side was Stanley Dawson's former office-turned-patient quarters, as yet unoccupied.

"What are we gonna do?" Cundiff asked in hushed urgency. "We can't..."

"I don't know," Klewes said, though indecision did little to slow him down. He neared the door. His partner followed close behind. The darkened room still gave no hint of Dykeman's whereabouts. He could have been hiding behind the door or against the wall, ready to grab at them, perhaps turn them into wretched and spoiled creatures like himself. How many times had they each touched him, carried him like a child from bed to chair, chair to bath? Now they pursued him into the darkness. They followed like hunters on safari would a dangerous beast.

Klewes reached the room first. Without hesitation, he pushed the door open. Cundiff told him to be careful, though he made no motion to take the lead. In fact, he stopped his advance when Klewes plunged his arm into the darkness. Both held a breath. Klewes reached the wall switch, curled a finger under it. What they had already witnessed would stain their psyche for the rest of their lives. It would be the subject of ongoing night terrors, provided they lived through this horrid event. Had they seen the worst of it, or was the worst waiting in the dark beyond?

Klewes flipped the switch.

The contents of the room flashed to being under the brilliance of the fixtures. Within the stark white walls were two cots and matching round-cornered dressers. There was a floor-to-ceiling privacy curtain between the two bed sets. It had been left open and bunched against the wall. Klewes stooped in the doorway and looked under the cots. Nothing—even the pristine cornflower-blue floor did not show the slightest smudge or footprint. The orderly stepped inside and yanked the door away from the wall to check behind it. The room was empty.

"How did…" Cundiff left his thought unspoken as he entered the room. He silently gestured at the curtain gathered between the beds. Klewes took his meaning and fell in behind Cundiff as he moved stealthily toward it. The curtain was scarcely enough to conceal a person. The orderlies were cautious all the same. After all, Dykeman had managed to pass through the meager gap in the transom window. Now anything was possible.

Cundiff raised his hands to the curtain. He pushed. The curtain went flat against the wall. Allowing himself to exhale, he pulled his hands back. They were trembling.

"Look," Klewes said, breaking the silence.

Cundiff turned to where Klewes was pointing. Because the room was once Stanley's office, it was different from the other patient quarters in one significant way. Its window could be opened. The point of egress had been an oversight during the renovation. It was open now. The men moved closer and were greeted by a gust of moist night air. They looked over the grounds from the second floor window, but there was nothing to see. Dykeman was long gone.

Out on the bay, vapors were massing. Soon a fog would form and it would inevitably invade the town, wrapping Saint Andrews in a bleak embrace.

"Oh, my God," Cundiff offered. "What the hell are we gonna do now?" Then he left Klewes at the window. He called for Darcy and hurried out of the room. Klewes wiped sweat from the sides of his face. His scrub top was wet across the back and the cool breeze off the water made him shiver.

Maybe it was not the breeze.

# Chapter Nineteen

*Dawson residence, Prince of Wales Street, Saint Andrews...*

He had regained the ability to see hours ago. More time passed before he could blink, so he had surrendered to the view of his former home from the vantage of the front hall, not waiting, just *being*. Just *being* a little more and a little more with each passing minute.

The squares of sunlight on the floor lazily drifted east as the day passed. When they reached the wall, they flared a glorious copper, then orange. Then the room began to dim and the air cooled. He became aware of the lamplight shining from behind the study door. He was thankful for it. It warmed him as night descended.

Aside from the glow, his only companion was pain. It started before he could see, before he could breathe, touch. Its beginning, a tiny ember in his very core, flickered and spread with the rest of his body. Bones formed from the marrow out. Musculature followed. Bundles of nerves snaked throughout, a road atlas of agony in the making. Until he could see, that was all he knew.

Vision, as it happened, was small consolation during his rebirth into death. It only allowed him to mark the passage of time as he was made whole again, one burning cell at a time.

By the time he was able to move a finger, any trace of sunlight had been wiped clear of the house. More hours ticked away before he could take a step. Then it happened all at once—Stanley Dawson was complete.

First he went to the framed photographs hanging by the staircase. He had watched them from the doorway all those long, torturous hours while the sun was still up. The pictures had got him through his ordeal of being reconstructed. It was the promise of looking closely on Susan and Matthew by the blooming cherry trees that sustained him. Seeing their faces, their smiles—he existed for it. Stanley stood before the pictures a while. He studied Susan's features and her colors. He did his best to brand this image of her on the tissue of his mind. He had to in order to replace the memory of the gruesome version of his wife he had encountered at Saint Michael's. Her beautiful eyes were melted, her hair scorched. The idea of it made him moan aloud.

"That wasn't her," he said, rubbing his brow roughly. "Please God...don't let that be her."

When he raised his head he saw himself, forty years younger and grinning like an idiot on the steps of his newly opened hospital. *Fool*, he thought. *Nothing but a dead fool, even then.*

From there, Stanley went to the kitchen. It was dark, but he saw the liquor bottles crowding the countertop well enough. He stood before the kitchen table and smiled on its two empty chairs. So much of his life with Susan was spent at that table. He learned so much about her while sitting in that very chair on the right. He learned even more about himself. Fitting that the room should be dark. It was here they had talked giddily about Matthew's college acceptance. It was here they had planned for a happy retirement spent travelling throughout Europe. In these chairs they each wept as they discussed the terminal illness that would see them part far too early.

He ascended the hardwood staircase, dismayed that the old treads did not creak like they had in life. He supposed he would have to concentrate to make that happen and he did not have it in him. In his bedroom, he looked down on the bed. He remembered waking in the night different times and finding that he was alone. There, he would listen for the stairs to creak. It was such a comfort when they finally did. They told him Susan was making her way back to bed after fetching a glass of water from the kitchen as she did so many nights. That may have been the worst thing to learn to live with after the cancer took her—waking alone at night and listening for the creaking that never came. He was an intelligent man, an educated man, but damn if he didn't forget she had died every time he woke in the night.

Stanley was in agony again. Not like before, this pain was localized in the center of his chest. All he wanted to do was cry. It would feel so good just to shed tears, but they defied him. He had found a way to pass through solid doors and cross the entire town, a disembodied essence, but he was robbed of the most basic of human functions.

In his study he looked at his earthly remains atop the mantel in the gaudy jug he had picked out of King's catalogue and he wondered if anyone had got the joke. Imagine a sensible man like Stanley Dawson wanting to spend eternity in a wine chiller. It did not seem all that funny now that he was confronted with it. He went behind his desk, where the well-worn chair was pulled out, and sat down. He thought about how he used to love this room and all the shelves holding all his most prized books and how he adored his rich mahogany desk. Had he known how important all this stuff really was, he would not have wasted his time collecting it. He looked down at the drawer Matthew had forced open. It was a broken mess of wood chips and splintered facing and Stanley did not care.

*What did it matter?* he thought. *You don't have anything when you can't shed a simple tear.*

Despite his every attempt to dwell on other things, Stanley kept going back to Saint Michael's and his encounter with the burned people. Susan and Phillip were there for *him,* but where did they intend to take him? Judging by their appearance, Stanley had only one guess where they came from. He was glad to make it here one last time, to look around his family's home, but he knew it offered little safety from those burned people. It would not be long before they emerged from the basement or dropped down from the attic. Regardless of their entrance, Stanley would not run the next time they appeared. It did not matter if he did. The outcome would be the same.

Had he really expected to outlive Morris Dykeman? Was that how he planned to deal with this lifelong menace—with a funeral? Did he think he would arrive at the hospital one morning to find Nurse Tait solemnly shaking her head when he asked about the patient? He should have known something so foul would be sustained through some unnatural means. He should have known he would be passing the vile burden down to Matthew.

Matthew...he found Dykeman's file, probably learned the whole ugly story. He was always so bright. Of course he took it upon himself to deal with Dykeman, the way Stanley never had the courage to. Matthew would not stand by and let a patient rot. Stanley frowned. For all the good intentions Matthew had, he was missing the one thing that could actually help. With good intentions of his own, Stanley had kept it secret. He had promised the others he would.

*Secrets will damn us all,* he thought.

Those secrets were now taking a toll on his son. Stanley had never seen Matthew look so poorly or so near his wit's end. As it turned out, Stanley's death was proving to be a quite the inconvenience for everyone. Perhaps it would all end again soon. Perhaps the burned people would arrive and hand him a second, permanent death. Stanley would welcome oblivion, but he doubted he would finally be granted peace. On some level he knew he would find no peace where he was going—only flame.

# Chapter Twenty

Matt rinsed his pills down with a handful of water from the stainless steel sink in the corner and sat down on his unforgiving cot. It was little more than a metal slab welded to the wall. It had a mattress, but offered little relief to his weary bones. He had thicker sweaters in his closet. These cells were clearly not designed with comfort in mind.

After Darcy's visit, Deason Klewes brought him back here from the interview room. He returned a few minutes later with the painkillers Matt so dearly needed for his fractured hand. Twenty minutes later, the throbbing in the shattered appendage died down, but now it was back with a vengeance. With nothing to distract him from the pain, it took center stage while he waited for his latest round of medication to kick in. He tried to occupy his mind by staring at the brick-and-mortar wall across from him then at the grillwork of the iron bars at the front of the cell. It only worsened his mood.

His was the first cell in the line and he could not tell if he had neighbors in the others. It was likely they were unoccupied. Quaint towns like Saint Andrews usually did not harbor much of a criminal element. All the same he remained as quiet as possible, trying not to encourage conversation if he was not alone. All he needed was to share in one of those *what are you in for?* conversations and he would know for certain he had hit rock bottom. Looking down at his shoes minus their laces was bad enough. They had been confiscated along with his belt, phone, wallet, and wristwatch. Even the pens in his pocket had been taken away. Were they worried he would add to the graffiti on the wall—perhaps come up with his own bawdy limerick to post beside the others?

What he really wanted was his watch. Only the small barred window in the hall that ran along the cells gave indication of whether it was night or day. The sunshine was long gone. It had been when Deason last paid him a visit to ask if he wanted something to eat. Matt's appetite was in hiding, though he asked for pizza in case it emerged later on. One look at the seatless metal toilet beside the sink made him leery of putting anything in his system for fear he would actually have to use it.

He just had to hold out until morning. That was when Mister Kelleher figured charges would be laid. They could only hold him for twenty-four hours without bringing formal charges, the lawyer assured him. After that, things would move fast. He would go before a judge and bail would be set, and then he would be back at home in the luxury of his clean and private bathroom facilities. Matt pictured his en suite, his shower in particular, and gave himself a whiff. Oh, how he needed a shower.

His cell was grimy—the whole police station was. Matt looked around at the yellowed walls and up at the dead bugs dotting the inside of the recessed light fixture. He felt somehow infected by the filth. How was he supposed to eat in here? If his appetite *had* been making a comeback, it was gone again.

Matt heard voices muffled by the door at the end of the hallway. Maybe Lumley had returned to ask him more questions to further his investigation. Matt remembered his lawyer's instructions to keep quiet for fear he would say the wrong thing and land himself in hotter water. He wondered if telling Lumley to go fuck himself was one of those things. Then Matt considered the possibility that Lumley was coming to tell him that another murder had been committed while he was behind bars and that he was to be released. Matt stood up and went to the front of his cell.

The door rattled subtly and Matt could hear a *clink* from the other side. He figured the police officers would have been as familiar with the keys as Deason had been, but it sounded like whoever was on the other side was trying different ones. Then there came a profound thump from the dead bolt being retracted. The door opened and Tyrone Klewes stepped through. It took a moment for Matt to realize that it was the Klewes in his employ and not the young turnkey.

"Wh—what are you doing here?" Matt said in disbelief as Saint Michael's two orderlies filed in. For a few seconds, he had trouble reckoning their appearance in their white hospital scrubs, so out of their element.

"We're getting you out of there," Cundiff said. He went to the door of the cell and Klewes threw him the ring of keys.

"Wait a minute, guys, where is Deason?" Matt asked while Cundiff went to work on unlocking the cage. "I'm not sure this is a good idea."

"Deason is tied to his chair out front," Klewes said. His tone suggested that he regretted putting his cousin there. "We had to make it look good for the cameras."

"You planned this?"

"It didn't take much planning," Cundiff said. "Klewey just asked him to let us take you. Lucky for you the Klewes family do for each other unconditionally."

"No...stop what you're doing. I have to stay. I'll get a trial. There's a good chance—"

"No can do. We need you now." Cundiff sighed, as though finishing his thought would take some effort. "Dykeman escaped."

Matt stumbled on those last two words. They were possibly the worst combination of words he could imagine. His flesh blanched. His gaze drifted as though he was searching the walls of his cell for some plan of action, now that the unthinkable had occurred. He looked up at his orderlies. "How did this happen? You were supposed to watch him."

"Oh, we watched him, all right," Klewes answered. "We watched him squeeze through the window over his door and then slither down the wall. Then we watched him leave."

"Now we gotta do something before he gets out of town," Cundiff said, trying another key in the cell lock.

Matt's mouth went dry as he pictured the old man making his escape, but it was his own memory of Dykeman that rattled him the most. He pictured those eyes, blacker than the deepest night. After shaking the image, he said, "I don't think he'll leave town, Mister Cundiff. He has business here." Still, Matt couldn't think of just who else Dykeman may want to deal with. He still did not see any connection to Phillip Prichard and Eric Fisher, let alone why he wanted them dead.

"I just hope he doesn't decide to make his way back to the hospital. We left Darcy and Nurse Tait there alone," Cundiff said.

Matt considered the dead men, and while what they meant to Dykeman was unclear, one thing was not. Matt was linked to both of them. He could be next on Dykeman's list. If that were the case, getting out of jail suddenly seemed like a good idea. If Dykeman caught up with him on the outside, he at least would not be a sitting duck. "Whatever his plans are, they don't involve him going back to Saint Michael's."

"You seem to know a lot more about him than you're letting on," Klewes said.

"I know some."

"Well, you better use it to find him. We wanted to call the police, but Darcy's betting on you. She thinks you can stop him and I hope to God she's right. Deason could get in some real shit for this—we all could. Don't let it be for nothing, Doc," he said. "Please."

*Clunk.*

"There it is," Cundiff announced. He clutched a bar and slid the cell door open. "Let's get outta here while we still can."

Matt waited a moment before crossing the threshold. He was already accused of two homicides, now he was about to add another federal offense to his growing rap sheet. Yet, that was not what gave him pause. His friends had freed him, Darcy believed in him, and now it was his turn to act. And he was terrified.

When he joined the orderlies in the hall, they passed through the doorway and turned right on the other side. That would take them to the rear exit. There, Cundiff attempted a few more keys before finding the right one. All the while Klewes berated his fumbling in what amounted to a harsh whisper. The door emptied into the parking lot and Klewes pointed to where they had left his Corolla. It was nestled between two police cars. *An unlikely spot for a getaway car*, Matt thought, *but this is an unlikely escape.*

Cundiff withdrew the station key from the lock and tossed the ring inside before pushing the door closed. Then he hurried across the lot to catch up to the others. "So, what's our plan, Doc?" he asked.

"I need you to drop me off at home so I can get something. Then I want you guys to go to the hospital and wait with Darcy." Matt spoke with a confidence that belied his fears. He did not know what to do next, but figured that sending someone to watch over Darcy and his patients was as good a place as any to start. "Once I get what I need, I'll call and we'll start searching the town for Dykeman."

Klewes unlocked the car doors with his key fob. "Okay, let's-"

His voice froze in his mouth, along with the rest of his body as the headlights washed over them. The three turned to the source of the blinding light. It came from the far end of the parking lot. Matt immediately pictured Chief Lumley behind the wheel of the vehicle, silently watching the jail break transpire, letting them go just far enough to make them think they made it, giving them just enough rope to hang themselves. Cundiff must have had the same idea.

"Oh, ssshhhit," wheezed out of him.

The vehicle came at them, tires screeching. Klewes threw his hands up to show they were not going to run. The headlights grew brighter and the engine pushing them forward roared. Matt raised his hands to shield his eyes, but he could move little else. It was like he was resigned to the fact that they would be run down. The parking lot was not very long and in a few more yards, they were going to be smears on a car bumper. He squinted his eyes tightly when the car was on top of them. He could feel the heat coming off it. Then there was another screech and instead of feeling the unyielding tonnage slam into him, he felt a gust of warm air.

When he opened his eyes, Matt found the vehicle stopped beside them. The car had swerved at the last second and skidded to a stop. It was not even a car, but a red pickup truck with a yellow design on the door. Cundiff and Klewes rose from their half-crouched, braced-for-impact positions. Before any of them could say a word, three men hopped from the truck and partially surrounded them. Matt bit his tongue. Two of them were holding rifles.

The unarmed man stepped forward confidently, like only a man with an armed entourage could. He wore grimy, green work pants and untied work boots. His plaid jack shirt was untucked and his longish hair fell from under a grease-spotted ball cap. His counterparts were similarly dressed and equally caked in dirt. Though the thing Matt noticed first was the overpowering stench they brought with them.

"What the hell do you want, Ricky?" Cundiff barked at the unarmed man.

"Well, *Cundt*," he said, clearly irked by the orderly's bold question. "The old man wants to talk to you fellahs. He sent us along to collect you."

It was then Matt placed the smell coming off of the men. He had caught a whiff of that same odor when he had spoken to a man outside Stanley's wake. *Fishermen*, he thought. Then he made out the symbol on the door of the truck and read the name at its center. "Your father is Arthur Sullivan, I take it," Matt said.

"That's right, Doctor."

"Easy with that!" Klewes howled as he was prodded closer to his friends by a gun barrel between the shoulder blades.

"You know, the guns aren't necessary," Matt said to Ricky Sullivan.

"Maybe they're not, but I figured they might get you in the truck a little faster."

"We're not going anywhere with you," Cundiff said flatly.

"I'll handle this, John," Matt said. "Now Ricky, I know your father and I'd be happy to meet with him, but not tonight. We have urgent business."

"I'll just bet you do," Ricky said with a hint of amusement. "The trouble is the old man wants to talk to you straight away. Now you're new here so maybe you haven't heard, but when the old man wants something, he gets it. Just ask *Cundt* or the *mountain man*, here."

"Maybe *you* don't know who you're talking to..." Matt started, but was cut short.

"I know who I'm talkin' to," Ricky interrupted. No trace of humor remained in his voice now. "You're the guy they arrested for them two murders. You're also the guy who just broke out of jail. Maybe you're the guy who got shot while trying to escape by some heroic local folk."

Matt looked from one of his orderlies to the other and suddenly he longed for his filthy cell. They were outmaneuvered and he told Ricky Sullivan just that.

* * * *

*This was a stupid idea*, Darcy thought. Saint Michael's was the last place on Earth she wanted to be, given the ghastly display Dykeman had put on during his escape. Still, someone had to stay behind for the patients who did not escape their rooms and the idea of joining the jailbreak gang did not appeal, either. A pleasant alternative would have been to go to the Lobster Bucket and have Chuck make her a cherry pie. She could use a drink. Make it several.

The others had only agreed to leave the hospital on Darcy's assurance that Nurse Tait was in the building to keep her company. The only problem now was finding the nurse. Of all times for the woman to pull one of her disappearing acts, why now? Darcy hoped the nurse's nap was worth the tongue-lashing she was in for when she found her.

As for the rest of the residents at Saint Michael's, it was well past lights-out and the orderlies had escorted them to their rooms for the night before Dykeman took his leave. Darcy was making rounds, half searching for the nurse who was supposed to be keeping her company, half checking on the patients to make sure they were all safely abed and accounted for. She was also locking the quarters—even those of the trustworthy patients—an act that raised a moral dilemma. She told herself that it was for the patient's wellbeing every time she keyed one of the dead bolts closed.

Darcy completed her rounds of the second floor in a state of numbed shock. She went about the task robotically as though a high dose of Novocaine was injected directly into the fear center of her brain. That stoic numbness, however, was flushed out of her system when she reached the bottom of the staircase and saw the sparsely lighted west wing. The very sight of it roused her from her coma like a slap in the face. It conjured the memory of Dianne calling to her from the darkness.

"It wasn't her," she told herself now. It had been some malevolent spirit playing on her fears—some evil thing that somehow had intimate knowledge of exactly what scared Darcy Collins. Whatever it was, it knew how much the idea of losing her sister frightened her, whether it was in a public place, or in the darkness, or to schizophrenia. Nothing could be more painful than watching Di dissolve into the murk of the disease until all trace of her was gone. The presence in the hospital knew that.

"Where the hell are you, Tait?" Darcy breathed as she went to the first quarters in the hallway and looked through the darkened observation window. Inside, Hannah Wilkins gawked back. Darcy nearly screamed as horror gripped her airways again. It took a few seconds for Darcy to recognize that the girl standing in the room was not Di or a ghost, but her teenaged patient. She opened the door and went inside where the low hallway nightlights were diffused further.

"Hannah, why are you out of bed? Do you need to visit the restroom?"

"D-Darcy…"

"Yes, dear," Darcy said, brushing her yellow hair from her eyes. "I'm here. What do you need?" That Hannah was still dopey from a medication change distressed Darcy more than a little as she waited for the girl to answer.

"Darcy...she's not here..."

The words sent icy waves down the back of Darcy's neck. "Who's not here, Hannah?" *Do you mean Dianne? How did you know I was thinking about her?* Darcy waited for the girl's lazy answer until her patience was near exhaustion. "Who, Hannah? *Who?*" Darcy held Hannah by the shoulders and fought the temptation to shake the answer out of her.

"She's upstairs...N-Nurse..."

"Tait?"

"...upstairs..."

Darcy put her patient to bed and locked her door as quickly as she could. Then she was climbing the staircase, thinking about where the nurse could possibly be on the second level and how in the world Hannah Wilkins could know it. She could rule out the entire west wing and most of the east up there. She had just locked them down. When she reached the top stair, the lurid epiphany struck her deep in the chest. There was one room she had not checked. Neither Cundiff nor Klewes had checked it, either. They all felt there had been no reason to search the room after its sole occupant had escaped.

"No...no...please." Darcy battled the urge to retreat downstairs. "Nurse Tait," she yelled. "Nurse Tait!"

Saint Michael's expressed the depths of its cruelty in the form of the silence that answered Darcy's pleas. It went as quiet as she imagined the frozen vacuum of outer space would be. All she could hear was her shallow, hurried breaths and the thumping in her breast. She flung her arms to her sides as the absolute futility of the situation settled on her. She wanted to screech until her poisonous frustrations bled from her body. None of them were safe. Then she pierced the perfect silence in the hospital.

*Click clack.*

Darcy started her approach toward Dykeman's quarters on legs she was sure would give out at any second. She remembered sending the orderlies off to get Matt, telling them it was okay, that she would not be alone. How incredibly foolish she had been. This moment was the very epitome of *alone.*

*Click clack.*

At the door to Dykeman's quarters, Darcy waited for her thrumming heart to calm. It was folly. Instead, she concentrated on mustering the courage to look through the observation window. *Why would he be in there?* She asked herself. *Think about it. Why would he return to his room after going to such lengths to escape it? He is not in there. There is no way he's in there.*

She opened her eyes. They scanned the room before falling to the cot where the white sheet appeared somewhat ballooned and bunched. Her hand felt up the wall until it came to the switch controlling the room's lighting. *No one is in there,* she told herself then she lit the room and found that she was wrong. She was not alone. Someone was in the cot.

The sheet was pulled all the way up but it could not hide the obvious human form—the twin ridges of legs, the valley between, the bulge of a torso. Darcy eyed the hallway east and west for someone, anyone who could offer help. She had not seen any staff members since the orderlies left. Rory was supposed to be in for his shift already, but she hadn't seen the janitor at all this evening and now Nurse Tait had vanished. Holding a breath, Darcy went to enter the room. The door rattled as it held to the jamb. It was locked.

Darcy watched the sheet for a sign that the sound had roused whoever was under it. There was no response to the noisy door or the jingling of her keys as she pressed one of them into the lock. It did not occur to her that it was a complete impossibility for someone to lock themselves in one of the patient's rooms. Darcy's concept of possible-impossible had blurred when she witnessed Dykeman's exit. She was, for the time being, insensitive to it.

The door creaked as she carefully pushed it open. No hint of acknowledgement issued from the sheeted specter on the cot. "Hello," she whispered. Her voice was shallow and high, like she had been replaced by a ten-year-old version of herself. She was ready to sprint from the room, ready should the figure suddenly fold upward on the cot and reveal itself to be some ghastly creature or worse yet, the man who called this room home. Her greeting went unreturned. She stepped inside the room with every fiber of her every muscle on alert and poised to vault her in the opposite direction should the sheet so much as twitch. If it did, she would run. She would run and not stop until she was out of the hospital. Even then she would not stop until she reached her condo and locked the doors and hid herself beneath her own sheets.

When she was within an arm's reach of the cot, her racing heart found another gear. It beat in her chest like humming bird wings, for if she was within touching distance of the cot it meant that whoever or whatever was in it was within touching distance of her. Despite her ongoing inner monologue insisting she do otherwise, Darcy grasped a handful of the sheet at the foot of the bed. She turned her body toward the door like an athlete would toe the track line. She would pull the sheet off and run, she decided. If at the doorway, she did not like what she saw in the cot, she would continue her retreat...all the way home. That was her plan. She hated it. Along with the icy fear coursing through her body, she felt foolish that it was the best ploy she could come up with, and besides that, it did not even work.

She yanked the sheet down, and her feet failed her at once. Somewhere deep within, the connections between brain and body were torn and Darcy's mind locked up while trying to reason through what she was seeing.

Nurse Tait lay lifeless before her.

Her body was positioned front-down on the cot, though her head was twisted around to face the ceiling. With her mouth stretched wide, her eyes near bursting, the woman wore a death mask of absolute horror. That same fear was boiling inside Darcy and when she looked at Nurse Tait's neck, purple and lined like the braids of a rope, that fear boiled over. She screamed like she did not know she was capable. It was the kind of scream born of only the purest dread. It jolted her from atrophy.

Seconds later she was nearing the stairwell in full flight. She nearly stumbled and kicked her shoes off to take the stairs. At the bottom, she did not dare hazard a look right or left for fear of what might be waiting for her under cover of the darkened corridors, behind the furniture in the patient lounge or behind the pedestal of the defaced angel sculpture. She bolted straight for the hospital entrance and beyond.

Outside, dank mists had crept in off the bay and now skirted the grounds. The vapors were cool on her skin but did nothing to soothe her. Instead the fog provided cover for whatever might be lurking on the fringes, ready to attack.

Nurse Tait had not expected to meet her end. Astonishment was plain to see in her contorted visage. The old nurse was probably going about her rounds when she was taken and violently twisted about. Who did the twisting did not matter to Darcy—whether it was Dykeman or the thing she thought was her sister. All that mattered to Darcy now was putting some distance between herself and Saint Michael's and then herself and Saint Andrews.

She darted down the front steps and onto the concrete walkway. The pain that accompanied her bare footfalls hardly registered as she made for the iron gate at the edge of the yard. No amount of money would have stopped her departure from the hospital, and yet stop she did when she saw the object in the center of the path. It was a shoe. A well-worn white leather shoe and she recognized it right away. It belonged to Wanda.

Without thinking, she bent and picked it up. It was cold to the touch, damp from the fog. "Wanda," she called. "Are you out here?" She immediately dropped the shoe on the grass as though it was the bait in a trap laid just for her. Turning, she searched helplessly for the trapper, ruefully aware that she had given up her position. Wave after wave of dense fog rolled in from the south. It worked to surround her. It concealed whatever may be stalking her. It clouded her view of the street and soon it would erase it, blot it out with ever-thickening tendrils. A moment ago the hospital was the last place on Earth she wanted to be, now in the midst of the invasive fog it seemed like the safer bet.

Darcy took a step back toward the building. She scanned the shrubbery that lined it. If there was a monster on her trail, what would make a better hiding place? She took another step, watching the cedars and boxwoods and willows for movement, then she stopped abruptly. It was no monster she found in the flower beds, it was Wanda. Her legs protruded from behind a row of boxwood. Though Darcy could only see her lower half, she knew it was Wanda from the white uniform skirt she wore daily and her footwear—on her left was a white shoe, on her right, only a stocking.

She stood watching for a moment, not sure of what to do. She should check on her, she thought. *What if she's not dead?* It seemed like someone at least had to make sure, like it was an inherent part of the dying process akin to a funeral or a viewing. Then Darcy imagined looking down on her and finding her head twisted in the wrong direction like Nurse Tait's...or something worse. The image was all it took to change her mind, to dash any thought of returning to Saint Michael's. No, she would go home and maybe she would regroup with John and the others later—or maybe not. Maybe she had enough of this gruesome business and this odd little town. Maybe she would just pack a bag when she got home. She turned on her heel and started for the gate and ran into something hard. A shriek burst from her and she was falling backward. The thing she bumped into had arms and they grabbed for her. They clutched her by one wrist and stopped her from falling. It pulled her forward. Then it spoke.

"Easy my dear...are you okay?"

It was not a *thing* but a man...a mayor. Robbie Bentley unhanded her when he was sure she had her footing. "I'm sorry if I frightened you, Doctor. That wasn't my intent."

"Mister Bentley," Darcy started. Her breath was in short supply, but she had a lot to tell the man. Unfortunately before she could, he interrupted.

"Call me Bud, my dear." A wide smile beamed on his round face. "Everyone does."

\* \* \* \*

The drive to Arthur Sullivan's office was brief. Matt was thankful for that. He found out the only thing he liked less than riding in the back of a truck was riding in the back of a truck with a rifle aimed at him. Their destination had only been a few blocks down King and across Water Street. The Sullivan Fisheries office was a single-story red brick building near the wharf. A weathered sign bearing the company name ran the length of the roof line. Beside its lone metal-clad door was a large picture window that would yield a wondrous view of the bay if its blinds were not shut tight.

The truck came to a stop close to the building and the passengers were urged out. Matt jumped down carefully so as not to jar his hand. It would soon be time to boost his painkillers and he did not want to cause more agony than was due.

The murky evening fog rolling off the bay surrounded them as deftly as Sullivan's men had. It breached the shoreline like an army advancing in broken formation, already crossing Water Street down by the fire station and close to taking the wharf. At the end of the long wooden structure a wall of haze rose from the bay like the head of a great leviathan hungering for a taste of the town.

Inside the office, they were greeted with a haze of a different sort. Cigarette smoke poisoned the air. On the round table at the center of the room was a large ashtray heaped with butts and still fuming. A desk strewn with loose papers stood in the corner and on the floor beside it, two cardboard boxes overflowed with more paperwork. Matt did not know how Arthur Sullivan operated on the water, but in the office, he did not exactly run a tight ship.

Ricky Sullivan disappeared through a door at the back of the office. Matt heard a brief exchange, then Ricky returned with his father in tow. It was not hard to see the family resemblance, especially when they seemed to share a common wardrobe. The elder Sullivan wore a thick beard scruff that was more white than gray except around his mouth where nicotine had stained it copper. His skin had an ashen hue that made him look generally unwell and he walked with a limp that implied bodily wear from years of hard work. Despite being diminished by age, he projected a strong presence and it commanded the full attention of his men.

"Leave us," he said to them. At first Ricky protested like a child being told there was no place for him at the grown-up's table, but obeyed when his father turned his scowl on him and said, "Wait outside!" Matt was so startled by Sullivan's teeming temper that he almost followed the others out the door. Instead, he sat at the table when Arthur invited him to.

"You want your boys to stay?" he asked.

"I do," Matt said. He nodded for the orderlies to join him at the table.

What felt like a long silence ensued once they were seated. Sullivan lit a cigarette and inhaled deeply, then let the smoke plume from his nostrils. He looked at Matt sidelong as though he was sizing him up. His calculating stare then drifted to Klewes and it lingered on him a while before it settled on Cundiff. "I know you," he said.

"I umm...used to work for you," Cundiff said, exhibiting a degree of trouble looking old Sullivan in the eyes.

"Right...John Cundiff." Sullivan turned back to Matt and said, "I hope you get more out of him than I ever did."

Matt gave Sullivan's look a stiff return that showed what he thought of the salty comment. "Why did you bring us here?" he demanded.

Sullivan took another drag off his smoke as though he was in no particular rush to answer. "Because I know what you're tryin' to do tonight," he said puffing exhaust, "and because you need my help to do it."

"Really, what do you think we are trying to do?"

"You're tryin' to catch a killer," Sullivan said flatly. "The problem is, if you find him—which you most likely won't—you don't know what to do with him."

"Do you know where he is?"

"I got a pretty good idea, but you can't just take him back to that little hospital of yours and expect he'll sit still for ya. There probably ain't no place that can hold him now. He's become more monster than man. I know because I watched it happen."

"You know about the book...what Dykeman and Stanley did with it?"

"I was there."

Klewes and Cundiff exchanged confused glances as the story was leaving them behind.

"Tell me. Don't leave anything out."

"Hmmm...that's goin' on sixty years ago, Dawson." Sullivan snickered and a whiff of smoke escaped his mouth. "I guess it goes back to Morry comin' across that bloody book. God *damn*...how I wish I never laid eyes on the friggin' thing. I don't know how it come to him, but his father used to work the freight boats and he turned up with unclaimed stuff all the time. Could be that book was in with somethin' he took home. Anyhow, Morry got readin' it. Well, he got Stan readin' it *for* him. Morry was too dumb to pick up on the wordin' of it. It was mostly English, but it was a hard read and Stan was the only kid smart enough to get a handle on it. Lookin' back, I guess the first mistake was Stan tellin' him what the book was about. If he said it was about teachin' dogs to dance, this whole thing never would have happened—but he didn't. He told the truth—Stan always did. He told him the book was about these...*ceremonies* you can do. They were all different, all supposed to do different things. If ya did this one, you'd live a long life. If ya did that one, you'd have the girls hangin' off ya."

"Dykeman didn't want to do either of those ones."

"Shit no. He was poor. His father drove their farm into the ground. Hell, as a farmer, he couldn't grow hair for Christ sake. The Dykemans hardly kept fed and Morry, well he figured he'd do somethin' about that. And wouldn't ya know it, that book had just the thing for it."

"Did he warn you of the dangers?"

"No...he just said, if we did this thing, we'd get rich. I didn't know what it was about and I didn't take it too seriously. Him and Stan got it all ready. They cleared a spot in the Dykeman's old barn and drew these things in the dirt for the ceremony. We all met up later that night." Sullivan ground his spent cigarette into the ash tray. "That was June 21, 1952."

"The summer solstice."

"That's right," Sullivan said, noticeably amused by Matt's knowledge. "Stan read in that book that it was a good time to do it. The *spirits* were supposed to have their ears on, or somethin' like that." The grin faded from Sullivan's face. "Too bad it was true."

Cundiff and Klewes exchanged puzzled looks again, each one confirming the other was just as lost.

"What happened?"

"They lit a bunch of candles, but it was real dark. Ya couldn't see as far as the walls or nothin'. Stan started readin' from the book. That part wasn't English. I don't know what it was, some kind of jibber-jabber. Morry went into this sack he brought along. Of all things, he pulled a bird out of it...a crow. The thing must have been clipped 'cause it didn't even try to get away. It should have tried to do somethin' to get loose, because the next thing ya know, Morry cut the damned thing's head off. He poured its blood into a wineglass. Right about then is when all hell broke loose. Things started moving around us in the shadows. At first I thought the Dykemans were keepin' sheep in the barn again, but it wasn't long before I figured out they weren't farm animals making them noises. For one thing, farm animals don't talk back to ya."

"You heard voices?"

"They were talkin' like Stan was. I couldn't tell how many there was. They were all around us, moving and not just around the walls, overhead too. They were up thumpin' around in the rafters. I can still remember that scurryin' sound, like a hundred pairs of feet draggin' in the dirt. There was this scrapin' too—like nails being raked over the barn boards. I was scared shitless—this close to wettin' myself in front of the boys. But the whole time Morry was cool as a cucumber. He didn't even blink. It was like he'd done it all before and knew what to expect.

"Next thing I know, Stan was holdin' that glassful of crow blood right in front of me. He dipped his thumb in it and drew somethin' on my forehead. Then somethin' weird happened. I couldn't see. It was too dark, but one of us dropped the glass. Then the inside of the barn went the blackest black I've ever seen. The boys start to panic, they're shoutin' stuff and whatever them critters were that were in there with us didn't like it too much either. They got to howlin' somethin' fierce.

"I dropped to the dirt and got a hold of one of the candles and tried to get my matches out, but hell if I could find 'em. Then there was a bang. I looked up and saw some light from outside. One of the boys got to the door and opened it. I just ran for it. We all did...except for Morry."

"Stan come outside behind me. He had that goddamned book in his hand. The crow's blood was drippin' off the page. Seein' it run like that, all that red, got my heart poundin' even harder. The sight of that blood made me realize we did somethin' real bad.

"Stan asked me what he should do with it and I told him I never wanted to see it again. Then I ran for home. I ran like them critters were right behind me the whole way. I didn't stop 'til I was through the door and in my bedroom. My old man hollered at me to slow down in the house and I didn't pay him no heed, so he whooped me for it. There I was, bent over my bed and gettin' the belt across my arse. I got a few extra licks 'cause I couldn't stop laughin'. I was never so happy to get a whippin' in all my life."

Cundiff was dumbstruck. Even if he had something to add, he could not find his voice to do it.

"Did you see what happened to Dykeman?"

"The next time I saw him, he was in shackles getting' loaded in a truck for Saint John to stand trial. Come to think of it, I never saw him again after that."

"Do you know what became of the book?"

"Yeah, the rest of us boys talked only one more time about what happened. We decided that Stan should hang onto it, hide it somewhere. He was the most trustworthy of us, anyhow. We figured if someone found out what happened was because of that book, it might land us in hot water. So, we made a pact to keep it secret and never so much as talk about it again, even to each other."

"So, you're pretty sure that the ritual getting screwed up had a lingering effect on Dykeman?"

"That's the thing. It didn't get screwed up. It worked. It was supposed to make all us boys rich, and it did. The God's honest truth is, I couldn't make a bad business decision, if I tried. And I *have* tried. Bet your arse, I tried." Sullivan went into his pocket for his cigarettes. He brought one to his mouth and paused before lighting it. His hand shook as he held the lighter. "Somethin' was listenin' to us that night and it got a hold of Morry just as surely as it sent buckets of money my way."

Matt was silent as he let the fantastic story sink in. He wondered if whatever *got a hold of* Dykeman got Stanley as well. "Mister Sullivan, who exactly was in the barn that night?"

"Well, you know about me and Morry and Stan. Philly Prichard was there too, and so was Bud Bentley."

\* \* \* \*

"Murder..." Darcy said.

"There's been a murder...two. Nurse Tait...and Wanda, I think." She fought to catch the breath that escaped her when the mayor surprised her on the walkway. She pointed to the pair of legs sprouting from between the shrubs in the flower bed near the front steps. The smile faded from the mayor's face when he saw them. He did not speak, merely walked cautiously toward the nurse's body. When he got to the flower bed, Darcy saw that he flinched. He reached for a handkerchief in the breast pocket of his sports coat and brought it to his mouth. Several seconds passed while he stood and looked over the body. He did not touch it. Evidently the nature of the injury made it clear there was no need to check for vital signs.

Bud returned to the path still wiping at his mouth. He looked like a different man without his customary full-of-good-cheer expression. He turned the bewildered look to Darcy then back to where Wanda lay.

"Who…did you see anything…anyone?" he asked.

"No, I didn't," she said. Technically it was the truth, but she had a pretty good idea of *who* was responsible. Getting Bud caught up on the whole uncanny series of events that transpired this evening was the least of her concerns. "I have to get out of here."

"You can't. You said something happened to Miss Tait, too. You have to show me. We have to call the police." Bud grew braver, more resolute with every word he spoke as though the duty of his civic position superseded his fears.

Darcy looked up at Saint Michael's. It was even more intimidating to her now. Shrouded in the night fog and looming over her, it made her breath run short again. Still, Bud was right, not about calling the police, or the need to show him Nurse Tait's body, but about staying for the sake of the patients. That was *her* duty. Her place was with them. She knew it was the right thing to do because it was the hard thing to do, another hurdle set before her. Her legs stiffened when she took a step toward the hospital. No doubt if she decided to run for home, they would function just fine, but going inside was a different story. Her body was rejecting it.

Bud moved up the front steps and waited for her at the door. When she joined him, he pulled it open. "It will be all right," he said in a most nurturing tone. "We're going to stick together through this."

Inside, the lobby seemed even darker and thick with shadow than it was when Darcy had fled the building. Despite Bud's promise of sticking together, she felt no comfort. She wondered what kind of protection the squat senior citizen had to offer against the likes of one who could inflict the sort of injury that killed Nurse Tait. With any sort of luck, the orderlies would soon return and provide her with a real sense of security. As Darcy and the mayor stood at the doorway, the silence inside the building emerged and folded in around them. She longed for John Cundiff's company. If he were here, he would not let any harm come her way. Instead, she was to settle for the pudgy mayor who just happened to drop by on a night that saw two people killed…

*Why?* she thought, stopping mid-step before crossing the threshold. *What is he doing here?*

"It's all right, Doctor. You just lead the way. I'll be right behind you."

"Bud…what brings you to the hospital tonight?"

"I wanted to have a word with Doctor Dawson about some town business."

"It's a little late for a business call, wouldn't you say?"

"Ordinarily…yes, but you know how the doctor keeps unusual hours."

"That's true, but surely you are aware that he's been arrested. I mean, I take it you've been following the murder cases in *your* town."

"Yeah…you got me. Truth be told, I thought you could use some company on a night like this with all the craziness that's been going on."

"Then you must have known I was alone."

"I *figured* you might be and this old hospital is no place for a young lady like yourself to be alone."

"Yeah, but how could you even know that I was here? Nurse Tait usually works the night shift, not me."

"Yes—"

"Unless you already knew they were dead."

"I-I heard screaming and I came to help. I..."

"Why don't we call the police now? We can use my cell." Darcy went into her jacket pocket and pulled her phone out.

"Stop," Bud said, and grabbed the phone away from her. In his other hand was a gleaming black revolver, its stubby barrel pointed at her midsection. Her legs went to jelly and she almost swooned at the sight of the gun. She did not even see him produce it. He was so fast.

"You're a clever girl," he said pocketing the phone, "but I'm clever, too. I knew you were alone because I was watching you. I saw your big dumb boy-friend leave with his big dumb nigger friend. Before that, I saw Wanda Cook laying in the bushes, just as dead as Good Friday. Before that, I saw one of your patients jump out a second floor window. I figured if Morris Dykeman was on the loose, Nurse Tait was more than likely done-for and quite possibly you were, too. Lucky I was wrong on that account."

"What do you want?"

"Just the pleasure of your company, my dear. I expect our good Doctor Dawson will supply the rest. You see, he's very fond of you. You may not know that because he has a great deal of trouble when it comes to women, but trust me, he is. I make it a point to know the little things about people in my town. He'd do just about anything to keep you out of harm's way. He might even give me what I want. That leaves us free to orchestrate a trade. It's really nothing personal. If you behave yourself, there's no reason we can't all walk away from this night with exactly what we want."

\* \* \* \*

"The mayor...*Bud* took part in the ritual?" A queasy sensation settled in Matt's belly. "He never told me. He explained what happened to Dykeman... and about Stanley transferring him to Saint Michael's, but he never told me *his* involvement." Matt tried to recall their conversations, to uncover some motive Bud may have had to keep his role quiet.

"Bud plays his cards pretty close to the vest," Sullivan said flatly, smoke billowing from his nose. "Especially when he's up to somethin'."

Matt had been met with deception left, right and center since coming to Saint Andrews. Stanley had deceived him, then Fisher did, and now Bud has. The common thread in all cases became abundantly clear just then. Matt's belly found a way to feel worse. "The book...Bud wants the book, too."

"I'd say so."

"Why didn't he just ask me for it? Why hide the truth?"

"Maybe he didn't want to leave gettin' his hands on it to chance. What if you said 'no'?"

"Why would I do that if there was any way it would help us deal with Dykeman?"

"I think you just answered your own question. He doesn't mean to deal with your problem. He has other plans for that book."

"So, now he's an expert on the occult?"

"I don't know about that, but if he fears for his life, he may be willin' to try anything."

"He thinks Dykeman will go after him next. That's what he's afraid of?"

"Whoever or whatever is pullin' Morry's strings is here for blood. Think about it, Dawson. First Stan died unexpectedly, not twenty feet from Morry's room. Phil Prichard got it next. That leaves Bud..."

"And you..."

"That's right. Bud and me are the only two survivors outta the boys who went into Dykeman's barn that night in '52." Sullivan extinguished his cigarette in the ashtray and gave Matt a frosty sidelong look. "Turns out, there was a price for what we did and now someone's here to collect."

Matt considered Stanley. *Could he have paid that price? Did he pay it with his soul?* "Do you think there is something in the book that can save you and Bud?"

Sullivan winced and his full set of wrinkles went on display as he shook his head. "Bah...don't know. Don't care, either. Bud, on the other hand, he's been workin' on it for years. He preserved everythin' in the barn just as it was that night, all the stuff drawn in the dirt, it's still all there, the wineglass, the candles. He hasn't moved a thing."

"In the barn?" Matt said. "Bud told me the barn and the house were demolished after the murders."

Sullivan only smiled at that. "He probably didn't want you snoopin' around and figurin' out what he's got on the go. That barn is still standin' on the very patch of dirt it was built on. So is the house. Bud bought the farm lock, stock and barrel more than fifty years ago. It was the first of many properties he'd get his name on around here, but to him, it was the most important one—the place that might give him a chance to mend the mistakes of the past."

"So now all he needs is the book."

"He went to Stan for it different times. Your father told him to go pound sand. He told him if he ever tried to take the book, he'd burn it double quick. Bud had to believe that, as honest as Stan was, he no doubt meant it."

"Did you ever ask Stanley for it to maybe help yourself?" The old salt grinned again and Matt wondered what he found amusing in any of this.

"Have you ever thought about damnation?" Sullivan asked, his cold stare still engaged. "Do you ever think about where ya go after this life ends? Well, I know where I'm goin'. I got a taste of it that night in the barn. I felt the darkness and I heard the things that live inside it. The memory of it is burned into me. Because of that night, I know I have nothin' to fear in this life. Makin' a living the way I have is a dangerous thing. I worked boats in storms and high water. I've seen fifty-foot swells break over bows. I've seen the fear in the eyes of the crew, but they don't know what it is to be truly *afraid*...not just for your life, but for your soul. I've lived with it every day since I was fourteen years old.

"I know what I got comin' to me and I don't want to be saved. All I want is to finish what we started in '52. I want to call out the thing that took hold of my friend, Morry and I want to send it back to hell."

# Chapter Twenty-One

Stanley was lying on the sofa in the front parlor when Matthew burst through the door. He got up and followed his son's urgent dash to the dining room and the precarious pile of cardboard boxes inside. Matthew lit the room and took a moment to look over the columns taller than either of them then he looked down at his hand. It was in a cast. He wiggled his fingers and his thumb as if to test them. Grimaced while he did. Then he went to work. Stanley felt compelled to tell him to stop what he was doing, but it was too late. Even if Stanley had been able to gather his voice in time, Matthew would not have heard it anyway. It was just Stanley's reflex action when he watched his son grab a hold of the top boxes in two columns and pull them down.

The flimsy cartons bearing the magic marker labels: *books*, exploded against their contents like a weakened dam overwhelmed by a raging river. Books fell everywhere, around Matthew, around the dinette set. Stanley winced when he saw some of his older, more delicate editions hit the floor. The sound of their spines breaking and pages bending was almost more than he could stand. True, they were mere possessions and mattered little at life's end, but still Stanley had no wish to see them damaged any more than he wanted to see his cherry trees cut down or his house burned.

Not satisfied with the tumbled mess of books he made, Matthew reached for the next tower of boxes and yanked it down just as violently as the others. The resulting mound of texts was up to his knees. He scanned the titles surrounding him, as though waiting for a needle to spring forth from the haystack. He released a long, drawn-out sigh when it did not. He waded out of the lump of literature and eased himself to the floor at its edge.

Stanley watched as Matthew picked up one volume at a time, inspected it ever so briefly then flung it to the opposite corner of the room.

"It's not there," Stanley said. "If you know what you're looking for, and I assume that you do, you know I'd never keep it in my office, on some shelf for anyone to see." Matthew continued his destructive sorting process of tossing valuable texts across the room. One after another they fluttered through the air like beating pigeon wings until their flight was abruptly halted by the unyielding plaster of the far wall.

Stanley slid down the wall and sat beside his son. He wanted to put an arm around him, to offer a father's comfort, though his touch would fail miserably. Stanley was beyond offering comfort now.

Matthew jarred his cast while handling a heavy volume and he wheezed with the fresh pain. Stanley wondered how he came by broken bones. *Did he have his own encounter with the burned people at Saint Michael's?* Whatever the case, he was scared and injured and searching feverishly for the *Sacra Obscurum*.

*Things on the outside must be getting bad*, Stanley thought.

\* \* \* \*

Matt took a break from his task. He went into his pocket for his bottle of painkillers and dry swallowed two of them. He figured he would do well to avoid addiction by the time his hand was healed, but he had to keep the disabling agony in check. He could not let it cloud his concentration. Tonight he would need all his wits about him. After stowing his pills, he inspected his cast. It was a day old and already showing the grime of a cast that was due to be removed. The white plaster was hopelessly stained about the thumb hole and palm. He blamed it on his stay in jail where every surface had a sticky film.

Judging by the mound of books he still had to search, he was nearly halfway through the pile. Only he was no closer to finding this magic devil book that everyone so desired. He told himself to focus. He had sent the orderlies to the hospital to keep Darcy company. He convinced the gun-toting fishermen who drove him here to wait outside while he located the book. Everyone had their place. His was here. His job was to find the book. He concentrated on that.

With renewed vigor, he resumed his search. William James' *Pragmatism* got tossed aside as did *Christianity: the First 3000 Years*. *The History of the Psychoanalytic Movement* he threw especially hard against the wall. Matt thought for a moment about how fitting it would be to throw it out the window. Then he could say he had done it literally as well as figuratively. Everything he thought he knew he had tossed aside since arriving in Saint Andrews. Why should the foundation of his profession endure?

After another twenty minutes of sifting, the mound diminished enough that Matt could see that none of the titles before him contained the words *sacra* or *obscurum*. He sat heavily against the wall and faced the ceiling, contemplating his next devil-book-seeking destination. He pictured himself toppling the books from the shelves in the study. It almost seemed satisfying—the act of sweeping an arm down the length of a shelf, sending all those volumes thumping to the floor—then he remembered his fractured hand. Searching the study would be no fun whatsoever. He granted himself a few minutes' respite. The air in the dining room was cool going on chilly, though he found it refreshing, like he had found the fog outside Sullivan's office refreshing, despite its gloomy, almost foreboding, presence.

\* \* \* \*

"Where are you going to look now, Matthew?" Stanley asked. "There are shelves full of books in the study. After that, you may want to check the bathroom. I used to keep reading material in there from time to time. Use your head, Boy!" Stanley knelt beside Matthew, who seemed to be thinking things over. He was doing his best in a difficult situation—one that was obviously taking such a steep toll. He had not seen any of this coming when he had returned to Saint Andrews to settle the estate. He was not the least bit prepared. Stanley had blindsided him with all of this. *If only there had been more time,* Stanley lamented. *If only...*

Matthew wiggled the fingers of his casted hand again, discomfort clear in his expression. Stanley nearly rejoiced in the one thing he was able to help with. He rubbed his spectral hands together in anticipation. This was the one time that an arctic touch may be welcomed. He may not be able to console his son with his cold-as-ice grip, but he could take some of the sting out of that broken hand.

Stanley positioned himself in front of Matthew and leaned toward him. Ghostly hands floated just above the cast resting on Matthew's lap. Stanley lowered them onto the plaster and he felt heat. Tremendous heat. He *saw* heat. He *saw* flame. It ebbed and flowed dangerously close. Then the flames parted and he saw Dykeman looking up at him from his white plastic deck chair, his human eyes eclipsed with the purest loathing. Dykeman seized Matthew's hand that was now Stanley's hand. The beast within the man stared at the ghost within the man.

Stanley felt intense shame, a sense of queer familiarity when he looked upon his monstrous patient. It was reminiscent of his confrontation with the burned people, only now he had the profound feeling that he was looking at the thing that had *burned* those people. Beast-Dykeman squeezed Stanley's hand—tight—tighter—tightest—*pop*. Stanley felt the small bone bridging his pinky finger to his wrist go to dust, and he yelled for release. Beast-Dykeman's face was stone, devoid of human traits like sympathy, mercy. He continued to squeeze—tight—tighter—tightest—*pop*. Howls erupted from him, Matthew's voice laced together with his, united in agony. Another bone was crushed to powder, but the beast within Dykeman would not relent. Tight—tighter—tightest—Stanley pulled his hands away from Matthew's cast and the momentum spilled him over backward.

He lay awkwardly on his side while the heat drained from his spirit body along with the sour sensation of broken hand bones. He looked at his son who was oblivious. *He deserves to be*, Stanley reasoned. *He lived through the ordeal.* Stanley gathered himself off the floor and went back to Matthew's side. He looked on his son with renewed admiration—and more guilt than ever. He considered touching the cast again and reliving the violent moment over and over. He deserved to suffer Dykeman's wrath more than anyone. He brought his hand close to Matthew's...

Stanley stopped as the full realization of what had just occurred sunk in. He had relived an experience from Matthew's life simply by touching him. Those times he had touched people in the past, he was able to pick up on their raw emotions, moods, basic thoughts. This was entirely different. What if that *transfer* was becoming stronger, more sophisticated with time and use? What if he was able to get more from physical contact as he gained more ability using his spectral body? Just like he had learned to pass through doors. Just like he found a way to reconstruct himself. There was no telling what the depths of his abilities may be. *And if I can* take *a memory from a person*, Stanley thought, *maybe I can* plant *one*.

\* \* \* \*

Matt sat on the floor with his back against the wall. He considered Morris Dykeman and wondered where he was now. *Was he stalking the mayor like Sullivan suggested? Could he be found in the bushes around Bud's house, leering through windows, lying in wait to ambush the mayor?* Matt looked to the windows on the west wall of the dining room. Dykeman could just as easily be watching *him* now. Just because Sullivan felt that Bud was a target did not necessarily make it so. The idea of his deranged patient watching him left Matt shivering as a frozen current ran from his head to his toes. Outside the window a hazy apparition marched by, then another. It set Matt's heart to pounding against his ribs. He knew immediately that it was only fog billowing past the house on the soft night breeze, yet its appearance rattled him, nonetheless.

As if there was a technician behind a curtain working the controls of an amusement park haunted house, the next special effect came right on cue. The low, rumbling moan rose from beneath the floorboards. Matt's thoughts went to the old coal chute door and what horrors it may contain. The sound that was so engraved in Matt's memory came again, louder, sorrowful. The dead boy trapped in his eternal hiding place voiced his displeasure. Despite his reasonable explanations for the noise, despite being a fully grown rational man, despite utter frustration in himself, profound fear gripped Matt's chest and it drew the breath from him. He became the boy cringing under bed sheets while the boy trapped in the coal chute lamented his fate.

*No*, Matt said to himself. *I can't do this tonight. I have a book to find.* He shifted to gather his legs under him, to get up and head to the study to resume the search. Before he could rise, the technician behind the curtain flipped the next switch. Matt exhaled and his breath wafted before him, a thin, white vapor. It danced on the air for a fleeting moment before dissipating, only to be followed by another plume. Then the cold bit him. He shuddered as icy fingers raked his flesh. It permeated his skin and spread through his torso. He pictured ice forming on his spinal cord, creeping up his brain stem until all neural activity was brought to a halt. Then came the moan again—loud enough to be generated in the kitchen or parlor next door, loud enough to send vibrations through the walls and sprinkle dust from the ceiling.

Matt found himself standing beside Chrissy in the dark, facing the coal chute door. He turned away. To the rickety basement stair he went, to climb out of the depths of this unwelcomed memory. The stairs were gone. The one exit from the foul cellar had been erased. He was guided back to the coal chute by unseen hands. Matt struggled against them, but he was far too weak to break their hold. He felt like a child again having been scooped up and carried to his bedroom for a disciplinary time-out.

He was beside Chrissy again.

"This is it," the sitter whispered. "The coal chute door."

Matthew shivered when she said the words.

"I told you we'd find it here."

"I believed you," Matthew said. *Can we go upstairs, now?*

"It is said that when the little boy's spirit moans, if you come down here and open the chute, you'll see him trapped inside waiting to be saved."

"Don't open it...my parents might get mad." *Why didn't they tell me about this?*

"They don't have to know. It could be our secret."

Chrissy raised a hand and touched the door. There was a scraping sound and a metallic *clink*.

"*Don't!*"

"Come on, Matthew, we might get to see him. I want to be able to tell the kids at school I did."

There was an awful screech as the door opened on its rusted hinges.

In his nightmares, Matthew saw the boy tumble to the floor. His skin was blue, moisture-less, and sucked up against his bones. His ribs could be counted, his vertebrae as well. He hit the concrete floor with a sickening thud, elbows and knees folding the wrong way as he piled before them like a grotesque marionette whose strings had been suddenly cut. His head wobbled on his broken neck and turned up toward them like a wiffle ball coming to rest. The boy's face had given up the features of youth for those of the mummified.

Chrissy kneeled beside him and looked up to Matthew. "See, I told you."

"I believed you," Matthew said, a pitiful whimper.

The boy's eyes peeled open.

Milky white orbs rolled in the bloated sockets and they turned on Matthew. "*Help...me,*" the boy hissed. "*Tell my parents...where I am.*"

"Wow..." Chrissy breathed. "Is that ever cool."

Matthew's horror erupted violently. He screamed and sat upright in his bed as though spring-loaded, waking his mom and dad for the third night in a row. He searched the dark corners of his bedroom for the boy from the chute. He was there lurking in the shadows behind Matthew's dresser or behind the laundry hamper...Matthew could *feel* him. He had escaped the chute somehow and crawled out of the basement and now he was coming for Matthew. All at once, his mother was there, bringing with her precious light from the hallway. It trickled into the bedroom, exposing the emptiness behind the dresser and hamper. His mother lit the lamp on his nightstand and it confirmed the absence of the ghoulish boy.

She sat on the edge of his bed and folded a nurturing embrace around him. He could not help but be soothed by her voice, the way she hushed him and told him he was safe. He almost *had* to believe her as she explained there was no such thing as ghosts and that he was letting his imagination get the better of him. But she had not been there. She had not been in the basement with him and Chrissy and she could not understand. Even when he told her about the boy who fell in the coal chute in his most serious grown-up voice, she could not understand. All she could do was threaten to take him down to the cellar and show him just what was inside that chute—a prospect that had him screaming again.

"There's nothing in there, Matthew."

"Chrissy...she saw him. She saw the boy. She said so."

"No sweetie, she didn't. I'm sorry, but she was only playing a cruel trick on you. She made you watch that scary movie and then she told you that ghost story. It isn't real, any of it."

"But I can hear him sometimes. He cries and I can hear him."

"Oh, that? That's only wind blowing through the house, down the chimney, through the cracks in the foundation. It's old. It makes a lot of strange noises, but they can all be explained and *none* of them are made by ghosts."

Matthew said nothing, thoroughly disappointed in his mother. She was supposed to protect him from the things that scared him and she did not even try, did not even care to.

"You'll feel better in the morning. You'll see."

"Can I sleep with you and Dad?"

"No sweetie, you're a big boy," she said, rising from the bed. "You have to learn there's nothing to be afraid of in this house."

"No," Matthew said when his mother went to the nightstand beside his bed. "Leave the lamp on, please."

His parents conferred in the hall outside his room. "What's the matter?" he heard his father ask.

"He had that nightmare again."

"Again?"

"He's still convinced there's a ghost in the basement. We never should have hired that little bitch to watch him. She's turned our son into a nervous wreck. He can't even sleep for more than a couple of hours. You're supposed to be the psychiatrist, see if you can get through to him."

"Rough night, eh Son?" his father said when he stepped into the room. He closed the door behind him and sat himself on the edge of the bed. Matthew was not used to seeing him in pajamas. Stanley Dawson was the sort who dressed in his suit and tie before coming down for breakfast, even on Christmas morning. "I understand you're concerned about something in the basement. Why don't you walk me through it?"

Matthew started his report, gladdened that his father did not simply tell him to hush or dismiss his fears right away. He related the story about the game of hide-and-seek that went horribly wrong and about the search party that was gathered and about the discovery of the boy's body. His father listened intently all the way through, never once telling him he was wrong or that his fears were unfounded. He listened carefully until Matthew had finished and looked up at him with pleading eyes, longing for help with a problem that only a parent could solve.

His father looked at the door behind him to make sure the Dawson men had the room to themselves then he turned back to Matthew and said, "Well... that sounds like some pretty scary stuff and when it comes from someone like Chrissy, an older person in a role of authority like she was, I'm sure it's all the more convincing. Add to all that a trip to the basement to actually look at that old coal chute and I can see why you'd be frightened. It's hard to see down there in the dark and when we can't see things clearly our minds sometimes like to invent what we see. Do you follow what I'm saying?"

"Yeah..."

"So, if you understand that Chrissy was simply trying to scare you with her story and that your senses play games with you in the dark, then you might come to see that there isn't a ghost down there, after all."

"Maybe..."

"Though, we can't say for certain, can we?"

Matthew looked into his father's eyes then and saw none of the warmth and comfort that was so evident in his mother's. Instead, Matthew saw a cold indifference in his father that was bordering on anger.

"Maybe there *are* ghosts...and maybe there aren't. I guess the only thing that we can be certain of, is that you should stay the *hell* away from that coal chute...just in case there *is* something in there waiting for you."

Matt was guided away from the bitter memory as surely as he was shoved into it. He was ushered back to the dining room and the scores of books thrown about the place. He found himself on his hands and knees, his forehead pressed to the floor. His eyes were wet and his face streaked with tears. He dried them with his good hand and sat up on his haunches. "You son of a bitch, Stanley," he said aloud. "You were a sorry excuse for a father. You son...of...a..."

Matt clamored to his feet, the epiphany hitting him like a slap across the face. He moved briskly into the hallway, leaning on the wall for support when he teetered badly on his weary legs. Then he stopped, facing the cellar door. He reflected on a childhood spent dreading the other side of this meager wooden slab, on the hundreds of windy nights spent wide awake in bed listening to the *moaning*, on the hundreds more occasions he woke slick with sweat from his latest night terror. It all could have been avoided with a reassuring word from his father. Instead, Stanley chose to frighten young Matthew. He chose to cultivate Matthew's crippling fear of the cellar, and of the coal chute, instead of simply finding another hiding place for the *Sacra Obscurum*.

It had all been a ploy to keep Matt away from the chute, so he would not stumble upon the dangerous book, so the son would not repeat the sins of the father. Armed with this knowledge, Matt threw open the cellar door. He was met with a rush of stale, dank air from below. There was nothing to fear down there. He knew that now. He had known that all of his adult years.

So why did he have such difficulty going down there? If a patient came to his office with a similar problem, he would have taken a logical approach to assessing the implied hazards associated with whatever he or she was afraid of. Ultimately, he would encourage that person to face the thing they fear in a safe manner, like recommending swimming lessons for one who was afraid of the water or visiting a puppy for one who feared dogs. It had always seemed so elementary to him. From this side of the desk, however, that all seemed like so much bullshit. There was nothing easy about confronting this. He took a deep breath and when he exhaled he could see his breath. He felt a strong chill, especially on his neck and brow where he was suddenly wet with sweat.

Matt reached inside the door and flipped on the staircase lights. He peeked inside the doorway. A fourteen-year-old Chrissy was descending the stairs ahead of him. When she was two treads from the bottom, she turned back to him and said, "Come on, Matthew. Don't be such a chicken."

"I'm coming," he whispered.

She faded into the shadows.

Matt took the steps slowly, each one creaking and cracking as if to herald his arrival to the black void. At the bottom, he fumbled for the light switch and threw it on. Weak globes of yellow light formed, but most of the cellar was still given to darkness. It was like the place preferred it that way.

He moved under the glow of the few bare bulbs, grit crunching under the souls of his shoes as he went. It sounded his presence to whatever may be hiding beyond the edge of the light. At the end of the large concrete room, beside the red brick chimney, Chrissy waited. "It's over here," she said. "Just where I said it would be."

Matt followed her behind the chimney where the reach of the light bulbs did not extend.

"This is it," Chrissy whispered. "The coal chute door."

Matt waited for his eyes to adjust to the dark.

"I told you we'd find it here."

"I believed you."

"It is said that when the little boy's spirit moans, if you come down here and open the chute, you'll see him trapped inside waiting to be saved."

"There is no dead boy in there."

"*Sure* there is. We might get to see him. I want to be able to tell the kids at school that I did."

"Trust me, there's no boy. There's no ghost. What *is* in there is much, much worse."

"What are you talking about, Matthew?"

"The thing in there...I think it's like a key. And this key can unlock the gateway to hell. Once that gate is open, there's no telling what things might come crawling out. The most wicked, unspeakable evil will be allowed to enter our world."

"No...they were playing hide and seek and—"

"It happened before, sixty years ago. Back then, some evil thing made a boy slaughter his whole family. Mother, father and brother—he diced them up with a pair of garden shears until there was nothing left. When he was taken away to an asylum, he attacked his nurses—bit one of their faces off."

"What...Matthew..."

"Now he's escaped. He's killed two more men—crushed their skulls as flat as pancakes."

"That's horrible. Is that true?"

"I'm afraid it is," he said soberly then he raised his cast for her to see. "Oh yeah, and he broke my hand."

The sitter gulped hard to swallow the lump in her throat. "Where do you think he might be now?"

Matt nodded at the coal chute. "Open it."

Chrissy raised a hand that was not at all steady and touched the door. She pulled back as though the surface of it was red-hot. "Maybe we shouldn't."

"Why not? We came down here to open it. It was your idea."

"Your parents might get mad."

"It can be our little secret. You like secrets, don't you? Of course you do. Everyone in Saint Andrews likes a good secret." Matt grabbed the door handle.

"Please don't!" Chrissy blurted, sheer anguish in her voice. "Whatever's in there...we should leave it alone."

There came an awful screech as the door opened on its atrophied hinges. The shrill sound spurred Chrissy into motion. She turned to run and faded silently into the ether.

A gust of stale air blew in from the opened chute. It was strong with the stench of mildew and decades-old coal dust. Matt steadied himself. He felt the unlikely combination of pride and dread swirling in him as he stood before the opening. It was the singular source of his childhood fears and conversely the source of a profound adult triumph. He took a breath of the sour air and reached inside.

There was nothing at the bottom of the chute save a silty layer of coal. He felt further up the walls of the chute, on one side then the other. At the limit of his reach, he finally felt something. It was cloth. His heart stopped beating for a few seconds when he pictured himself touching the dead boy's shirt. Then his hand reported that the object the cloth covered was too hard to be any decaying body part. This cloth was taped to the chute wall. It took some doing to pry it free. When he pulled it down, he brought it into the sparse light on the other side of the chimney for a look, though he had zero doubt what it was. He inspected the rectangular shape wrapped tightly in soot-stained, white fabric. Before leaving the cellar, he turned back to the chute and considered it briefly. He left the door wide open and went upstairs.

\* \* \* \*

Matt eyed the bundle on the desktop like it was some sort of science experiment about to yield a chemical reaction. He brought it to the study to unwrap and thoroughly inspect, though it was easier said than done. After carrying the thing from the cellar, feeling its queer weight, its faint but detectable inner warmth, it was finally hitting home for Matt that this book was indeed *real*. Up until now, it had been a concept, a variable in a bad dream, something abstract that on some level he could dismiss as bunk anytime. Now here it was—in the study with him, casting a small, yet defined shadow on the desk, occupying the same space and time he was.

Matt gathered his courage and went about unwrapping the soiled cloth. He tore the remaining strands of stubborn duct tape free and balled them up. Then he lifted the bundle and unfolded the fabric. He laid it down then pulled one flap off to the left. He paused. He would be face to face with the thing when he unfolded the final layer of cloth.

*Was this the point of no return?* he wondered, or had he passed that already—perhaps when he stuck his arm up the chute? Perhaps when he arrived in Saint Andrews after Stanley's death?

He turned his head to the side and squinted, half expecting the thing to spew flame when he opened it or fly up from the desk and clamp his face between its hungry pages. He freed it of its remaining covers and it did neither. Matt ogled it with one wide eye for a moment, then he faced it, confident it was at least not *physically* dangerous. In fact the book was rather unassuming. Only six inches by ten, it was sleeved in soft, supple black leather. The cover was scuffed in places, but looked as though a bit of oil would bring it to a polished luster. The inch-and-a-half-thick crosscut of pages in between was uneven, evidence of the book's age and the paper-cutting practices of its day. They were yellowed and spotted here and there with wine-colored blotches. Matt imagined the pages were brittle, and thus would be easily split by a careless touch. Fisher may have been accurate in his assessment of the book's age. Surely it had endured centuries. Its spine was well-preserved, wrapped in more taut, black leather, and it did not show a single crease or ridge, though it was mildly worn at the bands and joints.

It *was* the book he was looking for. Matt knew it could be nothing else. However, there was no marking or title text evident. It occurred to him that there would be no identification on the spine by design. It was a safeguard against detection—camouflage to hide it from those who would burn such volumes *and* their owners. He did not know where that knowledge came from. It just popped into his head as though the book had somehow told him.

He stood straight over it and examined the cover. It was blank also...no wait...there was something there. Matt looked at it sidelong, let the lamp light play across the surface of the leather. Then he saw the words. They were etched in the cover, tooled into its black skin, and the angle of the light coaxed them out. They remained bold even as Matt moved his perspective straight overhead again. He wondered how he could possibly have missed the title before. *Sacra Obscurum.* Reciting it, even silently, made his spine tingle.

It took Matt a couple of minutes before he mustered the nerve to actually open it. *Certainly this is the point of no return,* he reasoned. If he wrapped the thing back up and stuffed it in the coal chute again, could he just get on with his life like none of this ever happened? Could he get on a westbound plane and simply resume his career at the D. A. McLaughlin Center and put these black days behind him? It would not be that easy. He could feel the moment cutting through him. Scars would remain after this. They would overlap the scars left by his childhood fears. They would forever be there.

With one tentative finger, Matt lifted the cover. It raised a pair of end pages with it. He drew a breath and opened the cover fully. A bead of sweat rolled to his chin and he wiped it away, afraid it might have dropped onto the book. He did not want to make that sort of personal contact. On some level, he knew it would be unwise. Already he was sensing some peculiar energy, like there was a coiled antenna deep within him that was picking up frequencies in the air never before detected.

He turned a few pages. The cover hinge creaked. The rough, mushroom-colored pages rubbed together.

Only when he was certain nothing was going to jump out of the book at him did Matt sit at the desk. Soon he thumbed through the pages with increasing confidence, though unsure of what he was looking for. There was no table of contents—the book jumped right into detailed descriptions for communing with otherworldly beings. Perhaps, he thought, the boys had made handwritten notes in the margins or folded page corners or did something to indicate where in the book they centered their focus. The sections were titled in bold, black script. The rest of the text was a smaller typeset bracketed by narrow margins, though it was easy to read. As he leafed through the pages, he saw words in the title blocks that struck cords within him—*Leviathan*—*Baal*—*Beelzebub.* He did not know their significance, but his instincts told him he was looking at something purely evil. It was a primordial knowledge that came ingrained in him upon birth into the tribe of Man—a base instinct in the vein of breathing and suckling.

Suddenly the desk lamp did not offer enough light for Matt's taste. He went to the doorway and flipped the switch for the ceiling fixture. The new brilliance sent the shadows retreating into thin black lines beside the bookcases and window curtains.

Matt returned to the desk and got seated. The book was still centered in the dirty white cloth that had wrapped it for decades. He pulled it toward him by the cloth so as not to touch it any more than was necessary. When he resumed his perusal, he realized the book was not on the page he had left it open to. This page was badly wine-stained, half of it left crisp and wrinkled after the apparent spill dried. He read the title: *Entreaty for Belphegor*. He sounded the odd name aloud.

*Bell...fa...gore...*

Just as he was about to continue on to the next entry, a bone-deep chill fell upon his hand where he held the corner of the page. He laid the page down and the chill abated. Matt looked around the room, then set to reading the section closely.

He read through the details of preparing the site for the ritual. There was a good deal about arranging candles and laying out the proper runes. He skipped ahead to the ceremony itself. It directed the leader of the ritual, or the *Magician*, to pay homage to the four *princes of hell* before proceeding. Here, the text changed. *Is that Latin?* Matt thought. He skimmed through it and moved on to the next section. It made mention of preparing the sacrifice. Matt balked.

*Those boys arranged a sacrifice.*

Sullivan had told him about Dykeman killing a crow on that night. Matt went back to the introduction of the ritual and confirmed what he read, that this Belphegor character liked crows. Matt prayed that was all they presented him with. He flipped several pages back to where he had found a section entitled *offerings*.

In this section, the book went into morbid detail concerning sacrifice. The benefits of using animal offerings were described, but it reported the most valuable sacrifice was, by far, human—especially the infant human. On the adjacent page was an engraving depicting a baby being ritualistically offered. It was grotesque. Matt returned to the wine-stained page and continued learning the morbid details about what those boys did in 1952. He tried to get the brutal image of a human sacrifice out of his head—the image of an altar, of blood running...*blood. This is no wine stain*, he thought.

"Jesus Christ!" he said aloud, pushing his chair back from the desk. He looked at the book, opened to the page that had once been soaked in the life-blood of something...or someone. The sight of it sickened him. He buried his face in his hands and rubbed his eyes hard. "Stanley," he whispered into his palms. "How could you get involved with this madness?"

"Matt!"

The shout came from the front door. It was John Cundiff's voice.

"Matt, where are you?" Tyrone Klewes yelled next. "Darcy's missing!"

Matt stood up behind the desk. "In here," he shouted back. "What happened?"

The orderlies appeared in the doorway to the study, their faces twisted with anguish.

"We went to Saint Michael's like you said," Klewes started. "We found...we found..."

"Wanda," Cundiff spat. "She's dead. So is Nurse Tait. We saw them."

Matt went rigid. It was like an electrical current shot from his heels to the top of his head contracting his every muscle along the way. His tongue petrified in his mouth, not that he would have known what to say to the men.

Klewes seemed to be in a state of shock and Cundiff appeared on the edge of tears.

"Darcy...she was gone," Klewes labored to say. "She doesn't answer her phone. We went to her condo. It was empty. We drove around...searched the streets...the clinic."

"What are we going to do?" Cundiff said, his face stricken, childlike. "*What the hell are we going to do?*"

Matt's head swam with a torrent of images: Wanda, Tait, Darcy. He looked down at the *Sacra Obscurum* splayed open on the desktop to the gore-stained page. It seemed to call to him, and though he wanted to look away, he found that he couldn't. The book held his focus as if by some supernatural means—like he and it had formed some kind of bond the moment he laid eyes on it. Then he heard the voice. Little more than a raspy whisper, it wound its way through his head, dropping terrible words as it went.

*Darcy. Blood. Altar. Mayor. Barn. Blood.*

"She's still alive," he said meekly as he struggled to overcome his paralysis. "You would have found her body with the others if she was—She's still alive! She's with Bud. She's the..."

*Sacrifice.*

The foul word echoed through Matt's head.

"What do you know, Matt? Where is she?" Cundiff begged, those tears starting to get the better of him. Klewes clamped one of his long hands on his friend's shoulder.

"I think I know where," Matt said, "but we need Sullivan to show us the way." He walked around the desk. "We have to hurry." He reached for the book to close its cover.

And thunder followed.

It boomed as every door throughout the house slammed shut one after the other. The domino effect of the banging doors ended at the study where the oaken door flew closed in the orderlies' faces with such tremendous fury it threw the men backward to the hallway floor. Matt froze still again. A fierce cold wrapped the room and his breath billowed like thick white smoke.

"No," he said aloud. "Not now..."

Cundiff and Klewes pounded on the door with shouts for Matt to open it despite their failing attempts. The door shook in the jamb, the knob rattled uselessly. They called for him, asked if he was okay, though their voices were becoming distant. As they fought to rescue him, Matt was leaving the room.

# Chapter Twenty-Two

He was guided to a world without light, without sound.

Only the pulse in his broken hand told him he was awake.

He took a step and heard the dry scuffing of dirt beneath his feet.

Then came the strong scent of animals—hay, manure.

Then he saw tiny specks of light in the distance. He was drawn to them. He got closer and saw that they were candles. Several were placed on the ground at distinct intervals. Closer again, he saw people...boys. They wore drab-colored woolen coats and trousers. The five of them were huddled like an offensive line planning their next play. Matt sidled up to them. He spoke, but was not heard. Flagged their attention, but was not seen. They continued with their meeting in hushed voices—secretive voices, the sort that usually led to more harm than good.

Matt looked around and got his bearings with the aid of the candlelight. Walls of rough-hewn boards surrounded them to bear silent witness to their plans. He did not see a ceiling in the large room. The candlelight was too weak to pry it from the darkness, though he did see the thick wooden beams that supported it. They crossed the breadth of the space and some angled upward into the gloom. At the edge of his vision, Matt saw stalls lining one side of the space. They were vacant. Underfoot, he found clumps of straw. He was in a barn, he realized. He was in *the* barn.

He turned to the boys. "Hey," he hollered. "You don't want to do what you're planning to do."

The boys went about their secret business, paying no heed.

"You're going to ruin lives...*all* of your lives," he implored them. He went to their huddle—tried to grab at a pair of them by the shoulders. "Stop this!" His hands passed through the juvenile bodies like they were smoke...or like he was. He circled the group, trying to seize each boy's attention. To them, he was a mere phantom. Between the boys, he got a glimpse of what they were focused on. His pulse revved. One of them held the *Sacra Obscurum* open for the rest to study along. Even in the diminished light, Matt could read the boy's features, the pronounced nose, what one day would be a rigid jaw line.

It was Stanley.

Matt turned away. He never wanted to see this. No one would ever want to bear witness to his father's most shameful moment. It was enough for him to know it had happened.

Where he came from, in the world of the living, of the present day, people needed him. Darcy was missing, quite possibly hurt or worse. Dykeman was loose. He did not need to witness what these boys did sixty years ago. He did not have to, in order to face its repercussions. Despite his needs, some unnamable force brought him here, the same way it took him back to his childhood. Then, it helped him to find the book, but seeing this ritual go down was not going to help in any way. He raised his head to the shrouded ceiling and yelled, "I don't want to be here. Take me back!"

Matt's voice rang amid the high timbers and silence ensued like a nasty retort.

The huddle broke. For a fleeting second, Matt thought his warning had gotten through. Then each of the boys went about his duty. There was the youthful Arthur Sullivan, not yet showing the withering abuse of the sea across his brow. Phillip Prichard, unmistakable with his scrawny build and thick-framed glasses, joined Sullivan in inspecting a broad circle that had been etched in the dirt floor. The circle was lined with a white, powdery substance that Matt assumed was salt. Sugar was unlikely. In '52, it would be too expensive to dump on the floor, especially in that quantity. The white powdered etchings continued into the center of the circle. As the boys worried over the integrity of their design, Matt was able to see more of it—the lines and corners intersected and prevailed in the form of the pentacle star.

Matt felt very cold. The thin film of sweat on his neck began to frost over. He knew nothing of the significance of this symbol, only that it was bad news. He remembered some of the kids in his high school class carving it into desktops or drawing it on bathroom stall tiles. Back then, the symbol was so widely adopted by hard rock culture, that it was seen everywhere from album covers to patches on jeans jackets. Matt also recalled the time he drew one on the cover of a textbook. He had finished his handiwork in H2 pencil then stared at it in its defiant mockery of the mathematics within and he wondered how the other boys could be so glib about spreading the sign around. Even then, knowing nothing of Morris Dykeman or the *Sacra Obscurum* or the dark arts it extolled, he knew the symbol had power. Simply eyeing the thing conjured the feeling that he was being watched by something that dwelled just beyond the edge of his perception. So eerie was the feeling it stirred in his core that he erased the drawing and scratched over its leaden remnants with a black pen. Matt wished he could stomp and kick his way through the dirt and obliterate *this* pentagram where it laid. That would do no good. This night had already happened.

Young Stanley still read from the book while a tall, lanky boy hovered around him. Matt knew at once it was Morris Dykeman. Even in youth, Dykeman's eyes were sunken, his face long. His hair was in a brush cut, like Stanley's, and he wore a simple plaid shirt tucked into brown trousers. He looked like the other boys except for one thing. Matt saw something *behind* his eyes. It was a subtle glint that hinted at mischief or perhaps suppressed glee. He spoke in a low voice to Stanley. Their conversation was private from the rest of the group. Always did Dykeman have an arm around Stanley or a hand on his back, always displaying a bond that far exceeded those he shared with the other boys. Sullivan had told him that Dykeman needed Stanley to decipher the book. Did Dykeman goad him or lure him through the guise of friendship? Stanley kneeled to situate the book on the ground, and Matt caught a glimpse of that gleam in Dykeman's eye again. Matt recognized it this time. It was *knowing*. Dykeman *knew* that something was going to result from their little experiment with magic. Whether he had seen it in a dream or he had done his own homework on the subject, he knew something was going to happen. That little spark in the deep well of Dykeman's eye said it would be hell.

The pudgy boy, none other than Robbie Bentley, returned to the group having retrieved something from a sack. He showed it to Dykeman, as though eager for a pat on the head. It was Stanley who addressed Bentley's contribution. "You brought it," he said. "Good work, Bud."

"Do you think it will do the job, Morry?" Bud asked, not giving up on the possibility of praise from the leader of the pack. Dykeman did not raise his sight from the floor and the symbols etched in it. He was occupied with other details.

Stepping carefully over the salt lines in the dirt, Sullivan joined them. "Is that the cup thing?"

"The *chalice*, yes," Stanley answered, turning the large wine glass Bud had brought. He watched it sparkle in the candlelight as he turned it between his thumb and forefinger. "It's crystal."

"Hey, that's nice," Sullivan said.

"It's one of my mom's good glasses," Bud said. "Please be careful with it. I have to sneak it back into her set, after."

"Stan..."

The boys all stopped what they were doing and turned their combined attention to Dykeman.

"Are we ready?"

Stan thought for a moment. "Let's see...we have the chalice." He raised it and Dykeman looked at it for the first time and nodded. Stan pointed at other things on the dirt floor. "We have the *bell*. That old milking stool will serve as the *altar*. We have the candles all lit. You have the *sword*, you said." Dykeman nodded again. "Both symbols are drawn," Stan continued.

Matt searched the floor from his vantage a few yards away. He moved to his right and the second symbol that had been blocked from view by the group was there, lined in salt as well. Matt shuddered. The boys had etched a circle a quarter the size of the pentagram. It had two dissecting lines, one longer than the other. The wretched thing was becoming sickeningly familiar to Matt. It popped up in the most horrid, most purely evil places. Later, on this night, Dykeman would draw it in the blood of his family. Decades later, he would draw it in Prichard's blood and in Fisher's blood and in God knew who else's.

"We have prepared the *quill* and the *parchment* for the ritual," Stanley said, pointing at the pencil and paper atop the milking stool. "If you have the... umm..."

"I have it," Dykeman said.

"Then we have everything ready."

"Good, Stan," Dykeman said, applying another friendly slap to his back. Bud winced. "Why don't you drill into these slugs what we're doing here one last time?"

Stan turned to face the others and told them to gather in closely. "Okay boys, like I told you before, once I ring the bell, there can't be any talking. So if you have a question, now's the time to ask it." They all looked at each other, each seemingly sheepish to ask the first question and appear slower than the rest. Stan continued. "The first thing we're going to do is make sure the candles are all lit. We laid them out so that there are groups of three, positioned at the north, south, east, and west points. According to the book, three candles are burnt in a mockery of the holy trinity. One candle burns on the altar. That makes thirteen in total. We gotta make sure, too, that we don't step in the salt and screw up the lines of these symbols. They're important. This one we're standing on is supposed to protect us."

"Protect us?" Artie balked and turned to Dykeman. "Why do we need protection? This is safe, isn't it?"

Morris Dykeman turned his coy smile toward him.

Stan answered on their leader's behalf, "It's safe, but we have to take precautions. The book says, when we open a gate like we plan to do, there is no telling who might be listening on the other end. It's kind of like taking a phone call. You don't know who else might pick up a receiver."

"So this here is gonna keep 'em from droppin' in, then?"

"Not exactly, but it will keep us safe if they *do* drop in. Do you see what I mean, Artie?"

"He sees," Morry said, still smiling. "Keep going, Stan."

"Right...umm...to start, I will ring the bell nine times, turning counter-clockwise to face each compass point. It is supposed to purify the air."

"Why are the compass points important, again?" Bud asked.

Stan ignored him. It was clear that Morry was short on patience and not many questions away from losing his cool altogether. "Then, the *mage*, that's me, performs the Invocation to Sss...to...umm...to Satan." He had trouble even saying the word, though it brought a smile to the faces of the others. Phil even bounced on the balls of his feet like some maniacal jack-in-the-box. "It's right here in the book. They call it a prayer. After that, I pay homage to the Infernal Ones by reading their names, listed here."

"Holy shit," Artie piped up again. "There are like a hundred. You gotta read them all?"

"There are seventy-seven, and yes, I have to read them all."

Morry was smiling on Stan now. He seemed to detect Stan's discomfort, his reluctance to even say the names aloud.

Stan continued referencing the book. "Then the mage takes the sword and points it at all the compass points and calls forth the Four Princes of Hell."

"What are their names?" Morry said. "The Four Princes...the boys should know, don't you think?"

"Well..." Stan went back to the book and paused. Whether it was to read or whether he was nervous, he hid the distinction well. "There is Belial, Baseborn of the Earth, to the north. There is Leviathan, Serpent of the Depths, to the west. There is Lucifer, Bringer of Light, to the east." Stan paused again, then just started reading directly from the text. Perhaps he read the words so they would not be *his* words, *his* thoughts. "To the south dwells the Adversary...the Opposite...the Accuser...the Lord of Fire and of the Inferno...Satan."

"Whoa," Artie exclaimed. He nodded excitedly at Bud and Phil. "Now that's a handle."

"Good job, Stan. I think you might have been born for this," said Morry, another pat on the back followed. "Then what?"

"Then, I will read the request we wrote on the parchment. After that, Morry, you hold it to the thirteenth candle on the altar and burn it while I say, *shemhamforash* and you guys follow up with, *hail Satan.*"

"Hail Satan!" Artie boomed and laughed aloud.

"Not now, you dope," Morry said. "I don't know why I let you come. You're apt to foul this whole thing up."

"Yeah, dope," Bud put in.

Stan waited for the chatter to stop and Morry gave him a prodding look. "Then, Morry makes the sacrifice using the sword."

The dreadful word snatched Matt's attention. He had been pacing the dirt floor, listening to the foolish exchange of the boys, but that word stopped him dead in his tracks. *Sacrifice.* He had forgotten about that part of the ritual and now images of the minced bodies of Dykeman's family flooded his mind.

"We have to capture the blood in the chalice," Stanley continued. "Then we all use the blood to paint the inverted cross on our foreheads."

"What's inverted mean again?" Artie interrupted.

"Upside-down," Stan said sharply. Apparently he was tiring of Artie's dim wits also. He went on, "After that, we place the chalice in the center of the symbol for Belphegor over here."

"Just, please be careful with the glass when you put it down," Bud said.

"The blood is our gift to him."

"Yeah," Morry said. "So he'll give us a gift in return, right Stan?"

"Right..."

Morry laughed then, clapped his hands and rubbed them together. "All right boys, let's get this show on the road." The others followed his example and laughed too—all except Stan. Matt watched him turn away from them and raise the book to make final preparations. He did not read, Matt could tell that much. It was a ploy to hide his emotions from the others. It was clear to Matt that Stan was the only one of the group who had really read the *Sacra Obscurum.* He was the only one who had a firm grasp on what it was all about and the power it contained.

And he was the only one who was afraid.

Matt watched on, praying Stan would slam the book shut and run from the barn. Without him, the ritual would never be performed. Dykeman's family would live. So would he. How many times in his life had Stanley wished for the same thing? How many times did he wish he could take it back? Regardless of all the praying and wishing, Matt knew this *would* happen. It was history and he had a front row seat to watch it unfold.

"Here," Morry said to Stan. He thrust the bell into the smaller boy's hand. "Get started."

Stan studied the brass bell that Dykeman had likely stolen from the school-house after class. His face was distorted and stretched in its reflection.

"Just drop it, Stanley," Matt said. "Drop it and walk out of here."

Instead Stan faced the altar, turned counter-clockwise to the three candles burning at the south edge of the pentagram and rang the bell. Matt looked away, disgusted, as Stan continued to turn and sound the bell, just as the book instructed, just as Dykeman urged him. The others smiled in anticipation. Artie wore the widest grin and Phil put a finger to his lips to remind him to keep quiet.

Matt faced the darkness, unable to watch the action playing out amid the candles. The ringing finally ended and shortly after the tone faded, he heard pages rubbing together, turning over. Then he heard Stan clear his throat. Then Stan's voice rose—tremulous to start—then it grew strong and thick. And in Latin.

Matt turned to watch.

*"In nomine Die nostril Satanas Luciferi excelsi. In nomine Satanas, in dominatorem, terrae, rex mundi, ego praecipio copias Tenebrae impertiri eorum Infero potestatem super nos. Late aperiret portas inferi."*

*This* Stan was not the Stanley Matt had grown up with, the man he had known all his life. Now this old Stan was somehow different again. He read from the book in broken Latin with purpose, a conviction that made it seem as though he had been replaced with another boy—one who was hell-bent on performing the ritual to perfection. He turned a page and began listing peculiar names aloud. They had to be the Infernal Ones.

*"Astaroth...Belaam...Moloch..."*

Within Matt, they conjured images of goat-legged men with cloven feet and horned brows. Red-eyed, disease-spreading creatures with coarse fur and salivating maws.

*"Hecate...Sammael...Azazel..."*

Beings with blue skin and scaled appendages reared at the call. Leathery wings unfurled and spread on searing air currents. Pointed teeth gnashed in anticipation of the souls of tender youth.

*"Thamuz...Russitt...Bast..."*

Minutes passed as Stan continued to summon the demons to witness, calling their names with a rhythm like the marching of a platoon. Matt squatted in the dirt. Each name felt like a blow to his chest. He had no idea there were so many pitiful creatures in hell and each time he thought the list had ended another demon was called. He felt outnumbered. What were he and his orderlies and the Sullivans supposed to do against such organized and zealous evil? Hell had an army and these seventy-seven were merely its officers.

*"Damballa...Shamad...Gorgo..."*

The traces of animal scent in the barn strengthened. The reek of feces became pronounced and pungent. Matt covered his nose and mouth as the stench became overpowering. The boys surrounding Stan detected it also. They passed puzzled looks back and forth. Matt scanned the vicinity as far as the candlelight would allow. He sensed something else behind him—stirring. It was just beyond the reaches of the candles, though he sensed the presence. It intensified with each name Stan called.

*"Beelzebub...Baphomet...Demogorgon..."*

Soon Matt could *hear* them as well. The massing horde in the darkness gave up on secrecy as their numbers grew. Hissing, grunting, snorting—even the screech of a pig—sounded from all sides. Matt considered stepping inside the pentagram with the boys to share in its supposed protection.

*"Belphegor..."*

Stan fell silent. The final guest had been invited. The beast-of-honor joined his brethren in the shadows.

Matt still could not see even one of the seventy-seven, but he could certainly hear them. Their seething and panting and wheezing combined into a horrible din that left him feeling as though he had fallen into the bear den at the zoo.

Inside the salt circle, the boys continued the ritual in silence, despite the other-worldly company now sharing the barn. They wore the colors of fear—blanched faces, red necks—though they went about their foul business all the same. Perhaps it was fear that spurred them on.

Dykeman was the exception. He looked cool and controlled. His movements were smooth, succinct. He handed Stan a fold-up hunting knife as adeptly as a surgical assistant would pass on a scalpel. Stan, however, was no surgeon. His hand shook violently as he reached for the blade. Dykeman turned it handle-first so Stan would not cut himself on its edge.

With the *Sacra Obscurum* in his left hand and the *sword* in his right, Stan turned and addressed each compass point and called forth the Four Princes. When he faced the final group of three candles positioned south, he pointed with the sword and summoned the adversary of God Almighty and the Lord of the Inferno.

Amidst the shadows, a hush fell over the horde. There was a palpable shift in the energy in the barn. The fine hair on Matt's arms straightened and goose pimples formed up the back of his neck. His legs twitched as if his every sub-conscious instinct was urging them to burst into a sprint just as they did when he was a nine-year-old boy standing before the coal chute with Chrissy.

Dykeman took the knife from Stan and handed him a sheet of paper. Stan cleared his throat and read from it aloud. "Hail Belphegor, the Disputer, Bringer of Sloth. Grant wealth eternal to we subjects anointed in the blood of your gift. Let power over men and riches abundant follow us in all our Earthly days. So it be done." Stan handed the parchment to Dykeman and he put it to the flame of the thirteenth candle. He held the page up for the others to witness the fire consume it. The orange glow dancing on his face left his eyes dark and hollow, like those of a skull. When the last bit of paper was ash in Dykeman's hand, Stan referenced the book and said, *"Shemhamforash."*

The other boys took their cue and responded with an emphatic, "Hail Satan." Artie Sullivan grinned like a simple fool, having made his minute contribution.

The assembly in the darkness remained eerily silent. Matt wondered for a moment if they were still there, but his extra sense, that instinctual antenna all men were born with, quickly told him they were. They were waiting for something.

Dykeman knelt down and retrieved a burlap sack from behind the milking stool they were calling the altar. He reached inside and carefully pulled out a black bundle. Matt moved to get a better look at it. Stan had said the sacrifice would follow the burning of the parchment. That was done. This had to be the part Matt had been dreading most. Arthur Sullivan had told him they killed a bird during the ritual, but questions still nagged at Matt. *What if that bundle is something else? What if it is a baby?* That notion nearly stopped his heart. He continued to circle the boys, for the moment scarcely aware of the mob of demons at his back. He had heard of cults sacrificing babies, dissecting them in tribute to some wretched devil. Matt could not imagine these boys would be capable of such an act. He knew them as adults—Stanley, Phillip Prichard, Arthur Sullivan, Mayor Bud Bentley—surely as young men they could not al-low such a thing to happen.

Matt drew close to Dykeman and saw what he was holding. He saw jet black feathers. It *was* a crow. It gleamed in the light of the thirteenth candle. Matt exhaled, able to dismiss the idea of an infant sacrifice. The crow gawked about with clueless, glassy eyes. It did not put up any sort of fight, likely weakened from spending untold hours in the sack. Only when it was under the sword did it make a sound. It gave up a final caw that became more of a gurgle as Dykeman worked the blade through its neck. The horde murmured in response to the sacrifice, like an excited courtroom gallery. The headless bird gyrated in the farm boy's wide grip. With two hands, Dykeman held the bird over the chalice on the altar and squeezed it like a grapefruit. The bird's life essence spurted into the crystal wine glass in globs at first, then it turned to a steady seep as it ran dry. It half filled the glass while some dripped astray and coagulated in the dirt. Dykeman tossed the crow aside and picked up the chalice. He passed it carefully to Stan, using two hands like an altar boy would to a priest during a church service.

Stan put the book down on the altar and took the glass. His hand smeared the blood on the surface of it and he grimaced at the sticky mess. It was the first time he showed his discomfort outright and Dykeman did not like it. In fact, he shot Stan a look so vile and contemptuous that it would likely rival the demeanor of half the demons in attendance. Stan obeyed the unspoken command and turned the glass toward Artie.

Artie dipped his index finger in the contents. "Ooh, it's still warm," he said. Immediately, he recognized his mistake. He mouthed *sorry* to the boys who were now glaring at him. Blood dripped from his finger as he held it over the glass then he brought it to his forehead. He went cross-eyed trying to see what he was doing while he drew an upside-down cross on his brow. When he finished, he grinned at the others stupidly and bounced on his toes.

Next, Phil dipped his bony digit into the chalice. He did not let the excess blood drip off it, so when he drew on his brow, a trickle of blood ran down his nose.

When it was Bud's turn, he hesitated. He was sweating profusely. It matted the hair to his temples and his brow. He had to brush it away to make room for his cross. In silent communication, Bud nodded at the glass, then eyed Stan as if to ask him to draw it for him. Stan shook his head and pushed the glass closer to Bud's swollen belly. Each one must draw his own, was the intended message. Each one must anoint himself of his own free will. Bud did just that. His chubby finger made for a wide cross on his brow.

Matt watched closely now.

It was Stan's turn.

He peered into the contents of the glass and swished the dark red fluid around. Several seconds passed as he waged some inner war with himself. Once, he nearly plunged his finger in the glass only to reconsider and pull it back. The others began exchanging concerned looks. Even the host of otherworldly onlookers seemed displeased at the delay. Their murmuring soon turned to grumbling.

"Come on, Stan," Morry whispered. He stepped in front of the boy they had named the mage for this ritual—the boy who they would elect mage for all future rituals. "We need you to do this."

Matt saw the faintest glimmer of hope. He stepped closer to the boys to better hear their hushed conversation.

"I—I don't think I can," Stan breathed.

"What?"

"I've been reading the book like you said, Morry. I read it cover to cover. It—it's too dangerous to use like this. I don't know what's happening here, but it's...wrong. It's not a game...what we're doing. I can't take part in this. I...I'm a Christian."

"Godamnit, don't say that in here," Morry said, looking around the barn in hopes their guests had not heard his friend's statement. "Now I figured Fatso, here, would chicken out, but you Stan? No, we're in this together."

"No...no, I'm not doing this." Stan's voice rose beyond a whisper. He no longer seemed to care who heard him. "This is wrong. This is a *sin*! And if you want to continue to *sin* like this..." Stan pointed on the milking stool where the *Sacra Obscurum* rested, "...you'd better learn how to read for yourself!"

The other boys were shocked at meek Stanley's utter dissension. They watched, mouths agape, eyes wide, inverted blood crosses and all.

Dykeman dropped the guise of friendship he had shown Stan. Somehow he was able to contain his brimming fury—he still managed to whisper though it came out more a hiss, "Listen here, you little bastard, you're going to finish this thing or—"

Stanley yelled now. "I'm going home. I am going to pray for forgiveness from the *true* Lord...the *Christian* Lord, Jesus Christ." He thrust the wineglass toward Dykeman. The blood sloshed and spilled down his shirt and pants and onto the open page of the *Sacra Obscurum*.

A raucous howl erupted from the shadows like a thousand death screams.

"Oh, shit..." Matt said aloud.

The demons advanced from all sides and brought the darkness with them. The edge of the candlelight seemed to retreat from the combined fury of hell. Matt found himself backing toward the pentagram to stay within the ebbing tide of the light. Inside it, the boys panicked. Mrs. Bentley's crystal glass shattered as Stan threw it down. Bud did not care. He was balled up in the dirt, covering his head in his arms. Artie bolted in one direction only to stop abruptly and change course when he saw some terrible thing in his path. Phil clutched Stan's arm. He screamed, "What do we do? What do we do?" Stan crossed himself and looked around the barn at the coming blackness as it consumed more and more of their turf. It even came down from above, where demons could be heard clambering about the rafters.

Matt remembered some of their many titles from skimming through the book. There was the Deceiver and the Villain and the Sullied One. Others had worse titles. There was the Feaster and the Plague and the Taker of Children. They were the ones he feared to meet now.

Then the candles flared. Like torches fuelled by some arcane energy, they cast dim light to the walls of the barn. Matt prayed for them to burn out, for he preferred the dark over what he saw. Grotesque creatures teemed about the place. They crawled about the floor and walls and amid the rafters. One had the head of a ram. One had a second face on its belly. Another had three mouths. Another, three breasts. There was even a great worm with an oval maw edged in spiny teeth coiling itself around a roof beam. There were piked tails and webbed feet and horns and scales and reptilian eyes and drooping tongues.

To the south stood a man flanked by snarling beasts. For an instant, Matt thought it was one of the boys. No, this was a grown man. He was naked, lean and perfectly muscled, his long manhood hung slack and hairless. He looked directly at Matt with wide eyes that shone saffron in the firelight. His complexion was flawless, his face smooth and wreathed by a mane of blond curls. He smiled and his pink lips parted to reveal snow-white teeth beneath. Matt was unable to move as he shared this lingering look. How did this man see him? *This is a memory*, Matt kept thinking. *I'm not really here. This is a memory.* The man winked at him and spread a pair of great, fleshy wings behind him, opaque and branched with purple veins. The wings flapped twice and the man began to laugh. Matt's mouth dropped open, his eyes flooded with tears. He drew in a breath to scream, and he heard it sound off, terrible and desperate. Only it was not his. He turned to find it had come from Stan.

Dykeman had grabbed hold of Stan. Stan fought to free himself, but long arms and wide hands wrapped around him, pulled him this way and that. Stan screamed again and as the last note of his anguish faded, so too did the horrible din of the demon horde. The barn fell into silence. Dykeman and Stan stopped their grappling. Artie stopped his frantic galloping. Even Bud peeked up from his cowering, like a turtle from under its shell. Dykeman and Stan un-handed each other and looked around the barn at the encroaching darkness. Its steady march halted, though it remained close, poised to come crashing down on them.

Then Stan saw the reason.

"Morry...your feet," he said.

Dykeman looked down and found that he was standing outside the pentagram. During their wrestling he must have accidently stepped beyond the salt-marked lines.

"Get back in," Stan said.

All Dykeman could do was look up at Stan with the widest, most purely fearful eyes that Matt had ever seen. It was already too late. One demon was closing in. Matt watched it cross the room in the sparse light. He saw a long haired beast with a great, yawning, serrated mandible. It disappeared from sight. In an instant it reappeared, several feet closer to Dykeman like it was blinking in and out of this world. It vanished again.

It was Dykeman's turn to scream. Unseen hands hoisted him into the air. Around and around he spun violently and was raised beyond the range of the firelight. Then the world went black. The candles extinguished.

"Come on!" Artie could be heard yelling. "This way! Run!"

The stomping of feet in the dirt floor sounded as the boys made their frantic retreat for the barn doors. So utterly terrified were the boys that they risked running through the demon mob waiting in the darkness.

"Wait for me!" Bud hollered.

Matt felt him run past, breathing heavily. He followed, though he was also frightened half to death. Only he feared the prospect of meeting that beautiful specimen of a man with the unsightly bat wings. *This is a memory. How did he see me?* He ran, and as he did he braced himself to be hooked by a claw or bit on the leg or otherwise assaulted by one of the devils in his path. Attack did not come. He was allowed to pass through unmolested. So were the boys. Matt trailed behind them, following the sound of their footfalls and eventually the sound of the squealing barn door as it was shoved open.

Outside, the boys were illuminated by bright yard lights attached to the adjacent farmhouse some forty yards away. The bracing summer air was a welcome reprieve from the fecal stench of the barn. Stan and Artie doubled over, panted like dogs. Bud crumpled on the ground again, wheezing worse than before. Phil had kept running. He stopped several yards from the others and doubled back when he realized he was alone.

"Where's Morry?" he asked when he rejoined the group.

"He's still in there," Stan said. "We gotta get lights and go back for him."

"Bugger that!" Artie spat. "Didn't you see what got him?"

Bud rolled onto his side and between gasps he said, "I saw...things...in there. We gotta get...outta here. Help me. Help me get...outta here."

"Yeah. Who's to say those things are gonna stay in there?" Artie added. "Fatso's right. We should go."

Stan looked into the pocket of darkness beyond the barn door, then at the crow's blood that had splashed on the back of his hand when he spilled the wine glass. He rubbed it off on his pant leg and eyed the doorway again.

"Don't do it, Stan. Don't you go in there," Phil said.

Matt found himself saying the same thing.

Stan marched toward the doorway. He made it to the edge of darkness, then stopped short and fell over backward.

Morry Dykeman appeared in the threshold.

Bud scrambled to his feet, ready to flee the scene. Artie flinched as well.

"Morry, are you okay?" Stan asked as he propped himself on an elbow. "I saw you..."

"I gotta get home," Dykeman said. He offered nothing else, merely started for the farmhouse, his stride short and stiff legged.

"Whoa, Morry, are you hurt?" Phil asked.

"Yeah, you don't look so good," Artie said.

"I gotta get home," Dykeman repeated, not slowing or even looking back.

The other boys searched each other as Dykeman walked awkwardly away.

"He may have hit his head," Stan offered.

"Is that what you think, Doctor?" Artie quipped. "This whole thing gettin' fouled up is your fault, Stan. You made a mess outta that ri...that ri...outta that thing in there. What the hell got into you?"

"Some *sense* got into me."

"Morry never shoulda trusted you to do it. He shoulda got me to do it. I woulda at least gone through with it."

"Oh, Artie, you can't read any better than Morry can," Phil said.

Artie sneered at Phil, but had no retort.

"Well, we can't tell anyone about what we did here tonight. I'm not sure anyone would believe us, anyway," Stan said once he got up and dusted himself off. "I'll come back tomorrow in the daylight and clean up the barn."

"I'll hang on to *that*," Artie said. He pointed at Phil's hands. Phil was holding the *Sacra Obscurum*.

"How did you find that in the dark?" Stan asked.

Phil shrugged and said, "I was close when the candles went out. I just reached down and the next thing I knew, it was in my hand."

"Well, I'll keep it for Morry," Artie said. "Give it here."

Stan looked back to the barn. He rubbed a chin that did not yet show the faintest indication of peach fuzz and nibbled on his thumb for a moment, eyes never drifting from the black void beyond the door.

Phil held the book out for Artie.

"No," Stan said. He moved between them. "Give it to me, Phil."

"Why?" Artie whined.

"Because I know what it can do and I'll keep it out of the wrong hands."

"You don't know shit, Stan. We don't even know if what happened in there had anything to do with the book."

"Don't be stupid, Artie. You know we made that happen…and that book showed us how. It needs to be hidden away."

"I think maybe Stan should keep it, too," Phil said. "What do you think, Bud?"

Bud Bentley was eyeing the barn door uncomfortably, like he expected a slew of monsters to emerge any second. "Stan," he sputtered. "Give it to Stan."

Phil shook his head at Artie and handed the book to Stan. "Hide it. Keep it secret," he said.

"Fine, you can keep it until Morry wants it back," Artie said. "Just don't forget—it ain't yours."

Stan agreed, though Matt knew that book was not going to see the light of day again for sixty years. The boys went their separate ways, each running at his top speed. Matt watched them go, then he watched Morris Dykeman slowly climb the steps to the farmhouse, face the door for a few seconds and change course. Dykeman stepped to the corner of the wrap-around veranda and bent down. He picked up a pair of garden shears, strolled back to the door, and went inside.

# Chapter Twenty-Three

The study was frigid when he woke, balled on the floor. Cundiff and Klewes were still thumping on the door. He called to them, but his voice was a dry wheeze. His muscles were achy and his joints jittered as he rolled to his knees. How long had he been *away*? How long had it taken for him to relive the '52 summer solstice?

Already the terror of the barn was fading like a dream in morning light. A few waking hours would have it totally purged from his system. He would at least be to the point where he would question the things he had seen, and his rational mind would chalk it up to delirium from extreme fear or tricks of the shadow. No wonder Arthur Sullivan did not do the evening's activities justice when he described them to Matt. For him, it likely became an abstract concept more than fifty years ago. Over the years, there were likely many times he doubted the event even occurred.

Matt could understand how. Perhaps his vision had been a *rendition* of what happened that night, loosely based in fact. Perhaps not. He could not shake the image of the winged man—beautiful as an angel but for those demon wings. They shared that lingering look and that not-angel had smiled on him. He had looked *through* him. What was he trying to say? Even in the cold air of the study Matt felt a new chill building in his chest.

"I'm okay," he managed to shout after clearing his throat. He got to his feet and cradled the casted hand he had neglected while unconscious or asleep or whatever he was.

"Matt," he heard Cundiff call from the hallway. "What the hell happened?"

Matt eyed the urn mounted on the mantel and answered the question silently. *Stanley gave me his side of the story.* He laid a hand on the wooden base of the trophy-styled urn. "All these years, I was wrong," he whispered. "You cared. In your own way, you cared. Enough to send me away from here. And you tried to stop your friends that night." Matt felt an invisible ice pack come to rest on his shoulder. "You took responsibility for what happened in the barn and it changed your life. The burden shouldn't have been yours alone."

The study door gave up a *click*, its knob turned, and it swung lazily open to reveal the pair of stunned orderlies on the other side. They watched the door open of its own volition and turned their confusion toward their boss. Matt shook his head to ward off their questions before they even came. Cundiff and Klewes nodded subtly in agreement. Maybe in that brief nonverbal, exchange, they decided to never speak of it again.

The front door was thrown open and Arthur Sullivan appeared in the threshold, Ricky peeking over his shoulder. "What the hell is going on in here?" he boomed.

"Umm...two of our people were found dead, another is missing," Matt said, choosing not to relate the story of the doors slamming on their own.

Sullivan's stern countenance didn't waver. "Sounds like Bud made his move," he said.

"I think you're right," Matt said. He recalled the raspy whisper he had heard—the one that he feared came from the book. It spoke of *Darcy* and of *Blood*. "You know where to find him, don't you?"

Sullivan gave a stiff nod and said, "It's likely we'll find your friend there, too. You have something he wants."

"Now, he has something we want," Matt finished.

"Let's go then," Cundiff said, already starting for the door. Klewes followed.

Matt let the others go ahead. He turned to the desktop where the *Sacra Obscurum* waited. His instinct was to snatch it up and follow the orderlies, but he hesitated before touching it. Eric Fisher had told him what the book could do. Sullivan had too. After witnessing its works firsthand, Matt had garnered a true respect for it. It was what he would call a healthy fear. He ran a finger down the gutter of its pages and across the tail of its cover. That was when he noticed it was no longer opened to the page half stained with crow's blood. Somehow several pages had been turned to a new section. He read the bold black title of the entry and smiled.

He raised his head to the empty room and said, "Thank you, Father."

He folded the page to note the section and gathered the book under his arm. At the door, he took another look at the study that held so much of Stanley Dawson. He wondered if he would get to see it again.

\* \* \* \*

It was all Stanley could do to follow his son to the front door, but he wanted to lay eyes on him for every fleeting second he could. When Matthew had disappeared and the door closed behind him, Stanley went down on one knee in the entryway. He had done more parenting in twenty minutes than he had in the last twenty years. *Hopefully quality trumps quantity*, he mused.

He felt utterly depleted. It had taken every ounce of his strength to show Matthew the coal chute, and at that point, his job was only half done. After showing him the events in the barn, he felt thin and empty, even for a ghost, and he wondered if he had gone too far to recover. *What happens to a spirit when a spirit dies?*

Stanley slumped to the floor, too weak to even prop himself on his knees. He decided that his efforts were worth it, if they helped his boy even slightly. At least he now knew what kind of evil he was up against.

Stanley rolled onto his side. He recounted the mistakes he made in his youth—the ones that as Matt said, changed his life. Oh, there were regrets. The greatest of all was that he did not prepare his son for this day. Instead of hiding Matthew from the *Sacra Obscurum*, he should have taught him how to use it so that he would not be menaced by the greedy Bud Bentleys of the world or the Belphegors of the underworld. *That is the glory of hindsight*, he thought. In the moment, he did his level best to protect his son from harm like any parent would. He only wished now that he had done it in some way that would have still let him be a dad.

Stanley felt a burst of heat in the corners of his eyes. He rubbed at them and found moisture. They were wet with tears. On the cold, hard floor of the entryway, he wept tears filled by some long lost inner heat. He wept for his ruined family and that he should linger on to witness its end. "Still human," he said and chuckled despite himself.

A line of white-hot light spilled across him. It came shining from the gap at the bottom of the front door. It leaked through all sides of the entry until it formed a brilliant halo. Stanley felt warmth in its glow. It infused him with the power he needed to get to his feet. He crept toward the door and eyed the knob. He would never be able to muster the strength necessary to pass through the door. That ghostly act took far more energy than he had left. The knob may as well be a boat anchor for as much as he could move it. Still, he laid his spectral hand on it. It was thrilling how warm it was to the touch. The doorknob flooded his body with heat, and then it turned in his grip.

Stanley stepped backward as the door opened toward him. The brilliance beyond blinded him and he tried to shield his eyes against it. Never had he seen such luminance. It called to him. It showed him just how dark and drab the world in which he spent his life truly was. Suddenly his profound fatigue abated. He felt young again—ready to explore new horizons. Yet, when he stepped out the door, he found only the familiar old floorboards of the front veranda.

It was *his* porch, but also different. The front of the house was drenched in the most beautiful golden sunlight. A soft breeze teased his sparse hair and on it he could smell a thousand summer blooms. His skin tingled as he breathed in nature's perfume.

Down the steps, the flower beds were an artist's pallet of gorgeous hues, unlimited by human imagination. His eye wandered to the lush carpet of grass that spread out before him. Its long, sweeping expanse rolled like a subtle wave frozen in time. Down the vibrant pitch he was drawn to the three cherry trees exploding in pink and violet blossoms and alive with a plethora of ivory butterflies, flitting on the air like thrown confetti.

When he looked at the foot of the middle tree, any doubt he had that he was still alive melted away. The cold and dark life he had come from became only the memory of a perilous journey through a hostile land of angels and devils and men. The woman in the white sundress, who rose from the summer grass amid the snowing petals, welcomed him home.

# Chapter Twenty-Four

The text in Matt's lap jumped wildly as he tried to read it in the moving car. It was a hopeless endeavor and not just because of the inadequate dome light. Yet, he persisted. Soon, Arthur had promised, they would be at Dykeman's barn and then it would be too late to cram. He would face testing whether he was ready or not.

"Sorry Matt," Klewes said as he attempted to ease the car around the potholes in the road. Cundiff reached for his shoulder from the backseat and shushed him so he would not distract Matt from his studying. Matt had told the orderlies that he found something in the book that may prove useful and from that moment they had taken a vow of silence so he could give it his full attention. He did.

The only time he had looked up was when they first left the Dawson house. Matt had watched the Sullivan Fisheries pickup lead their car out of the driveway and onto Prince of Wales. The men in the back of the truck caught his attention. They were cradling their rifles like soldiers in a troop transport headed for the front line. While preparing to battle the forces of hell was daunting, seeing the armed men brought a reality-based sense of danger to their mission. Those guns were *real*. Their bullets were *real and* they would assuredly fly if things did not go well.

Whatever instruction Matt could glean from the book, he found himself applying to the vision he'd had in the study. He saw those boys, his father among them, as they worked through the steps of their ritual and it was proving invaluable. The process of saluting the unholy from the corners north, south, east and west. The significance of the symbols carved into the earth. Reading aloud the Latin segments as best one could, for it was the spirit of the incantation that was clearly important not proper enunciation. He would follow the example the boys had set, only he hoped for better results. There was a strong possibility that, while he attempted to rid their world of the demon inhabiting Dykeman, he would make things worse. He may open wide the gate to any number of the baddies on the other side.

Matt saw what had happened to young Morris Dykeman when he stepped outside the protection of the pentagram. He saw the beast that stalked him—its long reach, its fur-covered body, eyes as black as the abyss it came from. It seemed to shimmer, to jump from this dimension to another and back again. It moved as though it was under a strobe light, and though it was visible for only fractions of a second, Matt would never forget what he witnessed. Like it or not, he would be able to call upon the memory like it was a photograph saved to his hard drive.

He pictured the symbol—the circle with the two vertical lines running through it. That is the *symbol for Belphegor*, Stan had said before they started the ritual. That calling card was left at the murder scenes, scrawled in the victims' blood like an artist brimming with pride over a masterpiece would sign his initials.

The book bounced on Matt's lap as they hit an especially deep rut in the road. Klewes hissed a sort of apology and Matt sunk back to his thoughts.

Not to be lost in all of this was the fact that Dykeman was the first victim. He was somehow *chosen* when the ceremony got fouled up, thanks in large part to Stan's cold feet. Seventy-six demons—seventy-six repulsive creatures that had crawled from the pit to attend the ritual in the barn—stood by while the souls of five children were served up on a plate. *Why? Why didn't they close in like sharks on an injured seal?* Because, those souls were anointed for only one of them to consume...Belphegor. Matt had the demon's name. According to the page he'd folded in the *Sacra Obscurum*, that was a very important piece of the ritual he aimed to perform. That is, if he got the chance.

The steady hum of the car rolling over asphalt was broken when it made a left turn. The crackle of coarse rock under tire called Matt's attention away from the book in his lap. The pickup ahead of them continued on down the tree-lined dirt road. The tall trees stretching from either side of the road reached out, their limbs mingling over the center of the drive. The dense vegetation formed a sort of roof overhead that served to block the moonlight. In the dark, it looked like the truck before them was delving deeper and deeper into the mouth of a cave. The soldiers in the back, swaying with the swells of the road, paid little heed to the encroaching darkness. They continued to face the trailing car, still clutching rifles.

The dips and dives in the dirt road made it impossible for Matt to continue reading. No matter, for a minute later Klewes said, "I think we're here."

The pickup's brake lights came on solid and it slowed to a full stop on the roadside. Arthur Sullivan was the first one out. He guarded his eyes against the Corolla's headlights as he made his way toward it. Matt rolled down his window when the old salt got there.

"We'll go the rest of the way on foot," he said, puffing cigarette smoke. "Might be best if Bud don't know we're comin'."

\* \* \* \*

Matt would have called it *déjà vu*, but that hardly did the feeling justice when he saw the Dykeman place. It was more than scant familiarity—he had been here already tonight, only last time it was to watch the Bud and Artie of many years past. He stopped at the edge of the driveway where it split between the barn and the farmhouse and took it all in. It was exactly the same as it had been in his vision. The white clapboard siding on the house was dingy and weathered, but not rotten. The porch roof was sagging, but not fallen. The porch swing drooped lower on one end, but still it hung. Even the barn, with its sun dried boards missing in places throughout its vast walls, was basically unchanged. Arthur said Bud had kept the place up, but he must have gone to great lengths to keep it at the same level of decay it had shown in '52, as though it existed in its own secret bubble, unaffected by the passage of time.

Matt recognized the fruits of obsession when he saw them. It was a strong obsession indeed, one born of extreme fear that allowed Bud to pull this off.

The condition of the farm had been the solitary thing he could control in this whole unsettling situation and control it he did, even if the setting of the ritual did not matter one bit in the end. His fear would not leave it to chance. Matt wondered how the mayor was able to keep that lurking terror and obsession under wraps successfully enough to interact with people normally let alone win public office. In his experience, these symptoms always found a way to manifest and the results were never pretty.

Robbie "Bud" Bentley was a dangerous man. To make matters worse, he had abducted Darcy in all likelihood. If he wanted to trade her for the book as Sullivan suggested, Matt would oblige. Though he had a feeling Bud was going to be disappointed.

A slight breeze wafted streamers of fog between the gathered men as they took note of the forgotten farm. It seemed the fog had not forgotten it. It was here waiting for them as though it knew of some shortcut that allowed it to race their vehicles to the place. In the relative safety of the group, Matt easily dismissed the ghostly vapors swirling about them, though, if he were on his own, he would have been totally unnerved. The fog only added to the ambiance of the macabre scene. This long-abandoned farm was already sour, tainted by the presence of evil. It would not have surprised Matt to look out on the pasture and witness a spectral heard of cattle grazing, or to hear the caw of a phantom rooster, or to look on the porch and find Dykeman's butchered family emerging from the farmhouse, dropping limbs that were more bone than flesh and trailing gore from their abdominal cavities.

A gravelly voice chased the gruesome figments of Matt's imagination. "I'm sendin' these two around back," Sullivan said. "The rest of us will go in the front. Maybe we can get Bud surrounded and talk him out of whatever harebrained scheme he's come up with."

Cundiff did not care for the plan. "That's just stupid. If he has Darcy in there, surrounding him might provoke him. What if he's got a gun?"

"It does sound dangerous," Matt offered.

"I've known the man more years than I'd care to admit," Arthur said. "I know he'll be reasonable." He looked at the book under Matt's arm. "Besides, we know what he really wants, don't we? He won't risk losin' it now that it's so close."

"That's right," Matt said, "but don't forget, we're here to deal with Dykeman and we can't let Bud get in the way of that."

Sullivan turned his focus on the barn. "Well, I guess if Bud don't come around to our way of thinkin', I'll have to straighten him out." The old fisherman dug into his pants pocket and worked a stub-barreled revolver out. He rolled it open and checked the chamber. "But make no mistake—it'll be me or no one. He don't deserve to be done by the likes of you."

"You just be careful where you aim that thing," Cundiff said, his face as grim as the grave. "If anything happens to Darcy, I'll kill you with my bare hands. I don't care what your name is."

"Relax, *Cundt*," Ricky said, stepping forward. "Nothing's gonna happen to your little girlfriend...not tonight, anyhow."

Cundiff took a step toward the younger Sullivan. Before they were chest-to-chest Klewes got in between them to soothe matters. Matt also tried to calm his orderly, promising that Doctor Collins' safety was everyone's top priority. It was not until Sullivan barked his own order that Ricky stood down. "Go around back," he said and gestured at one of his henchmen. "You go with him. Make any noise and give up the surprise and I'll shoot you both."

Matt and the orderlies followed Sullivan to the front of the barn while his other hired gun held the rear. The porch light from the farmhouse lit their path until they got close to the double doors. There the corner of the barn blocked the solitary light and created a pocket of utter blindness. Sullivan disappeared into it. Matt went in next with no small measure of reluctance.

"Keep it down, boys," Sullivan whispered.

Matt could see none of him, but obeyed his detached voice all the same. Then there was a *clink* that could only be a latch of some kind opening. "Easy now," Sullivan murmured. Matt could sense he was pulling the broad barn door open slowly in hopes of keeping it quiet. It would only take one loud squawk from an old hinge to alert whoever may be inside to their presence.

A moment later Sullivan whispered, "Dawson, c'mere and look at this." He had silently opened the door by a couple of feet. Perhaps oiling those old hinges was a part of Bud's upkeep regimen.

Matt felt his way behind Sullivan and tried to figure out which direction he should be looking in. A slight draft carrying a familiar livestock aroma touched his face and led him to the opening where he craned his head inside. Then he saw the soft glow of a small gas lantern. It hung from one of the stalls, and in the dirt a few yards to its right, were the candles. The specks of light were arranged squarely at the center of the barn just like they had been in 1952.

"My God, it's like steppin' back in time," Sullivan said with discernable anguish. "My God Almighty, it's like a day never went by. What do you call that?"

Matt said in his lowest voice, "*Déjà vu.*"

"Yeah, it's like that all over again."

Matt heard one of the guys behind him sigh.

"It's like we were just here yesterday. Morry and Philly and Bud and Stan and me—it's like it all went to shit last night. But it was years ago, long before we started...droppin' like goddamned flies."

"Are you all right, Mister Sullivan?" Matt asked.

"Yeah...I'm good."

"You know Bud Bentley is still alive. In fact he might be inside here...and the two of you can still help Morry."

Sullivan was silent for a few seconds that passed more like minutes. Then he took a breath to gather himself and said, "Let's get this done."

Matt heard footsteps grinding in the dirt and he knew that Sullivan had gone inside. "Let's go," he whispered to the orderlies and he crept beyond the doorway, himself. Then he felt a rather large mitt on his shoulder and a scream threatened to pipe out of him like steam through a whistle. He was quick to stifle it when he realized that it was Klewes reaching out to keep his bearings in the dark.

Stepping inside the barn was like walking into some alien world where the gravity was not quite right and the air was comprised mostly of some gas other than oxygen. Matt felt the heavy atmosphere pressing on his lungs, weighing him down. The subtle lamplight allowed for some repressed vision, though he was undecided if it was better to squint or widen his eyes. Just like in the barn in his vision, the weak light did not cut the gloom very far. The outer walls remained shrouded and would again provide excellent cover for party crashers, be they human or otherwise.

Klewe's hand slid off Matt's shoulder. "What the fff—" escaped the orderly in a hushed voice. Cundiff came up with a similar response when he saw the arrangement of candles and the large symbol on the floor between them. Matt wondered if they sensed the palpable change in atmosphere, too, or if it was simply his nerves running amok. Though he would not share his apprehension with any of them, he feared the odd climate may have been caused by the presence of something that did not belong in their world.

Arthur Sullivan strode directly to the edge of the pentagram.

*So much for the element of surprise,* Matt thought. *Why had he insisted on secrecy if he wasn't going to use it?* Matt wondered what became of the pair that entered from the other end of the barn. *Did they lose their way in the dark?* Then he saw them as they emerged from the blackness across the pentagram from Sullivan. No wait, they were not Sullivan's men.

"Darcy!" Cundiff rushed past Matt to where Bud Bentley had a hold on Darcy's arm. Before the orderly could get close, Bud aimed a gun his way. It brought Cundiff to a sudden stop.

"You stay put there, John Cundiff," the mayor said. The sweat coating his jowly cheeks glistened in the candlelight. "That goes for the rest of you, too. Don't make me use this."

"Darcy, are you okay?" Cundiff said.

"I'm fine, but Saint Michael's...there's no one there. Wanda and Nurse Tait..."

"We saw. We called Elmer. He's there with the patients," Cundiff said, turning an icy stare on Bud. "Did he hurt you?"

"No...really...I'm okay. John, just do as he says. I just want this over with."

"Yes my dear, me too," Bud assured her. "It will be over soon, that is if your Doctor Dawson does as he's asked."

Matt and Klewes flanked Cundiff at the edge of the salt-lined symbol in the dirt. Bud eyed the book under Matt's arm. "That's it...isn't it," he said, unblinking. "That's the book. It's here." He lowered the gun as if he suddenly struggled with the weight of it. "Oh God, that's it...thank God."

Matt had never seen the mayor like this. He had witnessed momentary lapses in the man's public façade, but any trace of his wide smiles and warm kind eyes was undetectable. The friendly features had been replaced by those of a desperate and terrified man. Darcy saw it too. "Bud, I'll do what you ask, but you have to let my friends go. They have no part in this."

"That's where you're wrong, Doctor." He smiled at Darcy with his new, unkind smile. "The ritual calls for blood."

"You son of a bitch," Cundiff blurted.

"Let's rush him," Klewes said. "He can't hit all of us."

Darcy yelled for them to stop.

Matt threw his arms out to bar their advance and begged them to keep level heads. "Bud, you're not getting any closer to this book until you let Darcy go. You should know that there's a rifle behind you."

Bud released a sick laugh that smacked of desperation. "Wrong again, Doctor. The rifle is behind *you*."

It took a few seconds for Matt to get his meaning. *There is no way. The Sullivans are with us. They're on our side. Arthur wouldn't have...*Matt looked at Sullivan and found that the old salt had pulled his revolver and turned it his direction. The hard look in the old man's eyes, made more sinister by the dance of the candle flames, said it all. "You...lied..." was all Matt could manage.

"It's nothin' personal, Dawson," Sullivan said, nodding a direction to the rifleman behind them as he herded the orderlies aside at gun point. "I tried tellin' you how important that book is to us. If me and Bud don't get the use of it, we're as good as dead." Ricky Sullivan and the other gunman appeared from the gloom and stood by their master. "I don't feel like dyin' just yet."

"Me neither," Bud added.

Matt looked at the book in his hand. The title on the black leather cover caught the light just right and it seemed to glow. He wondered how he ever could have missed the etched title block the first time he inspected the book.

*So much trouble was caused by such an innocent-looking thing*, Matt mused. *It almost seemed unbelievable, but one look in the eyes of these men told you it was all too real.*

Matt turned to where the orderlies stood with their hands up. They shared a common expression of total confusion. Not Darcy, though. She was becoming despondent. It was clear that the situation was beyond her ability to manage. She would have to leave her fate up to these men and it did not sit well with her at all.

"I don't suppose we can just leave you the book and walk out of here," Matt said, knowing escape would not be that easy.

"We need you to perform the ritual like your old man did," Sullivan answered. "If you work magic half as good as him, it should go off without a hitch."

"Still can't read for yourself, Artie?"

Sullivan's jaw clinched as though the words slapped him in the face. "I'll read your goddamned eulogy good enough."

"True enough, we never did get a handle on the thing," Bud said. "Of course we never had a real good look at it. Not for lack of trying, though. We even hired us a professional witchcraft expert to pry that book out of your hands."

"Who..." Matt already knew, it just took him a second to process. He saw the wry smile slanting across Eric Fisher's face. "Fisher worked for you?"

"Yes he did, although he didn't work out long term. Good kid though, he was even willing to help us do the ritual for a handsome fee." Bud shook his head in feigned grief. "Too bad about him."

*That rotten bastard*, Matt thought. *Was every word that came out of his mouth a lie? And to think I tried to find the book for him. I would have given it to him had Dykeman not...*

"Yeah, too bad," Sullivan added. "Morry, or whoever is behind Morry's wheel these days, squashed his fuckin' head like a grape."

"Well," Matt said. "You mess with the bull, sometimes you get the horn."

"That's it exactly," Bud agreed excitedly.

Darcy looked at Bud, her face blanched. It seemed she suddenly understood the kind of violence he was capable of.

"Anyhow, we lost our expert, so we had to move on to plan B. That's you, Dawson," Sullivan said. "We figured Stanley showed you a thing or two outta that book over the years. Could be you're a better magician than Fisher, for all we know."

Matt snickered and said, "You're idiots..."

"Yeah, sick fucking idiots," Klewes added and it earned him a hard poke in the sternum from a gun barrel.

"Until two hours ago, I'd never laid eyes on this book in my life."

Arthur Sullivan did not like that news at all, but he did his best to remain calm. "Hmm, I guess old Stan wanted to save all the fun for himself."

"He sure as hell kept it from us," Bud said. "I think he liked to watch us suffer."

"Suffer? You fools prayed to some devil for money and power...and what do you know, you got it in spades. What happened to the others? Well, Morris Dykeman killed his family and was locked away for his entire life. Tonight, he got loose and killed two good people. Before them, Phillip Prichard, like Fisher, got his head—how did you put it—squashed like a grape. All Stanley got was the burden of keeping this book out of the wrong hands, out of your hands. It ruined his life. How can either of you say that you suffered? What in the name of God do you think you deserve?"

"Hey, we didn't ask for this. Do you think Morry wanted to share this magic book with us because we were his dearest friends? He was no saint. He *used* us. He couldn't read so he got Stan to do it for him and he was nervous, so he got the rest of us to share in the risk."

"We were kids...stupid kids and we made a mistake," Bud blurted, his face starting to twist with genuine grief.

"Oh sure, we got some money out of the deal, but it ain't worth nothing when you live in constant fear, always wonderin' if there are things hidin' in the shadows..."

"Wondering what they'd do to ya if they ever got their hands on ya..."

"Where you're going when you die..."

"Where Philly Prichard is right now..."

"If heaven is shut to people like us..."

"If we're going to burn...forever."

Everyone else in the barn went quiet while Sullivan and Bud studied each other across the pentagram. Ricky rubbed at his eyes and turned away from the light. Even Darcy shed the frightened expression that had strained her face. She now seemed to have a degree of pity for her captor.

Matt thought about his father and the relationship they never got to share because Stanley had lived in fear, too. He was afraid of his son getting drawn into the mess he created. He did everything he could to keep Matt out of it and yet here he was, in the very barn where it all started. Stanley had failed and Matt felt no pity for these men.

"I...umm...I read about a ritual in here that might help you both," Matt said. He watched the relief wash over their red faces. "I'll just need a little time to prepare."

\* \* \* \*

Sullivan and Bud stepped into the pentagram with Matt. "Careful you don't mess the lines, my dear," Bud told Darcy when he dragged her in, as well. His face was now frozen in a demented grin like a nervous contestant on a game show. In contrast, Sullivan was stone-faced and all business. He knew there was no jackpot at the end of this, but if it worked out, he would be getting off death row. The orderlies and Sullivan's men were left outside. Matt knew what that meant—they would not be protected from whatever hell-dwelling creatures the ritual may summon. There was no love lost between these men and the orderlies, so it made sense that they would not be invited in. Yet, Ricky was Arthur's son, his own blood, and he was left out and completely ignorant of the danger coming his way. Matt looked from one Slullivan to the other. The elder met his eyes then turned away.

"I guess we're ready to start," Matt said. "No talking from here on."

"Matt, are you fucking nuts?" Cundiff shouted. "You can't go through with this."

That earned him a blow to the belly with a rifle stalk.

Bud said, "If either of them says another word, shoot 'em both." Sullivan's men looked to their boss and he nodded in agreement.

Matt looked to the orderlies, barely visible at the edge of the candlelight, and wished he could apologize for all they had been through and what they were about to face. He could not bring himself to look at Darcy and feel her judgment. Instead, he opened the *Sacra Obscurum* to the folded page to read it over and make final preparations. The set up from '52 was still carefully laid out with the exception of the chalice. The one the boys dropped had been replaced by an identical crystal wineglass. It sat atop the milking-stool-altar along with the thirteenth candle, the hunting knife, a schoolyard bell, a pencil and a few blank sheets of paper. Matt bent down and gathered the bell.

Just as he witnessed Stan do, Matt rang the bell to begin the ritual, first at the cluster of candles to the south then he turned counter-clockwise and sounded the bell to the west.

When the cycle of bell-tolling was complete, he referenced the book and read aloud. *"In nomine Die nostril Satanas Luciferi excelsi..."* His pulse accelerated as he said the words. What they meant, he had no clue, but it was clear the words held power—they flowed out of him as though he was fluent in Latin. *"In nomine Satanas, in dominatorem, terrae, rex mundi, ego praecipio copias Tenebrae impertiri eorum Infero potestatem super nos..."* His voice swelled with conviction as though he wanted nothing less than to raise Hell to the Earth.

*"Late aperiret portas inferi!"*

Matt gasped for breath like he had run a lap of the barn at a full gallop. Arthur and Bud seemed to appreciate his efforts thus far. Bud was still grinning like a fool, Arthur nodded his approval. Darcy, however, was less than impressed with his new-found talent. She looked on him like he was a broken thing that could not be mended. It was the same way she regarded poor, sick Bud. The expression wounded Matt.

He pressed on. The book demanded it.

Next he was prompted to call upon the Infernal Ones. He had watched Stan call them out in sequence, all seventy-seven of them. He had listened to them massing in the dark corners of the barn until all were in attendance and the ruckus of their unearthly chatter was almost unbearable. This night, Matt would have no use for such a large group. For this particular ritual, only one guest would be invited. He looked up from the book, faced west and called unto him.

"*Belphegor...*"

Neither Arthur nor Bud so much as batted an eye at the deviation from the ritual they had participated in with Dykeman. As Matt expected, neither of them detected it. He wondered, if he showed them the title on the page he read from, if they would understand what he was doing then. If they read *The Infernal Exorcism*, then would they get it? They thought the *Sacra Obscurum* was a book of magic spells, but it was so much more to whoever possessed it. It could bring the darkness, but it could also send it away.

Matt listened carefully for some sign that their guest had joined them in the barn. None was forthcoming. He knelt, laid the book carefully on the ground and retrieved the knife from the altar. With only one fully functioning hand, he had difficulty opening the blade. Sullivan stepped forward to offer help, but Matt waved him off. He got the thing open with his teeth and eyed its shiny bite. If the ritual had not worked to this point, blood would spill and the thought of it turned his stomach. He had to trust in the book and that left him feeling worse.

As he rose from his knee, he dragged his foot on the ground and scuffed one point of the pentacle star under him. Salt mixed with dirt as he smeared the slanting lines under foot. All eyes were on the blade in Matt's hand. He moved toward Darcy, subtly dragging his foot as he went and extended his casted hand for her to take. She did not. Instead, she looked on her employer with disgust and a faint undertone of fear. Matt wondered if she thought he really had it in him to cut her and use her blood in this perverted prayer. Bud and Arthur seemed to think so. One, or both of them, pushed her toward Matt where he waited with the ceremonial sword in hand.

Matt caught her in his arms and their eyes locked.

It was then Bud noticed the broken lines of the pentagram. "Oh, my...G—" he stuttered. "Artie, look!" He leveled his revolver on the two and drew the hammer back. The *click* it made grabbed Matt's attention. It spurred him to action. He yanked Darcy around and turned his back to the gun. He cringed as he waited to hear the shot. In an instant, he expected to feel a bullet slam into his back. He imagined it would feel like a searing hot poker piercing his flesh and organs. What he heard next was not a shot. It was Sullivan. He released a ruinous noise that Matt could only describe as death's door-terror. It was the kind of noise a man only made once. And he was not sure he wanted to see what caused it, but in reflex, he was already turning to look.

He saw Sullivan, his face drawn, his mouth in an *O* shape. Beside him, Bud was much the same only a blot of darkened fabric steadily expanded at the crotch of his trousers. He still had the gun aimed at Matt, but like Sullivan, he was looking to his right. Matt followed their gaze and what he saw paralyzed him with fear as well.

Morris Dykeman stood at the edge of the darkness.

He smiled on his old friends, showing his yellow teeth, few and far between.

His pale blue hospital johnny was a smear of blood work. It looked like the canvas of a painter who tried to capture an eruption of lava. Unblinking eyes—black as the bottom of the bay—studied the two men. Webs of blue veins branched from their sockets to either side of his hairless head. Matt swallowed hard, and his mouth went desert-dry. He watched as Dykeman stood unnaturally still, his gangly limbs poised and taut, with pasty flesh nearing translucence stretched tight over bone.

Then he was gone.

Bud's trance lifted and he scanned his surroundings, recklessly panning his gun back and forth in search of a target. Sullivan did the same, having pulled his revolver from his pocket.

"What the hell was that?" Ricky shouted.

"Dykeman," Cundiff told him.

As if lured by saying his name, Dykeman reappeared, this time closer to Bud and Sullivan. He vanished just as quickly. Matt recognized the sporadic movements. He had watched the demon doing the same thing as he stalked Morry Dykeman in 1952. The thing flashed in and out of sight until it reached the boy with his long, furred appendages and grabbed him up. Matt tried to speak, but his voice failed him. Utter shock had over-ridden his systems.

Then Dykeman reappeared—this time between the two men. He crossed the broken pentagram without pause. Sullivan spun around with his gun, but Dykeman swatted him to the dirt as he would an insect. He then turned on Bud. The mayor was hopelessly slow in his defense. Dykeman knocked the revolver from his grip and clutched a handful of his jacket. He pulled Bud in and laid a wide hand on top of his sweaty head. *Call me Bud* Bentley never smiled again. Dykeman squeezed that big mitt closed and blood and bone and tissue sprayed in all directions.

Matt was close enough to get misted by the mayor's fluids, and still, he could not move. In fact, he was on the verge of passing out and only Darcy's scream kept him from a full-on swoon. It preceded the gunshots by only a fraction of a second. The report of rifles filled the barn as the Sullivan men opened up on the thing that felled the mayor. Their target disappeared again, but still they fired into the darkness.

"Run," Matt yelled at Darcy, hoping his voice would cut through the sound of gunshots.

Darcy heard. She bolted to where Cundiff was waiting. Klewes was already leading their escape toward the double barn doors. The gunmen paid them no attention, their focus entirely on firing at nothing, reloading and firing again.

Matt was tempted to fall in behind his friends, but he could not leave yet. Summoning the demon was only his first goal. If he was going to stop it for good and all, he needed to finish the ritual. He turned and scooped up the book, then he went about fixing the pentagram in the places he'd scuffed its lines. The firing of guns faded while he dug with his fingers to make the final repairs. He heard Ricky shout, "Dad, are you okay?"

And the old salt answered with a growl.

*He's still alive.*

He said, "Get after them and get 'em back here."

Matt turned to face Arthur Sullivan while his men obediently beat it for the doors. Sullivan got up gingerly and dusted himself off. He had nothing but hate in his eyes when he looked at Matt. They eyed each other a moment in the safety of the newly repaired pentagram then both men dropped their gaze to the dirt and the revolver that lay between them.

In a split second they were in motion. Matt was younger and relatively un-harmed—he should have been the quicker. Yet, Sullivan obviously had a hun-ger for life in him that few men ever knew. He beat Matt to the gun by inches. Then it was all hands and arms vying for control of it. The advantage went to Sullivan. Matt gritted his teeth and squealed as he tried to get some fight out of his broken hand. It failed him.

Sullivan pulled the gun away and with it, pistol-whipped Matt across the jaw. His head hit the dirt and he was left with an up-close view of the three candles burning to the south. He told himself to get up—that if he wanted to live, he *had* to get up. Still, darkness crept in and he watched the southern candles fade and fade.

* * * *

"Hurry," Klewes yelled. The shooting in the barn stopped and he did not necessarily think that was a good sign. "Jesus Christ, did you see what hap-pened to Bud?" Cundiff came out of the darkness with Darcy in hand. They stopped in the faint light from the farmhouse porch. It lit the fog around them as it flowed on the breeze like a tattered gray flag. It was nearly waist high, and thick enough for someone to hide in without much trouble.

"Matt's still in there," Darcy said. "We can't just leave him."

"We don't have much choice," Cundiff said, fighting for his breath. "We don't have guns."

"I know where we can get some," Klewes said. "Let's get the car. We'll come back for Matt when we can shoot back."

Darcy glared at him. "You're going to have a gunfight with the Sullivans? Is that the plan? Well, that's a great way to get Matt killed if he isn't already."

"Well, I don't know what to do. I don't see this kinda shit go down every day."

"We have to call the police," Darcy said. "This stopped being something we can handle the minute guns came into it."

"Either way," Cundiff said. "Matt gave us a chance to get away. Let's not waste it. We can decide what to do in the car."

Klewes said, "Finally someone's talking some sense." He turned on his heel to start out the driveway and did not get two steps before he was stopped cold.

Dykeman blocked their path.

He stared at them with his dead eyes, their blackness spread into his slack cheeks like cancer. The fog curled around him like obedient dragons, seething smoke from their mouths.

"Holy shit," Cundiff said. He grabbed Darcy's hand and pulled her close. "Now what?"

Klewes was already backing up. "The house," he said. "Go...go."

They walked backward several paces until they were certain Dykeman was not giving chase, then they turned and sprinted for the porch.

# Chapter Twenty-Five

The door may have been locked, but once Tyrone Klewes put his shoulder into it, it acted like a door anxious to be open. Slivers of wood from the jamb that held it went skittering across the foyer floor.

"Damn it, Klewey," Cundiff said. "How are we supposed to lock it now?"

"Shit. I don't know. I wasn't thinking."

The three of them piled inside and Cundiff swung the door shut behind them. The hammer in the doorknob had nothing to seat in and the door started to drift open again. He leaned against it and said, "Is there something we can brace it with...a desk or a table?"

Darcy found a light switch that lit a bare bulb overhead. Then she looked around the entryway and the room adjoining. It was the parlor. There were a few dingy pieces of furniture and a short coffee table, but nothing heavy enough to fortify the door. Klewes ventured down the short hallway adjacent the foyer and reported, "I got nothing here, either."

"Okay," Cundiff said, "Maybe if we—"

A shout from the other side of the door interrupted him.

Ricky Sullivan did the shouting and he said, "We saw you go in there, *Cundt.*"

Darcy turned her frantic expression toward Cundiff and she wondered where the unnoticeable shift in her life had occurred. Where did she go from being a hard working young professional to a person so many people wanted dead? Was it the company she was keeping?

"You might as well come out—you and the mountain man and that little piece of ass you got," Ricky went on. "We'll go easier on you if we don't have to go in there."

"Klewey, is there a back door?" Cundiff asked.

"I'm on it." The orderly went back down the hallway and disappeared.

"Come on, *Cundt.* The old man needs you in that barn..."

"Go to hell, Ricky," Cundiff yelled through the door.

Then it shook against the orderlies' hold. There was a lot of thumping but he held the door shut without breaking a sweat. He looked up at Darcy who had no idea what to do with herself. "Go upstairs and find a place to hide," he said.

Darcy went to the darkened stairwell with its drooping handrail and crooked treads. The light did not reach the top—the steps could have carried on into oblivion for all she knew, and the prospect of finding out did not appeal in the least.

When the first window smashed in, she changed her mind.

\* \* \* \*

"Hurry," Cundiff said, but Darcy was already on the stairs, taking them in twos. "Klewey, they're in," he shouted next. No answer came back.

In the parlor, another window burst and its shards scattered across the floor like dice on a game board. Cundiff abandoned the door, and when he spied the parlor, he saw two figures climbing in through the windows. He hit the stairs running. Darcy must have found another switch up there, for a sparse yellow glow fell down the stairs from above.

There was no sign of her in the hallway when he reached the top—just some doors, every one closed. The light socket overhead was surrounded by broken plaster as though someone had just punched a hole in the ceiling and pulled the wiring down. Cundiff entertained the idea of shutting the light off to confuse their stalkers, but the sound of boots on the stairs told him he had no time for trickery. He opened the door to his right as quietly as he could and stepped inside.

\* \* \* \*

When Klewes heard the glass shatter, he knew bracing the back door had become a pointless endeavor. He looked around the small mud room, first for a place to hide, then for a weapon. He found little and less. En route to the back door, he had passed by a closet or pantry or the like. While it was a place he could lay low, getting there unseen might pose a challenge. The stomping of work boots emanating from the front end of the farmhouse made it obvious the Sullivans were inside.

He went to the threshold of the mudroom to hazard a peek down the hallway. He saw two black silhouettes of men—armed men—moving toward the stairs. They were not hunched or moving with any kind of intended stealth. They walked in a workman-like manner, a confidence that came with being the only armed men in the gunfight.

After the shadows drifted by, Klewes made his move. He slipped into the hallway, crossed it and went for the closet door. He was suddenly thankful that the uniform of the Saint Michael's orderly included tennis shoes. They were a necessity for any hospital worker that spent most of the day on his feet, but they were an absolute godsend when that worker needed to do some stealthy sneaking. He grasped the doorknob and winced as he gave it a slow turn. He heard a slight ticking like the uncoiling of a rusted spring. Then the breath ran out of him like he had taken a kick in the gut.

The doorknob came off in his hand.

The knob on the inside would surely fall to the floor with nothing to hold it. The ensuing clamor would be loud enough to bring the Sullivans. He would be caught and taken back to the barn. Maybe they would just shoot him where he stood. He would die with a busted doorknob in his hand and a stunned look on his face. He waited, too scared to move for fear the slightest twitch of a muscle would cause that doorknob to come loose and fall. He pictured all those cartoons he'd watched as a kid and he imagined the doorknob was teetering on the edge of a cliff like the Acme anvil always seemed to. Would it fall on him—was he the Roadrunner or the Coyote?

Klewes tried to rein in his erratic breathing. He carefully slid the doorknob into his pocket. Then he warily hooked a finger in the cavity left by the broken knob. Above him, footsteps thumped and the ceiling whined like it might cave any second. *Noise is good*, Klewes thought. *If they're making enough of their own, they won't hear mine.* He didn't dwell on the possibility that one of Sullivan's men stayed behind on the ground floor or that Morris Dykeman in his blood-drenched johnny may have made his way inside behind them. He focused on pulling that door open—and doing it as quietly as possible.

The door hinges sang softly and Klewes winced again. Overhead, the footfalls went silent and started back in the other direction. Klewes pulled the door a little more. The tone of the hinges climbed higher. He could scarcely abide it any longer. The pitch of the squealing quickened his heart rate. A gap in the door had widened enough that he could pass his hand through. He reached inside and palmed the doorknob. It did not come loose in his grip, in fact it held fast, apparently seized to the mechanism by years of disuse. Klewes released a silent sigh, opened the door and stepped inside.

The clomping of work boots sounded from the stairs.

Klewes gingerly pulled the door closed behind him and the hinges sang again. He wasn't sure if the Sullivans heard. He listened for their footsteps to come closer. His pulse ran faster still.

His hideout was larger than a closet. Though it was pitch black in there, he could sense it was bigger. He could smell mold and food rot, the essence of which had leached into the walls and floor. It was definitely a pantry. That meant it likely had a light, but Klewes was not foolish enough to switch it on and spill a new glow onto the hallway floor.

Footfalls hammered the hallway—two distinct sets.

Klewes held his breath. He feared the banging in his chest would give his position away.

The marching of boots grew louder. The floor creaked.

He bit his lip—held the door precariously shut by the broken knob.

The report of boots stopped abruptly.

And there was a scuffing sound that could only be a hand sliding across the surface of the door.

\* \* \* \*

Cundiff braced the door closed with his shoulder and looked around the space. Enough light from the porch bled through the window to show him that he was in a bedroom—and that he was alone.

*Where did Darcy go?*

The room was a desolate place. The walls revealed the slats where the plaster had crumbled away. The floor was bowed and littered with debris. There was a disheveled bed near the far wall that Cundiff figured was a posh resort for many a rat.

*She shouldn't be left alone in this house. Hiding in a place like this may prove just as dangerous as the men hunting her—the floor could give out, the roof could fall in.*

Those same men had crested the stairs. Cundiff could hear their approach. He leaned harder into the door. Perhaps they would think it was locked or warped shut, if he held it firmly enough. Perhaps they would give up trying to open it and move on. Perhaps they would find Darcy behind the next door.

Cundiff looked to his feet where a line of light from the hallway lit the floor. It was broken by shadow. Someone was right outside.

He waited for their attempt to get in, watching his feet, the slight movements of the shadow. *Come on*, he thought. *Let's get this over with. Maybe I should let them in. The gunshots might urge Darcy to get out of the house and run for safety. The place is only so big. Eventually they'll find her in here. They'll find us all.*

The shadow at his feet remained, though whoever shed it had not tried to get in. It was odd torture, making him wait like this, playing on his nerves.

Then something *did* get in.

It was water.

It flooded under the door as though the man on the other side had poured a pail of it on the floor. Cundiff watched as the dark fluid foamed and fizzed. It washed over his tennis shoes and pushed further in the room before receding back under the door.

*What kind of sick game are they playing?* He wondered. As soon as he finished the thought, water came spilling back in. There was more this time. It ran over his shoes and when the flow turned back to the door, much of it remained in the room. More gushed in. Cundiff could smell salt as it splashed up his pant legs. It was bay water—ocean water. His eyes darted about the place, desperately seeking an explanation for the rising surf. It was freezing— no more than two degrees—the temperature of the North Atlantic in winter.

Had the farmhouse been plucked up and dropped in the harbor? That unlikely scenario was the only one Cundiff could conjure as the rising tide threatened to soak his thighs. The dark water sloshed from one end of the room to the other like the constant ebb and flow of the bay or of a flooded ship's hull that was doomed to sink to the bottom of her.

Gone was any fear Cundiff had of the gunmen outside. Gone was any fear of the murderous Morris Dykeman. Even the fear that something bad may happen to Darcy was driven from Cundiff's heart. When it came to the fear of drowning, it was so immense that it occupied every square inch of the man, saving room for nothing else. He even tried to get the door open, preferring a hail of rifle fire to facing the rising water.

It wouldn't budge.

The bastard on the other side must have been holding it shut. Cundiff pounded on the door and yelled for release, promising a beating for whoever was holding him in the sinking bedroom.

*Thunk, thunk, thunk.*

The sound grabbed Cundiff's attention away from the door. He turned, praying the noise was not what he thought it was.

*Thunk, thunk, thunk.*

The banging took him back to a frosty morning aboard the *Pact* where he pulled lobster traps with a mysterious deckhand, until the workday was cut short by disaster. He had fallen in, but that was a dream, a nightmare he had while sleeping on the job.

*Thunk, thunk, thunk.*

Cundiff turned and faced his nightmare made flesh. The deckhand stood by the bottom of the bed, clad in yellow rain gear and hat, slamming his hook against the footboard without the slightest regard for the water level climbing his legs.

Cundiff shook his head. "No," he said aloud. "This isn't real. This is a..." he said firmly, even as very real and frigid water reached his crotch, "...a dream."

The deckhand denied the statement by beating his hook again, gouging the bed frame and flicking wood chips about. The very sight of that steel hook, tapered to its wicked point, was enough to rev the young man's heart. The deckhand raised his head and eyed the orderly with cannonball eyes, sunken deep in a pasty and bloated face. He spread a yellow grin that looked like a seven—ten split.

*Dykeman.*

Cundiff tried to shake off what he was seeing. He laid a hand over his eyes and rubbed vigorously before looking again. Dykeman remained. The rising tide remained. It was wet and it was cold and, by God, it was real. Dykeman raised his hook and as far as Cundiff was concerned, it was real, too.

The hand moved in, led by the hook, arcing down in a vicious attack. Cundiff threw hands up to block it. He still struggled to accept what was happening, but he saw what Dykeman had done to Mayor Bud, and if he could do a thing like that maybe he could summon the bay, too. Dykeman's forearm slammed against Cundiff's. The orderly grabbed his wrist and tried to wrest the hook from him. The old man grunted and wrenched back, then came in with another slash, this one across the body. The orderly leaned back and the hook missed by inches. Another downward slash, another dodge—this one an even closer call.

The water continued to swell, making meager movements a challenge. It was like a third participant in the fight with a mind to claim them both. It sloshed to and fro, slammed into the men and when it grew strong enough, it broke out the bedroom window. Dykeman waded in again, this time grabbing at Cundiff with his free hand. He clutched the shoulder of Cundiff's scrubs and yanked him in close. Cundiff could not believe the old man's strength as he was pulled through the water, legs trailing behind. The hook raised overhead, poised to come chopping down. It came.

Cundiff caught it with both hands. For a moment their fight reached a stalemate—Dykeman's boom lowered, Cundiff's pistons opposed it. The younger man broke the tie. He won some desperately needed leverage, twisted Dykeman's wrist and the hook dropped into the black water. The orderly was relieved to watch the cruel weapon disappear into the murk, but the feeling was short lived. He was off balance and Dykeman took full advantage. He threw Cundiff down, under the surf.

The world went dark and silent, save the murmur of the bay. It sounded like a thousand hushed voices inviting him deeper and deeper. That kind of rhythmic chanting could have lulled him into a sense of euphoria and eventually into oblivion, if he had not felt Dykeman's massive hands wrap around his throat. Cundiff tried to break his hold. He beat with his arms and kicked with his legs, but under water no man hits hard. The first mouthful of water rushed in. It was his first taste of the brine, of impending death. His body reacted by thrashing violently, fighting for all he was worth. He felt the grip on his neck weaken and he pushed himself up.

Breaking the surface, he was rewarded with a gulp of air, so fresh and sweet. A split second later, he was under again. Dykeman resumed his hold and pressed Cundiff down to the floor face first. An unforgiving boot piled on the small of his back and he felt the wind getting squeezed out of him. The precious air bubbled from of the corners of his mouth. Soon a fire would ignite in his lungs and burn up the rest. Convulsions would follow and after that, he would try to breathe ocean water. Then Darcy would be alone at the mercy of Dykeman and Ricky Sullivan and his henchmen.

The thought enraged the orderly. He tensed, fought to get his knees under him. Then his anger took over, fuelling his body to rise to one shaking leg then to the other until he thrust through the surface of the water. Dykeman's hold was broken again and Cundiff engaged him, firing lefts and rights. He swung wildly, his sight encumbered by salt water, but he also connected. One blow landed, then a second, then he no longer missed. He pummeled the would-be deckhand with every ounce of strength his hatred could muster. The old man was staggered—his knees buckled under him and Cundiff moved in to put him down. His hands closed around Dykeman's neck and he drove him under the black water.

Arms flailed and hands grabbed and nails scratched, but the orderly's grip was iron. Once he had Dykeman down, he would not let the wretch up. Cundiff's mind was set. This monster had wrought too much pain, caused too much suffering, death. A patient he may have been, but this was the only treatment he ever deserved. It should have come to him far sooner. He should have drowned him in his bath water or suffocated him with a pillow long before he had the chance to hurt Wanda or Nurse Tait or Phillip Prichard or Mayor Bud.

Dykeman's thrashing continued, but with fading intensity. Cundiff wondered if he would make a final show of superhuman strength or some other devilry—one last push for self-preservation. Maybe the rabid dog knew it was time to be put down. Much of the fight had gone out of him, but the orderly would make sure he was good and dead before he let him above the water.

He watched Dykeman's arms slump, the top of his rain hat ceased moving. Cundiff was certain this outcome was best one for all involved, except for one little voice inside him. That soft voice implored him to stop. It told him that he was not a murderer, that he was better than that. He figured it was only his conscience playing devil's advocate and did his best to ignore it. Yet, the longer that incessant voice went on, the stronger its message became. Did the voice say, *Let him go?* He loosened his hold on Dykeman's throat. In that moment, the bay water stopped pumping into the bedroom. It ceased churning, its surface calmed and became placid. The voice overpowered all other sounds now. It was clear and distinct and it said, "John, let him go."

"You're killing him!" it shrieked.

Cundiff spun around to find Darcy standing in the doorway. The ocean water that flooded the room was gone—the walls, the floor, everything was bone dry. Darcy looked on him as though he was a stranger and it shamed him deeply. He looked back to the wretch he was holding in his death-grip and found, not the twisted and vile visage of the monster Dykeman, but that of

Ricky Sullivan. His face was red and his eyes wandered aimlessly.

"Let him go, John!"

He obeyed. Ricky crumpled to the floor where he sprawled and labored to breathe. He wheezed when he drew air through a black-and-blue throat. Cundiff looked at his hands, then up to Darcy, and he too fell.

\* \* \* \*

Matt awoke to darkness.

From what he could gather, Sullivan had rolled him out of the pentagram after his lights went out. As his wits returned, he realized he was hearing a voice, sounding in stops and starts. Arthur Sullivan was reading.

"I will...renounce...the false god and all of his works. I will not state—no—*sate* the starving nor will I clothe the naked. I will con-consume the weak that I may prosper...for it is the strong that are truly blessed among men."

Matt flexed his jaw, which was now doing even more complaining than his fractured hand. The slightest twitch of his mandible sent flashes of agony up either side of his skull. He tongued a split in the side of his lip and tasted blood, yet he fought the urge to spit for fear Sullivan would hear and give him another whack to the head. The longer he thought Matt was unconscious, the better.

"It just goes on and on like that. It's called the En-En...lightened Pro-clam-ation, it is."

Matt heard the shuffle of the book's dry pages.

"Jesus Christ, Dawson, how much of this damned thing did you read, anyhow?"

All of Matt's muscles tensed. He tried not to budge.

"Come on, Doctor. Quit playin' dead. I know you're awake."

Matt grudgingly rolled over in the dirt toward the sound of Sullivan's voice. He found the old salt sitting on his rear end, smoking a cigarette and perusing the book by the light of the thirteenth candle. Even candlelight proved too harsh for Matt's aching head, and he squinted against it. "I didn't get to read much of it," Matt said, wincing and with a noticeable lisp. Somehow his tongue was too fat for his mouth. He must have bitten it when Sullivan struck him or when he fell. "Though...there seems to be a lot of that kind of thing in there," he finished.

"Blasphemin'," Sullivan said matter-of-factly. "That's what Father Higgins used to call it. I remember that much from my church-goin' days. You know, I haven't been in a church since the night we...ah...I just felt like it wasn't for people like me anymore and I'd be insulting God if I went."

"Maybe the Almighty would have struck you down with a bolt of lightning," Matt said, getting seated on his own rump. He saw that Sullivan had removed Bud from the pentagram as well. He had even pulled Bud's coat up to cover his ruin of a head.

Sullivan met Matt's comment with a smile. "That might have been the best thing for me, to get...what is it when the Big Guy smacks you a good one?"

"Umm...*smote*, I think."

"Yeah, that's it. It might have been best if He smote me the very next day. I would have missed out on a lot of livin', though..." He seemed to consider his many years. "Well, I would have missed a lot of *fishin'*, anyhow. You know, I bought my first boat before I was old enough to captain it. I paid one of them coons from up the mountain to hold the papers on it. Then I worked my old man's license. He wasn't using it much. Of course you don't need a fishin' license to lie around and drink rum all day. I had that old trawler paid off in three years and on the day I made my last payment I bought two more—forty footers. They made my fortune. Then I got more boats and they made it bigger."

*How nice for you,* Matt thought.

"There was a lot of money comin' in—so much I didn't know what to do with it. Turns out my favorite things are free—salty spray off the bay, bunkin' out on the banks overnight, the way the gulls come out to greet you when you get home." He flicked his finished cigarette and it drew an orange line on the darkness.

"Far as spendin' money, I have two ex-wives that sure as hell know how. Truth be told, I never paid too much attention to it myself. It was the catches that amazed me. To this day, I never pulled a trap outta that bay that wasn't two thirds full. Even when the lobster stocks were down in the mid-nineties and the other boats were pullin' jack shit, I always put in with my hull burstin' at the seams. That was magic...*black* magic, I guess. Them other captains— Fuller, MacDevitt, that prick, Ernie Cole—they heard the rumors about me and my...unholy deal, but that's not why they hate me. Greed and envy is why they hate me. Seems there's a lot about that in this here book, too."

"The sins of Man..." Matt offered. He gathered his knees to his chest and wrapped his arms around them. He tried to get comfortable, but couldn't. Something poked his thigh. Then he remembered the hunting knife was in his pocket.

"Sloth is the only sin most men need to worry about. Everyone comes up against it," Sullivan went on. "You know, that son of mine would lose his shirt if I retired. He doesn't have the drive or the sense to work the boats without me and the...good luck I've been havin' all these years." He eyed the book in his hand ruefully, then tossed it aside. "I never wanted him to get caught up in this. I suppose Stan didn't want that for you, either." Matt slid his hand to the opening of his pocket.

Sullivan looked at Bud's body. "I'm the last one. We finally got the damned book and it's me it came to—the one who's too muddle-headed to figure it out. It might as well be writ in Chinese for all the good it does me. I can hardly read it, let alone put it to use." He grinned sourly and shook his head. "Now you tell me there's no Captain at the helm of this ship. Tell me He doesn't have a sense of humor."

"It's hard to deny."

"That it is," Sullivan said and he started getting to his feet. He moved slowly as though his old joints were seizing up on him. Matt took the opportunity to get up, too. His head swam mightily as he rose and it took him a few seconds to get his feet planted under him. Then he slipped his hand into his pocket and touched the handle of the knife. Sullivan dusted himself off and bent down to scoop up the revolver from the dirt. He rolled it open and took inventory of the chamber. Satisfied, he closed it up and cocked the hammer and started toward Matt.

"So that *thing* took Morry...then Philly," he said, counting on his left hand, the gun hung in his right. "Now poor old Bud. That *devil* has taken them all." Sullivan shuffled closer and outside the protection of the pentagram. Matt wrapped his hand around the handle of the knife. He clenched his jaw and it sent another wave of pain shooting through his head. He shrugged it off. Nothing mattered but the gun in Sullivan's hand and the knife in his own pocket.

Sullivan stopped a few feet from Matt. He turned his hard eyes on the doctor and said, "You know he didn't really get your father, right? Stan was the only one of us who didn't owe him anything. He had the good sense to back out of the deal before it was struck. So...the devil never got him."

Matt glanced at the gun at Sullivan's side. The old man's fingers seemed to tighten around the grip now. "I think I..." Matt started. He tried to swallow the unmoving mass in his throat. "I know that," he said. "I know...he's okay now."

"Good," Sullivan said with a stiff nod. "The devil ain't gettin' me, either."

Sullivan put the gun to his head and pulled the trigger.

\* \* \* \*

Tyrone Klewes dared not take a breath. Outside the pantry door, Sullivan's men continued their search of the farmhouse for him and his friends. They were close. One had even slid a hand across the surface of the door. It prompted Klewes to back away from it. The small room was darker than the crypt and smelled every bit as foul, but he stepped further inside, praying he could find a place to hide if that door came open. The scent of mildew and rot grew stronger as he stepped toward the rear of the pantry, feeling his way with both hands. He found shelving to either side, some of which held web-covered tins and boxes. He touched these with extreme care. All he needed to do was topple a stack of old cans and his foray into survival hiding would fail.

He continued on, no longer touching the racks, hands out front. And he found something else. It fell across his face like a snake hanging from a tree branch, and it had the orderly flinching backward. He realized it was only the pull string for a light fixture, and he pressed on. His mind conjured more images of what he would find at the rear of the storage room. There would be a box on the floor that he would stub his foot on. There would be a crate of dusty bottles that he would tip over. There would be a few brooms and mops leaned against the wall that he would knock down. He planned for it all and his probing hands were ready for any of these. Though, they were not ready for what they *did* find in the darkness—another hand.

Klewes went fence post rigid when he felt the familiar shape of fingers and knuckles hanging in the dark before him. It took a moment for his brain to translate the data it was receiving. It was a hand all right, attached to a sleeved arm, but it was cold, clammy. It was a dead hand.

He jerked backwards and clamped his hand over his mouth to keep from letting out a blood-chilling howl. Then he remembered the men outside the pantry and he went as still as he could.

"I thought I heard something," a muffled voice said.

"I didn't hear nothing," another voice answered.

"Hey, look. This doorknob's broken off."

"Well then, they can't be in there, can they?"

Footfalls in the hallway signaled their moving on.

Klewes uncovered his mouth and a fit of ragged breathing followed. *Sneak out*, he told himself. *Just get out of this tomb. Sneak to the door and run for it. Cundiff and Darcy probably did already. They're probably waiting by the car. Yeah, that settles it. I'm leaving. I'm not turning the light on. I don't need to know who's in here with me*, he thought. *Dead or alive I can't help them, anyway.* At that he figured his debate was over, even as his hand groped blindly for the pull string. He couldn't help himself.

The pantry lit up.

He saw the hand he had felt in the dark. He saw four of them. They belonged to Chief Lumley and one of his deputies—which one, Klewes could not tell. The man's face had been mangled beyond recognition. They hung from storage hooks intended for flour sacks or bags of turnips or onions, their skin blue and purpled, toes dragging on the floor. An expression of utmost horror was permanently etched on Lumley's face, just like the one Mayor Bud wore seconds before his head was caved in, just like the one Klewes now wore as he backed away from the officers swaying subtly like sides of beef in a cooler.

Klewes continued to back up. Escaping the grotesque scene became paramount—turning away from Lumley's bulging eyes and protruding tongue, his only priority. He backed until he thudded into the door behind him. When it did not open, he put his shoulder into it.

The pantry door flew open like it was spring-loaded and the orderly fell awkwardly into the hallway. He could not register the pain of his fall anymore than he could look away from the chief, his blood-soaked uniform, his still-holstered sidearm. Lumley's blood-pooled eyes held Klewes' attention captive even as Sullivan's men came upon him.

They aimed their rifles and shouted things that Klewes failed to decipher, but their threats were quelled as they too were ensnared by the bloody spectacle in the pantry. Klewes watched on from the floor as the gunmen stepped inside. They poked and prodded the officers with rifle barrels, intensifying their swaying. One of the men relieved the deputy's holster of its pistol while the other barked questions that Klewes couldn't answer. Both men stopped what they were doing when the light flickered overhead. They looked at each other. A second later the light failed completely. Next, the door slammed shut.

Klewes heard the men bellowing within. The gunshots came next, followed by a thrashing that sounded like the shelves coming down. Another shot resounded, and with it followed silence. Too afraid to move, apart from the profound shiver that vibrated his body, Klewes could do nothing but lie on the floor and pray for the pantry door to remain closed. In the eerie quiet that settled over the farmhouse, his short frantic breaths became all he could hear. That sound was more welcome than the blasting of guns and the wailing of men and far better than the squealing the pantry door did as it slowly opened again.

\* \* \* \*

Cundiff and Darcy watched over Ricky Sullivan as he faded to and from consciousness. His breathing was shallow and raspy. Even in the poor light, it was obvious how bruised Ricky's neck was.

"It wasn't him," Cundiff said for what must have been the tenth time. "It wasn't Ricky." *At least I don't think it was.* Yet, how could he explain what had been happening in the room when Darcy walked in? The deckhand, the ocean water, the hook, it was all gone without the slightest indication any of it was ever there. His pants had been wet, he had felt the freezing water, he was even sore from his bout with the deckhand. It had all vanished like some kind of waking dream. What did remain in the room after all else disappeared was Ricky— beaten and prone and getting the life choked out of him. Cundiff could not deny that. "Is he going to be okay?"

"I don't know, John." Darcy had instructed him to roll Ricky on his side and bend his knees up close to his chest. It did not seem to be helping the fisherman all that much. His struggle to breathe was painful to listen to. "We can't do anything for him."

"Oh, my God." Cundiff rubbed his brow with the heels of his hands. "I was hiding...and one of them got in here and..." *Actually, the North Atlantic got in here.* "It's so dark in here...I got fighting with the guy, but it wasn't Ricky, I swear. I thought...I thought it was *Dykeman.* I thought I was fighting with..." *It was Dykeman. He tried to gut me with a hook. Then he tried to drown me.*

"Either way, we're not safe here," Darcy said as she made for the door. "We need to get out of this house and get help."

"I was scared, Darcy." Cundiff shook his head. He was indeed scared, but not of Ricky or his men, but what the future might hold for a man who can suffer a hallucination so vivid. He feared that, judging by what he did to Ricky, he was a danger to his friends. Moreover, he feared his next trip to Saint Michael's may not be to perform the duties of an orderly, but to take up residence.

"John, we have to move. You can help Ricky by getting an ambulance to him." She hooked his arm with her own. "Now come on before we—"

Darcy was cut short by the crack of gunfire. She looked at Cundiff as another shot went off. The thunderous sounds froze them in place. They were unsure what to do as silence crowded back into the room. Then it was broken again. This time, a heart-stopping howl boomed throughout the farmhouse.

Cundiff recognized the voice. Despite the absolute terror that distorted it, he knew instantly who it belonged to. "Klewey," he said to Darcy, wide eyed. He raced for the door. He roared back, "I'm coming, Klewey. Hang on!"

Cundiff hit the hall and thundered down the stairs without the slightest regard for the whereabouts of Sullivan's gunmen or Dykeman. He raised storm clouds of dust as he bound down the rickety risers.

"Where are you?" he yelled.

Another gut-wrenching howl answered for Klewes.

\* \* \* \*

Darcy was right behind Cundiff. She moved as fast as her feet could afford, through the door, into the hallway and until she got to the stairs. Then her focus was yanked away when she glimpsed a person standing at the far end of the hall.

In the diffused light, Darcy could only make out that it was a woman. She was tall and thin and had long brown hair that fell loosely down her back. Another sense kicked in at that point. It was that extra sense that most twins possess. This sense tells them when they are in the presence of their other half. She had felt it in the darkened halls of Saint Michael's and it was no less potent in the derelict farmhouse. Darcy took a step down the hallway. She called her name. *Di.* The woman turned a corner and receded into shadow.

* * * *

Cundiff found his friend on the floor of the downstairs hall. He had his back against the wall and his feet firmly planted against a closed door. "What happened?" Cundiff said. He knelt beside Klewes and asked if he was all right. By the time Cundiff got the question out, he had gathered the answer himself and it was a big *no.*

Klewes was drenched in sweat. The wet coating was all over his skin—terror sweat. His lips curled downward in a grimace that implied he had been crying, but he shed no tears. Cundiff had never seen him this frightened in all the twenty years he had known him. Cundiff was there when Mister Finch at the corner store caught a teenaged Klewes stealing. Cundiff was there the countless times school bullies chased him after class. He was there earlier tonight as well, when they witnessed Dykeman's carnage in the barn. Even then, Klewes had managed to stay in control and show the leadership that came so naturally to him. This hardly seemed like the same guy, shaking and snot-nosed. He looked as though he had aged thirty years since the orderlies parted ways. His hair had even grayed at the sides. Cundiff took Klewes' trembling chin in his hand and turned his head for a better look at the hair at his temples and over his ears. It was more white than gray. It ran like a skunk stripe down the back of his head. Klewes snapped his head back so he could face the door again.

"Talk to me Klewey. What happened?"

Klewes just shook his head and continued to hold the door shut with his feet.

"Darcy, we gotta—" Cundiff started, turning around to talk to her. She was not there. He lamented that keeping track of his friends was akin to herding cats. He called her name up the staircase. No answer returned. He cursed the prospect of searching the house for Darcy. First, he decided, he would get Klewes outside, where with any luck he would sit still until he could collect Darcy.

Just what personal hell Klewes had lived through, Cundiff could only imagine. He had endured his fair share of hell, himself. They were both no doubt injured, but to this point the hurts had not been physical and Cundiff intended to keep it that way. "Okay buddy...we're outta here," he said getting to his feet. He reached down and grabbed Klewes under the arms. If he had to drag his friend outside, so be it.

"No!" Klewes yelled and pushed Cundiff off him. "I gotta keep it closed."

Cundiff looked at the door. It was unremarkable other than its missing doorknob. He put his ear to it, but heard nothing inside.

"He's in there," Klewes said.

Cundiff looked at the floor where it met the bottom of the door. From under it, a dark red pool was slowly creeping outward. "Jesus...is that..."

Klewes looked up at him, wild-eyed. He was still shaking, although Cundiff gathered it was not from fear, but from the force his legs were exerting to keep the door shut. Klewes whispered to him as though the very word he said was a curse, "Dykeman."

\* \* \* \*

Matt wiped the long strand of spittle that hung from his lip. The image of Arthur Sullivan shooting himself replayed over and over in his head. It happened so fast—too fast for Matt to even yell *stop*. Instead, he had yelled a nonsensical series of vowels as the shot went off. That was when things slowed down. It seemed to take forever for Sullivan to drop. The globe of red mist floated on the air to his left while his legs folded under him and he collapsed like the bones had been removed from his body. He hit the dirt and raised a plume of dust that still clouded the air. Matt retched but nothing came up, so he merely spat. That is when he realized he had fallen, too. More than likely he had passed out at the sight of Sullivan's suicide. His swoon may have offered a few precious pain-free moments, but now the aching of his hand and jaw were back with gusto.

*He ain't getting me, either.*

Those were Sullivan's final words. It may have been a small victory to avoid a death at Dykeman's hand, but Matt could not imagine a more surefire way for Sullivan to secure his place in hell than by taking his own life. Maybe for Sullivan hell was inevitable. Maybe Matt was a fool to think it was not.

He crawled on hands and knees to the fisherman's crumpled remains, taking care not to look closely on the body—specifically the grisly head wound. He batted the revolver free of Sullivan's grip and collected it before dragging himself to the protection of the pentagram.

Once beyond the sweeping arc of its border, he rolled onto his back for a breather. Unconsciousness threatened to take him again, and he fought it off. He had unfinished business and rest was a luxury he could ill afford, at least not while the demon was on the wrong side of the gate. Matt's friends may have fled, but they would never be safe from Dykeman so long as he was controlled by one of the infernal.

Matt got himself to the altar and did a quick inspection of the set up. The pentagram was intact. The candles burned. He reached for the *Sacra Obscurum.*

With a confidence that surprised even him, Matt fanned the pages toward the back of the book as he drew the knife from his pocket.

\* \* \* \*

Darcy peeked down over the staircase railing. The steps were narrower than those at the front of the farmhouse and looked even more treacherous. The treads were short, the risers steep. They had danger written all over them.

Yet, the woman she followed took them without hesitation. That is, *Di* took them. Because whether Darcy was willing to accept it or not, every fiber in her body told her that she was following her sister.

Darcy looked back into the hallway. She was compelled to find Cundiff, to seek out his protection, but the urge to follow Di was overwhelming. Before she knew it, she was stepping onto the top tread. The staircase groaned as it took her weight. The railing did little to ease her apprehension—it swayed like a deep sea buoy when she put a hand on it. Still she descended.

When last they had met in the corridor at Saint Michael's, Di asked why Darcy had left her all alone. Darcy had not known a question could hurt so much. She found herself on the perilous stairs, braving her armed hunters, all to trail Di in the hopes she would ask that question again. Darcy needed to face her, to tell her that she *didn't*—scream it at the top of her lungs. She *didn't* leave Di alone. She left her with their parents.

*That's totally different.*

*Right?*

*I didn't leave her alone, I...left her...with our parents.*

Darcy stepped down from the stairs and into the kitchen. It was in the worst shape of any of the rooms she had seen by far. The faded wallpaper was torn and sagging. Some of the cabinet doors, once white, were now grimy yellow spotted with black mold clusters and hanging askew. Some were missing altogether. Bits of crumbled plaster from the ceiling littered the floor and counters. The old Kelvinator stood, door ajar, revealing what looked like a science experiment gone awry on its shelves. The table and chairs remained as well, equally peppered with debris, the floor around it sporting dark blotches where something had spilled and dried. That same dark stain was on the wall over the table. Darcy decided it looked less like a stain and more like someone had drawn a..."symbol."

She remembered Dykeman's file and the police report from the night he had allegedly massacred his family. She had been especially disturbed by the gruesome photographs in it. Darcy's blood ran cold. The dark blotches on the floor, the hand-drawn symbol on the wall—it was *blood*. She was standing in the room where Dykeman had dismembered his mother, his father and his brother.

Di was standing in it too.

Di faced the blood-scrawled symbol as if admiring it. "You're right, Darce," she said. "This is where young Morry behaved so badly." She turned.

The first really good look Darcy got of her would-be sister was enough to freeze her heart. It was her—Darcy's mirror image. Her sullen face, sans makeup—her hair was the way she used to brush it—her voice was that flat, unwavering tone that offered no highs or lows. It was Di. Part of Darcy wanted to go to her and embrace her, another part wanted to run from the room and leave the horrid farmhouse behind her, while yet another part—the greater part—could not bring herself to move in any direction.

*Tell her,* Darcy thought. *Tell her you didn't leave her alone. Tell her it's not your fault she's sick.*

Darcy's voice caught in her throat and a *croak* was all she could manage.

Imposter or no, Di's voice worked just fine. "Would you like to watch?" she asked. "Of course you would. Nobody would come all this way only to miss out on the show."

Darcy still could not make a sound. She watched as Di moved beside her in anticipation. Then it started.

A woman appeared in one of the chairs. She was radiant, like she was comprised entirely of a soft flickering light. The edges of her arms, legs, and flower-print dress were blurred as though she was projected *onto* the kitchen rather than occupying it. The woman leisurely raised a teacup to her lips and sipped. She did not detect the twins watching her. How could she? She was merely part of the show.

Two men appeared and joined her at the table, one significantly older than the other. They had the same low-light, fuzzy glow as the woman. Darcy understood then that she was watching the Dykeman family and she knew how this story would end. She turned to Di who smiled on her wryly. "It's about to get good," she said.

The family soundlessly sipped tea and ate cookies, completely unaware of the horrible end they were about to face. Could there have been any warning signs that their youngest son and brother was messing with dangerous powers he did not respect or understand? Was there any indication that such evil was blossoming under their roof? The silent film family continued their snacking, oblivious to the peril from the character who now entered from stage left.

Morris Dykeman strode into the kitchen. The tall, wiry kid carried a pair of garden shears at his side. They swung casually in his hand as he walked behind his father's chair. None of his family raised an eye until Morry thrust the shears between Mister Dykeman's shoulder blades. Mrs. Dykeman's mouth stretched in a silent scream. Big brother rose from his seat. The shears ran him through the belly, and he went down. Next the yard tool was turned on Mother and, with the stronger men unable to defend her, Morry was free to take his time.

Darcy found her voice.

"*No...no more,*" she shouted at Di. "Stop it!"

Di stuck out her bottom lip and gave her an exaggerated frown. "What, you don't like the show? Granted, it's not a talkie like you kids prefer watching today, but I thought it had some pretty good action." She waved a hand and the grotesqueries paused.

Darcy backed away from her. "Who are you?" she asked.

"Why I'm your sister, of course," Di said with mock insult. "Your *little* sister, to be exact. You were born two minutes before me, remember? Somehow that's important to Mom and Dad. Oh, and speaking of Dad—he still thinks I'm crazy—anyway, he put me on a new antipsychotic. It's a generic brand so it's a lot lighter on his pocketbook. That amounts to a lot more wine money in the run of a month, so it makes him happy. Too bad the new pills make my hair fall out. See?" She pulled a handful of chestnut hair free and showed it to Darcy.

"That's not the worst thing, though. Do you remember Mister Jitters?"

"Don't do this."

"Well, Mister Jitters has started coming around again since you left."

"Don't..."

"He comes at night and gets in bed with me. He thinks I'm you." She cocked her head to the side as though this revelation just struck her.

"Stop this."

"Yeah, that's what I say. I tell him to stop—but, he doesn't."

"No! If you're going to be Dianne then *be* Dianne." Darcy balled her fists at her sides defiantly. "Tell me what happened on *Ellen* yesterday or what the cat did to the neighbor's dog. Let's talk about *Reader's Digest* and gourmet coffee and why you hate spring almost as much as you hate fall. That's what *we* talk about. *That's Di!*"

"He keeps me awake...Mister Jitters. Sometimes he just tickles me. Sometimes he sticks his dick in my ass. He says your name over and over... 'Darcy...ooh Darcy. That's a good girl,' he says."

"Damn you." Fresh tears streaked Darcy's face and with them she shed the last of her strength. She dropped to her knees.

"I do what you told me to do, to make him go away, but it doesn't work anymore. It's just not the same since you've been gone."

Darcy remembered helping her sister shoo all the baddies that haunt schizophrenics. They took up their mantra many times to rid Dianne of strange animals, personal messages from the television and, of course, that dirty, old Mister Jitters. They would repeat their words again and again and Darcy would try like hell to pass a little of her sanity into Dianne's body.

"I had to leave," Darcy managed between sobs. "I had to get away from them. They never gave you as much attention as you needed, but they gave me *too much*. It may be hard for you to understand, but believe me, that was way worse. They were smothering me. That's why I went away for university. That's why I took the job at Saint Michael's."

"You said if I held my heart pendant and told Jitters he isn't real, he'd go away..."

Darcy reached for her own pendant and clutched it tightly. If Di—the real Dianne Collins—was there, she would have done the same. She would have helped her sister dispel this demon. Darcy thought of her and said, "*You're* not real."

"...but it's not true," Imposter-Di continued. "The monsters never really go away, do they?"

"You're not real." Darcy stood up. "Come on, Di. Say it with me, for old time's sake. Say it with me like we did when we chased away the monsters together. Let's say it until our voices become one—until we're almost the same person."

Di fell silent and gave Darcy a smirk that looked more like a sneer.

"*You're not real.*"

"Fine. If that's your attitude, then we can't be friends anymore." Di turned on her heel and walked to the kitchen table where the projection of Morry Dykeman had paused obediently. Di put out her hand. The show resumed, only Dykeman did not continue attacking his mother. He stood straight, looked at Di and handed her the garden shears.

"*You're not real.*"

"Perhaps not, Sis, but these snips are going to feel real enough," Di said, starting back toward her. She cut the air with the shears.

Cundiff appeared in the kitchen entry. "Klewey," he shouted. "Dykeman's in the kitchen." The orderly ran at Di from behind. He lunged.

Without even looking Cundiff's way, Di batted him out of the air with one hand. He stumbled wildly through the image of Morry Dykeman and crashed into the table and chairs.

Despite the clamor of Cundiff's hard landing, Darcy said again, *"You're not real."* She squeezed her pendant and closed her eyes as the phony Di drew dangerously close. She heard steel sliding on steel as the shears opened wide to bite her.

*"You're not real."*

Then she heard nothing.

# Chapter Twenty-Six

Matt closed the *Sacra Obscurum* on the summoning ritual, then adeptly fanned its pages to another section. He looked up to find Dykeman standing just beyond the border of the pentagram, gore-stained johnny shirt and all. The old man had a pair of yawning garden shears in his hands, poised to cut. He inspected the shears briefly and dropped them in the dirt.

Matt felt Dykeman's cold stare pierce him.

"You have miserable timing, Doctor," Dykeman said. "I was right in the middle of something. It was just getting good."

"I didn't know you could speak," Matt said to his former patient. "Why didn't you say something before?"

"Speech isn't the only ability I hid from you. The lisp is new. Did I miss your coming-out party?"

"I bit my tongue."

Dykeman stepped along the edge of the pentagram and tested its boundary. Matt tracked his movements. "It really works. You can't cross the line?"

"Not any more than you can jump off a cliff. You have done your homework, just like Stanley did."

"I learned a few things from him."

"You sure did. I thought I knew a thing or two about torture, but you doctors have a *real* talent for it. Your medicines can to do some pretty terrible things. I never thought the poisons you pumped into this body would leave me incapacitated for fifty years. And I have been around, you know? I've spent three hundred lives of men between here and there. *Fifty years,* though, is still a long time to be out of the game. Think of all the suffering I missed. I missed *wars.* I didn't see one disease outbreak, or one measly infant death, not even one lousy car accident. Oh, I longed to hear the whining of men—like *why do bad things happen to good people?* or, *he was such a quiet neighbor, how could he do this?* That was my personal favorite."

"I guess that's the risk you take when you steal someone's body."

"Yeah, Morry Dykeman—the broken little toy that he was. Alas, taking his body wasn't part of the plan. We had such high hopes for the boy. He was showing all the signs of becoming a real all-star once he ripened. Watching him operate was going to be a hoot, especially with his penchant for hating all things female. But there was only one skin between us when the music stopped, and I wasn't going to be caught without a chair. I'd just got here and I had no desire to go home."

"You couldn't leave those kids alone, either."

"Of course not—they were *mine!*" His voice suddenly peaked with rage and just as quickly, it softened again. "One, two, three, four, five tasty morsels—the young always make the finest fare."

"You didn't get them *young.*"

"True. It wasn't quite worth the wait, either. Yet, I had a job to do. They sold their souls willingly and it was my responsibility to collect them. If I didn't hold up my end of the bargain, well, the whole system would just fall apart." Dykeman looked on the bodies on the ground. "Thanks to my efforts, they are exactly where they should be."

Matt winced. He had no fond feelings for the mayor or the fisherman, but their deaths were nothing to rejoice in.

"Though, Doctor Stanley—your father—*he* would have been the real treat. So righteous and pious, devouring his soul would have been utter ecstasy." Dykeman licked his lips with a tongue that was long enough to touch his nose. "You know, I thought he would weaken when your mother died, but he was too rigid, too stubborn. He just kept injecting me with his poisons and keeping his distance."

"He did the right thing."

"He did the *easy* thing."

"Oh, there was nothing *easy* about Stanley's life."

"So it would appear that you have forgiven him for all of his fatherly blunders? Bygones, yes?"

"I understand why he did what he did."

"You think he sent you away because he loved you? How do you figure, Doctor? He loved your mother deeply, but he didn't send her away, now did he?"

"Save your bullshit."

"Right, bygones. Well, I'm glad I could facilitate such a touching father-son reconciliation. I supposed it's the least I could do. After all, it was me who tore your family asunder before it was even born."

"I'm well aware of your history with my family."

"Ah...that's what this is really about, isn't it? The valiant heir rushes into battle to defend the legacy of the patriarch. How many sons have been led to the spit by such noble intent? It's just so...delicious.

"I shouldn't tease, though. I should be thanking you. It was *you*, after all, who set me free. *You* let that fool writer awaken me. *You* stopped squirting Stanley's chemicals into Dykeman. No longer an invalid, I could soon walk. Then I could run. Then I could *kill*. Then I broke your fucking hand." He snickered at the memory. "The look on your face was priceless—*how is this old man doing this to me? Let me go. Ahhhh...*"

Matt did not see the humor. He eyed his casted hand and sneered.

"Look Dawson, I don't want any hard feelings," Dykeman said, having suppressed his laughter. "I'm a businessman. We could cut a deal, you and me."

"I don't want anything from you."

"Rubbish. Everyone wants something. I just have to figure out what *your* something is. What does Matthew Dawson really want?" Dykeman's liver-spotted head began to melt. It became a molten, pliable mass before reforming into the spiraling blond curls of Matt's former sitter. Chrissy stood before him and gave a sultry smile. "I think I know what you want," she said.

Matt's body went rigid at the sight of the young woman he still feared on some deep-buried level.

"No?' she asked. "Maybe this is a little too young for your particular perversions. How about..." her curls uncoiled and darkened into warm brown tresses. "...this?" Darcy Collins asked. "I'm a driven professional who enjoys reading psychiatric journals and working my ass off and I'm about to discover problem drinking. Oh, and you must love dogs and psychotic sisters." Matt's blank expression left her frowning. "Still not interested? Hmm..." Her hair shortened along with her overall height and her skin paled a bit. "Maybe this is what you've always wanted," said Matt's mother. "Sorry son, but I'm married, off the market as they say. You'll never get your hands on this," she said raising the johnny shirt above her waist.

"You son of a bitch!" Matt abruptly looked away.

"Oh, Doctor, I so enjoy spending time with you. You're fun!" Dykeman's morbid mug returned and Matt was actually relieved for it.

"I've had enough of you."

"That's too bad, Doctor." His twisted yellow grin faded and he leveled his bleak stare on Matt. "I'm not going anywhere," he hissed.

"Oh, I think so." Matt held up the book for him to see. "You're not messing with children this time around."

"What have you got there? Oh, *the Obscurum*...nice. That's a *big* book, but you know, it ain't size that matters. It's how you use it. Do you, Doctor Matthew, do you know how to use it?"

"I'm getting a pretty good handle on it."

"Good, good. I love it. I can feel the heat coming off those pages from here. That Prussian kid sure knew what he was doing when he wrote it. Of course, it was a colleague of mine, from upper management, who helped him with the hard parts. You might know him—a real asshole, carries a pitchfork? Anyway, the *Sacra Obscurum* is that gift that keeps on giving. Let me tell you, it has been in some pretty maniacal hands over the years. Even so, it was a big day at the office when the book found its way to young Morry Dykeman. There were high fives all 'round. The potential for mayhem had us wringing our little paws together. But, I got to be honest with you, it was your old man who had management really excited. Dykeman may have had the, how should I put it, *mean streak*, to make the book work, but Stanley could make the fucking thing sing."

"Well, I'm not too shabby with it myself."

"*That*, I would believe. When it comes to matters of magic, apples never fall far from their trees."

"That's convenient, because I'm going to use this thing to drive you out of Dykeman."

"Oh, the confidence. At least you stopped short of calling him a *servant of God*." Dykeman looked on the cluster of candles nearest him. "Maybe you will send me packing. Maybe you won't. Either way, it's still a win for our side that you're even using the *Obscurum*. Think about it, you could be standing there holding the Holy fucking Bible...but you're not." He sang the last part, tauntingly, waggling his finger. "Tisk, tisk. Shame on you, Doctor. Perhaps you're not *clean* enough to hide behind the Cross. After all, you may be Stanley's seed, but you're definitely not him. You don't have thick-shitting angels like Mikey in your corner, do you? All you have is that book of sweet, sexy evil and every time you crack it open my side grows a little stronger."

"Well, I hope you all appreciate this," Matt said opening the book.

That had Dykeman grinning from ear to ear. "What do you think you can do with it, anyway? Let me give you a hint, because I know what's in that thing better than anyone in this world, I'll tell you. It holds only one ritual that could possibly get me to leave this body."

"The Infernal Exorcism," Matt confirmed.

"Ooh that's the one, all right, but moving me from one vessel to another calls for blood, Doctor. You know it does as well as I do. Only I don't see any donors around here...other than *you*, of course. Tell me, are you prepared to offer up your blood, your *soul*? Are you willing to sacrifice yourself to save a grotesque like Morris Dykeman? Does ousting me from this rotten old bag mean that much to you?"

The gleam of anticipation in Dykeman's eyes spurred Matt to back up a step, even though he was relatively safe within the borders of the pentagram. He had never been ogled like he was a meal before.

"Don't get me wrong," Dykeman continued. "I hope you do it. Just think of the fun we could have, me and you. The very first thing we'll do is visit Doctor Collins..." he said, grabbing at his crotch.

"I had something else in mind," Matt interrupted. He tucked the book under his arm and reached into his pants pocket and pulled Sullivan's revolver from it. "This calls for blood, too." He aimed the gun at Dykeman. "There won't be a chair for you when the music stops this time."

"What are you doing, Doctor?" Dykeman said, chuckling at the absurdity of Matthew Dawson aiming a gun at him.

Matt pulled the hammer back.

"Now put that away." Dykeman's voice had taken on the slightest nervous edge. "You're no murderer."

"For once, I agree with you. I know when I pull this trigger, I'll be saving lives." Matt was no marksman, but as close as he was, it did not matter. He was already squinting, anticipating the damage he was about to inflict.

"No!"

He fired.

The small gun kicked hard against his hand. It surprised him, as did the flinty smell it made. For a moment, he thought he had missed his target. Then a fresh rose blossomed on Dykeman's johnny shirt.

Dykeman staggered back a few steps, a look of disbelief etched on his face. When the situation finally sunk in, so did panic. He gawked about the barn for a destination, a new body to inhabit, while the life poured out of his. In a few moments his host would be dead, and so would he, if he remained there. He howled again and glared at Matt. His teeth gnashed, now wet with blood.

Matt carefully laid the gun in the dirt and retrieved the pencil and a sheet of paper from the altar. "You know what's interesting? It may be very difficult to exorcise a demon when it inhabits a body of the living, but it is quite simple to send one back to hell when it doesn't." Dykeman swayed on his feet, head lolling. His lifeblood now dripped steadily from the tail of his johnny. "According to the book, all I have to do," Matt went on, "is learn the demon's name, write it down and burn the parchment. So, how do you spell Belphegor?"

Dykeman fell over backward. He thudded heavily in the dirt. Matt watched his chest slowly rise and fall until he was sure he had taken his final breath.

The barn went quiet, crypt-like, though Matt knew he was not alone. He could feel it. The demon was still there, hiding somewhere in the barn, ready to descend on him as soon as he left the safety of the pentagram. Matt could not let it remain. He finished writing on the parchment and took a deep breath. After all the trouble he had seen, it was the simplest of tasks that would put things right. All he had to do was burn a small sheet of paper. In just seconds it would be over and he could go back to his old life—back to the realm of the normal.

Matt knelt before the thirteenth candle.

He held a corner of the parchment to the flame.

A gust of wind threw the barn doors violently open. The gale screamed through the barn and snuffed many of the candles around him. The ancient structure shook as legions of wind marched through it. Matt threw himself down at the altar and cupped his hands around the thirteenth to protect it. He shielded the flame even as it licked his fingers. The candle blackened the cast on one hand and reddened the palm of the other, though he refused move them away. If the candle went out, there would be nothing inside the pentagram to burn the parchment. He yelled with the fresh agony in his hands, but only huddled closer around the flickering flame. Then, with as much warning as it gave when it first appeared, wind began to recede. It calmed to a gentle soothing current before it dissipated altogether. Matt released a heavy breath. He assumed he had witnessed the demon's final tantrum.

He had not.

The candle flared like a brush fire in a dry field. The flame stretched three feet high—into Matt's face. He jerked backward, but not before losing his eyelashes and most of his brows. Thinking his hair had caught, he batted frantically to put it out. As he rolled in the dirt, slapping at his smoldering hair, he could have sworn he heard laughter.

Matt raised his head in search of the demon. He did not see it, but he saw its handiwork. The gas lantern that was hung from one of the stalls now went careening into the hay bales piled against the barn wall. It burst like a bomb on contact. Matt watched helplessly as the dry hay fuelled the spreading flames. He did not dare leave the pentagram to fight the fire, and in moments it grew too big to stop, anyway. It climbed the rough-timbered wall and soon reached hungrily for the rafters. The fire advanced and consumed the barn boards like a living, breathing entity. It captivated Matt. He was unable to look away until a more dire thought broke his trance.

He had lost the parchment.

Desperately, Matt scanned the floor around him for the sheet. His heart sank when he came up empty and he realized he would need to broaden his search to the ground outside his safe zone. He rose from the dirt, taking care not to break the precious continuity of the symbol under him. He found the paper when he turned, a yard beyond the arc of the pentagram. It lay on the ground, one singed corner bent upward, taunting him. It was a mere yard away and yet it was miles away at the same time.

Matt kneeled at the edge of the symbol and looked around the barn, now aglow with seething orange flame. He looked to the parchment, around the barn, back to the parchment, the barn again. *All clear?* He reached for the paper, his left arm extended, teetering on his knees. It was barely within reach. He touched it with one finger, then two, tweezed it between them. The hairs on his forearm rose. They stood letter-straight as though the air around him was suddenly charged. Matt yanked his arm back just as the demon appeared before him.

In that frantic moment, Matt could discern few features of the hideous face. Dark, matted fur, sunken black eyes, but it was the thing's mouth that would invade Matt's dreams for his remaining nights. The maw gaped from the center of the demon's brow, lined with a perfect gleaming set of human teeth. Matt winced and braced himself for the bite of incisors and only when it did not come did he realize he was on the right side of the border. The demon hissed in Matt's face. Its putrid breath reeked of feces and the acidic tinge of vomit. It fanned Matt's singed hair and flecked his face with spittle until he recoiled.

Matt fell to his side. He refused to look upon the creature one second longer. He felt its eyes on him, heard it panting as it waited on the other side of the boundary. Matt was eager to end its wait, its time on earth. He opened his left fist and eyed the crumpled parchment within it. The sight of it evoked a series of grunts from the demon. Matt ignored them as he crawled toward the thirteenth candle, minding the lines of the pentagram that guarded him from certain death. He crawled past the *Sacra Obscurum* and recalled the words to recite once the parchment was reduced to ashes. With those words on the tip of his tongue, he held the paper to the candle.

And the winds returned.

Matt watched in disbelief as the ribbon of gray smoke tailed from the extinguished wick. His temper flared and he spun around toward the demon. It was gone again and Matt released a long scream that was born of rage and ended in utter anguish. He dropped onto his back and, this time, he was certain he heard laughter. He laughed, too. While tears started to run freely from his eyes, he laughed.

When he opened his eyes, he saw flames combine into one horrendous monster that fully engulfed the roof of the barn. Searching tentacles intertwined between the rafters and stretched up to the peak. The barn had become a cathedral of fire. It was hell. The ever-growing fire monster sucked up more and more air, stealing Matt's breath. It left him light-headed, drowsy. He so badly wanted to sleep.

Matt read the paper in his hand. *Belphegor.* Before tonight the name was only a concept, an idea. Having come face to disgusting face with the demon, it was now *too* real—as real as the barn and the fire consuming it. It waited for him somewhere in the dark on the other side of Matt's safe zone. He knew full well that if he made a run for it, the demon would run too—and faster.

*Belphegor,* he read again then looked from the crinkled sheet to the wall of fire beside the bales. He got to his feet. Beads of sweat threatened to sting his eyes and he wiped them away. The heat in the barn had become unbearable, but Matt figured he would not have to abide it much longer. He eyed his destination, the distance between. *Twenty feet, give or take*. It was a little longer than the cellar stairs in Stanley's house, and every bit the challenge. *I've already been brave tonight*, he thought. *Now I must be foolish.*

He looked to the barn doors. The brilliance of the inferno around him turned the outside world into a black hole. He saw that he was still alone and was thankful for it. If he could make one more wish, it would be that his friends were safe, and by now, very far from the Dykeman farm. He took a breath and collected his nerve. Then he turned to the barn wall where the now-scorched hay bales had fed the fledgling fire monster. The high wall was fully involved with flame and the mere sight of it seemed to burn Matt's eyes. He drew another smoky breath, balled his fist around the parchment and ran toward it.

He looked down as he crossed the border of the pentagram. He was now in the lion's den—fair game. The feeling was palpable. It welled up every fear Matt had ever experienced and blended them together in his stomach. It drove him. *Three feet...five...*he was getting there...*seven.* The heat intensified. He sucked air and got only carbon exhaust. *Ten feet...twelve...*The notion that he might actually make it hit him. It burned within him as much as the fire without. Only a second later, it was doused when the cold breath blew on his neck. The demon was on top of him and a half a dozen feet might as well have been a hundred yards.

It slammed into Matt's side and he went down hard. Precious oxygen was squeezed out of him and he croaked dryly when he tried to recover it. He crawled forward on his knees until a heavy weight pinned him down. He felt ribs and spine bend under the force, yet Matt was more concerned with the ball of paper lying in the dirt before him. He reached for it with his casted hand, his other helplessly pinned under him. The parchment was just within his range, but the cast prevented him from closing his hand around it.

A fierce cold rushed through his body like a winter storm. His chest swelled and his muscles tensed. A voice came to life in his head, speaking a foreign yet vaguely familiar language. He last heard it on a recording Eric Fisher had played for him. The voices on the sound file had been chanting. This was different. The voice was talking...or perhaps *thinking.*

Matt was invaded.

He reached for the parchment, tried desperately to grab it before the demon took full control of his body. The paper played in and out of his awkward grip, rolling the slightest bit closer. Matt's legs went stiff as broomsticks while his arm folded behind him and his spine contorted. He struggled futilely against the atrophy spreading through his body. Much of his motor control was lost and he would get no closer to the parchment. He eyed it where it lay in the dirt as his vision began to cloud over and, before he lost sight of it, reached for it one final time, and batted it toward the flaming hay bales.

Howls erupted from his body. Though it was not of his doing, Matt heard himself scream, "No!"

The parchment rolled to the foot of the wall and was instantly wrapped in fire.

Matt scrambled to his knees and lurched toward the flames. He was a spectator of his own actions as he went to retrieve the parchment, now fully aflame and opening like a spring bloom. Matt went headlong into the wall and fell in the fire. He watched his good hand scoop up the remains of the parchment. It turned to ash and flaked through his fingers. He roared again. Just as the ringing of his voice faded, Matt felt the heat. Sensation returned to his body and it screamed for him to get out of the fire. He rolled to the dirt and slapped at his pant leg where the flames had grabbed on. His hand, still numb, worked feebly as he patted his smoldering legs. Once the fire was out, he dragged himself away from the wall.

Crawling back to the pentagram, Matt was reminded of the words to close the ritual. He sat on his haunches and said aloud, "So it be done." He looked around the barn, unsure of what to expect, if anything. "So it be done?" he said again.

Across the barn, sprawled in the dirt, Dykeman stirred. It was just a twitch, the slightest movement of his foot, though Matt saw it, and he knew what it meant. He fought his way to his feet and laid in a course for his old patient. He stumbled mightily on rubbery legs, stopping briefly to collect Arthur Sullivan's revolver from the ground. He dropped to his knees when he reached Dykeman's side and wrapped his good hand around the gun grip and steadied it with his cast. He held the barrel inches from Dykeman's forehead and pulled the hammer back. The *click* it made cued Dykeman to open his eyes.

*It's still here. It's still alive. A bullet won't stop it*, Matt thought. *If the ritual from the Sacra Obscurum failed to expel this demon, another gunshot won't help matters.* He ran through the rite in his head, trying to figure where he had made the fatal mistake. It was too late for that, he decided. Whatever happened, whatever he did wrong, there was no making it right this late in the game. His gun hand fell slack to his lap. He closed his eyes.

"S-Stan...Stan..."

Matt looked down at Dykeman, met his cool gray eyes. They were clear. For the first time, Matt knew Morris Dykeman was looking back at him and not the malevolent presence that had possessed him. Matt dropped the gun and rested his hand on Dykeman's shoulder.

"Stan...your f-face," Dykeman struggled to say. "You're old."

"I'm not Stan," Matt said. "I'm...Stan was my father."

Matt figured Dykeman did not understand. He looked up at Matt, then beyond him to the flaming barn roof. His eyes reflected its golden hue. He coughed and a fresh trickle of blood ran from the corner of his mouth. "What happened..."

"There was an accident," Matt offered. "You've been gone a long time."

"Oh...I gotta...get home..."

Matt watched the light go out of Dykeman's eyes and his head slumped to the side.

From overhead came a loud crack followed by a heavy thump, and sparks rained all around them. The fire was eating through the rafters and would soon bring the roof down. Matt got up and found the air thick with smoke. He went back to his knees, but before he could make for the door, he saw a figure, a man, leaning against the burning wall, of all things. The sight locked up Matt's joints and held him in place. His every breath was of noxious gas and still he could not move. He recognized the man standing in the flames and he was terrified beyond any concept of self-preservation.

The man stepped forward from the fire, and he was unburned despite being nude. Even his blonde mane was untouched by the flames. He fluttered furled leathery wings, this not-angel, this anti-angel. Matt was held captive by his stare. Eyes, the yellow of the sun, faded to green and to red then yellow again. He smiled the faintest lilting smile at Matt, and that was what frightened him the most. It was, Matt knew, an expression of endearment. Without so much as blinking, the not-angel watched Matt as he stepped backward and blended into the flames.

A hand clamped on Matt's shoulder, then another. He screamed and flailed his arms wildly in feeble defense. He could do little else in his weakened state. The fight had all but bled out of him. His attacker dragged him through the dirt. He imagined getting hauled into the flames and being transported to the bowels of some hell where doctors who fail their patients go to toil in heat greater than that of the burning barn. Instead, the air around him grew gradually cooler. He was hit by the damp chill of outside air. Matt craned his neck and looked up to find John Cundiff pulling him across the threshold of the barn door. The fog slithered around them then and he took to coughing. He had all but forgotten the taste of fresh air, and now it had him gagging as his lungs tried to process it. They stopped several yards from the barn and he came to rest on dewy grass. Tyrone Klewes was seated beside him. He didn't acknowledge Matt's presence. Darcy stood to his side. Cundiff joined her and the three of them watched the fire in silence.

# Epilogue

Matt listened politely to Mrs. Finney as she listed the town's most eligible and unattached young ladies. "...any number of whom would love to meet a handsome, young doctor like yourself," she said. "At risk of over-stepping, you've been spending far too much time knocking around that big, old house alone." Matt thanked Mrs. Finney for her concern and made a hasty escape.

He rubbed his freshly shaven chin and made sure his hair was fixed neatly as he went to the pedestal beside the stairs. It was where the statue of Saint Michael had kept his solemn vigil for over thirty years. The statue had been covered by a sheet since being vandalized by an unruly patient, according to the official record. Matt flexed his mended right hand, grasped the sheet, and addressed the gathering in the lobby.

"Let me start by thanking everybody for coming," Matt said. The modest group turned their focus on him and the murmur of chatter was quelled. "It means a great deal to me that our little hospital still gets such tremendous support from the community. Thanks to that support, this hospital will continue to serve Saint Andrews and her people the way my father had intended. So, on that note, it is with great pride that I officially rename this facility the Dr. Stanley Dawson Center." Matt pulled the sheet from the statue to a smattering of applause. Instead of uncovering the archangel, Saint Michael, Matt revealed a bust of his father.

Most of the group stepped toward the sculpture for a closer look. Impressed gasps spread among them. "I see my father in every corner of this hospital and I hope that this sculpture serves to remind everyone, staff and patient alike, that he is still here, watching over us. So let's continue to deliver care that reaches the lofty standard that he set."

Darcy and Cundiff circulated champagne among the group. When everyone had something to toast with, Cundiff raised his voice, "To Stanley!"

"Stanley," everyone agreed.

Matt made his way toward Darcy, but he was intercepted by Rick Bowman from the *Daily Tide* who asked who had commissioned the sculpture and how long it had taken to create.

"I'll call you this afternoon," Matt promised. "Just now, I have some goodbyes to make." He continued on his way to Darcy who held up a champagne flute in salute. "Doctor," he said, touching his glass to hers.

"Cheers," she said. "The sculpture looks great. You must be very pleased."

"I am," he said. "It turned out better than I ever hoped. Unfortunately, that was the end of the good news."

She winced and said, "I'm so sorry about that. I know I dropped a bomb on you, but I've given it a lot of thought and it's really the right thing for me to do."

"It was tough news, but I know you're right. I could never begrudge you for wanting to personally see to your sister's care. It's very noble and I'd expect nothing less from you. God help your parents if they get in your way."

"I told them I was coming home to take care of Dianne. I didn't ask, I *told* them. It felt so good." Darcy reined in her glee and said, "The only downside is leaving you like this. You thought you found a head doctor for the hospital and I'm letting you down."

"Nonsense. This hospital has a head doctor. I guess it always did. I just didn't know it until now." They drank to that. "You're destined for great things in this field," Matt told her. "I just wish you weren't taking my best orderly with you."

Darcy looked to where Cundiff was conversing with Elmer Savoie. "John needs to get away from the ocean for a while and Stratford is nicely inland." Her smile faded altogether. "Have you made any progress with Klewey?"

"None to speak of. I'm working with him, but he has put up some strong barriers. He doesn't remember anything from the farmhouse."

"Maybe he's the lucky one."

"Don't feel badly about taking John. I'm glad you two are...not parting ways."

"Thanks, Matt."

"Umm, besides, Klewey's cousin Deason is coming aboard to help out. It seems his career in law enforcement was cut short for some reason."

\* \* \* \*

Matt saw the last of his guests to the door and locked it behind them. He looked fondly on the bust of his father as he passed through the lobby en route to his office. The further he went into the hospital, the more the unanswered questions seemed to crowd in around him. How was he going to replace the staff he had lost? How was he going to replace the combined experience of Wanda Cooke and Nurse Tait?

These were relatively easy questions compared to the ones he had to answer during the police investigation and subsequent government inquiry. He had his new-found talent for persuasion to thank for his freedom, and for keeping the hospital open. He had blamed housing the dangerous Morris Dykeman in an ill-equipped facility for the resultant killing spree. When officials checked into the patient transfer records, they dropped their case. He did not need to know any more than that.

Matt got seated at his desk and began sifting through the loose papers atop it. He scribbled his signature on a few before he was distracted by other thoughts. He tossed his pen and leaned back in his chair. Every time he was behind a closed door, truly alone, the events of the summer came rushing back. They were not events he could simply share with anyone—even with those who were there—and yet he wanted to talk about them endlessly, like veterans retold the same war stories time and time again.

However Matt's stories were off limits. They were secrets.

He drew his top drawer open and looked inside at a modest book bound in black leather. He traced his finger over the etching in the cover—first the S, then the A and C.

Soon, he thought, men like Eric Fisher would descend on Saint Andrews like vultures to get the story of those events. Matt figured it would be a hard story to get.

*Around here, we're good at keeping secrets.*

## About the Author:

This is Todd Allen's first novel. He, his wife Michelle, and their daughter Maya currently reside in southern New Brunswick, Canada—a safe distance from the town of Saint Andrews.

Visit him online at:
http://www.toddallenbooks.com

# *Also from Damnation Books:*

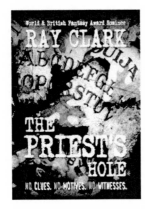

## The Priest's Hole
by Ray Clark

eBook ISBN: 9781615726240
Print ISBN: 9781615726257

Horror Supernatural/Occult
Novel of 75,316 words

If you're willing to unlock the gates of hell, be prepared.

Four charred bodies in the middle of a field. The evidence suggested a ritual killing.

The body of a young constable with his head smashed to a pulp. He was investigating with his colleagues and he was on the other side of the oak tree from the four charred bodies. No one saw or heard anything!

A registered charity collector, bloodless and deflated, stretched out on the driveway of the house of a famous, well-known, local writer.

With each of the mysterious slayings, there are no clues, no motives, and no witnesses.

The police have no ideas, until their investigation takes them to Mark Farnham's house, the author, a man who has everything...including more than enough secrets...and one of those is a Ouija-Board. Have the police found the answer to their problem?

Or have they found an even bigger headache?

# *Also from Damnation Books:*

## Red Dahlia
by Ross Simon

eBook ISBN: 9781615728916
Print ISBN: 9781615728923

Horror Supernatural/Occult
Novel of 61,749 words

She has chosen us, at last...as her banquet of flesh.

First World War to a colonial Indian life of peace, Commodore Clifford Selickton RN is unaware of the blood about to be spilled through that which he unleashes. Selickton takes a beautiful young priestess, Virhynda, for a wife, and they bear a darling little child...a child who, horrifyingly, is prophesized to become the very incarnation of the dread Kali-Ma, East Indian goddess of blood sacrifice. The mind-bending examples they witness of random people receiving their doom are, in fact, only preludes to the hideous, demonic goal of the Blood-Mother: conquest of the Earth, to cover it in a maelstrom of hellish flame and mangled flesh that will consume all mankind. Worst of all, Kali aims to achieve this by striking at the very heart of the civilized world... and it might take a miracle from the Hindu gods themselves to stop her once and for all.

## Visit Damnation Books online at:

Our Blog—
http://www.damnationbooks.com/blog/

DB Reader's Yahoogroup—
http://groups.yahoo.com/group/DamnationBooks/

Twitter—
http://twitter.com/DamnationBooks

Google+—
https://plus.google.com/u/0/115524941844122973800

Facebook—
https://www.facebook.com/pages/Damnation-Books/80339241586

Tumblr—
http://eternalpress-damnationbooks.tumblr.com

Pinterest—
http://www.pinterest.com/EPandDB

Instagram—
http://instagram.com/eternalpress_damnationbooks

Youtube—
http://www.youtube.com/channel/UC9mxZ4W-WaKHeML_f9-9CpA

Goodreads—
http://www.goodreads.com/DamnationBooks

Shelfari—
http://www.shelfari.com/damnationbooks

Library Thing—
http://www.librarything.com/DamnationBooks

HorrorWorld Forums—
http://horrorworld.org/phpBB3/viewforum.php?f=134

Our Ebay Store—
http://www.ebay.com/usr/ep-dbbooks

CPSIA information can be obtained at www.ICGtesting.com
Printed in the USA
BVOW02s1830120415

395708BV00001B/190/P